BRIDGE OF DREAMS

"Let go of my hand. *Now*," Cathlin snapped.

"Maybe I don't want to let go," Dominic said cockily.

"There are two kinds of women in this world. Those who say no and mean it. And those who say no and mean it."

"Very clever, Ms. O'Neill. But there are two kinds of men in the world: those who think there are two kinds of women, and those who know they'll never understand the first thing about the incredible subtlety of the female mind. I happen to fall into the second group. Now what about my proposition?"

Cathlin shook her head in disbelief. "There are probably four hundred women in this room right now. Most of them would seriously consider armed robbery to hear a proposition from you. Go pick one of them."

His jade eyes glinted. "I don't want one of them. I want you."

"Christina Skye has become a master
of delivering wonderfully unique
and spellbinding tales . . .
a truly unforgettable novel.
Don't miss it!"
Romantic Times

crossed romance
Abbey, read
na Skye's
the Rose

D1051709

Other Avon Books by
Christina Skye

Hour of the Rose

Avon Books are available at special quantity discounts for bulk purchases for sales promotions, premiums, fund raising or educational use. Special books, or book excerpts, can also be created to fit specific needs.

For details write or telephone the office of the Director of Special Markets, Avon Books, Dept. FP, 1350 Avenue of the Americas, New York, New York 10019, 1-800-238-0658.

CHRISTINA SKYE

BRIDGE OF DREAMS

AVON BOOKS ◆ NEW YORK

If you purchased this book without a cover, you should be aware that
this book is stolen property. It was reported as "unsold and destroyed"
to the publisher, and neither the author nor the publisher has received
any payment for this "stripped book."

BRIDGE OF DREAMS is an original publication of Avon Books. This
work has never before appeared in book form.

AVON BOOKS
A division of
The Hearst Corporation
1350 Avenue of the Americas
New York, New York 10019

Copyright © 1995 by Roberta Helmer
Published by arrangement with the author
Library of Congress Catalog Card Number: 94-96566
ISBN: 0-380-77386-4

All rights reserved, which includes the right to reproduce this book or
portions thereof in any form whatsoever except as provided by the U.S.
Copyright Law. For information address The Elaine Davie Literary
Agency, Village Gate Square, 274 North Goodman Street, Rochester,
New York 14607.

First Avon Books Printing: May 1995

AVON TRADEMARK REG. U.S. PAT. OFF. AND IN OTHER COUNTRIES, MARCA REGIS-
TRADA, HECHO EN U.S.A.

Printed in the U.S.A.

RA   10   9   8   7   6   5   4   3   2   1

In memoriam,

Paul M. Helmer
(1904–1994)

WITH WARMEST THANKS ...

to Helen Wolverton, for braving a deluge of wine trivia;

to Judy Spagnola and Diane Manziano, for information on Venetian Murano glass;

to Ed Lorne and Earl Martin, who introduced me to the arcane world of security and firearms;

to Rick Tucci, bodyguard and founder of Princeton Academy of Martial Arts, who along with Jeff Jones demonstrated the elegance and flawless power of French kickboxing *savate* (I wouldn't want to meet *these* guys down a dark alley);

and finally to Ellen Edwards and Maggie Lichota, the best in the business, for sharing my vision of Cathlin and Dominic.

PART I

A Door
of Shadows

Prologue ～

Gabriel Montserrat, the fifth earl of Ashton, stood in the candlelight, letting the silence wash around him.

He was going to die. There was no escaping it now.

But it didn't matter. Everything he had loved and valued was already gone, so what greater pain could death hold?

He touched the damp stone walls of Draycott's wine cellar, feeling everywhere its vast age. A grand old house, it had witnessed so much of his life's joy—and all its bitter sorrow.

Draycott Abbey alone he might miss. And also its arrogant master. But the rest?

No, not the London glitter. Not the jeweled, laughing women who ever sought his bed. Not the gaming, nor the vice. Certainly not the heady danger he had taken to courting ever more recklessly of late. He was the Rook, after all. Such excesses were expected of the man famous for saving French aristocrats from the guillotine. Yes, Gabriel was a man who would dare all, even if his exploits in revolutionary France left nothing but ashes in his mouth.

3

Now that *she* was gone.

Gabriel's head was pounding and the wound in his side had settled into a vast, icy chill. Something was sticking to the lace of his shirt. Glancing down, he saw that it was his own drying blood. He raised a glass of wine to the darkness. "To you, Devere. You have won, damn you. I shall die in here behind this wall with my wine."

He should have been terrified or furious, but he wasn't. He'd lost too much to care. And, as he studied the case of wine, a strange smile twisted Ashton's lips. Yes, it was over. Devere had seen to that when he'd shot the one woman Gabriel had ever loved.

But maybe there was a different way. Maybe in some other time, everything could be different. Maybe somewhere in the soul everyone carried memories of lovers lost and vows shared in palaces that had long since turned to dust.

For a moment the tall man with the sun-bronzed face and the unfashionably unpowdered hair studied the bottles nestled in a case of wood shavings and cotton batting—bottles which he had escorted all the way from the misty valleys of the Garonne in France, where the fires of revolution yet raged.

He had slipped through death, eluding his pursuers again and again, and in the process he had saved the family of the woman he loved. But he had returned to find death leering from his own doorstep.

Still, maybe there was a way.

A wild blaze filled his eyes. As hope lit his face, a fragment of the earl of Ashton's notorious bravado returned.

The recklessness that Geneva had loved so well.

Before she'd breathed her last. Before she'd died in his arms. *Yes, I will manage it somehow, my love,* he vowed.

Because some things had power beyond belief or explaining. Perhaps beyond time itself.

Gritting his teeth against the pain tearing through his chest, Ashton pulled quill and ink from the small writing desk that Adrian Draycott kept by the far wall of his wine cellar. Slowly he began to write . . .

I, Gabriel Ashton, being whole of body and sound in mind and spirit, do hereby warrant this document as the final addition to my legal disposition of worldly goods and lands. Only one change is to be made, and that will be entered below . . .

His face gaunt with strain, the dying earl wrote on by the light of a guttering candle. Each sharp stroke that slashed at the vellum sent fresh blood oozing onto his white lace.

The contents of the case of superior Sauternes wine from the Garonne Valley of France, lately acquired by myself and now settled at my feet, are to be handled exactly as detailed below. Let it be recorded that ANY DEVIATIONS FROM MY WISHES WILL NEGATE THE TERMS OF THIS WILL. In that event, this wine is to be destroyed, with no benefit accruing to anyone. I hereby charge the heirs of my friend, Adrian Draycott, to see to the terms, and warn that WHOSOEVER SHALL TAMPER WITH THESE WORDS WILL FEEL THE FULL FORCE OF MY FURY.

Ashton coughed painfully. A dark blotch slid onto the sheet that was an addendum to his last will and testament, a document as reckless and outrageous as the fifth earl of Ashton had been in life.

And when he was finally done, when the last word lay like a black gash upon the page, the man who had once been the most dashing scoundrel and the greatest hero in all England gave a despairing cry and fell forward onto the desk, where his lifeblood mingled with the still-wet ink.

He whispered Geneva's name with his last breath.

Kent, England
Draycott Abbey
April 16, 1994

Somewhere over the Wealden hills of Kent a church bell was chiming.

The brawny mason from London barely noticed, too busy looking for the end of the rusted water pipe. Cursing, he inched along the wall, reaching fruitlessly through the suffocating darkness of Draycott Abbey's wine cellars. With every cramped movement his oaths grew more colorful.

Suddenly his foot caught on a slab of uneven granite. He toppled forward, his ten-pound wrench slamming against the wall.

Somewhere beyond the granite slab came a low rumble, then the heave of rotting mortar. Moments later a six-foot section of wall gave way, toppling to the stone floor.

A square of darkness gaped from the far side of the cellar, where a narrow room now lay revealed.

"Well, I'll be blowed," the big man whispered.

"Bloody likely," his companion answered. But as he spoke, he surreptitiously made the sign of the cross.

Suddenly, William Jones wasn't feeling so grand himself. "Go and fetch his lordship. Reckon he's going to want to see this for himself."

But the man at his side didn't move, transfixed by the opening in the wall that led away into darkness.

To a room that had lain sealed and secret for two hundred years.

"Whatta you reckon's hidden in there, Will?"

"How in bleedin' hell should *I* know?" There was nervousness in the big man's voice now. Suddenly he wanted to be back in London, back in the crowded streets filled with lights and laughter and people.

Anywhere but *here*, with its odd silence.

With its strange, clinging darkness.

"Will?"

"Just go and *get* him, blast you!"

With the other man gone, the silence in the wine cellar grew choking. And although the brawny stonemason would forever afterward try to deny his memories and convince himself it had been no more than a freak of his imagination, at that moment he found himself implacably drawn toward that cold square of darkness.

Slowly, he raised his flashlight. Just beyond the jagged edge of the wall, light played over an old wooden crate thick with dust and cobwebs. Inside the rough planks he could just make out the outline of eight bottles of wine, dark streaks of mold straddling their corks.

And draped across the case, quill intact, lay a set of white bones, still cradled in fragments of lace and velvet.

Will Jones's broad face went pale. His flashlight glinted off a jewel winking amid the network of bones, all that remained of a man who had died here two centuries ago and had been interred in this dusty grave. Then the stonemason saw the diamond ring and the sheet of vellum that lay scrolled between the white, bony fingers.

Not much frightened William Jones. He had fought in the Falklands and done a tour of hard labor in the emerald mines of Brazil, where greed and death lay thick as the stink of human sweat. But he had never known real terror until now as he stood with his flashlight playing through Draycott's inky darkness.

Because suddenly he had the feeling he was not alone. Something seemed to push him inexorably forward, almost as if a hand had settled on his shoulder, forcing him toward that jagged piece of darkness. His jaw clenched as he fought the urge. Muscles bunched over his brawny shoulders. Against every wish, he felt his hand rise toward the dusty crate of wine. As it did, William Jones felt something move past his fingers, almost like the brush of cold water.

With a cry, he lashed out with his hammer, fighting the insane urge he couldn't even name. "No, damn it. I won't. I *won't!*"

Stumbling like a drunken man, he lurched around and fought his way back toward the cellar door.

Toward the lights. Toward the noise and the life.

Not all the money in the world could keep him in that cold, restless tomb full of secrets.

Outside Draycott Abbey the wind played through the elms and hawthorns. A bird cried once, high and shrill.

But within the shimmering moat, within the circling walls, all was silent. Deep in the wine cellars, light tore away from darkness, form from nothingness.

A shape emerged. A man, yet not quite a man.

His eyes glinted with the clear, azure of a tropical sea and his hair shone the unrelenting black of a northern sky.

Alive, he was, light shimmering about his shoulders, catching in the fine lace that fell across his wrists.

Alive, yet not quite alive.

Back and forth the ghost of Draycott Abbey paced the cold floor, brows knit, hands locked behind his back. His eyes were fixed on a past half-forgotten and a future that refused to be revealed.

For a moment anger filled the darkness. Anger and a wanting that stretched down through the long, sad centuries.

I tried, Gabriel, but God help me I came too late. By then you were both gone. But where? What happened here in my absence?

The words drifted on the soft wind. They sighed through the roses wrapped about the abbey walls.

Of course, there was no answer. Adrian Draycott had long ago given up expecting one.

Only now the past stood open, unsealed with the stroke of a wrench, and Adrian was determined to see the old mystery solved. It was his sworn duty, in fact, as the guardian ghost of Draycott Abbey. On and on he paced, fire in his eyes and cold in his heart, walking this house he loved so well.

He wished he could change the past, but it was not possible. One could only go forward, trying desperately to remember all the old lessons while mastering the new ones. Sometimes the process left him very tired.

He made his way to the gray parapets. There he touched the lace that drifted at his cuff, lost in memories of a bolder time, when the abbey had rung to his shouted commands and fourscore servants had rushed to do his slightest bidding.

But no more. Now he was just another shadow at the edge of the roof, just another memory among all the others that filled this great, grand house. And he found himself wondering if his long-dead friend Gabriel had been right. Maybe there was a way that the past could finally be set to rights.

It all depended on the wine, of course. And the hearts of two stubborn people. But Adrian swore that if it was even remotely possible to see Gabriel's mystery solved, he would somehow see it done.

Deep in the night the church bells chimed, twelve times and then once more, a low, ghostly hum. The scent of lilacs seemed to drift upon the still air, while the dreaming house slept on. And Adrian's tall form shimmered, moving restlessly among the abbey's shadows.

One ～

"*One million pounds?*" Dominic Alexander Montserrat, the tenth earl of Ashton, sank down in a chintz wing chair at the sunny corner of Nicholas Draycott's study. Below the window, Draycott Abbey's moat shimmered and danced, but Dominic barely noticed. "I don't believe it."

Nicholas Draycott smiled broadly. "Then you'd better start. As a matter of fact, the solicitor tells me the figure might be closer to *two* million."

Dominic's strong fingers, callused from months of stripping oak casks and pruning grapevines, dived through his long black hair. "But *how*, Nicholas? Why? And when—"

His old friend, now the twelfth Viscount Draycott and devoted inheritor of the beautiful Jacobean moat house called Draycott Abbey, interrupted with a laugh. "Hold on, Dominic. I realize this must be a huge shock—it bloody well was to me, too. At least *you* didn't have to go down and confront a skeleton that had been immured for two hundred years in your wine cellar."

"I still can't believe it!"

"According to the date on the will, that's when he died. And this man Gabriel, your ancestor, was most precise in how he wanted that wine of his to be

11

treated. With a million pounds at stake, I suggest that it's worth taking the trouble to comply with his conditions. Not to mention the fact that he threatened anyone who tried to obstruct his plans. 'Whosoever shall tamper with these words will feel the full force of my fury,' was how he phrased it."

"Sounds damned Gothic." Dominic's lean, suntanned face still carried signs of disbelief. "Look, Nicholas, I'm finding all this very hard to accept. Maybe I've been too long at my vineyards and I'm accustomed to hearing nothing but French morning, noon, and night." There was indeed a hint of an accent in his voice. "Let's try it again, shall we? You're telling me that an ancestor of mine left a case of Château d'Yquem 1792 down in your cellars. A case of vintage Sauternes in perfect condition that could bring, even conservatively, over a million pounds at auction?"

"That's what I said. The man was Gabriel Ashton. The fifth earl of Ashton, to be exact."

"Bloody hell." Dominic ran his hands through his hair, burned by the French sun to a rich mahogany. "Since I was a boy I've heard stories about mad Uncle Gabriel. Many a night my sister and I went to sleep shivering from some horrendous tale our father had told us. The man was either a black-hearted scoundrel or the most reckless hero England ever knew, snatching French aristocrats from the very shadow of the guillotine. But no one in the family ever knew what happened to him. He simply vanished one day without a trace."

"Well, now you know *where* he died, at least," Nicholas said grimly. "The why remains a mystery, however." He sat back, noticing how fit his old friend looked sporting a new set of muscles and skin baked copper by the French sun. The last time they'd met, Dominic had been guarding the Prince of Wales on a state visit to Thailand, and the strain of Dominic's work as a royal bodyguard had been all too apparent.

That vineyard he'd bought in France three years ago had to be good for him, Nicholas decided. La Trouvaille, wasn't it called? "That's it in a nutshell. And it's all yours, Dominic." A speculative light entered Nicholas's green eyes. "Well, half of it at least."

"Mad Uncle Gabriel. A million bloody pounds." Dominic stared blankly at his glass of sherry. "My God, I could finally start setting in those new Sémillon vines that I've been wanting to get my hands on. Then maybe I'll commission some new oak casks for—" Abruptly his head rose. "*Half?* What happens to the rest of the money?"

"I'm afraid that's where things turn a bit tricky. As I said, your ancestor was most precise about how the funds were to be disposed of." Nicholas cleared his throat, turning a jewel-studded Fabergé egg in his fingers.

"Out with it, Nicky. What do I have to do, spend a night down in that haunted wine cellar with Mad Uncle Gabriel's ghost?" Dominic laughed softly. "For a million pounds, I'd spend a *week* down there, ghosts and all."

"You'd be surprised what you might find in this house, Dominic. But it's not so simple. Someone else is involved in the bequest. And I feel that the two of you are honor bound to solve the mystery of that skeleton I happened across."

Dominic barked out a laugh. "I have to split with you, is that what you're saying? If so, out with it, my friend. After all, I owe you Draycotts something for keeping that wine safe all these years."

"No, not me." Nicholas looked at his friend, noting the calluses from hard field work and the little lines at the edges of his eyes. From days squinting in the sun, days of backbreaking physical labor setting in vines, stringing protective nets, and harvesting grapes, Nicholas knew.

If he didn't love Draycott Abbey so well, Nicholas would envy his friend, who had beautiful rolling acres of vines in one of the loveliest valleys in France. He worked hard, lived well, ate wonderfully, and the little lines at his eyes attested to the fact that Dominic Montserrat laughed often and hard. Life didn't get much better than that, Nicholas thought. Surely that was the right kind of work, healthy labor that made things grow where before there had been nothing. Not like the other kind, the work that had carried Dominic to tense meetings with suspicious men in far-flung cities with unpronounceable names.

But Nicholas knew he couldn't put off the rest of his news any longer.

"So who's the lucky man? He's going to get one hell of a surprise when he finds he's just inherited a case of priceless sweet white Bordeaux." Dominic's eyes crinkled at the thought. "*I* certainly did."

"Not he, *she*."

"That's better yet. Maybe she'll be so overcome with delight at the news that she—"

"It's someone we both know." Nicholas's fingers tightened. "Donnell O'Neill's daughter."

Dominic went very still, his eyes on the sunlight spilling through the study windows. "Cathlin O'Neill?"

"One and the same."

The silence unraveled until the whole room was filled with it.

Dominic strode to the window and stared out at the moat. "Cathlin O'Neill, the girl whose mother died here? I remember your father was off in Brazil at the time, buying a copper mine. We were up at school when you found out. Bloody awful."

Nicholas nodded grimly. "We never found out exactly what happened to the mother. When my father came back, the police told him it was probably a simple accident. Or . . ."

"Or what?"

Nicholas shrugged. "Or it might have been something else. Elizabeth Russell O'Neill was here to examine some textile samples that needed restoring. My father was very keen that it should be done right and had insisted on hiring the best authority, which Elizabeth O'Neill was. She'd brought her young daughter along with her for the weekend and even though Cathlin was only ten, she loved this place as much as her mother did." Nicholas turned the priceless jeweled egg, frowning as it caught the light. "You know the rest. That first night they were here, her mother went out and never came back. There were only a few servants on duty in my father's absence, but none of them saw or heard anything odd and there was no sign of foul play. But the next morning little Cathlin found her mother's body beside the moat, where she'd plunged from the roof."

"Good God." Dominic looked at his friend. "Possibly suicide?"

Nicholas shook his head. "She had no history of instability and she was happy in her marriage, by all accounts."

"And there's nothing more? You never discovered how it happened?"

"Never. The girl remembered nothing—the result of trauma, we were told. At the time there was some talk of a political connection, since her father had been involved in government work. But nothing concrete ever turned up. I can't believe this is all coming up again." Nicholas glared out the window. "I'm almost tempted to pitch that wine into the moat, since the last thing I want is all this muck dredged up again. Believe me, the press will have a field day when they find out." He sighed and set down the jeweled egg. "I don't want Kacey and little Genevieve upset by this either.'' Nicholas studied a framed photo of his laughing wife and five-year-old daughter. ''I think it best we leave as soon as the conditions of your ancestor's will have been put into motion. Perhaps some digging in London will turn up new answers about the mystery of Gabriel Ashton.''

''But what do Cathlin O'Neill and I have to do with this wine? I don't understand.''

''Your ancestor insisted that the two eldest living descendants of himself and one Geneva Russell spend seven days and nights here at Draycott Abbey. Then—and only then—the wine would be theirs. Cathlin is the oldest living relative of that Geneva Russell, through her mother.''

Dominic stared at his friend. ''You're kidding, aren't you?''

''I'm afraid not. And this will was quite specific, Dominic. In fact, the legal terms are enforceable even today. You can see why I feel I have to carry out those terms exactly as Gabriel Ashton asked.''

Dominic cursed softly. Already he could see his hopes of expansion at La Trouvaille vanishing like early morning mist in the French sun. ''But what's all this business about seven days and nights?''

''Assuming that these descendants are of an age of independence and of sound mind and body, they must spend seven nights together here at Draycott Abbey. It was Gabriel's express wish.''

''Isn't this all rather farfetched, Nicky? The man's been dead for two hundred years and from all I've heard he was far from a saint himself. Why not just forget all this folderol? *He* certainly isn't going to know.''

A frown worked down Nicholas's handsome face. ''He won't, but I will. Dominic, the man wrote his will as he lay dying. He signed his name in his own blood. How can I ignore such a request?''

"It's probably some kind of trick one of your demented ancestors thought up. You Draycotts seem to have a damned morbid sense of humor, especially that ghost you always talked about as a boy."

"This is no trick, Dominic. I had an architect in to look at that wall, and the bricks were authentic for their period, and the mortar was brittle with age—two hundred years of age."

"I don't *believe* this."

"You'd better start. La Trouvaille's future is going to depend on how seriously you take what I'm telling you. A great old vintage like that Château d'Yquem is worth a fortune now."

Dominic's jaw hardened. "You don't have to tell *me* what a rare Sauternes is worth!"

"Stop it, Dominic. I know this is hard for you, but it's the very thing to get you back on your feet at La Trouvaille. That vineyard has drained your pockets since day one, and you know it. Your father left you damned comfortable, but a million pounds will buy a hell of a lot of new vines and every kind of technology you could ever want."

"But why do we have to go through with this farce about the will? I've got grapes to tend and wine to get into cask. Can't we just take the wine and sell it now?"

"Out of the question. The heirs of Adrian Draycott were assigned to oversee the terms of the will, and I mean to comply with the man's wishes." A challenging gleam lit Nicholas's eyes. "Which means I'll just have to toss the wine off the abbey roof and leave it in the moat to feed the fish."

Dominic went still. "The will specified *that?*"

"Afraid so."

The earl of Ashton rubbed his jaw, calculating exactly how many oak casks, stainless steel distilling vats, and computer-scanned irrigation pumps he could buy with half a million pounds. "Damned expensive fish food."

"Isn't it though."

Dominic muttered something low and graphic and shoved his hands into his pockets, trying not to think about how much good that money would do at La Trouvaille.

"There's something else you should know, Dominic."

"Sweet God, what *now*?"

Nicholas looked grim. "This kind of news is going to interest a whole lot of people. I'll try to keep the wine secret as long as I can. I've already paid the plumbers to keep their mouths shut, in fact, but eventually one of them is bound to let something slip. And since the will is a legal document, I will eventually have to see that it is publicly recorded. When I do . . ."

"Go on, Nicholas."

"Let's just say that I suggest you find Cathlin O'Neill and get her up here where you can keep your eye on her."

"You think she's in danger?"

"It's only logical, considering the value of this wine. Wouldn't you be interested in possessing such a treasure?"

"If I had the money to spare, of course."

"There are other people with fewer scruples. They'll try to get it any way they can."

"Kidnappers?"

"Would you give up the wine if Cathlin were taken?"

"Of course. But it won't come to that." Dominic thought about the dangers he had confronted while guarding presidents and kings in every corner of the globe. He found it hard to imagine that he'd meet his end back in sedate, stuffy England, trying to protect a case of wine.

Then again, he hadn't made it to the relatively ripe old age of thirty-five by underestimating any kind of danger. "Have you spoken to Cathlin O'Neill about any of this?"

"I've tried, but she hasn't returned my calls. Draycott Abbey can hardly hold fond memories for her, of course."

Dominic's jaw clenched. "If I should decide to look up Cathlin O'Neill—and I do mean *if*—where would I find her?"

"She has a wine shop on Regent Street. No, wait a minute." Nicholas delved through a pile of papers on the edge of his desk and pulled out a sheet of thick vellum stock. "If I remember correctly—yes, here it is. Cathlin's on the program of a charity auction to be held at the British Museum next week." Nicholas held out the engraved invitation. "And do it right, if you please. I don't want any more restless ghosts pacing the parapets and wrecking my sleep."

"Any more? You mean those stories you told me in school were true?"

Nicholas frowned. "Never mind. Just find Cathlin and convince her somehow. Use that famous Ashton charm I keep hearing about."

Dominic shook his head. "I'm making no promises, Nicholas." He swung his jacket over his shoulder. "How can you expect her to come back here after what happened? Who would want to face all that again? I certainly wouldn't."

"Maybe it's time she did. No matter what she decides, she's involved, and she's going to need someone to keep her safe when this news gets out. And you were always the very best, Dominic."

"Not anymore. I'm out of that world, Nicholas. You'll have to find another bulletcatcher."

"Why? You never told me what happened," Nicholas said softly.

Dominic watched his shadow slant across the lush

peach carpet. Outside, the air filled with birdsong. "Because it almost killed me, Nicholas. After a while I saw shadows everywhere and I couldn't tell my friends from my enemies. I can't go back, not to the shadows, not to the adrenaline highs and the cold sweats. Not even for a million pounds."

And when Dominic left the abbey, he didn't look back. Danger had once been a way of life for him. He had been a cold professional, a man who had learned the hard way to trust no one.

But France had softened him, taught him balance. The long sunny days and lazy velvet nights of his fields along the Garonne had wiped away some of the anger and most of the bad memories.

And Dominic liked it that way.

So he would go see Ms. Cathlin O'Neill in all her glory at a society wine auction. He was curious to see how good she really was. But that was the beginning and end to it.

Nothing was going to pull him back into the shadows, not even the last, desperate words of a dying ancestor.

Or so he told himself.

Two ⌇

The stately vestibule of the British Museum was filled with the glitterati of four continents. Amid the Indonesian orchids and dwarf oranges, royal dukes rubbed elbows with English rock stars, California winemakers, and unsmiling Japanese investors. Champagne flowed, diamonds glittered; the suits were strictly Armani and the gowns were all haute couture.

Cathlin O'Neill looked on and stifled a sigh. It was the world she'd made her own, the world she'd become intimately familiar with since she'd come to England to expand her business as an appraiser and dealer in rare old wines. She knew that tonight the bidding would be fierce, all proceeds from the charity auction going to benefit a popular wildlife trust. It didn't hurt that more than a few in attendance expected the Prince of Wales to put in an appearance before the evening was out.

Cathlin entered the antique-strewn ladies' room and turned before the mirror, straightening her elegantly severe black velvet suit. She looked like what she was: young and clever and very American. If the stuffed shirts around her didn't like it, then too bad for them. She'd had to deal with too many condescending aristocrats since coming to London and she had done it smoothly and well—but she hadn't liked

21

it. She was tired of the formality and tired of the condescension. All she wanted was to finish her work here and go back to her little apartment off Piccadilly Circle, kick off her heels, and finish an article commissioned by a major wine journal on the pitfalls of sulfites in the winemaking process.

Hardly light reading, Cathlin thought.

But most of her thoughts had been far from light these last months. She had begun to have serious doubts about staying on in England. She disliked the climate and disliked the tone of the city and wanted nothing more than to return to her plant-filled rooms in the sunny Philadelphia shop she kept off Rittenhouse Square.

In addition to her subjective biases against London, the last months had stirred up memories of her English mother, memories that Cathlin preferred to leave buried. But she found she had little choice. The images seemed to come and go at will, and they'd been coming more often since she'd returned to England. Cathlin knew she'd have to make up her mind soon just how much longer to stay. When her friend, formerly the head of Harrods Wine Department, had first called, a partnership had seemed a good idea. Now Cathlin wasn't so sure.

She shoved back her glossy black hair and frowned into the mirror. Outside, the premiere auction event of the season was about to begin, and her partner, an old friend from college days in Ithaca, had talked Cathlin into gaveling the Sauternes segment. As an expert in the early sweet white wines of Bordeaux, Cathlin knew how to fill her patter with a running commentary on good wines, bad wines, and how to know the difference between them. She named names and quoted prices, when no one else dared. As a result, she'd been the hit of two similar London auctions, especially when she'd poured out a sample taste of one of the offerings, then tossed the bottle over her shoulder, saying no one needed to be afflicted with an unfortunate mistake like that year was.

The charity council had nearly succumbed to cardiac arrest and the owning wine company had been apoplectic. But Cathlin had been dead on target and the rest of the audience had laughed wholeheartedly.

The next day the phone at her shop on Regent Street had rung right off the wall.

So tonight Cathlin forced a smile and straightened her hair, reminding herself that this exposure helped her business and gave her access to the stuffed shirts she needed, even if she *did* find them incredibly irritating.

"Ready to go?" A jeweled finger pressed her shoulder.

"Serita, you pest, why do I ever agree to do these things? If I die of Joy inhalation, it will be your fault and yours alone."

"But what a way to go." Serita McCall, Cathlin's partner, stood six feet tall and drop-dead gorgeous in gold lamé. She knew everyone worth knowing and all their various wine preferences. For five years she'd badgered Cathlin to come to London, and now that Cathlin was here, her friend was determined to see her paired off and happy.

Cathlin had very different ideas. Serita's string of introductions had left her utterly bored, and she was having no more of them.

But suspicion was a hard habit to break, and Serita had that old gleam in her eye again. "What is it, Serita? Don't tell me there's another sweet, dear man you want me to meet. I warn you, I've had it with making small talk with strangers."

Her friend gave her a sympathetic look. "I was terrible, wasn't I? Well, you can breathe easily, because I'm done with all that. I'm only thinking about that man who's been asking about you. See, over there." She opened the door and pointed. "Beside the Japanese contingent."

Cathlin studied the tall man striding past a marble column. She had time for only a dim impression of broad shoulders and dark hair before he disappeared into the jeweled throng. "Am I supposed to know him?"

"No, but I am. His name is Dominic Alexander Montserrat. He's the tenth earl of Ashton, actually."

Cathlin's lips pursed.

"Don't go all New World snob on *me*, Cathlin O'Neill. Dominic is a perfectly nice man who asked me to point you out. For purely business reasons, I might add. He owns a vineyard himself."

"Great. Another dissipated absentee landlord. Forget it, Serita."

"You're wrong, Cathlin. He's very quiet about his involvement, but he does take a great interest in his wine and he's very knowledgeable, believe me. I'd tell you more, but he'd shoot me, since he's very sensitive about his privacy."

"So am *I*."

Serita smiled. "As a matter of fact, he said you were far too young to be an expert on anything so subtle as nineteenth century Sauternes."

"Just what I need, another pompous ass. I dearly love you, Serita, but really, you English seem to grow pompous asses the way we grow Florida oranges. And these auctions just seem to pull them out in droves."

"But he is a most attractive man, Cathlin. There's something different about Dominic. It's his eyes, I think. He looks at you and really *sees* you. There's something seductive, but dangerous about that kind of total focus in a man." She shrugged. "Then again, I've already had two glasses of Taittinger, so my judgment is probably a tad hazy. Now I must be off. There's a man waiting for me outside who has a blank check from a very fine department store in Texas and I mean to see he spends every cent of it here tonight." She winked at Cathlin. "And a few more after that."

Knowing Serita, she'd do just that, Cathlin thought, as her partner moved back into the crowd. For a moment Cathlin was envious of her ebullient friend, who always seemed to know just how to put people at their ease and bring out their best points.

Unlike Cathlin, who seemed too serious, too competent, too—

Capable. Yes, that was the word. She'd had to be capable, losing her mother so young. Worrying about her footloose father. Then losing him, too.

Sighing, Cathlin picked up her repoussé gold evening bag and headed for the columned auction room. Capable or not, she had made a promise to Serita and that meant she had some very old and very valuable Bordeaux to sell.

Halfway between the potted palms and the carved ice swans a man blocked her way. A very tall man with hair the color of the oak casks used to age the finest Dom Pérignon.

"Ms. O'Neill?" His black brow arched.

Cathlin looked into his cool green eyes and thought they were too knowing, far too confident. Not that he didn't have reason to be. His formal black jacket was just about perfection and his bronzed face spoke of just the right amount of time shuttling between Cap d'Antibes and the latest haunt in Mustique.

Which meant that in Cathlin's eyes he was a grade-A washout.

"Maybe." Her eyes skimmed his body, noting the exquisitely cut white shirt that came from one of the finest tailors on Savile Row. His wrist held a worn but extremely valuable Swiss designer watch that would have bought a year's lease on her shop back in Rittenhouse Square. "But probably not."

There was a flare of emotion in his eyes, something that Cathlin decided was a mix of anger and humor. She found the combination startling.

"Why not?"

"Because I don't like how you talk."

A muscle flashed at his bronzed jaw. "You haven't heard me talk yet."

Cathlin pursed her lips. "Then because I don't like how you look."

"I can take off the suit if it will help."

"Not interested. You're too high on the food chain and I don't like your attitude." Cathlin smiled sweetly. "Is that reason enough?"

Again the flare of mingled emotions, only this time the anger was winning out over the humor. "My credit is good and my references are excellent. As for my attitude—" His lips curved slightly. "I'd be glad to discuss that further over dinner."

Cathlin had heard it all too many times before. As a woman in a man's world, she was considered fair game for every Bond Street Lothario and would-be Don Juan with a storefront and a two-line wine list. It was true back in Philadelphia and it was equally true here in London. "Sorry, I never mix business with pleasure." She turned to leave.

He moved in front of her with a silent grace that left Cathlin frowning. "Then let's leave the pleasure for later and focus on business. I have a proposition for you."

"I'll just bet you do."

"A business proposition."

"Let me guess. You need to decide between an imperial of Château Lafite-Rothschild '71 and a 1912 Château d'Yquem Sauternes and you simply *must* ask my advice."

His eyes weren't just green, Cathlin saw then. They were smoky, the color of the finest China jade. Too hard to be carved, the stone could only be shaped by the slow and laborious abrasion of some harder substance like crushed garnets or rubies.

The result was objects of phenomenal price but extraordinary beauty.

Looking into those eyes, Cathlin thought of the imperial archer's ring her father had brought back to her after one of his frequent Far Eastern trips.

Cathlin had found the piece lovely—at first. Soon she had come to hate it, because it represented the government work that kept him away from home for months at a time, constantly on the move—and perpetually in danger.

And the work had finally killed him, before Cathlin had ever really gotten a chance to know him.

The green eyes narrowed, hardened. "Sorry, no Lafite."

"No? How disappointing. Good-bye." Cathlin saw his eyes change again. She sensed a raw edge of violence, not quite hidden by that sleek, cool veneer.

If so, that was *his* problem.

She was turning away when his hand snagged her wrist. She felt the hard palm and the ridge of calluses lining his fingers. Not exactly the hand of a playboy, she thought. But he'd probably gotten the calluses from counting tax write-offs and opening bottles of tanning oil for Victoria's Secret models. "Let go of my hand."

"The Lafite '71 has definite potential, but hasn't opened up and come into its own yet. The d'Yquem '12 was a flat-out disappointment." A slow, cocky grin. The kind of grin that said he was smart and good to look at and he knew it.

"*Now.*"

"Maybe I don't want to let go of your hand."

"There are two kinds of women in this world. Those who say no and mean it. And those who say no and mean it."

"Very clever, Ms. O'Neill. But there are two kinds

of men in the world: those who think there are two kinds of women, and those who know they'll never know the first thing about the incredible subtlety of the female mind. I happen to fall in the second group. Now what about my proposition?''

Cathlin shook her head in disbelief. ''There are probably four hundred women in this room right now. Most of them would seriously consider armed robbery to hear a proposition from you. Go pick on one of them.''

The jade eyes glinted. ''I don't want one of them. I want you.''

''So call my shop. It's on Regent Street. Right under H for hard to get.''

''This is important, damn it. I need to talk to you.''

Somewhere out in the auction area, a man's voice announced that the final lot of champagnes had just been sold, tallying up to a grand total of fifty thousand pounds.

Which meant Cathlin was on next.

She stared at their overlaid hands, trying to ignore his carefully controlled power. Her jaw hardened. ''For your information, the Lafite '71 is more than passable even now and its potential is tremendous. The d'Yquem '12 was intense but quite uneven. Both are better than anything that could be said for *you*.'' She jerked her hand from beneath his. ''And if you ever try that again, I'll break your wrist.''

Dark glints lit the jade eyes. ''What if I let you be on top next time?''

''Certainly. *If* I were wearing cement boots—with a whole lot of spikes.''

''Have you ever eaten Bordeaux oysters fresh from the salt marshes on the Seudre River, Ms. O'Neill? With just a hint of lemon juice and nothing more. You'd like them. Then we'd add some hot sausages and a little pastry from Gascony. Maybe a *foie gras* or two and a big white Burgundy. Or perhaps a bottle of Sauternes, since that's your specialty." His eyes narrowed, considering. "A Château Climens '71, I'd say. Big and gorgeous and magnificently well bred." His eyes followed the curves suggested but not quite revealed by the black velvet of Cathlin's jacket. "Chilled just fractionally to give an edge, of course."

The man was smooth, all right. And he bloody well knew his wines. He also didn't give up. "I don't eat oysters and I don't mix business with pleasure, Mr—"

"Montserrat," he finished smoothly. "Dominic, since we're going to be on a first name basis."

"Not in this lifetime we aren't. Lord Ashton," Cathlin added a moment later, remembering what Serita had told her of the man's background.

In the next room a very Oxonian voice announced that the Sauternes category was next and that this year's auctioneer would be Ms. Cathlin O'Neill of Nonesuch Wines, Philadelphia and London.

There was a ripple of applause.

"Very impressive, Ms. O'Neill."

"Not as impressive as I'm going to be if you hold me up any longer."

"Tell me which Sauternes I should bid on."

She looked him over thoroughly. "A '61 Climens, I think. Pleasant but hardly exciting. Impeccable opening aroma, but a thoroughly disappointing finish."

With that, she pushed off through the crowds already thronging the auction floor.

Dominic Montserrat's lips curved up in a hard smile. "Tough, aren't you? But let's see how a case of Château d'Yquem vintage 1792 worth two million dollars grabs you, Ms. O'Neill."

"Next on our program we have a very fine Château Climens '71. This, as you all know, is a superb sweet white Bordeaux with excellent balance, exquisite overtones, and a fine finish. It would make a perfect companion to some of the chocolate trifle I had here earlier. Now who will give me fifty? No one? Come, come, Mr. Smythe-Hampton." Cathlin made the words a sultry caress as she smiled at a tall man in an $8,000 Patek Phillipe watch.

He smiled. His pale fingers wobbled.

The man beside him muttered something and stabbed at the air.

Two minutes later the sale was closed at two thousand pounds.

Cathlin breathed an inward sigh of relief. Her feet were killing her and her shoulder itched. But there was one lot left to go.

"Our last lot tonight is a very special bottle of Château d'Yquem 1870. It is, quite simply, a legend that deserves being a legend, with marvelous texture, perfect balance, and wonderful finesse. It is also distinguished by a resolute finish. I suggest you offer it with a wedge of Grand Marnier soufflé and a bit of Vivaldi. In a Georgian drawn-stem wineglass, of course." Her lips curved. "Except for you, Reginald." She gestured at Mr. Smythe-Hampton, who was sweating openly now. "You can drink it out of that gold bullion you keep in your vault. My partner Serita will no doubt be happy to help you carve it into a suitable-size container."

Amid the laughter, the rare bottle was carefully lifted for display, to a host of muffled sighs.

"Let's be dangerous, shall we? No need for preliminaries." Cathlin swept a curve of satin hair back off her cheek. "Do I hear, say, three hundred pounds?"

"Five hundred."

Heads crooked. Women whispered at the unorthodox size of the bid.

And Cathlin felt a sinking sensation in her stomach.

The voice was cool and correct and utterly brash. It could belong to only one man.

Dominic Montserrat.

Cathlin made a point of not looking. "Do I hear six? Six hundred pounds?"

Mr. Smythe-Hampton nodded.

"Six hundred. Do I hear—"

"A thousand."

Cathlin looked up and met piercing jade eyes. "Perhaps our mystery bidder has a few chunks of gold bullion of his own lying around among the Bentleys. I have a thousand," she repeated. "Do I hear a thousand one?"

Smythe-Hampton wiggled uncomfortably and inched up one finger.

"One thousand one."

Two rows away a well-groomed man in a Turnbull and Asser shirt raised a manicured finger.

"I have one thousand two. You'd like this one, Richard." Cathlin smiled at the well-groomed international financier she had worked with on several occasions. "Much better than that last batch of erratic '83 Burgundies you bought."

Richard Severance smiled tightly and raised his hand. Cathlin's comments were dead on target, of course, so he shrugged gracefully.

"I have one thousand two. Do I hear one thousand three for this brilliant Château d'Yquem? Come now, ladies and gentlemen. One of our most famous statesmen and presidents admired this wine greatly. You do remember Thomas Jefferson, don't you? He was on the other side of that little war we fought a few years back. But really, no hard feelings. You got to keep the peerage and we got to keep the tea, even if it was at the bottom of Boston Harbor. So now, for Mr. Jefferson, do I hear—"

"Five thousand pounds."

Cathlin swallowed. The man was mad, utterly mad.

She saw heads bend and mouths gape open. She saw bejeweled women turn clear around in their seats.

And she saw the president of the wildlife fund

smiling broadly in the front row, already counting his money.

Cathlin took a breath. "Five thousand pounds. Do I hear six? Six thousand for this memorable vintage?" She waited, glancing at Mr. Smythe-Hampton, who looked flushed and sulky. He shook his head.

Cathlin's eyes swept the room. "Do I hear six?"

Richard Severance frowned and looked away.

Cathlin brought down her silver gavel. "Sold for five thousand pounds. End of lot. End of category. Thank you for all your warm participation. I'm sure our lucky buyers will enjoy these exceptional Sauternes and that the proceeds will go to help a very good cause."

She moved out, fast and silent, but she wasn't fast enough.

He closed in on her before she even got to the bottom of the stairs. "Go away," she hissed. A countess in too many opals and too little silk blinked at her and sniffed.

"Now that one's a Chablis." Dominic moved right in behind her. "An '82, I'd say. Overweight and overpriced." He slid into step, his breath tickling the soft skin at her neck.

Cathlin tried to ignore him.

"That one's an '80." He pointed to a man in polished loafers and a head of hair that was obviously not his own. "He's had his good moments, but now he's fading fast."

Cathlin felt her lips curve into a reluctant smile.

"And then there's that one." Dominic pointed to a woman in a black dress whose brevity barely qualified as decent. She looked very glossy and expensive to maintain. "Definitely a '75."

"A keep-away vintage?"

"At all costs."

So he really did know his wines. Cathlin studied him closer, noting the tiny lines around his mouth and eyes. From too much beach time or something else? "And what exactly are you, Mr. Montserrat?" Not that it mattered, of course.

"Oh, I'm definitely Château d'Yquem 1870, the exact lot you sold to me. I'm all marvelous texture and wonderful finesse." His eyes burned over her face and settled on her full lips. "Especially the resolute finish. Care to try it out with me?"

"The wine?"

"Of course. Did you think I meant something else?"

Definitely. His eyes were hinting at something much more earthy. Cathlin shrugged. She'd heard all the innuendos before. At least this man did it with panache. "You're asking me to share the bottle you just bought for five thousand pounds?"

"I could always get something more expensive, if it's not enough."

"Are you serious? Does money mean nothing to you?"

"You might be surprised."

"I doubt it."

He moved ahead of her, blocking her way. "I've just spent a great deal of money to secure your good opinion, Ms. O'Neill, but it looks like I'm failing. Help me a little here." The mockery was gone from his voice. He seemed almost sincere.

As sincere as a car dealer at a convention of little old ladies, Cathlin thought sourly. "Listen closely, Lord Ashton. I can't. I won't. I'm not interested. End of lot. End of category." The bluntness had always worked before. Somehow Cathlin found herself regretting that it would work again now.

"It's important, damn it. I need to talk to you. Now."

This time his voice was taut. Could he possibly be serious? She looked pointedly at her watch. "You have thirty seconds."

He glanced at the throngs around them. "I can't. Not like this."

"Five seconds."

"Not here, damn it."

"Ten."

"It's—confidential. I have a letter to show you, but it will have to be done somewhere more private."

Cathlin shook her head, angry at herself for believing him, even for a moment. He was just like all the others, men with smooth smiles and sleazy agendas. "I see, someplace private. Back at your apartment, no doubt. Probably with our clothes off on the middle of the bed." She stepped forward and ran her hand along his lapel. "Sorry, Lord Ashton, but I'm not impressed. You're several centuries too late with that Don Juan routine." She smiled sweetly. "But maybe the Chablis '75 would think differently. She hasn't looked away from you once. Good night—and happy hunting."

Cathlin felt his eyes burn into her all the way to the door.

He cursed.

Softly. Then not so softly.

Two men frowned at him and a woman in a backless Yves St. Laurent sheath giggled.

Dominic saw a familiar face and caught her wrist. "Serita? Come here and talk to me."

"You found her, I see."

"I found her all right. I have the wounds to prove it."

"Sorry, Dominic. I'm afraid Cathlin's a little prickly these days."

"Prickly wasn't exactly the word I had in mind," Dominic said grimly.

"It hasn't been easy for her, you know. She's young and lovely and very honest, Dominic. That's a difficult combination for this set. It's still very much a man's world over here, you know. Half the men in this room act as if Lord Nelson still rules the seas and America is just one of our colonies."

Dominic cocked a brow dramatically. "You mean it isn't?"

"Repulsive insect." But her eyes were admiring. "That tan becomes you. How are you doing? Really doing?"

"A decent yield." Dominic thought of his neat rows of vines marching over the hills of his holding in the Garonne. He was turning out his fourth vintage this year and already his vineyard, La Trouvaille, was making a solid profit from its rich, complex wines. It had been hard work, but the very best work of his life. "The sugar levels could be better, but we're working on that. So far no problem with quality, but—"

"No, I mean *you*. You inside."

He shrugged. "I'm surviving."

"That tells me next to nothing."

"Maybe I like it that way." Dominic gave her a lopsided smile that took the sting from his answer. "Tell me about her, Serita." He said the words tightly.

"Look, Dominic, she's not one of your usual runway beauties or extrovert actresses. She's nice and she's vulnerable. Leave her alone." Serita's voice was surprisingly hard.

"I don't plan on bodily physical harm, my dear. I have a business offer for her, that's all. But the lady seems determined not to hear it. Tell me why."

Serita sighed. "She lost her mother young, Dominic. Then she lost her father when she was just getting to know him. He was in security, I gather. Among other things," Serita said. "Oh, she doesn't talk about it much. She says she's put it all behind her. But she's lying. And that's one of the reasons she doesn't care for pomp and circumstance English-style."

Dominic laughed shortly. "So I've noticed."

"Unfortunately, *you're* very long on both, my dear man."

"Who me? I'm just your average working stiff."

Serita studied his lean, chiseled face. "Not in a million years. You're too bloody handsome for comfort. You're also too arrogant."

Dominic frowned as he saw Richard Severance stride up to Cathlin and slide his arm casually around her shoulder. When he laughed—and he seemed to laugh a great deal—Dominic saw that he had very regular white teeth. "What about *him?"*

Serita turned. "Richard? Oh, there might have been something between them once. I didn't ask and Cathlin never told me. But if so, it was nothing serious. Now it's just business."

Dominic watched Cathlin's slender back disappear through the doorway. She was beautiful and clever and he'd be a bloody fool to get within two counties of her. "I heard a saying over in Thailand once, Serita. It went something like this. Woe to any man who trusts a clever woman, because she'll drive him to all fours and leave him howling like a scrawny dog in the market square." Particularly, Dominic added silently, if the woman in question had black hair as soft as China satin and burning amber eyes.

Serita brushed his cheek. "Maybe, with the right person, howling can be fun."

"About as much fun as taking a heavy caliber .357 Magnum slug in the leg," Dominic muttered. He knew, because he'd done it. More than once.

But that life was behind him. Wine was what he cared about now, and if getting the funds to improve his acreage in France meant being nice to bloody Miss High-and-Mighty O'Neill, maybe he'd have to consider it. Besides, he had a personal score to settle now. "Where's she spending the weekend?" he asked tightly.

"Forget it. You'll never find her."

Dominic turned, his eyes urgent. "Please, Serita. I won't charm her and I won't push her. I just need a chance to talk to her in private, away from all this. It's important. To *both* of us."

Something about the urgency in his voice cut through Serita's obvious reluctance. "I don't suppose you'd care to be more specific."

"Sorry, Serita, I can't."

She sighed. "You promise you won't be an utter pest?"

"Who, me?" He gave her an innocent look.

"*You.*"

"I promise. On my honor as a good Etonian."

"Etonians don't *have* any honor, only a universe of charm. Dangerous charm." Serita had been involved with enough of them to know.

Dominic frowned. "If I have any charm, Cathlin O'Neill didn't see it."

"Didn't fall for you? Come to think of it, this might be a very salutary experience for you, Dominic." Serita nodded decisively. "She's got a big, rambling house on the southeast coast, overlooking Romney Marsh."

"Near Rye? How in the world did she manage that?"

"Seacliffe came to her through her mother's family. Cathlin hasn't been there often since her father's death last year. Oh, the place is beautiful, but very expensive. The house itself is early seventeenth century and there's a ruined thirteenth century priory on the grounds."

Since Dominic had just finished renovating a fourteenth century chateau in France at La Trouvaille, he'd seen enough crumbling plaster and rotting wood to last a lifetime. He also knew firsthand just how expensive—and how infuriating—such a project could be.

Which meant that things were definitely looking up. "So she'll need lots of money?"

"Don't we all?" Serita asked cynically.

"I can help her then. Tell me how to find her, Serita. Just to talk to her. It's urgent."

After a moment Serita sighed and reached into her purse. "She'll kill me if she finds out I gave this to you, but—" She pulled out a pen and scribbled on a sheet of paper. "Good luck. You're definitely going to need it."

"Thanks, my dearest Serita." Dominic bent and kissed his companion's cheek. Smiling slightly, he pocketed the precious address.

And now I have you, Ms. O'Neill, he vowed darkly.

Three ~

Southeastern England
Romney Marsh

Water.

Reeds.

A thin black ribbon of road and beyond it the coast of Kent in May, all shadows and cold silver.

Out in the English Channel, lightning forked through the darkening afternoon sky. A storm over Dieppe, Dominic thought. Or maybe above Dunkirk to the north.

Some days in summer, France must look close enough to touch, he mused. But not today, with rain racing over the channel and the thermometer dropping by the hour.

He squinted into the windshield, past the fingers of mist that drifted over the glimmering silver pools. How far was it to Seacliffe? He'd stopped in Rye for directions and had been told to take the coast road. Now, as the sun slanted low and golden over the hillside, over the barren marshes where two hundred years before smugglers must have plied their desperate trade, Dominic felt as if he'd stepped straight back into the past, a past without highways, electric wires, or telephone poles. And there was something very beautiful about that past.

He swung his battered Triumph around a sharp curve and crossed a narrow granite bridge. To his right a pair of Sussex sheep stood grazing beside a granite boulder that marked the gravel road up to Seacliffe. Slowing, Dominic studied the landscape. The wind was picking up now, and through the tossing reeds he finally made out a winding drive that led up the hill.

He was a fool to have come here, Dominic thought as he eased the Triumph over the deep ruts. His old car, which he kept at his family estate near Tunbridge, was well loved. He had hand-nursed it for too many years to see it wrecked on a gravel road now.

Suddenly there was a crack of lightning and a wave of sand struck the windshield, driven by the first gusts of the coming storm. Dominic downshifted, trying to see in front of him, and cursed when he heard a thump, followed by the hiss of leaves. The next moment the Triumph struck what felt like a wall of cement and his head smashed down against the windshield.

Slowly, Dominic fought his way back to consciousness. His head was throbbing and through the sand scattered on the cracked glass he made out a tree blocking the road five feet ahead of him.

So that's what had left him with the fifty-piece orchestra hammering inside his head, he thought irritably.

Scowling, he shoved opened the door, but his initial hope of moving the tree aside quickly faded. The lightning had broken, but not severed, the huge trunk and the roots were still half-embedded in the sandy soil. It would take at least three men to wrench them free and cart the tree off the road.

He would just have to walk the rest of the way.

Muttering uncharitable words against a woman

who kept a house in such isolated countryside, Dominic grabbed his single bag, turned toward the hill, and began to walk.

But as he strode through the wild, beautiful terrain of the marsh and the lapping sea, his thoughts grew calmer. Even with the rising wind, the place had a brooding beauty that went right to Dominic's soul. With every cool cry of a passing kestrel, Dominic again felt that strange sense that he had been carried back in time.

He laughed softly and hiked his bag over his shoulder. Places of beauty and isolation had always intrigued him. It was half the reason he'd fallen in love with La Trouvaille, gleaming in the early morning sun.

Off to his right came the distant clang of sheep bells. The sound rose and fell, carried on the gusting wind, first loud then wavering sharply. Strange, Dominic thought, he'd never been here before. In spite of that, the sound was almost familiar.

Shrugging, he walked on, letting the low hiss of his feet on the sand settle into a rhythm.

Again the bells rose. *Clang-clang*, they called out, tugging at his mind. He frowned, studying the hills that rose lush and green above the sandy slope. Where had he heard that sound before?

Again it came, making him think of the wood slamming against stone. The sound was restless and sad in the last hour of daylight.

Clang-clang.

Suddenly, as sweat trickled over his forehead, Dominic knew that something about the sound was infinitely important to him.

He closed his eyes, letting the noise roll over him, opening deeply to its meaning.

He had a sudden image of a house. A house with no lights.

Clang-clang.

A big gray house with weathered green shutters. A house by water, full of noisy people. A house where something very important had once happened to him.

He cut off his reverie with a low laugh. He'd never seen any house like that, although he'd been in enough grimy waterfronts in his life.

Yet with every distant clang Dominic felt his hair rise at his neck.

Clang-clang. Clang-clang.

What did it mean? And why did the sound seem to mock him, rising in gray waves that filled his head until he could think of nothing else.

Tendrils of mist curled about his feet and the wind pulled at his clothes. He thought of water and night and an infinite loneliness.

Most of all Dominic thought of honor—and a vow betrayed. On he walked, fog at his feet, wind in his hair. And as he walked, his mind drifted, coiling like the mist.

Imagining.

Or was he really remembering?

London
The Crown and Dragon
April 1794

Outside the inn a loose shutter was banging in the wind.

Frowning, Gabriel Ashton tossed off the last of his brandy, cursing the noise, cursing the ache in his side, most of all cursing his memories. For once he'd actually succeeded in forgetting, putting the death and blood of the Paris streets out of his head.

Then she had swept into the noisy inn that squatted on the mist-covered bank of the Thames.

Clang-clang.

The same wind that banged the shutters sent her per-

*fume wafting through the smoky room filled with game-
sters and footpads and thieves. Roses, perhaps? Or was it
something more subtle?*

The fifth earl of Ashton scowled down at his empty
glass. Damned if he cared. He was only here to forget. To
drink himself into the darkness of utter oblivion, where he
could finally escape the cries of the hungry children in the
Paris streets.

As he poured himself another drink, her perfume mocked
him yet again. Lilacs, he decided, with just a hint of cinna-
mon. It was as unusual as the woman herself, her fine-
boned face framed by the hood of her velvet cloak, with
blue satin shimmering at one hem.

Hardly the usual attire of the women who conducted
their profitable trade at the Crown and Dragon, Gabriel
thought grimly.

And those eyes of hers. Dear God, they reminded him
of Baltic amber shot through with flecks of gold. How
young those eyes were. And how achingly innocent. But
beneath the cloak came the shimmer of satin that hinted
at a body tantalizingly ripe.

He must be drunk, Ashton thought cynically. Not that
it had helped him forget.

A slender shadow fell against the grimy table where
he sat.

"May I sit down?"

Gabriel looked the woman up and down, striving to be
as rude as possible. Her face was even finer than he'd
thought, which meant she had no business being in a place
like the Crown and Dragon. "No," he snapped.

Color flared across those impossibly creamy cheeks, but
for some reason Dominic wasn't pleased at the sight.

She gnawed at her full lower lip, then sat down anyway.
"I am looking for someone, you see." Her voice was cultured, yet with a rural softness.

"Aren't we all?" Gabriel was surprised to hear that his
words were faintly slurred. Ah, well, a bottle of brandy
would make even King George himself slur his words.

Except that these days the unfortunate, mad king always slurred his words.

"My name is Geneva Ru—"

He cut her off abruptly. "Not a place f'r real names. Not by the likes of you anyway." Gabriel scowled at her, wishing she would go away. Wishing she would stop blushing.

Most of all wishing he could see the color of her hair beneath that soft, flowing hood she wore.

"You are drunk, sir!"

"That was my plan," the earl agreed easily. "Care to join me, m'lady?"

Her eyes widened. Ashton saw her lips tremble in their haste to form a denial. And then she went quite still. "I see. This is the test he told me about."

"Test? I should like to offer you many things, my dear," the earl said huskily, "starting with a roll between my sheets. But not a test."

"You are vastly rude."

"That was also my intention." And so it was, Ashton thought. Perhaps the bloodstained streets of France had left him unable to look upon such innocence without feeling resentful.

Abruptly the candle fluttered. A cold wind rushed through the room, and the door was thrown open by a crowd of noisy sailors.

Drunk, no doubt, Gabriel thought. And so would he have been if she had not interrupted him like some avenging angel. "Go away."

"But I need your help."

Ashton's eyes narrowed on her fine kid gloves. "If you're looking for help, you've come to the wrong place. Certainly to the wrong man."

But she was as stubborn as she was unsuited to her sordid setting. "I think not. I have heard about the many brave things you've done." She glanced about and lowered her voice. "You once helped a friend of mine." She drew

something from her pocket and laid it on the grimy table.
"He said to show you this."

It was a rook's feather, the sign of the man who was
wanted throughout France for snatching aristocrats from
the very shadow of the guillotine.

Gabriel's eyes hardened. "How come you by that,
young woman?"

"From my friend, Lord Draycott."

"From Adrian, you say?" Gabriel finished his brandy.
Determined to be discourteous, he immediately poured another. "Are you lovers?" Adrian Draycott, plump of pocket
and striking in his dark good looks, was notorious for his
unquenchable appetites.

"That is none of your affair, I believe."

"Ah, but it is. If you ask a man's help, then everything
becomes his business." He steepled his hands. "Well, are
you?"

"No," she said flatly. "Though for his part—" She
looked down, coloring.

"So he wants you for his bed, does he?" Maybe it was
the brandy that made Gabriel speak so crudely. Or maybe
it was the fineness of her eyes, eyes that urged him to be
the hero she took him for.

Which, of course, was entirely absurd. Gabriel Ashton
was no hero.

"Go back to Adrian. His wealth will buy all the assistance you need. I can do nothing for you."

"But it is an affair most grave!"

"Aren't they all?" The earl studied her over the rim of
his glass. "Have you lost a bundle of love letters and fear
that your husband will find them and toss you out on
your lovely backside? Or have you been indiscreet with a
mercenary cad who means you to buy his silence after a
night of passion?"

Her chin rose and she clasped her hands before her with
infinite dignity. "Lord Draycott told me it would be exactly so with you. First you would bait me, then you
would be vastly cynical and refuse me. But I told him he

must be wrong. The man called the Rook would never turn down such a desperate request. And you are that man," she said firmly. "You are the hero I seek."

"My dear woman," Ashton said, his voice as cynical as she'd predicted, "the notorious Lord Draycott was correct for once. I do refuse you. And I know nothing of this person you call the Rook. Now if you will kindly hie yourself off, I have a glass of brandy here that requires my immediate attention."

And a host of nightmares to forget, *Gabriel* thought bitterly.

"But you can't! Truly, you are my last hope."

The earl turned away, hardening his heart. He'd heard too many sad tales over the last two years. Why should he take time for hers?

Frowning, he tossed back the last of his brandy, then refilled his glass. As he emptied it, he felt a pleasant numbness steal over him.

Much better, he decided.

Looking up, he saw blue satin blur into white lace. "What? You still here? Go away. 've got no time f'r angels."

Somewhere there were three more angels tonight, he thought dimly. Three children with frightened faces who'd fallen to the blades of the Tribunal, their only crime to be born with blood too blue. Gabriel knew he'd never forget them.

Her gloved fingers settled resolutely on the table. "I see I must make myself very clear. I am prepared to give you whatever fee you ask for your services, my lord. Anything at all."

"Anything?" the earl asked brutally. "Best be careful with that particular word, m' dear."

"I am. I would only make the offer to a man of honor like yourself."

"Then your faith is sadly misplaced."

"Not at all. The Rook is a man of great honor!"

Ashton laughed bitterly. "He might be, but I'm not."

"I think not. You are known to a cousin of mine, you see. You must remember the comte de Broussard. Last month the two of you were engaged to fight a duel. Although he is little more than a boy, his honor was touched, and nothing would do but for him to call you out." Her eyes took on a gleam. "You devolved most nobly, after appearing to stumble."

"Didn't pretend anything," Ashton muttered. "Exceedingly drunk at the time and m' hand slipped."

"On the contrary, my lord. You merely pretended to be drunk."

"And on what d' you base this masterpiece of deduction?"

"One simple fact: when you entered your carriage after the seconds had been satisfied, you were again the soul of sobriety."

An odd look crossed Ashton's face. "And how, young woman, would you know a thing like that?"

"Because I was right behind you."

"You?"

"You do not recall me?"

"I think not!"

"Hardly surprising, I suppose, since I was dressed in the yellow livery of your house at the time."

"Impossible!"

Her amber eyes gleamed. "Not at all, my lord. You were wearing a vastly elegant sapphire waistcoat with an exquisite fall of white lace about your neck. In the lace was nestled a diamond stickpin carrying the Ashton crest. In addition you wore one of the Ashton emeralds on your left forefinger."

The earl shrugged. "Anyone could have told you that."

"But you cursed as the stairs were lowered. And then you vowed that you would never again drink port at White's with young cubs just up from Sussex."

An arrested look crossed Ashton's face. "You were the clumsy cockney lad? The one who earned my abuse for failing to see the coach door fastened properly?"

Miss Geneva Russell nodded gracefully. "Verbal abuse only, for which I much thank you. Other masters would have used a cane on me. I fear I would have found that most unpleasant."

"What audacity! You are monstrous impertinent, miss."

Her chin rose defiantly. "And you, my lord, are monstrous foxed."

"Not foxed enough." But Gabriel knew he'd have to be dead drunk to be immune to this woman's charm. "What d'y say y'r name was?"

"I didn't. You warned me that I should not."

"Did I? Can't think why. Unless y've something to hide."

"I do not," Geneva said with great dignity. "My name is Geneva R—"

Gabriel sat forward so swiftly that his head swam. "No names," he said gravely, in blithe ignorance of his own pronouncement. "Dressed as a footman, you say? By God, I should turn you over my knee to repay such trickery."

"You would have to catch me first."

"Did I catch you, you would soon be sorry. Now off with you!"

"Not until you agree to help me. It is the Rook I need and the Rook I mean to have."

Gabriel's eyes narrowed in anger, but she met his gaze without flinching. "You were very kind to let my poor cousin go free, for he is a dreadful shot and he did malign your honor most shamefully. In truth, I thought you most handsome. And wonderfully noble."

Gabriel Simon Montserrat, Lord Ashton, hardened roué and lifelong cynic, could only stare in disbelief. "Noble?" He thought of the three soldiers he'd left in the mud outside Calais. He thought of the French children whose cries still haunted his dreams.

Bottle in hand, he pushed away from the table. She would betray him, as all other women had done. He could not trust her or anyone else with his dangerous secret. "Enough of this. I've a bottle to finish and a pair of willing

arms to find. Unless you'd care to join me in my bed?"
He tossed down a gold sovereign as a final insult. He saw
her cheeks darken and laughed harshly. "No? I thought
not. Women like you always offer the world, then forget
it a moment later."

"But—"

Gabriel turned away. "Go back where you came from,
Geneva of the golden eyes. Go back to your satins and
velvets and forget you ever saw me." His jaw hardened
and he lied to her with the cool ease of a man whose lies
had often saved his life. "For my part, I've already forgot-
ten that I ever met you."

The sun had gone by the time Dominic felt himself
slip out of his odd reverie. His head was aching
where he'd struck the dashboard and he couldn't
seem to clear the odd fragments of images from his
mind. It must be the strange desolation of the marsh,
hugging the shore of the channel. Perhaps its weight
of ghostly history had played tricks with his mind.
Or perhaps it was the thought of his ancestor's exploits, resurfacing in all this attention to the will.

Dominic was near the crest of the hill now, and a
cold wind drove over the reeds, carrying the sharp
salt tang of the sea. Yes, it was simply the storm and
the shadows that brought him such odd thoughts.

As he walked through the gathering shadows he
tried not to think about a woman with golden eyes.
He tried not to hear the distant clang of a wooden
shutter.

But he didn't quite succeed.

Four ~

Cathlin frowned as she trudged over the crest of the hill that ran from a copse of gnarled oaks down to the lawn skirting Seacliffe's weathered walls.

Out to sea dark clouds piled in toward the land. Just what she needed, more rain! Seacliffe's gabled old roof already leaked in half a dozen places and Cathlin doubted it would bear the assault of another full-fledged gale.

She gnawed at her lip, calculating the cost of the repairs that would be required after another storm. More money than she had, certainly, which meant that she'd have to take on new clients.

She sighed. She and Serita had finally built up a successful list of customers with the palate and the pocketbook to appreciate their choices. But with the demands of renovating Seacliffe, all that would have to change. Cathlin knew she'd have to take on additional commissions and broaden her clientele, taking on the high rollers she had always avoided, men with far more money than taste, whose only concern was buying high-ticket and making sure everyone knew it.

Was this wonderful old house she'd inherited worth it? True, it was a thing of beauty and her only concrete connection to the mother she'd lost so young, but would Seacliffe simply awaken the old memories?

Cathlin shivered and hunched her shoulders against the rising wind, then set off through a tangle of berry vines. Seacliffe's broad green lawns were only yards away, but the air was filled with fine bits of sand and gravel, which left her cheeks flushed and stinging.

She stared out at the marsh, looking for a car. She was expecting a structural engineer from Hastings later that afternoon, but it was possible that with the coming storm, he might not make the trip. She only prayed that if he came, he wouldn't ask for a bank draft up front.

And then Cathlin went still as she saw someone striding up the hill. Some instinct made her pull back behind a hawthorn tree so that she could watch unobserved. He ran for the porticoed front entrance just as the first fat drops hit the gravel drive. Frowning, he propped one broad shoulder against the weathered granite and turned to survey the house. Fawn corduroy trousers hugged his lean hips below a shirt of tailored blue denim. A slash of dark hair curved down into his eyes. In the gloom of the storm, Cathlin couldn't make out much more than this—except that he looked cool and quiet and dangerous.

Then he turned toward the sea, and Cathlin felt her breath catch.

Dominic Montserrat? How had *he* gotten her address?

She strode over the gravel, not bothering with a smile. "What do *you* want?"

One dark brow crooked. "How about shelter from the storm?"

"I'm waiting, Mr. Montserrat." Cathlin didn't like the peerage in general and she certainly wasn't going to make an exception for *him*.

Dominic sighed. "As I told you in London, I need

to talk to you about some wine. You didn't return my calls, remember?"

"I've been busy," Cathlin said curtly.

"This is no game, Ms. O'Neill."

"Talk to Serita. She's got a tremendous knowledge of wine. Besides that, she actually appears to like you."

Her visitor looked Cathlin over slowly, taking in her faded blue jeans and baggy Montreal Canadiens sweatshirt. His gaze went to the matching Canadiens cap that covered her sleek black hair. "Very nice. I think I like it even more than the black velvet."

"Good-bye, Lord Ashton."

"You can't just throw me out. The road is blocked down there by a fallen tree, and I can't go anywhere."

"So walk back to Rye. You're certainly not staying here. As you can see, I'm busy. I've got to see a man about my roof. Assuming that it's still there, of course."

Dominic's keen eyes narrowed. "What's wrong with your roof?"

"Rain damage from our last gale. And about two hundred or so before that one." Cathlin shoved the Canadiens cap lower on her head. "Something like a century of neglect isn't helping either. Why?"

"Just curious."

"Don't tell me. In addition to dabbling in wines, you just happen to be an authority on roofs."

"As it happens, I am."

The man's gall was beyond belief. "And I'm the Royal Mum," Cathlin snapped. She stiffened as his eyes slid over her. "May I ask why you're staring at me?"

"You're different out here. Younger. Softer. Then again, appearances are usually a trap."

Great, now he was a philosopher. A philosopher with something cold and hard at the back of his eyes.

Maybe he could brandish a quote from Descartes to patch that three-foot gap in the south roof, Cathlin thought bitterly. She pushed past him and shoved open Seacliffe's massive, rose-covered door. "It's been nice to know you, Mr. Montserrat. Walk carefully."

The door wedged open beneath the firm force of his foot. "I happen to be great with roofs, O'Neill, and it sounds like you're going to need an expert."

"This is a bad dream," she said, closing her eyes. "I'm going to wake up and you'll be gone, I know it." She opened her eyes and sighed.

"Still here. Tell me why you haven't returned any of my calls."

"Because I don't want to talk to you," Cathlin said very clearly, the way one would speak to a sulky child.

"What is it with you Americans?"

"Ask Ben Franklin. He didn't like you aristocrats much either."

"Can we stop the warfare and get back to business?"

"What business? You were milling around trying to convince me you're seriously interested in my roof and I was trying to convince you that I don't believe a word you say."

Dominic frowned as he stood angled in the doorway. Over his shoulder he had seen a glint of metal down the hill.

Coincidence, or something more?

"What's wrong?"

"There's something moving out there."

"Of course there is. With white fur and four legs. They're called sheep."

"What I saw was no sheep."

"Then it was probably a hiker. We get them down here occasionally. It's certainly nothing to worry about."

His eyes swept the reed-filled pools along the coast. "A strange time for a hiker to be enjoying the scenery, considering the wind that's kicking up. Still, you might be right."

"Of course, I'm right. And now I have a roof to look at before it starts to rain."

Dominic Montserrat, however, was one step ahead of her. He pushed the door wide and strode past her, moving easily down the polished corridor. "Where are the stairs?"

"*What* stairs?"

"To the roof, of course." He moved in utter silence, and something about that silence made Cathlin's neck prickle. "I'm going to need a ladder and some kind of light."

"You're not going to need anything, because you're not taking another step inside my house!"

He turned. His shoulder brushed hers. "A deal, all right? I check your roof and you listen to what I have to tell you. How about it?"

"Then you leave?"

"If you still want me to."

Cathlin felt his anger but even deeper she felt his raw determination. He was a man who would always get what he wanted, she sensed. There was strength in every move he made, iron control in every word and look. He was a man comfortable in his power and comfortable using it over others.

But not on *her.* Because she wasn't going to listen to one word more. "The answer's no. I've got to go. The door's right back there."

A muscle tensed at his jaw. So Lord Ashton didn't like losing, did he? His eyes locked on her face and Cathlin felt the full force of his will directed over her, searching for her deepest strengths and secret weaknesses, like a hunter assessing his prey. And Cathlin found herself attracted to that basic power in some deep, elemental way.

Raw physical power.

Raw confidence.

Raw skill.

Cathlin hated to admit it, but those things struck a chord in her, subtly stirring her senses until she wanted to offer a counterchallenge, female to male, and find out what it would take to break that iron control. Instinct whispered that this man would be a warrior in bed as in all else. He would possess ruthlessly and demand total honesty from the woman he loved. There would be no secrets and no holding back. And that same instinct told Cathlin that he would offer all of himself in turn, body and soul.

She swallowed, trying to break the spell of her swift fantasies, trying to fight the dark, wordless current of sensation that bound them as they stood silent, shoulder to shoulder, in Seacliffe's quiet halls. What would it feel like to be loved that way? What would it take for a woman to claim such a man in turn, strength to strength, heat to heat, challenging his granite control until he felt the same blind, wild need that she did?

Dangerous, O'Neill. Very dangerous.

A wedge of plaster peeled away from the ceiling and struck her head.

"Maybe you'd better not take too long to make up your mind, O'Neill."

An abrupt fragment of memory stole over Cathlin. Something about a dark room. Low voices. *Fear.*

She was fighting a shudder when a pair of hard hands settled on her shoulders. "Let me go."

"You're covered with plaster. You can't just—"

"Can't I?" Cathlin's heart was pounding as she shoved past him. Why in heaven's name did this man affect her so? And what was it about him that had just triggered those dim memories of the day her mother had died?

She wasn't going to wait around to find out. She took the last few feet in a rush, following the narrow staircase up to a dim attic, illuminated by three large oriel windows. *Steady O'Neill.* It was just one of the old memories, the kind that skittered through her mind late at night when the doors were locked and the moon inched over the horizon.

"You all right?" Somehow he was right behind her, as silent as a cat.

"I'm fine."

"You don't look fine."

Cathlin swallowed, uncomfortable beneath that intent green gaze that seemed to miss nothing. "Oh, very well. Have a look at the roof. Then I'll hear you out." *But don't expect me to believe a word,* she thought grimly. *And definitely don't expect to be staying on afterward.*

Dominic swung a heavy wooden ladder over his back as if it were no more than cardboard, then carried it to the far wall, which was speckled with damp rot. A blizzard of fallen plaster covered the floor at his feet.

He shook his head. "Not good. Exactly how old is this place?"

"Nearly four hundred years. I'd say the structure has held up exceedingly well for that kind of age."

"Sorry, Ms. O'Neill, but I've seen buildings demolished when they were in better shape than this."

"You probably enjoyed it, too," Cathlin said angrily. Damn the man! This was all a game to him, like his wine dabbling and his womanizing. "Look, don't let me keep you. This was a mistake from the start. I'll take my chances with the structural engineer from Hastings."

Dominic's eyes didn't leave her face as he opened the ladder. Casually he stripped off his leather jacket. "What's wrong? Do you want someone older? Someone more polite?" One hand rose to the neck of his tailored denim shirt. "Or do you just want someone who'll agree with whatever you say?"

The soft blue cloth hiked up over his flat stomach.

Cathlin's breath hissed free. "Just what do you think you're doing now?"

"Taking off a few clothes. You don't mind, do you, Ms. O'Neill?" His eyes held hers, shining with challenge. His chest was lean, deeply indented with muscle. And his shoulders . . . sweet heaven, they were a perfect fantasy, full and beautifully hard.

Warrior's chest. Warrior's body.

One look was enough to tell Cathlin that he'd earned those muscles anywhere except in a gym.

Cathlin took a steadying breath. He *wasn't* going to get to her. So the man had nice shoulders. Okay, so they were *phenomenal* shoulders. It would take a lot more than that to worm through her reserve, Cathlin told herself sternly. "I *do* mind, as a matter of fact."

"Sorry, but it can't be helped." He shrugged off his shirt and tossed it to the floor. The movement made the deeply sculpted muscles flex and curve.

Cathlin couldn't pull her eyes away.

"Do you have a problem with that, Ms. O'Neill?"

Cathlin swallowed. "No. No problem at all."

With a shrug, she swung the flashlight beam up toward the roof, intent on ignoring him. *He'll look, you'll listen, then he'll give up and go away,* she told herself. *It's not exactly World War Three, after all.*

"Are there any alarm systems up here I should be worrying about?"

"There's never been a need."

"It's the twentieth century. Nowhere is safe anymore." It sounded as if he'd had personal experience with the fact, but that was absurd. He didn't look like a man who thought about anything more serious than where he'd find the next night's bed partner.

Cathlin sniffed. She ignored the way his chest glinted, misted with sweat as he climbed the ladder and stretched up to feel the exposed beams in the ceiling.

That was when she decided it could be closer to World War Three than she'd thought.

"This house must hold a lot of memories for you."

"Enough." She wasn't about to discuss her past with him or anyone else.

His eyes narrowed at the chill in her voice. "Growing up in a place like this can be wonderful, even with the leaking roofs and ancient plumbing."

"Don't tell me, you just happen to have a drafty old castle of your own back in Sussex."

He smiled faintly. "Near Tunbridge, actually." He leaned back and braced an arm against the ladder. "Something wrong, Ms. O'Neill?"

"Wrong?"

"You're staring."

"No, I'm not." But she had been, Cathlin knew. No matter what she said, this was a different man from the one she'd met in London. This man was competent and cool and very intent. And there was something seductive about that kind of intensity, about the way he ran his hands through his hair, leaving it a rumpled mess when he was thinking. Or maybe it was the way he studied her, as if he were looking past the words, probing all the way inside her.

Suddenly she remembered Serita's description: *It's his eyes, I think. He looks at you and really sees you. There's something seductive, but dangerous about that kind of total focus in a man.*

Not for *her*, Cathlin vowed.

"Look, just finish checking the roof, if you don't mind."

Dominic shrugged and pulled a knife from his pocket. It looked comfortable in the palm of his hand. He gave the damaged ceiling an experimental jab. Instantly, plaster rained down over his neck and chest. He backed down the ladder, coughing all the

way, then surveyed the roof in silence. "Not good,"
he said finally. "Not good at all."

"Can it be fixed?"

He rubbed his jaw and Cathlin tried not to notice
the play of muscles across his chest. "We're probably
looking at a new beam structure and a new tin alloy
undersurfacing. Maybe even a whole new slate exterior.
It's damp rot all right, and it's gone all the way
through. It's going to take lots of money to repair it."

"How much money?"

His eyes darkened. For a fleeting moment Cathlin
saw something like reluctance there. He hiked one
powerful shoulder against a rung. "Two hundred
thousand, give or take."

"Give or take *what*, the Crown jewels?" Cathlin
moved to the window and gripped the sill. She'd
never be able to put together that kind of money.
And expensive or not, this old house was the only
real connection she had left to her mother. How
could she bear to lose it? "You're sure about that?
Maybe it's not as bad as you think."

He laughed harshly. "Ms. O'Neill, I also happen
to own an old château in the Garonne Valley in
France. It was beautiful, too, right down to the rotten
beams and crumbling foundation. Even the mice
nesting in the walls were kind of cute. But the place
was derelict. We had to rip out two complete walls
and most of the top floor before we could even start
on the roof. Believe me, I've waded through enough
wood dust and ruined plaster to know damp rot
when I see it."

Every word was a physical blow. The man clearly
knew what he was talking about.

Cathlin's heart fell. Two hundred thousand pounds!
Even if she signed up a hundred new clients, she
couldn't scrape together that kind of money.

Which meant she would lose Seacliffe.

She sank down in the rickety armchair at the window, her visitor forgotten. She felt the dim press of images, of sounds and colors too faint to be real memories. Long ago Cathlin and her mother had come up to these attics. Seacliffe had belonged to Cathlin's grandmother then, and the house had been a happy place, ringing with laughter.

When Cathlin's mother had been alive. When they'd been a family, and she'd seen her father smile.

"What am I going to do?" she whispered.

More plaster exploded beside her foot. Cathlin didn't move, staring down at the white mound, her eyes haunted.

"Maybe it's time you listened to me. I think I can help you."

Cathlin shoved at the plaster with her toe. "How?"

"There might be a way." Dominic gave an experimental tap on the wall.

"Do you mean I could manage it for less? If I helped out with the work perhaps."

"It's too dangerous to allow amateurs up here once the beams are removed and the construction's under way. No, I was thinking of something else. All it will take is a week of your time."

Anger replaced the empty ache in Cathlin's chest. "I see. How very imaginative," she said acidly. "But I'm afraid it would take a whole lot more than two hundred thousand pounds to tempt me to do that."

"Damn it, will you listen to me?" Dominic frowned and ran a hand through his long hair. As he did, flecks of plaster skittered over his chest. "It's not what you think. I'm talking about seven days together under one roof, nothing more."

"Right. And I'm an emissary from the Martian base hidden on the far side of the moon."

There was a sudden curve to his lips. "Are you always this prickly, O'Neill?"

"Depends on my company. After all, I'm not a complete idiot. Who would pay that kind of money for a week of my time? I'm not exactly centerfold material."

Dominic's green eyes narrowed. "Who told you that?"

"Two hundred thousand pounds for the pleasure of my company, in bed or otherwise?" Cathlin laughed rather unsteadily. "I rather think not."

"You rate yourself far too low in that case." His eyes were hard, his voice deadly serious.

Goose bumps rose along Cathlin's neck. He *wanted* her. She could almost taste the force of his desire, so attuned were they at that moment. And Cathlin discovered what a potent aphrodisiac that kind of hunger could be.

But she forced herself out of her sensual haze. What was happening to her? She was a competent professional who dealt with powerful people every day. She was responsible for rare objects worth thousands of dollars. She was capable and intelligent and utterly in control of her life.

Up until the moment you met this man, you were.

"I don't believe anything you've told me, Lord Ashton, but I'll listen anyway. As you see I'm rather desperate. So now maybe you'll be specific. How exactly are you proposing I make that vast sum of money you mentioned?" Cathlin spoke tightly, not wanting to believe he could be telling the truth.

"Actually, it's a little difficult to explain. Hell, it's more than a *little* difficult."

"Try me." Behind Cathlin another clump of plaster struck the floor. She muttered something graphic and slid her hands into her pockets.

"If you'd answered my messages, I could have told you all this a week ago," Dominic said irritably. "What it comes down to is this. You and I are the beneficiaries of a two-hundred–year-old will that stipulates the ownership of a very precious old case of wine. A Château d'Yquem, to be exact. Vintage 1792," he added, in the coup de grace.

"Château d'Yquem?" Cathlin's eyes widened. "But a wine of that age and quality would be worth about . . ."

"A million pounds at least. I know the figures too," Dominic said tightly.

"But why? And how?"

Dominic turned to pace the dusty attic. "It has to do with one of my ancestors. Mad Uncle Gabriel, we always called him, though he wasn't an uncle and I have no idea if he was mad. But he was reckless, mysterious, and a bit of a firebrand. And then, about a week ago . . ."

He stopped, rubbing the back of his neck irritably. Cathlin tried to focus on what he was saying, but she kept seeing the soft hair that swirled over his chest. "What happened then?"

"We found out when he died—and where. His skeleton was discovered hidden inside a walled-in cellar along with his wine. And with it was his last will and testament, stipulating the way the wine should be handled."

"Good heaven above."

"I was a little surprised too," Dominic said wryly. "But there's more, I'm afraid. According to the will you, as the descendant of one Geneva Russell, and I, as Gabriel Ashton's oldest living descendant, must spend seven days together at the site of the buried wine. Otherwise, the will is negated."

"Is that legal?"

Dominic smiled faintly. "Hell if I know. I'm told it is. The point is that the man who found the wine considers himself honor bound to comply with Gabriel's last request. I expect you would, too, if you found a two-hundred–year-old skeleton buried in your cellar."

Cathlin took an unsteady breath. "But it all seems so . . . so odd."

Dominic shrugged. "Don't look at me. I'm not exactly thrilled about taking a week away from my own work right now."

Cathlin looked out the window, listening to the wind rise. "One million pounds," she repeated softly. Then she looked up. "Is this some kind of joke? If it is, so help me I'm going to—"

"It's no joke. I've got the documents to prove it. I can even arrange for you to see the will, which was signed in Gabriel's blood," Dominic said grimly.

"You're kidding, surely."

His hard look told her just the opposite.

"My God, you're telling the truth, aren't you?" Cathlin watched a cloud of plaster swirl up, carried by a gust of wind from one of the holes in the roof. "But why us? What was the connection between our ancestors? They weren't married, by the sound of things. What happened to them?"

"That's part of the puzzle, I'm afraid. I've done some checking into the Ashton family records, but came up with nothing. I was hoping that you might be able to supply some answers about this Geneva Russell."

Cathlin frowned. "I don't know much about that side of the family. My mother was an only child, you see. And then, after she . . ." Cathlin cleared her throat. "After she died, my father and I moved to Philadelphia. He had scads of relatives there and it simply seemed the best thing to do." She glanced around the attic. "I suppose there might be some kinds of records around here. I haven't had much time to go through things." She looked at Dominic and gnawed at her lip. "Not that I'm agreeing, mind you, but where would this hypothetical week be spent?"

"Here in England."

"Where here in England?"

He seemed very concerned with closing the catch on the ladder all of a sudden. Cathlin's eyes narrowed. "I'm waiting."

"Someplace north of here. Nice grounds. A moat and a beautiful granite abbey."

A gust of air swirled down from the roof, ruffling the fine hairs at Cathlin's neck.

Moat. Granite. Abbey.

She shivered slightly. "Just give me the name."

Slowly her visitor wrapped one broad hand around the ladder. "Draycott," he said finally. "Draycott Abbey."

"No." Cathlin's face had gone very pale. "That's impossible. Draycott is where my mother was . . . murdered."

Five ❦

Dominic shoved a hand in his pocket and cursed softly. It wasn't going to work, he could feel it already. Still something kept him from walking out. Maybe it was the pain Cathlin O'Neill was trying valiantly to keep from filling her eyes.

"I'm sorry." He ran a hand through his hair. "I can imagine how painful this is for you." He frowned at how that sounded. "Hell, probably I can't begin to imagine. But this is a chance for *you*, for your future. Your mother would want that kind of chance for you."

Cathlin turned and rested her head against the windowpane. The movement sent her hair sliding over her cheeks.

Dominic felt the force of that single gesture through his whole body. Even now there was a grace to her, a vitality that pulled him like a magnet. He'd felt aware of her as a woman since the first second he'd seen her, but the awareness had soon turned to something more. It was dark and elemental, like this beautiful wild landscape around them.

That's crazy, Montserrat. You're strangers with a business deal to consider, and nothing more.

He shoved a hand against the ladder, reminding himself that he was a man who prided himself on being in control. It was part of him by nature and profession. He couldn't think of one other woman who had managed to shake his control like this one, and he damned well didn't like the feeling. "Well?" he said.

He saw her brush at her eye, then study the six-inch crack of sky showing through the broken roof. "I can't. Not ... *there*." She started toward the stairs.

Her foot was on the threshold when Dominic caught up with her. As his fingers wrapped around her wrist, he could feel her anger and uncertainty pulsing through every bone in his body.

How did he tap into her feelings like this? They were two strangers, after all. They didn't even *like* each other, for God's sake.

Scowling, he looked down at his fingers circling her wrist. The sight of their locked hands was like being kicked in the stomach by a horse.

By a very *angry* horse.

Dominic went stock-still, feeling sweat bead his brow. He had to fight an urge to pull her against him and find out how she tasted, how she would fit, molded hot and naked against him. "Give me an answer," he said harshly.

"The answer's no!"

Dominic felt her trembling and bit back a curse. Was she remembering Draycott and her mother? No matter what happened, she'd have to face those memories some day, he told himself. Maybe the best time was right now. "Not even for a million pounds?"

"Didn't you *hear* me? My mother died there! I never even found out why," she said bitterly.

"Maybe this is your chance to find out. Maybe—"

"And maybe there's a tooth fairy," she said in a low, hard voice. "No, don't." She raised her hand, almost as if to ward off a physical blow. "No more, please." Dominic had a glimpse of the depth of her pain then. He knew that on some level he had just stumbled across some of those buried memories of hers.

But burying wouldn't work. He could have told her that from personal experience. The memories always came back to haunt you.

"You'll have to leave." Her voice was tight with anger, but beneath it was an edge of panic.

"You'd be crazy to turn this down. I'd have to be crazy to *let* you. This house is beautiful, but it isn't going to last another five years in this condition. Maybe not another five months."

"Why do you care?"

"Because I don't like to lose, Ms. O'Neill. Not in life, not in business." Some angry force made him add, "Not in love. And I'm not giving up. I'm going down to check on my car, then I'll be back."

"The answer will be just the same. I'm never setting foot on Draycott land again." She raised her head and Dominic saw pain seep through her eyes. He hated being the one to cause anyone that kind of pain. But something drew him, something made it impossible for him to turn his back and walk away from her the way he wanted.

"You love wine. I heard it in your voice at the auction in London. And this involves a wine of the very rarest sort. Just think of owning a wine like that, touching and holding it in your hands. It would be something beyond imagining."

Why was he making this harder for her? Dominic wondered. Why couldn't he just accept her answer and be done with it? Or had it already gone too far for that?

"I don't want to hear this! Not for any amount of money! I don't care who you are or what you're offering, the answer's still no."

"Cathlin, wait—"

She shoved past him, one hand locked to her

mouth. The hammering of her feet down the stairs sent another slab of plaster hurtling to the attic floor.

Dominic didn't try to stop her. Something told him that once he touched her, once he felt her body shiver and then yield to his, all his years of careful experience at control would be swept away in a second.

Impossible, of course. And yet somehow he already knew exactly how she would feel wrapped against him.

Almost as clearly as if it had already happened.

Cathlin watched him stride down the long gravel drive toward the coast road. Gravel and dust flew up around him, driven by the wind.

The tears didn't come, just as they hadn't come after that day fifteen years ago. She had never found out what had led to her mother's fall from the roof at Draycott Abbey, though she had spent years wondering.

Suicide? Cathlin shivered. It couldn't possibly be. Her mother had always seemed so happy, ready with laughter and a hug. But perhaps a child couldn't see the pain that a grown-up learned to hide.

When she was older, Cathlin's father had explained what he knew of the events of that night. Somehow Elizabeth Russell O'Neill had fallen or been pushed to her death from the roof. But Donnell O'Neill had steadfastly refused to believe that what had happened had been an act of suicide. He had gone on searching for clues for months, but neither he nor the investigating officers had ever solved the mystery of what had occurred up on that dark and silent roof.

Though she had no conscious memory of that night, Cathlin had been the one who found her mother's body, motionless and silent against the soft green grass by the moat. Yet the night remained one great blank. Over the years Cathlin came to consider it a blessing that her memories were locked away where they couldn't torment her.

And now in a matter of minutes this hard-faced stranger came striding into her life, touching those dark places in ways that Cathlin couldn't begin to imagine.

Or to bear.

Overhead a curlew shrieked and darted over a tidal pool. Cathlin looked down at her hands, angry when she saw the fine tremor that shook them.

She had to accept the hard truth then. It wasn't going to go away. Even though the memories were buried, they were still very much alive.

Cathlin watched angry clouds race in from the channel. Just like the storm, dark and gathering speed, there were things that couldn't be put off any longer. The doctors had told her one day everything would come back to her. As an adult, Cathlin finally had to consider other methods of remembering, things like drugs and deep hypnosis. Maybe it was time she had an answer to those years of shadows. If so, the whole process would have to begin at Draycott Abbey.

Maybe she owed it to her mother to find out what no one else could.

She was waiting, fists tight, when Dominic strode back up the drive. "There's one other thing you'd better understand, O'Neill." His hair was raked back by the wind and a fine sheen of sand covered his face. "Like it or not, we're in this together. You're not the *only* one who stands to gain from that will." Abruptly Dominic stopped. Over Cathlin's shoulder he studied the eerie sweep of reeds and silver water. "Come inside."

"Why."

He bit off a curse. "*Now*, O'Neill. There's someone out there."

"It's not exactly a crime. As I told you, we get lots of lost hikers this time of year."

Dominic's eyes were cold and hard. "In this kind of weather? I doubt it. But if they're just hikers, they won't mind answering a few questions." He pulled her around, shielding her with his body. "Keep walking, slowly and very casually." He draped an arm around Cathlin's shoulder and began moving her toward the house.

As they neared her old Jeep, he bent low and pulled a backpack from the car. Turning quickly, he moved his body between Cathlin and whoever was out there on the marsh.

"What are you doing?"

Dominic ignored her, pushing her along toward the house. "Is there a door that will let me out on the north side of the property?"

Cathlin nodded. The confusion in her eyes began to be replaced by fear. "If you're trying to frighten me, you're succeeding."

"I'm not trying to frighten you," he said harshly. "I'm trying to protect you."

"From what?"

His mouth hardened. "That's always the question, isn't it? Now show me how to get to the north side of the house."

It was soft but it was an order, and they both knew it.

Cathlin led him wordlessly through high, wood-beamed rooms full of Georgian furniture, along a corridor that had once been lined with portraits but now held only a few proud faces. Even now the house contained a fragile beauty and a vast dignity, offering comparisons with its beautiful, stubborn owner.

When they emerged onto the lawn at the far side of Seacliffe a few moments later, Dominic's face was unreadable. "Stay here."

And then he sprinted off into the trees.

Cathlin started to stop him, but the memory of his eyes kept her still. In an instant the friendliness had slid out of them, leaving them wintry and hard.

Warrior's eyes.

A stranger's eyes.

Cathlin shivered slightly as his tall figure vanished into the dense woods above the house. She found herself wondering what Dominic Montserrat's real business was here at Seacliffe.

Because if his proposal was as simple as it sounded, then she was a lost Romanov princess named Anastasia.

Six

*S*tay low.

Aim where they'll least expect you.

Always keep them guessing.

As Dominic entered the woods, all the old habits slammed into play.

Close protection work wasn't like in the movies, all speed and gleam and the slam of pumped-up bodies. In real life it was usually a test of patience, of agonizing minutes spent squatting in utter stillness, waiting to see who would get bored or careless or just plain hungry and give away their position first.

Dominic's jaw hardened. Memories . . .

He crawled into a canal ringed by waist-high reeds, and there he waited.

Five minutes.

Ten. Twenty.

A bird skimmed toward the channel. Wind whined through the reeds. And then he heard the faint growl of a car motor, gunned and abruptly silenced.

Across the reeds, across the quiet tidal pools, Dominic felt something waiting. There was no mistaking the prickling in his neck. When there was no noticeable movement, he worked down the slope. Soundless, he dropped to the ground and began to belly

72

his way along the winding canal, the same way he'd moved in jungles from Asia to Colombia.

He'd gone nearly a mile and darkness was closing in over the marsh when he saw the dusty Saab with a deflated front tire and a broken jack tossed beside it on the ground. So this was what he'd seen from Seacliffe. Patient scrutiny told him no one was in the area. Probably the owner had gone off to the coast road for help.

He looked up the hill. Seacliffe's roofs were not visible from here, hidden entirely by the trees and the slope of the hill.

Even then, Dominic was taking no chances. He waited by the narrow stone bridge to see if anyone appeared. After fifteen more minutes of silence, Dominic decided that all was as it seemed, a simple auto malfunction. He emerged from the water wearing a layer of mud, slipping as he crawled up the wet bank. He was just heading back up the hill to Cathlin when the soil he was standing on gave way. He cursed, swaying wildly as his ankle struck something in the dark. Thrown off-balance, he fell sideways and rolled downhill.

He only had time to curse his stupidity once before his head slammed down against the unforgiving granite of the bridge.

Cathlin paced the living room, her eyes locked on the marsh. She had long since gone through the nail-biting stage and was now muttering a stream of graphic oaths about the moral fiber and questionable parentage of one Dominic Montserrat.

Where *was* the bloody man? He'd been gone two hours already. Outside lights were winking in the channel, but the winding gravel drive that ran past the seawall was a sheer wall of black. Those pools could be deceiving and the ground unstable.

Cathlin made her mind up in that moment. Something was desperately wrong.

Cathlin took the gravel road far too fast, squinting out into thirty miles of fog-swept tidal pools lapped by the cold sea. Suddenly something moved, out in the darkness.

Out in the lonely silence where no one should be moving.

Wind-driven sand pelted the windshield. Cursing, Cathlin flipped on the wipers and looked again, but whatever had been there was gone.

She sighed, rubbing her shoulders. Just nerves from too much caffeine and too little sleep, she told herself. Muttering, she jammed the gear into third and shoved her hair out of her eyes. From here it was only a mile to the coast road. Three turns, through the narrow fringe of yew trees, then over the little stone bridge. He *had* to be there somewhere.

She was talking to herself, repeating the words like a litany while her hands clutched the wheel, nursing the sturdy old Jeep over the pitted road. Gravel and dust flew up as she downshifted, passed the skeletal oak, now ringed with a ghostly drapery of fog, and swung onto the tidal flats that hugged the seawall.

Then she saw him, a black blotch against the night. Any faster and she'd have plowed right into him. As Cathlin threw open the door, fog coiled around her ankles.

He was upright but swaying tiredly.

"Dominic, what happened to you?"

Around them the wind hissed and whined, rippling the quiet pools.

Dominic swayed forward, hands clenched on his dark jacket.

Cathlin caught him with an arm around his waist. His body was rigid and he seemed to be trying to tell her something.

"Come on, big guy, let's get you home." She worked one shoulder behind his back and began maneuvering him toward the car. "A little help might be nice about now, okay?"

No answer.

"Dominic?"

Still no answer.

It was hard going; he seemed to have become dead-weight. And then Cathlin felt something warm slide over her fingers. Something thick and wet.

Blood. Sweet God, he was bleeding. No wonder he hadn't answered her.

"Oh, Lord, just hold on." Fighting for calm, Cathlin shoved Dominic into the passenger seat and slammed the door shut.

His eyes opened just as the moon broke from behind a fringe of clouds. Cathlin felt his desperate intensity of will as he tried to clear his mind. "Bank . . . out." His fingers tightened on her wrist. "Stupid . . . bloody bridge."

Then his eyes closed and he sprawled back against Cathlin's shoulder.

She fought to keep her hands from shaking as she swung the Jeep around, gravel flying. She slammed back up the road, taking the stone bridge too fast, and veered into a shortcut that skirted the fallen tree.

It took her nearly ten minutes to haul Dominic from the car and maneuver him into the house. The stairs would have been impossible to manage, so she stretched him out on a big chintz couch in the front study.

Unfortunately the storm had downed the power lines, and she couldn't reach a doctor for advice about his wound. He was still unconscious and very pale, but his only wound was a narrow gash over one temple, which she cleaned and bandaged. Then Cathlin found the lump at the base of his neck.

All her fears returned in a rush.

What could she do for him, stranded out here miles from a hospital? What if he didn't wake up? What if he *died*? What if he—

One smoky green eye opened. "F-found me." He searched for her hands. "Knew—you'd come." Then his eyes closed once more.

But his fingers stayed wrapped around hers.

Dominic awoke to moonlight on his pillow.

He blinked and looked about him in confusion. Where was the huge armoire at the far side of his room? Where were the cut flowers his French housekeeper always kept in a careless profusion by the window?

Where were his *clothes?*

Dominic frowned and looked down. His shoulder was covered by something bulky and his throat felt like old shoe leather. He sat up dizzily and glanced around the dark room. His jaw locked.

In the moonlight, he saw a chair where a woman with black satin hair lay sleeping in a long white gown.

For some reason, Dominic thought of candlelit rooms. Of fine blue satin and soft kid gloves and rare pink pearls set in triple strands.

All of it far, far away.

Her dark hair gleamed, lit by flames and a bar of lambent moonlight. Her head was angled against the back of an old armchair and a book lay open on her lap.

Lord, she was beautiful. Her name was as wild and lovely as the rest of her. His eyes drank in the sight of her: strong hands, flashing eyes. Full, high breasts. Would they fill his fingers, all warmth and silk? Would her nipples tighten and peak as he caressed them?

Dominic cursed harshly. In spite of what she thought of him, he was no cool playboy. He was not a man who treated intimacy casually or women lightly. This woman had undoubtedly saved his hide out there on the marsh after his stupidity in cracking his head against the bridge. Spinning X-rated fantasies wasn't exactly the best way to repay her.

But once begun, the heated images wouldn't stop. Images of white skin tormented him, fantasies of Cathlin moaning beneath him, sheathing his heat. And all of them felt achingly *familiar*. He twisted angrily, seizing his pillow and fighting the hot, deadly tide of desire.

Finally the pain at his forehead accomplished what raw discipline had not. His head caught in a vise of pain and, clenching his fists, he sank back against the bed.

Clang-clang.

Tired. So bloody tired.

Clang-clang.

Sweat clung to his brow. Pain, regret, and something far darker mingled in the gray waves that filled his head.

Dark things. Pain and secrets that wouldn't stay buried.

And then it was so close he could taste it, a memory that hung rich as fruit, but always out of reach. And somehow Dominic knew he had to make himself remember. It was almost as if his life—and Cathlin's—depended upon it.

But how?

Clang-clang.

Sweat broke from his brow and skated down his neck. Close, so close.

And it had something to do with *her*.

Gabriel's head was aching and his mood was dark as he turned up the steps to his town house. Somewhere in the night a church bell struck three times.

He scowled. A bottle of claret at White's had not soothed

*his memories of France, nor had three offers of companion-
ship to share his bed.*

*All he found himself thinking of was a pair of burnished
golden eyes.*

*As he came to the top step, the polished oak door was
thrown open and his butler's long face appeared in the
sudden light.* "My lord, there's a person—a person in
the study!"

Gabriel's dark brow crooked. "Then put the person
out, Stanton."

"I tried, most decisively. But the person would not—
that is, she—"

"A woman?" Gabriel's voice hardened. "Not here. You
know better than to allow her in, Stanton."

The old servant wrung his hands. "Of course, my lord.
But this female was most persistent. And she said you
knew she was coming. Indeed, she vowed that you were
expecting her!"

"Persistent?" Gabriel laughed grimly. So his defiant
angel had come to track him down, had she? Ashton tossed
his gloves and hat onto the mahogany side table and smiled
darkly. "Where is she?"

"She insisted on waiting in your study, my lord. I tried
to dissuade her, but—"

"Never mind, Stanton. I suspect it would take a cavalry
regiment to dissuade this visitor from a goal. I shall deal
with her, however." The grim smile played over his lips
as he strode down the hall toward the rear of the house.

The study was in shadow, lit only by the three candles
in a silver candelabrum. Gabriel stood motionless in the
doorway, while his eyes grew accustomed to the shadows.
"Since you've taken the trouble of pushing your way in,
you might as well show yourself," he said harshly.

There was a rustle of silk. The light, sweet fragrance of
lilacs drifted toward him.

And then she was before him, even more beautiful than
he remembered. In the darkness her pale features shimmered, and her eyes glinted like rare old Roman coins.

Gabriel refused to be enticed. "What do you want of me?" he demanded.

She wore a velvet cloak with a hood lined in satin. Beneath, her shoulders gleamed white and elegant. "Your help."

The earl of Ashton shrugged. "Find someone else."

"I can't. I need a man who knows the boulevards and byways of France. A man who knows Jacobin and Girondist alike. And that man is the Rook."

"Never heard of the fellow."

Geneva studied his face thoughtfully. "Adrian Draycott told me you would continue to be difficult."

"My dear, I haven't even begun to be difficult." Gabriel strode to a lacquered chest and poured himself a glass of wine. Blast Adrian for his interfering ways, he thought grimly as he emptied the glass. She was the third person Draycott had referred to him this month. All of them had equally desperate stories of relatives or friends caught in the terrors of the revolution in France. But Ashton was not about to be pulled in again.

Not even for a good friend like Adrian Draycott.

Geneva's lips curved. "Is that your usual way of dealing with encroaching females?"

Ashton felt a strange tickling sensation in his chest, a blend of hot and cold and purest hunger. The truth was that no other female had ever been so rash as to bait him in his lair as this woman had done.

"On the contrary." Gabriel moved soundlessly through the room and tossed off her domino, then stood studying the perfect ivory sweep of her shoulders and her full breasts. As his hand brushed her chin, he watched color tinge her creamy cheeks.

Curiosity. Determination. But no fear. Not a trace of that.

Maybe it was time the woman began to see what danger she was courting. He touched a powdered curl that lay coiled on her bosom. As his fingers moved, he watched the curl tremble, rising and falling rapidly on the full breasts confined against low, lace-trimmed satin. "To be perfectly blunt, my dear, this is how I treat encroaching females."

He caught her with a hand to her slender waist, pulling her into the shadows, pulling her to his heat, to his fury. There was not even a hint of subtlety in his fingers circling her neck and holding her still beneath his exploration.

But he did not touch her red lips, not then. Instead he worked along her jaw, her neck, her shoulder. Slowly he caressed the soft powdered curl at her bosom.

Geneva's breath caught sharply. His was not a touch but a possession. Later, she would realize it was not so much a kiss as a conquest. But for the moment, she did not think or analyze, swept along on the dark power of his touch. She did not flinch, not even when Gabriel's mouth shifted the powdered strand aside and tasted the lush rise of her breast.

Her hands slid to his shoulders. Her blood was a storm in her veins. She hated the man for his arrogance and his harshness, but Adrian had told her this was the only person who could help her, and Geneva knew he was right. Only a man of utter ruthlessness would face the terrors of revolutionary France. Only a man of total callousness could snatch her sister and her sister's children from the looming shadow of the guillotine. And the darkness in Gabriel Montserrat's eyes told Geneva that he had witnessed the fury of the guillotine many times.

For that service she would pay any price he named.

But Geneva had not been prepared to like the task, to feel her pulse sing and her blood drum as an utter stranger bent her to his will.

Inches away, Gabriel cursed harshly. She was even more sweet than he had imagined, a creature of silk and spring-time. Her skin rose and fell, flushed and hot with her arousal.

She would be his, Gabriel knew. She did not even understand the significance of her fingers threading through his hair and the pebbling of her nipples beneath the tight satin.

But Gabriel did, only too well. The sight of her passion,

so sweet and new and untried, was like a brand to his groin. He traced the thrust of her breast with his lips and felt her shiver, her fingers sliding deeper into his hair.

Right now, she could be his, all ivory skin and breathless moans as he shoved up her skirts and brought them both to reckless passion. Suddenly Gabriel was shocked by how much he wanted that.

But he did not allow himself to pursue it by even one more motion. It was Geneva's very response as she trembled against him that made him curse and release her.

Because she was too young and he was vastly too old.

He looked down and cursed to see that his fingers were shaking, while hers were perfectly steady. Grimly he caught up her domino and tossed it over her pale shoulders. "Leave."

"I don't understand." Her voice was husky with passion. "What you did—how it made me feel—"

"Was wrong. Damnably wrong. And unless you leave, it will happen again. Along with something far worse."

"Worse?" Her eyes were dazed, confused. "It was very nearly heaven, my lord. How can you call it wrong?"

"Damn it, have you no sense? My reputation is as black as that domino you wear. People whisper that I consume innocent virgins by the dozen. And if you are even glimpsed in my company, then your reputation will be blackened, too. What would your parents say then?"

"My parents and family are dead, swept away in one of the cruel waves of cholera that ravaged the East India Company settlement in Madras."

"And you are left alone in the world?"

"Except for my sister in France." Her chin rose. "But you needn't worry about me. I have a substantial inheritance from my father."

"All the inheritance in the world won't protect your reputation as a woman alone here in London, you little fool. Leave now, now while you still can."

Geneva did not move. "Is it true?" she asked softly. "Are you truly as black as everyone says?"

Gabriel laughed bitterly. "What does the truth matter? Either way you will still be ruined."

"It matters to me, my lord."

"In that case, you are a greater fool than you seem," Gabriel said harshly, striding across the room and drinking from the glass of fine Bordeaux that he'd poured, even though he knew it would taste like the cheapest vinegar to him.

Without a word Geneva slid her hand into the folds of her domino. Her eyes glinting, she held out a pistol, silver-etched and double-barreled. "Now, my lord, you will gratify me by sitting down and listening for once."

Gabriel did not betray his surprise by the slightest motion. "Is that weapon you are clutching supposed to frighten me?"

"Without question."

He threw back his head and laughed.

And as he did Geneva took an angry breath, leveled the sight, and shot the glass from between his fingers. "Does that? I am a crack shot, I assure you. The next bullet will land between your eyes!"

"Shoot away. I'll be of no use to you laid out in a coffin."

"I am serious. I will shoot."

"I am quaking in my boots, as you can see."

"As if you would ever quake," Geneva scoffed. "But you are far too practical a man not to do exactly as I say. As long as I hold this pistol, at least." She smiled grimly. "And I do not mean to let it go, I assure you."

At that moment Gabriel's butler appeared at the door, his face the color of raw dough. "My lord? I was certain that I heard a—" His voice trailed away as he saw the broken glass and crimson stain spreading over the fine Persian carpet. "Then I did hear it. You are wounded!"

"Go away, Stanton. That is only a glass of Bordeaux down there, not my blood. There are those who say my blood is not red, but black, after all."

"But my lord—"

"Begone! And close the door behind you."

As the servant fled, shaking his head, Gabriel settled his long length into a wing chair. Templing his fingers, he looked measuringly at Geneva. "Well? You have me captive. My attention is all yours, Miss—" His brow rose in a mocking question.

"Miss Russell." Geneva felt the bite of his sarcasm, but raised her chin defiantly. "It was necessary. I am sorry to spoil your wine and your carpet, but my sister's life is at stake."

"How enormously affecting," Gabriel said with a yawn.

"Only the man known as the Rook can save her."

"As I said before, I've never heard of the fellow."

"No?" Smiling grimly, Geneva reached to the desk behind her. "Then perhaps you will explain this black silk mask, which the Rook is well known to fancy."

Although Gabriel's mouth hardened, he merely shrugged. "Left over from some masquerade, no doubt. I do not keep track of such things."

"Indeed." Geneva tossed the mask onto his lap and held up a letter written in French and sealed with a bloodred crest in the shape of a rook. "And this is from the same masquerade, I suppose?"

Gabriel pushed to his feet, his body tense. "Where did you get the key to my desk?"

"I had no need for a key. I merely picked the lock. One of our servants used to be an attic thief and he enjoyed teaching me his tricks. All it took was a corset stay, worked in exactly the right place," she explained.

Gabriel's eyes darkened as he moved toward her.

"Stay back," Geneva ordered. "I still have my pistol and there's a bullet in the second chamber."

Gabriel's pace did not slow.

"I'll shoot, I warn you."

"Be my guest."

His chest was before her. All she had to do was pull back the trigger. Geneva swallowed, focusing, preparing.

Did the man know no fear? "Stop tempting me, blast you!"

The earl only laughed.

Her finger tightened. Sweat dotted her brow. She had to shoot, if that's what it took to make him listen. The situation was too desperate, and she had no one else to turn to.

Gabriel's hand circled her wrist. "Go on and shoot," he ordered, his chest level with the barrel of her pistol. "I fancy you couldn't miss at this distance."

"I would not miss at two hundred paces," she said irritably. "In this position, I would certainly blow away half of your chest."

"As I said, my dear, fire away."

"You're mad."

"So I am told. But don't let that stop you."

She felt his heat and his utter indifference to her choice. Geneva knew then that there was no doubt he was the man who had time and again bested the finest officers of revolutionary France. "I will, I tell you!"

His eyes were coldest granite. "So you have said."

She meant to. She tried with every shred of her being. But her finger locked and would not close.

And then she let the barrel waver.

He moved in utter silence, shoving the pistol aside and wrapping his hand around her chin. His eyes glinted, gray and savage upon her face. "And now, my little hellion, you'll learn two lessons. Never make promises you can't keep. And never carry a weapon if you do not mean to fire it. Especially," he added grimly, "when it is leveled against your worst enemy."

"Are we enemies?"

He looked down at the naked sweep of her shoulders, and his eyes darkened. "Without a hint of a doubt."

"But why? I came here for your help, not as an enemy."

"Women and men are always enemies."

"Only because you think of them so. Indeed, you treat

women most shabbily. You have had your pick of far too many, I think."

"So now you are a philosopher?" Gabriel pulled her hands to his chest, drawing her toward him. "I merely treat women as they wish to be treated, Miss Russell, as beautiful jeweled objects to be coveted, admired, and beautifully maintained. Never do I treat them more seriously than that." His eyes darkened. "Except in bed, of course. And there I treat them very seriously."

Geneva swallowed. A dark tendril of sensation coiled through her chest. "You are intolerable!"

He offered her a mocking smile. "One tries."

"Let me go."

"Not just yet, I think." He eased her backward until the mantel brushed her shoulder. "Not until I've had my fill of that honeyed mouth of yours."

"But I don't want to—"

"You will," he said silkily. And then his mouth hardened, fell, joined to hers. In conquest it began, but in silken exploration it grew. Geneva put one hand to his chest and shoved, but her strength was as nothing against his. She felt the cold metal at her fingers and remembered the pistol. She would use it, she swore. This time he would not escape her. But only if she had no other choice. Only if he continued to mock her, to tease her.

To run his lips so hotly, so sweetly across hers, until she wanted to cry out in wonder.

Heat spiraled through her. Inside her satin slippers her toes curled. Never before had she felt such a touch, such perfect skill that left her thoughts reeling. If only her head weren't suddenly so muddled, and her knees so weak.

On a sigh of breath, she rose to her toes and brought her fingers to his shoulders. Only for stability, she told herself.

Her forgotten pistol lay balanced precariously beside Gabriel's head.

He didn't even notice.

Geneva's eyes closed as his tongue touched the soft center of her lips and teased an entrance. She shivered beneath his heat and raw power, driven by a wild curiosity. What would he taste like? What would he do if she, too, tasted his heat?

Still holding the pistol, she brought her hand to his neck and ran her tongue gently over the hard curve of his lower lip. He muttered a curse and brought their bodies together, thigh to thigh, working her backward until her shoulders were crushed against the mantel.

His heat surprised her, as did the shudder that tore through his angry muscles. She had expected power and confidence and ease, but not that betraying moment of shock, nor the lash of his own desire. He wanted her, she realized. At that moment his body told her he wanted her very badly.

Geneva felt a wild surge of triumph. She had thought to tempt him, to yield to whatever price he wished to extract for his services in saving her sister. But never had she thought to taste such heaven in the process.

He muttered hoarsely, his fingers molding her soft hips, his lips pure velvet.

Geneva's hands trembled. Her pistol dropped forgotten from her fingers. An instant later the barrel discharged and a bullet cracked through the silence, sending a rain of plaster from the hole that now marred the damask-covered wall.

Somewhere a door creaked open. The butler's voice rose in panic from the corridor. "My lord! You cannot—the pistol—"

"Get out, Stanton. I'm busy."

"But the wall!"

Gabriel spun about. "Out!" he ordered.

"Yes, my lord." The door slammed shut.

The sound was like cold water hitting Geneva's face. She stared at Gabriel, her face pale, her eyes amber and gold in the firelight. "It meant nothing," she said hoarsely. "Nor did I feel anything."

"On the contrary," Gabriel said silkily. "You felt every-

thing I did, and that was vastly more than I had expected."

She gave a calculated laugh, which broke slightly at the end. "La, my lord, how easy you are to fool." Her voice rose in a titter. "'Twas all an act, I vow, just to entrap you. And you have fallen for it."

His fingers bit into her shoulders. "It was no act, my sweet. And no pretense of passion. I felt it in the heat of your body pressed against me, and in the drum of your blood."

"A lie," Geneva gasped, shoving at his chest.

His fingers settled on the pale curve of her cheek. "A lie, you call it? No, by heaven, I'll have the truth."

"Does it matter?" she said bitterly. "You've had your sport with me, and now it's over. For myself, I don't choose to waste words on a man with no heart and no scruples."

Gabriel laughed grimly. "You're right in that, for I have neither. But I have a great curiosity about this mission you've been so busy tossing in my face."

He watched pride war with need in her face. She turned away. Picking up a poker, she nudged a log in the grate and watched sparks shoot up the chimney. "It's my sister, you see. She is married to the duc de Verney, whose estates run along the Garonne Valley in France. She assured me that she and the children were fine, but last month I received a letter written in desperate haste. She wrote that the villagers were in turmoil and she feared for her life."

Gabriel's jaw hardened. "Am I supposed to find this story interesting?" He lifted his glass and tossed down the fine wine as if it had no taste at all, wishing she would leave him, wishing he could forget the sight of the blood he'd seen darkening the Place de la Concorde the week before. "Besides, I'm foxed. I'd like to enjoy my inebriation in peace."

"I do not believe that you are cup-shot," Geneva said softly. "I think that you are tired and very sad."

Ashton felt impaled on the clarity of those fine gold

eyes. He cursed silently. How did she see so much, things that no one else even suspected? "Well, you're wrong," he said, pouring himself another glass. "I'm three sheets to the wind and I mean to stay that way till morning. If you have any sense of self-preservation, you'll get yourself gone while you still can."

"I'm not leaving. Not until you hear the whole tale. It is the children that my sister fears for most."

Always it was the children who suffered. Ashton frowned as he remembered three dark-eyed children he had lost in Paris. His coachman had been an accomplice of long standing, and Gabriel had never had reason to doubt his loyalty.

But he'd been wrong, and three innocent children had died because of it.

Never again.

He pulled the poker from her hand and raised her face to his. "It's no good, Miss Russell. The valley of the Garonne is impossible to enter. I know from personal experience that the peasants are rioting there. No foreigner would get a mile before they stopped him."

"But for *you* anything *is* possible."

Ashton tried to ignore the hope and admiration in her eyes but found he could not turn away. Suddenly he wished that he were all she thought him. He wished he could see the people she loved spirited away to freedom. But he had failed too often of late. He had been forced to watch the prisoners fall, one by one, as the new leaders in Paris offered a bitter example to all who offered any hint of opposition. Now even women and children were murdered under the ruthless tyranny begun by Marat.

No, he could not help her. The plan was impossible. He turned to the fireplace and stared down at the red embers. "Go home, Miss Russell," he ordered. "Go home to your balls and your beaux. You've come to the wrong place and you've found the wrong man to play at hero." He was exhausted from three weeks of continual travel and the endless horrors he had endured on France's muddy roads.

But Gabriel knew he was sick of life as well. Perhaps he'd seen too many things that no man should ever have to see. "I want nothing to do with you and your schemes."

But even as he spoke, her scent assailed him, all sweetness and summer lilacs and the infinite innocence of youth. He knew she must be close behind him, for he heard the faint rustling of silk.

In the small, still room it was a damnably intimate sound and it sent a wild stirring through his blood.

"I fear I have not made myself plain enough, Lord Ashton. I do not ask you to risk your life for nothing. I would of course be beside you to help in every way I can. In addition I offer you anything among my possessions—or myself. All this I give freely and willingly, if only you will aid my sister and her children."

A muscle flashed at Gabriel's jaw. She was too damnably close, her scent a torment. The little fool could have no idea what she was saying.

Yet her offer lingered, haunting him. He wondered how it would feel to hold her and hear her breathless little sigh when he sank deep inside her. "Damn it, don't you understand English?" *he said harshly.* "Be gone."

"Then I shall simply find someone else," *she said flatly.*

"There is no one else. It is hopeless, and the sooner you accept it the better."

"I thought I'd found a hero. I thought I'd found a man who would risk all for honor. Instead I've found a man with no heart at all." *Her voice held a mix of fury and despair.*

Though Gabriel had thought his softer sentiments long since dead, her scorn cut deep. "You have found exactly what I warned you you would find, a man without principles or honor."

Her eyes shimmered gold with fury as she studied him. "So you did. But I thought it was simply a test of my determination. How you must have laughed at my worthless offer of my body."

The man beside her did not look up, keeping his gaze on the fire.

"Look at me," she challenged. "Or is even that task beyond you?"

Gabriel's hand tightened on the mantel. He didn't turn. It was dangerous to look at her when he was so susceptible. "Go away."

"One look. Can it be so very difficult?"

The man in Gabriel refused to ignore such a challenge.

As if in a dream he turned. And his breath fled.

She was haloed in the light of the candles. Her eyes were dark with shadows and some other unnameable emotion. "I would have given you anything you asked."

Ashton closed his eyes, trying not to see her vibrant face, trying not to smell that haunting scent of lilacs. "Damn it, begone."

He heard the rustle of lace. Her fichu slowly came free and slipped from her shoulders. "I would have been glad to come to you, glad to render any price you named." The pale fabric slipped to the floor, bright against the shadows.

Gabriel closed his eyes, trying not to see the curves suddenly revealed, pressing against the lustrous folds of blue satin. But he found that imagining them was even worse.

"It would have been my pleasure, in truth. When our parents died, Isabel raised me as a mother, putting every other interest behind mine. Now I must do the same for her." She laughed bitterly. "I am only glad that I discovered your true measure before it was too late."

Gabriel shrugged. "Consider yourself lucky." It took more effort than he would have imagined to keep his voice steady before her scorn. "And now that you've discovered my villainy, perhaps you'll leave me in peace."

"Peace?" She laughed grimly and Gabriel knew the sound would haunt him forever. "For such a man as you, there will be no peace, not in this world or the next."

She was right. He was honest enough to admit it. But

her accuracy only fueled his fury. "My peace will begin the first moment I am rid of you."

She turned in a swirl of satin skirts and wrenched her domino about her shoulders.

"Haven't you forgotten something?" Dominic said icily. A moment later her silver-mounted pistol went hurtling through the air.

She caught it deftly. "So it would seem. My only regret is that my bullet hit the wall instead of your black heart."

Gabriel was still standing before the fire when Stanton opened the door long minutes later. He did not turn. "Is she gone?"

"Yes, my lord."

Regret tightened his throat, but Gabriel ignored it. "Very good. She is not to be admitted again. Now you may go, Stanton. I shall need nothing else tonight." Nothing, at least, that he had any hope of obtaining.

"Very good, my lord."

As the door closed, Gabriel stared deep into the dancing firelight, trying to forget the smell of lilacs, trying to ignore the heat that still washed through his blood from the nearness of a woman who would hold him in scorn for the rest of her days.

Below him the amber sparks snapped and hissed.

And every one left behind a bitter memory of haunting golden eyes.

As night closed around the marsh and lightning lit the distant sky, Dominic Montserrat shifted on the couch, gray-faced and sweating.

The dreams clawed at him. He heard the echo of shouted curses and the pounding of feet. And always there was the banging of a shutter, somewhere in the distance. He fought on through the pain, through the storm of dark images, knowing some part of that was dreadfully important.

But he had no idea what.

And as he fought, the bandage at his head tore open and his wound began to bleed anew.

But the fallen blood Dominic saw in his dreams was hundreds of years old.

And he could have sworn that he caught the faint, drifting scent of white lilacs carried on the still air.

Seven ~

Thunder boomed overhead, angry against the roar of the wind. The sound wrenched Dominic Montserrat from restless sleep.

He stared about him in confusion.

Stone fireplace. Old Peking carpets. Fine etchings of English wildflowers on the walls.

Rain hammered at the window, and as he sat up, Dominic discovered his head felt roughly the size of Outer Mongolia.

Grimacing, he focused on the woman bent before the fire, prodding the dying embers to life.

Cathlin.

"What day is it?"

She whirled around. "Welcome back. It's either very late Saturday night or very early Sunday morning. The clocks have stopped because of the storm. I'm glad to see you've rejoined the living."

"I'm not entirely sure I have." Dominic scowled as pain slammed through his head. "What truck ran over me?"

"No truck, just a bridge. You hit your head and I found you wandering on the road just this side of the tidal plain."

"Grand." Dominic frowned as he felt the white bandage around his head. He shoved back the covers and tried to sit up, only to feel the blood flow summarily from his head.

Cathlin caught his shoulders. "You're not going anywhere, you fool. You're bleeding again and your neck's the color of ripe eggplant."

He pushed her hands away. "I'll be fine." He pushed back the bedding, oblivious to his near nakedness.

Cathlin flushed and looked away. "So go ahead and bleed to death. But before you do, I'd like to know just what happened out there."

"So would I." Dominic ran his hands over the painful lump at his neck. It was a fight to remember much of anything. There had been the roar of the wind, then the sickening jolt of the bank giving way. And then—nothing. "Still storming?"

"Straight through till morning, no doubt."

Dominic frowned. The ache in his head made him curse, the sound all but swallowed up by the howl of the storm outside. Grimly, he focused on trying to stand up.

"Are you crazy? You can't—"

"Just watch me, O'Neill." As he rose carefully to his feet, his head felt as if it had been kicked several times around a soccer field.

"Oh, that's very smart. Who do I call to pick up your body?"

"Beats me. Try the pope. I'm going to need someone with lots of clout."

"He won't have any clout," Cathlin snapped. "Not where *you're* going."

Dominic pulled himself forward. Something warm oozed down his forehead.

"You're *bleeding*."

What was a little blood compared to the pain in his forehead, Dominic thought grimly. Even that was better than the strange dream he'd had, something to do with pistols and blue satin.

And amber eyes. The same eyes he'd seen as he walked along the marsh in the rising wind.

A dream? Dominic thought. Or something more than a dream? "Where are my clothes?" he demanded irritably, pushing away a question he wasn't prepared to face.

"Why? It's the middle of the night. Besides, you won't even make the door."

The problem was that she might be right, but he still had to try. There were things he had to tell her about Gabriel Montserrat's will, and he wasn't about to hold the discussion half-naked and flat on his back, no matter how much his head hurt.

He took another awkward step. "See, I'm fine. I'm fabulous, in fact. The reports of my death have been greatly exaggerated." He wavered and caught himself with a hand on the back of a wing chair. "Hand me my clothes."

"Forget it. You're not going *anywhere*." Cathlin blocked his way, her hands crossed over her chest.

They glared at each other as the angry seconds crawled past.

Outside, lights dotted the hills. In the distance the streets of Rye gleamed faintly, a crown of color atop the gray blur of the marsh.

"Did you see anyone else out there? Tire tracks, or any sign of a hiker?" he asked.

"As I told you, there was only you and me and a heck of a lot of blood."

"How vastly romantic."

"Listen, this is an incredibly entertaining conversation, but it would be even more entertaining if you weren't about to pass out."

"I'm just bloody fine." Dominic stood back from the chair and raised his hands over his head. "See, no hands."

"Well, if the phone weren't out, I'd ask you to call

a doctor for *me*, because I'm getting weak just looking at you."

"Look, we have to talk and I'd like to be on a little more equal terms when we do it. After that, we need to start going through whatever family records you can find around here. Gabriel Montserrat was murdered and I want to know why."

"So now you're blaming someone in my family?"

"No, I just want some answers."

"Be my guest. Get dressed and go look. At least you'll be fully dressed when you succumb to blood loss and complications from a cranial concussion."

Dominic cursed. "Just tell me where my clothes are, will you? I've got a letter in the pocket of my shirt that I'd like you to read."

"Get back on that couch and I'll consider it."

He swayed slightly. "First we talk."

"*Now.*" Her eyes were fierce. "No couch, no deal."

Dominic gave her a crooked smile. "From anyone else, O'Neill, that statement might be promising." With a sigh, he turned and made his way back to the sofa. "I doubt if I could manage a serious response right at the moment, anyway."

His eyes were closed before his head met the pillow.

Damned stubborn fool.

Cathlin glared down at the man filling her faded chintz settee. At least his color was good and his breathing steady. Yes, Dominic Montserrat would be fine. He just needed some rest. It was *herself* she was worried about, especially if there were any more shocks like this in store.

She was supposed to be here for a quiet weekend, but nothing had gone right since that wretched wine auction. Richard Severance had already called her three times, persistent as usual, and now *this* man showed up on her doorstep with this wild talk about a two-hundred–year-old wine.

Cathlin frowned. What had he said about a letter that he wanted her to read? Feeling slightly guilty, she pulled his shirt from the wing chair and went through the pockets.

Nothing.

And that was probably how much truth there was to this whole ridiculous story. So much for Lord Ashton's honesty!

She sank down in a chair across from Dominic, listening to sand and pebbles clatter against the window. Suddenly Cathlin remembered how Seacliffe used to be, full of joy and laughter when her mother was alive. Every morning her father had risen early and dressed in an oilcloth jacket, red tartan scarf, and battered Wellies. He had liked nothing more than to tramp the marsh as the first mists drifted up from the sea, reminding him of the Galway Coast where he'd been born.

She looked out into the darkness, imagining the green reeds and tidal pools her father had loved so well. But he'd been a stubborn man in a dangerous profession, and that profession had finally caught up with him. When an old colleague had called him back for one last job, Donnell O'Neill had reluctantly agreed.

He'd never come back, felled by a sniper's bullet in a country whose name Cathlin couldn't even pronounce. She hadn't forgiven the men who'd pulled him back in, not then and not ever. She had never understood what made a man take that kind of risk, and she would never stop feeling bitter toward the country that had stolen him from her.

But all the anger in the world wouldn't bring him back.

She brushed a tear from her cheek, staring out into the night. Yes, her father had loved this old house and the deserted marsh, whose fierce storms and blustery moods were so much like his own. Perhaps it came from the memories of the five years in his youth when he'd appeared on every police blotter in Europe. Paintings by the old masters, Fabergé eggs, or uncut emeralds, none of them had been safe from the quick, clever fingers of Donnell O'Neill.

Or Patrick McKee, as he had called himself then.

But he had seen the error of his ways in time. One night a bossy female art student from Oxford had caught him rifling her jewelry chest.

Donnell had been lost before he'd gotten one full look at the striking, ebony-haired beauty. They'd spent the next twelve hours arguing over the morality of theft—and the following twelve making passionate love in Elizabeth Russell's lavender-filled room overlooking the canal.

Afterward Donnell joked that he'd stolen Oxford's brightest jewel that night, and there was always a trace of seriousness in his voice when he said it.

Soon Cathlin had come howling into the world, the product of an irrepressible Irish love and an adoring English heart. She'd thrived on that love and over the years she had learned to expect the occasional shouting and broken dishes, knowing that afterward would come the sudden, abrupt silences, when they did some unknown thing called "making up."

Under Elizabeth's pressure, Donnell had turned his back on crime and begun working for the English government, which always had jobs for a man with light fingers like his.

Jobs like planting a false set of documents at the Russian Embassy, replacing the attaché case of Tito's private courier to Albania, and filching a set of incriminating negatives from an East German who was blackmailing a very high-level English cabinet minister had come in quick order.

The big Irishman had come and gone like a

shadow in the night, and with every success his handlers had grown more greedy. Just one more job, they'd swear. And he had agreed, because it was the only career he knew.

So the months had stretched into years. Cathlin grew to a fine girl of ten and began fretting to be out of London and into a cottage where she could have her own pony and a half dozen cats.

But it had never come to pass.

The week before Cathlin's eleventh Christmas, Elizabeth had taken Cathlin with her to Draycott Abbey, where she was to examine some Elizabethan textile samples at the request of the old viscount. And sometime during that night, while the servants slept and Cathlin lay lost in childish dreams, Elizabeth Russell O'Neill had been murdered, by whom it was never discovered.

No words could assuage Donnell's grief. Only little Cathlin kept him from crossing over the edge to madness. Together they had left England, settling in Philadelphia. There Donnell had established his private security business, among a grand extended family who had come over from Ireland years before. But even then, the painful memories of Elizabeth had persisted.

Three years ago Seacliffe had come into Donnell's hands with the death of Elizabeth's brother, and Cathlin and Donnell had moved back to England, to the old stone house perched on the rolling hills overlooking Romney Marsh and the silver sweep of the southern coast.

After twelve years in America, Cathlin had no ties to her mother's country and with the death of her father, her bitterness toward England had grown. But she had thrown herself into her work and stayed on, knowing her father would have wished it. And finally her wine business had prospered.

She smiled faintly, remembering how he had railed

at her choice of career, saying she spent too much time in dark, cold cellars and too little with living, breathing people. "It's not healthy, a woman like you caught down there verifying humidity and cork conditions from morning to night. There's more to life than that—flesh and blood things. And if you don't reach out and take them, you'll wake up one morning and find it's too late, *macushla*."

Macushla. My dear. The sweet word still brought a tear to her eye. And her father had been right. One day Cathlin had awakened to find both her parents gone and this great old house hers to maintain.

But the cellars at Seacliffe had precious secrets, a vast cache of old wines and brandy laid down over a century ago. Undisturbed and perfectly preserved, those dusty old bottles had provided the capital to repair the house, and Cathlin had sold the old vintages judiciously. The business had grown swiftly, supported by her fine palate and ability to ferret out old bits of research and documentation. Soon she had commissions from around the world, and returned to America to set up shop in Philadelphia.

Staring out at the rainswept night, Cathlin frowned. She still didn't like England much. Its climate was dour, its food unremarkable. But the real reason she was uncomfortable here was because England represented too keenly the loss of those she'd loved most.

As Cathlin stood in the window, listening to the wind and the churning sea, she shivered, feeling a sudden premonition that she was about to lose something precious yet again. And then she heard a crack from high overhead. Dear God, not the roof, she prayed.

The roof was exactly the problem.

Cold wind and a hail of sand poured into the attic as Cathlin rounded the top of the stairs, candle in hand. It took her long moments to trace the source of the draft, a jagged hole in the south wall, where wind rushed in from the outside, fraying the rapidly eroding layer of plaster.

Muttering words that wouldn't bear overhearing, Cathlin dragged hammer, nails, and a roll of heavy plastic from a corner storage closet and set about sealing the hole.

When she had pounded in the last nail through plaster that felt as though it might pull away at any second, she sank down against the wet wooden floor. And there, strangely enough, she began to laugh, caught by the utter absurdity of trying to hold out a sky full of rain and a marsh full of sand. It wouldn't work, of course. Cathlin was far too practical not to see that. But she laughed on, clutching her sodden sides until tears rolled down her cheeks and the candle guttered beside her.

And as she laughed, she seemed to feel a presence beside her, almost as if someone were laughing with her—maybe the moody old house itself. Or maybe it was some dimly remembered ancestor who'd long ago walked these attics and played games under the old eaves.

She sprawled backward and kicked off her wet slippers, wriggling her toes. When the laughter vanished, there wasn't much reason to live, so her father used to say. Maybe it was even that rakish Irishman Donnell O'Neill himself whom Cathlin felt hovering about the attic. If so, she hoped he liked what he saw.

Still smiling, Cathlin reached for the slipper which she'd kicked off into the corner. In the process she snagged a loose floorboard jutting up near the base of the wall. *Probably warped by the rain*, she thought. She had found one shoe and was looking for the other, when she heard a hollow crack.

Without warning the old wood gave way and she was tossed painfully onto her side. When Cathlin raised her candle, she found not one but four panels of wood rotted through. Beneath them lay a recess long hidden under the old floor.

Cathlin's hands trembled with excitement as she probed the dark hole, wincing when something skittered lightly across her fingers. Pushing through dust and cobwebs and heaven knew what else, she reached deeper until she touched something shoved into the recess.

Cathlin worked the heavy object toward her, then eased its smooth bulk up onto the floor. In the candlelight she saw it was a large chest of etched leather with brass fittings.

Her breath caught when she opened it. Did it hold letters from some long-forgotten relative? A treasure hidden from the days when Seacliffe had been a haven for smugglers?

A hint of lilacs teased the air as Cathlin pulled back a layer of velvet. Inside, snuggled against the chest's silk-covered walls, lay neat tiers of costly silk clothing wrapped in fine paper. But whose?

Item after item she pulled from the chest, delighting in the glint of figured damasks and lustrous satins. Full-skirted and tightly fitted at the waist, the gowns were sewn in the grand style of the period paintings of Gainsborough and Constable. Cathlin ran loving fingers over the elegant garments. Pulling aside another layer of velvet, she found a pair of navy slippers with diamond buckles. Nestled between the slippers was a blue velvet ribbon with a cameo worked in precious amber and outlined with tiny diamonds.

Cathlin's breath caught as the diamonds burned in the candlelight, giving the cameo a warm golden glow. For a moment she did not move, awed by the sense that she had somehow stepped back into time, caught in the drama of a stranger's life, which she had opened with the discovery of this trunk. And something called to her, urging her to run her hands over the soft satin and stroke the velvet ribbon.

She could not resist. She was too much a woman to ignore such a temptation. She caught up the candle and ran to fetch the wobbly old mirror leaning against the top of the stairs. With the blotchy glass settled firmly in place, she stripped off her nightgown and slid on the most beautiful of the gowns, an elaborate creation of navy satin stiff with lace and rosettes and seed pearls.

It might have been sewn just for her, Cathlin thought, as the last soft fold fell into place. Its long sleeves ran full to her elbows, then spilled into clouds of creamy lace. The same lace decorated the low bodice, over full skirts in a bright satin cascade. *In for a penny, in for a pound*, she thought as she pulled on the satin slippers with their tiny heels. She watched, entranced. The diamond buckles caught the light, making her feel like an entirely different person.

Her fingers trembled on the cameo. The delicate features made something tighten in her chest. She lifted the heavy stone to her neck.

Instantly the stone warmed beneath her touch.

The diamonds burned and the mirror seemed to shimmer, light-ringed. In that extraordinary instant, while the moon rose over the marsh and a kestrel called in lonely splendor, Cathlin felt beautiful, admired, loved in every atom of her being. It was almost as if this dress, hidden safely away for centuries, was meant only for her, a message of love and protection.

Who had owned these things? Were they keepsakes of a very special evening, a night when two lovers had danced beneath crystal chandeliers and exchanged whispered vows by candlelight?

She would never know.

Hypnotized, Cathlin studied her image in the old, cracked mirror, watching the diamonds glitter. So absorbed was she that the creak of the stairs went unnoticed, as did the low, checked breath from the doorway.

"How did you get here?" came a low, harsh voice. "I warned you not to come. Now it's too late."

Eight ~

Cathlin looked up, startled.

Dominic's angry face was reflected in the mirror.

"Dominic? What are you doing up here?" She crossed her arms, feeling enormously silly pirouetting in the majestic gown before a cracked mirror.

There was a hint of madness in his eyes. He was acting very oddly, almost as if he didn't hear her, his whole attention focused on the dress.

"You have no right to be here." Sweat beaded his brow and he swayed slightly.

"Dominic, you're not well. Go back down to bed."

This was getting crazier by the second, Cathlin thought. The man was obviously delirious, and she would have to talk him back to the sofa before he passed out cold.

"You should never have come," he said hoarsely. "I warned you what would happen if you came back."

Warned me? Cathlin went very still. "You did?"

"I told you it was hopeless, but you wouldn't give up. And I told you what would happen if you returned."

"Tell me again."

He ran a hand through his hair, frowning. He frowned, as if he had to concentrate to speak. "I told

105

you if you returned, I'd accept your bargain and there'd be no turning back. Not for either of us." His eyes were feverish.

He put out his hand, as if mesmerized by the sight of her in the candlelight. "You look even more beautiful than I remember. But your hair is all wrong." He caught her glowing black hair, letting it flow through his fingers like sand. "How odd it looks cut so short. And you've left off your powder."

"You're wrong. I—"

Dominic—who didn't seem like Dominic at all—went very still. He studied her face with fierce intensity. "Why didn't you stay away?" With a groan, he pulled her to him. His hands trembled as he kissed the creamy curve of her neck.

Cathlin shivered, hearing the voice of a stranger, feeling the hands of a stranger. What had happened to him? Who was this woman he took her for? And who in heaven's name was *he*?

He was simply delirious after falling down the hill, she told herself sternly. But the explanation didn't make her feel any better. It certainly didn't explain Dominic's strange behavior or the dark glitter in his eyes.

"Why didn't you put on my cameo?" he demanded.

"Cameo?" For a moment Cathlin had trouble breathing. She felt him pull the jeweled ornament from her fingers and fasten it at her neck. She shivered as the heavy piece of amber settled onto the fragile bones at her throat. "You mean . . . it's yours?"

"Have you forgotten so soon?"

"But you didn't—" Cathlin broke off, swallowing sharply as his mouth brushed her shoulder. He touched her with the cool certainty of a man who has touched many women—and has brought all of them pleasure.

Well, he wouldn't pleasure *her*, Cathlin vowed irritably. But she couldn't seem to think straight, not with his hands tracing the curve of her throat and his mouth doing slow, carnal things to the lobe of her ear. "St-stop," she said huskily. "I can't think when you do that."

"Then don't," he growled. "Just close your eyes and let me love you. I've thought of nothing else since you came to me at the Crown and Dragon."

At the Crown and Dragon? "Mr., er—exactly *who* did you say you were?"

"Have you forgotten already?" A muscle flashed at his jaw.

"No, of course not." Cathlin thought wildly. "I just like to hear you say it."

His dark brow rose. "I am the fifth earl of Ashton, of course."

The *fifth* earl? Dominic was the tenth earl. That would make him . . .

Gabriel.

A tremor went through her. He was delirious. He had had an accident and this business of the will had made him hallucinate that he was his ancestor. There was no other possible answer. "Don't you mean you're the tenth earl?"

"I am the fifth, woman. And in case you've forgotten, let me remind you that exactly three days ago you offered me the pleasures of your body if I would agree to a desperate effort to rescue your sister from France."

"I did *what?*"

"Do you pretend to have forgotten?" he demanded.

Just great, Cathlin thought wildly. *Put on a pair of diamond-buckled shoes and find yourself caught in a deserted house with a madman.*

Correction. A madman who had been dead for something like two hundred years, if her peerage math was correct. She held up a warning hand. "Now I'm not saying that I disagree with anything you've told me, Lord Ashton. It's just that I have a tiny problem with, well, promising my body to anyone. It's nothing personal, you understand."

His lips brushed her ear and Cathlin suddenly found it hard to breathe. "It will be. It will be exquisitely personal when I take you. I can't get you out of my blood, and I mean to see that you want this as much as I do."

"You're not listening." Cathlin felt the sensual slide of satin atop her naked skin and the cameo pressed against her throat. She had to get Dominic back downstairs before he collapsed. Then she was probably going to collapse herself. "No matter what you say, I think it's time you got some rest."

"No," he said hoarsely. With a groan, he pulled the lace kerchief from the bodice of her gown. Cathlin watched, dazed, as satin and lace parted cleanly. How had he known the two were unattached? In fact, how had he known about the cameo? When he'd come in, the ornament had still been hidden in her hand.

She took a steadying breath. *Get a grip, O'Neill.* It's just a coincidence. "Look, we've got a little problem here."

"No, you look," he commanded, turning her to face the mirror. "Look at us together."

Cathlin did. He stood behind her now, his hands in her hair, his head bent as he planted little kisses over her neck. She shivered at his exquisite touch, watching their images dance as the candle sputtered behind them.

An odd dry ache gathered in her throat.

Suddenly she found she wanted him to touch her. "Stop this. We can't—" Her breath caught. "I don't want—"

"I've fought this with every shred of my being,"

he whispered. "But you've won, woman. You'll have your way."

Cathlin watched his bronzed hands slide over the creamy skin at her chest and felt her breasts tighten and ache as a man who looked like Dominic but was not Dominic brushed his lips gently across them. "Th-this is crazy."

His lips nudged the high swell of her breast. She caught back a breathless sigh and found her fingers buried in his midnight hair. "Dominic, this isn't what you think."

"Dominic? So now you confuse me for another. Have you made your wanton offer to so many men?"

"No! That is—"

"Gabriel," he said harshly. "Gabriel is the name of the man who is kissing you now, and, I'll see you don't forget it."

Cathlin caught a shaky breath. Through the smooth satin she felt the press of his callused fingers. They stroked and pulled, until her nipples hardened. His desire was a tangible wave as she stared at their joined images in the old mirror.

She had to stop him. She had to get out of this beautiful old dress and back to her old, everyday self.

But somehow Cathlin couldn't take her eyes from the lustrous folds of satin where Dominic's hands lay clenched. She couldn't ignore the jolt of her heart as his mouth brushed the velvet ribbon at her neck. All unbidden, her neck arched and she curved into the hardness of his body.

"Yes. Like that, my love. Let me feel your passion."

Cathlin shuddered. What was happening to her?

"You have won, I confess it freely. You have but to command me." His hands were hot and not quite steady as they burned over her sensitive skin.

"No. That wasn't me. This—this is all unreal."

Smothering a curse, he pressed his mouth to the rise of her breast. "Does this feel unreal? Or this?"

Cathlin saw his hands taut at her shoulders. She saw her own face, wearing a mix of shock and desire. And as the candlelight played over their images, she felt the tug of the cameo, warm and heavy at her neck. With it came the brush of a phantom curl at her shoulder.

She had a sudden sense of voices and distant laughter, along with faint lilting notes of music. She blinked, watching the mirror dance, feeling her mind open until the shadows fled. Before her she saw a beautiful room with frescoed ceilings and candles caught in golden wall sconces.

She struggled, caught in the nightmare, acutely aware of the tug of the cameo at her neck and the cool weight of the satin gown on her naked skin.

And then the mirror shivered and swayed, and there was only darkness.

"Cathlin?" Something was striking her cheeks. "Cathlin, wake up."

"No!" She struggled blindly. "I won't do it!"

"You won't do what?"

"I can't. I won't betray him."

Cool liquid brushed her eyes and face, trickling into her mouth. "Look at me, Cathlin." It was a different voice, a voice that carried the soft hint of French vowels. "You are safe."

Safe? Cathlin cracked open one eye. No curtains, no wall sconces, thank God. Only Seacliffe's damp old floorboards and a trunk lying open at her feet.

And a man. A man whose eyes blazed with urgency.

Cathlin let out a long, low breath, fighting a wave of nausea. What in heaven's name had happened to her?

"Are you all right?"

"I'm getting there."

Dominic eased her back against his chest. "What happened up here? And where did you find all this?"

Cathlin hadn't a clue. Was it something to do with these old clothes and the cameo she'd found in the trunk? An hallucination perhaps?

She tried vainly to pull away. "I'm fine. I'd also like to get up."

"Not yet."

Cathlin glared at him. "Maybe you should be explaining what happened to *you*. You were the one who came charging up here like a man possessed. In fact, you acted like—" Cathlin started to tell him about the fragmented images she'd had, and her suspicion that Dominic in some way had assumed the identity of his ancestor Gabriel.

Right, O'Neill. Then he'll really be convinced you've had a major cerebral concussion. "Like a complete stranger," she finished.

Dominic frowned. "I did? All I remember was being caught in a hellish sort of dream, something with music and laughter and blurred lights. Then I found myself up here. And you were lying on the floor, dressed like that."

"It's not exactly a crime to dress in old clothes."

"I didn't say it was. I'm just trying to figure out how I got up here."

Cathlin ran shaky fingers through her hair. "Okay, I'm sorry. I'm still a little shaken." Abruptly she sat forward. "Where's the cameo?"

"What cameo?"

"The one I was wearing. A velvet ribbon with a carved amber stone. I had it on before I—" She swallowed. "Before I woke up."

Dominic frowned, looking at the floor around them. "Maybe it slipped off. It won't be easy to find. Some of the floorboards have broken right through."

"I know. That's where I found the chest with all these things."

Dominic gave a silent whistle. "Good work."

Cathlin wasn't so sure. Something about that gown and cameo left her distinctly uneasy. "That cameo has to be here somewhere."

"You're staying put," Dominic said tautly. "You must have fainted a few minutes ago and knocked over that old mirror against the wall."

Cathlin noticed the frame that lay on the floor, candlelight caught in a thousand shattered shards of glass.

It doesn't matter, she told herself sternly. It was just a mirror. "Can you see that cameo anywhere?"

"Maybe it's in the chest. I'll look, if you're sure you can—"

"Breathe without your assistance? I think I *might* be able to manage it." She caught a breath. "Look, I'm sorry. I suppose I should thank you. It's just—"

Just what? That I feel as if I've been tossed into a nightmare. That this gown feels somehow familiar. That I keep trying to hate you and I don't succeed. "Oh, forget it."

"No, let's not forget it." Dominic's voice hardened. "I didn't mean to upset you, Cathlin. Not from the first. It just seems everything I do rubs you the wrong way."

"It's not you. Coming back here always brings back a lot of memories."

"This is one beautiful house. You must have been very happy here."

Had she? A very long time ago, maybe, when she'd visited her mother and her family. But not in the last years. Then Seacliffe had been full of ghosts, reminding her of the parents she'd lost too soon.

Dominic watched her face intently. "What else happened up here just now?"

"Nothing." Too swiftly.

"I find you passed out on the floor, dead to the world, wearing a dress probably two hundred years old and you tell me *nothing*?"

"That's right."

Dominic shook his head. "O'Neill, when are you going to start trusting me?"

Rather than lie, Cathlin stayed silent.

"Great," he said grimly. After a moment he moved over to the chest and dug inside. His brow arched as he held up a fine cambric chemise with a white embroidered border. "Sure you wouldn't care to model this one for me?"

"Forget it."

Dominic's head disappeared back into the trunk. "Another pair of shoes. A mask of silk and feathers. An enamel box of some sort. And—damnation!"

"What did you find?"

Dominic sat up, frowning at his hand. "Some kind of pin. Bloody sharp, too. It's cut me." Carefully, he lifted a scrap of yellowing linen from the dark interior of the chest. Attached to the fabric was a diamond stickpin that shot cold fire into the attic shadows.

Cathlin's breath caught. "It's . . . beautiful."

"Thirty carats at least." Dominic ran his finger slowly over the fine silver mounting, watching the facets gleam. "I've seen this before."

"How could you? This chest has been hidden here for years. My mother and her parents didn't even know about it."

"It's familiar." Dominic's eyes narrowed. "My God, it's Mad Uncle Gabriel's."

"Your ancestor's? The one who . . ."

"That's the one."

Cathlin's mind rebelled. She sat forward awkwardly, her fingers tense. "It can't be."

"It is. There's a full-length portrait of the man back at our estate and he's wearing that exact pin." Dominic looked at Cathlin oddly. "A pin, if I may add, that we have never been able to find. We always assumed that he'd run into bad luck at the gaming tables and been forced to pawn it. Apparently not."

Cathlin surged to her feet. "Are you accusing someone in *my* family of stealing it?"

"I'm not accusing anyone. I'm just curious."

"There could be dozens of pins like that. Who says that it belonged to this ancestor of yours?"

Dominic's fingers closed around the beautiful old ornament. He stared down at his closed fist, thinking about the dark legends he had heard about the Ashton diamond ever since he was a boy. They had given him more than a few bad nights. As he'd grown up, it hadn't helped that he bore the same brooding, dark good looks of the fifth earl. Only their eye color was different. "Look, it's—rather a long story, and you're shivering already. You'd better change and then get some sleep."

"But—" Cathlin sighed, knowing he was right. Half of the wind in Sussex had to be gusting through that hole in the roof, in spite of her efforts with the plastic. Staying here any longer might be distinctly unhealthy.

On the other hand, Cathlin wasn't taking another step in this beautiful, disturbing gown. "First I want to change."

"Fine. I'll go down and get a fire going while you—"

"*No.*" Cathlin caught his hand, her eyes very wide. "I—I don't want to be up here alone."

Dominic's eyes narrowed. "Still not going to tell me what happened?"

Cathlin ignored him, reaching for her clothes.

"We'll never get anything done this way. Damn it, O'Neill, you're going to have to trust me."

"I'll keep that in mind. Now turn your head, if you please."

A glint went through Dominic's eyes. "What if I don't please?"

Color filled Cathlin's cheeks. "Don't," she whispered. "Not now."

Dominic cursed. "It wouldn't be any good anyway, would it? Not if you couldn't look me in the face. Not if you couldn't trust me." He strode to the chair at the far wall, his shoulders tense with anger.

Maybe she did trust him, Cathlin thought. Maybe it was herself she didn't have much confidence in.

She worked awkwardly at the laces at the back of the dress, freeing it slowly. As the satin slid away, a great weight seemed to lift. After a quick glance at Dominic, she eased out of the billowing satin skirts and tugged on her nightgown, relieved to feel the thick, practical cotton instead of rich satin.

She was buttoning up the front when she heard a hiss behind her. Without warning, one end of the plastic tore free, slapping across her cheek so hard that Cathlin bit back a cry of pain.

Dominic caught the flapping sheet and shoved it away from her face. "Are you okay?"

"It just frightened me, that's all."

"Hardly. You're shaking like a leaf and you've got a nasty welt on your cheek." Cathlin winced at even the gentle brush of his finger.

She looked up. His hair was unruly where the wind gusted over it. His eyes were flecked with gold by the candlelight. She wanted to hate him. She hated everything he stood for: men with easy fortunes, grand birthrights, and too much charm for a woman's safety. In spite of all that, Cathlin couldn't close herself off from him. He was too near, too overpowering. She'd never had a problem putting men in their place in the past, but with this man she didn't know where to begin.

Or if she even wanted to.

"Cathlin . . ." His fingers opened, eased across her cheek. They were trembling slightly.

Something sharp and sweet passed between them.

Dear God, he's going to kiss me, Cathlin thought dimly. *He's going to pull me to him and touch me as I've never been touched before. If I don't want it, I've got to stop him now, before it's too late.*

If I don't want it . . .

But the words wouldn't come.

Their eyes held, a universe of emotion slamming between them while their bodies stood frozen and the sea air gusted around them.

Dominic swallowed, his eyes hard. *God help me, I'm going to kiss her. How can I help it, when she looks at me with that crazy blend of innocence and passion, with eyes that go right through me and make me feel I've known her forever?*

Even then he fought it, telling himself he was a fool and worse, but she touched some deep corner of his heart, calling out to him, seducing him in ways that went far beyond the physical. He shouldn't touch her. He couldn't.

But he did.

Even the faintest brush of skin hit him like a jolt, made heat ripple through Dominic's body. He caught a low breath and eased her closer. When he heard her sigh, he covered her mouth completely.

She was all softness and need, all hunger and woman, and she fired his blood as it had never been fired before. He pulled her against his body, sliding his hands along her hips.

"Cathlin." It was a wave of need, of protest, of wild discovery. "God help me . . ."

Her lips opened beneath his. Somehow her fingers were in his hair. He felt her ease against him, her breath feathering against his mouth.

Her response made him harden with agonizing rapidity. Breathing heavily, he ran his fingers beneath the thick cotton and met cool silken skin. Her ragged little moan was loud in the taut silence between them and had the effect of gas poured on an open fire. Dominic told himself he was crazy to want her like this, but all the cold reasoning in the world didn't change the way she made him feel.

Hungry. Possessive. Like a man who'd found something precious that he didn't even know he'd lost.

What the hell was happening here? He drew a ragged breath and eased away.

He wondered if she even heard. Her hips moved restlessly. Her head fell back as she offered him the cool arch of her throat and the thrust of her breasts.

Dominic fought for sanity when all he wanted was to throw her down on the bare wood floor and bury himself inside her. And some crazy voice whispered that if he did, it would be unforgettable. And also somehow familiar.

He cursed. "Let's go."

"Go?" She looked dazed.

"You need food." He took a tight step backward and smoothed down her nightgown, cursing when he saw the tight jut of her aroused nipples against the soft cotton.

"Food?"

"Food," he repeated hoarsely. "Then a fire."

"Fire," she muttered dimly.

"And then we talk, Cathlin. Really talk."

She blinked, as if having trouble focusing. "Talk. Yes—have to talk." But her eyes were dark with desire.

Dominic cursed. Any more looks like that and they would end up naked on the floor. Maybe talking wasn't such a good idea either. Dominic wanted nothing more than to pull Cathlin against him and kiss her back into blissful insensibility.

But he didn't. He couldn't, not with all the questions hanging over them. He caught a ragged breath, wondering how much more torture he could take. She was looking at him, just looking, her eyes wide and haunted. And the sight of her eyes was like getting a roundhouse kick to the groin.

"What's . . . happening, Dominic?"

"You're asking me, the man you love to hate? Why start trusting me now?"

Cathlin ran shaky fingers through her hair. "Because like it or not, we're both involved. You knew about that pin. And something about that gown . . . affected you. Can't you feel it?"

In Dominic's hand the Ashton diamond felt cold and sharp. Frowning, he caught up the old shoes and satin dress and stowed them back in the chest, along with the diamond ornament. "Damned if I know *what* I feel right now, except tired." After a moment he shoved the lid down on the chest.

Somehow it left him feeling a hell of a lot better.

"It's probably just the effects of sleep deprivation. We'll talk in the morning, O'Neill. Tomorrow everything will look a whole lot better."

Dominic didn't believe it, but he hoped it sounded good to Cathlin.

Nine ~

The moon hung over the marsh, veiled in clouds. It was a night such as smugglers might have plied their desperate trade and excise officers made their equally desperate pursuit. But now the sea was quiet. In the wake of the storm, only the night birds cried, winging low over the lonely curve of sand and cold canal.

While Dominic Montserrat twisted restlessly in dreams, the scent of lilacs filled the sleeping house.

"Help me."

"No one can help you, Geneva." A tall man with pale, hard features stood before Geneva Russell in the candlelit study of one of London's most prominent hostesses. Henry Devere was clad in black satin that was not half as cold as his eyes. He smiled mirthlessly as he toyed with an enameled watch on a silver chain. "Your sister's life is in your hands now. Find me the Rook and she lives. Refuse me and she dies." He smiled darkly. "And her children will die along with her."

"Monster! You can't do such a thing!"

"Oh, but I can, my sweet Geneva. And so I shall, unless you find me the Rook tonight. There is a reward of one thousand gold guineas on his head, and by God it shall be mine."

"But I don't know the man. I cannot do as you ask."

"Ah, but you can. With your sister's life in danger, you went straight to the Rook. I have had your movements watched, my dear. You spoke to the man and you can identify him tonight. I want no question in my mind when he is taken."

Geneva's breath caught. *"Tonight?"*

"Of course. My informers say he will be here among the guests at the masquerade, dressed as Marc Antony. A most appropriate jest, don't you think, since he is soon to fall before your charms just as Antony did before his Cleopatra?"

Geneva felt her flesh crawl as she studied the heavy-lidded eyes and fleshy lips. She had known Henry Devere slightly in India, where he had been a merchant like her father. After her parents' death, she had come back to England to find her sister, only to discover she had gone back to France with her husband.

Henry Devere had been only too kind, only too glad to help her communicate with her sister.

At first.

Then he had begun to press her with more personal attentions. When Geneva had repelled his advances, Devere's manner had changed. Instead of the condescending advisor, he had become a cold-blooded bully. When he threatened harm to her sister, Geneva knew it was within his power, since his business contacts with the new, revolutionary government in France were extensive.

She wanted to scream, to turn, to flee, but she could not. Not while her sister's life hung in the balance. *"There could be dozens of such costumes,"* she said desperately. *"How shall I know which one is the Rook?"*

"That, my sweet Geneva, is your problem." The man in black ran a finger down her shoulder. *"I suggest that you use your very lush charms to entrap him."*

Geneva shivered as the diamonds glinted on her shoes, reflected in the dancing light of a dozen wall sconces. *"Don't touch me,"* she hissed, feeling bile fill her throat.

His nail bit into her skin. "Oh, but I shall touch you, my little beauty. And you'll fulfill my every command gladly, or you'll watch your sister die."

Fear tore through her. She was trapped, horribly trapped. Only one man could help her, but she knew that to ask him would amount to betraying him. "Go away."

"Not just yet, I think." Cold hands slid over her neck. "You will kiss me first."

Fury filled her. Such a beast deserved only one response. She lashed out with her knee, catching him full in the groin. Instantly, he bent double, his face tight with agony.

But her hopes were dashed as he came upright, the triumph in his eyes replaced with blind fury.

"Bitch. I'll see you pay for that. I'll make you beg for my forgiveness before I'm done with you." He swept up a heavy silver candlestick from the lacquered table beside him.

"I think not, Devere." A shadowed figure stepped from the heavy curtains of the French doors to her left. "The lady does not seem to care for your presence. In view of that, I insist you leave."

"Who are you to order me about? By God, I'll teach you to interfere."

"Take another step and I rather think you'll die." Candlelight glinted off a pistol as Geneva's rescuer moved from the shadows of the window.

Her breath caught as she saw the draping folds of linen that stretched across his powerful chest. Above his masked face was set a garland of olive leaves.

"Marc Antony," she whispered.

"Of course." His voice was smooth, silken. It was a voice to sway men and entice women, she thought. A voice born to bear the weight of command. "But why are you not in costume?"

She did not speak, her hands clenched in the folds of satin. "I—I had no time," she heard her voice answer, as *if from a great distance. It was a stranger's voice, full of fear. "I did not plan to attend."*

"A pity." His eyes darkened. "You would have been magnificent as my Cleopatra." He turned to the man in black. "Good-bye, Devere." There was a hard note of warning in his tone.

For a moment Henry Devere stood motionless, his body stiff with fury. Then a cold, sly smile eased across his lips. "As you wish. All Rome must bow to Antony, after all." He looked at Geneva. "Be certain that you do not succumb as easily as Cleopatra did, my dear. You know what happened to her." Still smiling, he made his way back out into the hallway.

Geneva shuddered, clasping her hands to her waist. Evil clung to the man and filled the room even after his departure.

"You're shivering and you've dropped your shawl." A length of lace slid gently around her shoulders. "And you are bleeding." Carefully, her rescuer caught the bead of blood left by Devere's nail. Raising her arm, he ran his tongue lightly over the tiny prick.

Geneva shivered at the shocking intimacy of his touch. "It—it's nothing," she whispered.

"He was importuning you?"

She nodded, unable to speak, still repelled by the memory.

"The man is an animal. But perhaps you do not wish to speak of it."

Words came finally. "How . . . much did you hear?"

The silver eyes were unreadable. "How much should I have heard?"

She gave a careless shrug. "It is of no importance."

"You would do well not to find yourself alone with him in the future."

"And what of you, my lord? Need a woman fear if she finds herself alone with you?"

His low laugh seduced her flushed skin. "Perhaps. Does that make you want to run, Geneva of the golden eyes?"

"I can defend myself."

He did not laugh as other men would have, but only nodded gravely. "Against some, yes. But not against such a man as Devere." His hand slid over a powdered curl of her hair. "And perhaps not against a man like myself." His jaw hardened. "I think it best that I leave you now."

"No." She spoke quickly, remembering Devere's threat. "Not yet. I . . . I do not care to join the others."

His dark brow rose. "You play a dangerous game."

Dear heaven, how much had he heard?

Just then voices came from the hallway. A drunken couple swayed into the room, arms entwined.

Her rescuer cursed. Pressing a finger to his lips, he pulled her back behind the heavy damask curtains. Molded against him, with his faint scent of lemon and tobacco in her throat, Geneva felt cut off from the world, cut off from herself, cut off from all she'd been and known and felt before.

By some spell of night and candlelight she had become a stranger in a satin gown, a woman falling inch by inch under this man's potent spell. She turned slightly, feeling her hip nudge his hard thigh.

Heat burned out from those inches of contact, heat that left her pulse hammering.

Outside she heard the rustle of silk and a woman's soft moan of pleasure. Her own heartbeat quickened at the sound. She thought of what it would be like if this man took her into his arms. Would she know the same pleasure and moan softly?

"Look at your image," he whispered, pointing to the glass pane behind them. His fingers moved to her neck. Something cool and hard slid over her skin.

She turned, as if in a dream. A beautiful cameo of carved amber hung about her neck, strung from a velvet ribbon. "It's . . . beautiful. But I cannot—"

"Hush, beauty," he said with a trace of his habitual arrogance. "It pleases me to please you." He stood behind her now, his hands in her hair, his head bent as he planted *little kisses along her ear. "Wear it always, and think of me."*

Geneva shivered at his exquisite touch, watching their images meld and dance in the candlelight. She would wear it. Just as she would always think of him. Even after she betrayed him?

She shuddered.

"You are cold?"

"No, not cold."

"Then this is fear, fear of me?" His voice was suddenly taut.

"No, not fear. But surely, we cannot." Her breath caught. "Not here. I don't want—"

"You will," he whispered. "I have fought you with every shred of my being and failed." His voice hardened. "May God help us both."

Geneva watched his hands slide over the creamy skin at her chest. She closed her eyes, her breasts grown tight and aching beneath his touch.

As if in a dream, she felt his mouth tease one crest of crimson. She caught back a breathless sigh, and sank trembling fingers into the blackness of his hair. "This isn't what you think."

Outside their curtained bower came a low, choked moan and the indrawn breaths of cresting passion. Geneva flushed, horrified.

But the man beside her barely noticed. "Gabriel," he said harshly. "Say my name, and let me know you think of me."

"You," she whispered. Then, more huskily, "Gabriel."

"Yes, my love. That is the name of the man who is kissing you, the man whose cameo you wear. I mean to see you don't forget it."

His fingers brushed against her hardened nipples. She shivered, filled with heat as she stared at their images in the long glass window.

She had to stop this. She had to make him understand.

But her body mocked her. She could not deny him what she had long ago determined to give freely, in order to save her sister's life. Her neck arched. The cameo swayed, cool and heavy as she curved into the hardness of his body.

"Yes. Like that, my love. Come to me. Let me feel your passion."

Geneva shuddered, fighting the dark pull of his sensuality. Even if he left now, could he be swifter than Henry Devere, who would use every connection he had in France to see her sister brought to harm? Geneva knew she could not risk her sister's death. She would have to be clever and cool, using both men to her own ends.

With a low curse Gabriel caught her shoulders, his eyes burning over her face. "I have thought of nothing else since I saw you at the Crown and Dragon. You have but to command me, for whatever I have is yours. But in return you must fulfill your part of the bargain."

Geneva felt her throat tighten. A choked sigh emerged instead of words as his lips met the swell of her breast.

Outside there came a low hum of voices and the rustle of clothing. Then only silence. Geneva gave a silent sigh of thanks that they were finally alone.

"No more tricks. God help me, I'm not up to them. You have beaten me."

Dimly she saw Gabriel ease her dress from her shoulders and free her straining skin.

"Was any woman ever so beautiful?" he said hoarsely.

Geneva choked back a moan.

He wanted her.

And dear God, she wanted him, with a passion equal to his own. When had it happened? And how was she ever to escape this nightmare choice that Henry Devere had forced upon her?

The cameo dug into her neck, dense stone and cold diamonds. A jolting tension crept along her spine. But Geneva knew she must say the words that would spell his ruin. "Are you truly the man called the Rook?"

A powdered curl brushed against her shoulder. She felt the tension of his hard arms braced at her shoulders and was achingly aware of his fingers as they eased beneath the warm satin to cup the weight of her full breasts.

"Yes," he said hoarsely. "I am the man you seek. Now you hold my secret and my very life in your hands. Do not betray me."

Geneva knew with a vast and terrible clarity that she would do just that. She had no choice. She could not let her sister die.

"No," she whispered, her throat dry.

He took her answer for assurance, instead of the protest that it was. He smiled darkly, studying her sweet, up-thrust nipples. "Your body shows its passion most eloquently. But I must see all of you."

"Someone might come. That monster Devere—"

"There is no need to fear. I'll keep you safe. At a masquerade such as this, nearly everyone has similar ideas," he said darkly.

Beneath the brush of his hands the satin folds moved. As they did, the heavy cameo swayed and came free. With a low hiss the ornament slid over the yards of satin and landed on the carpet.

The movement caught Geneva from her sensual haze. "No," she said wildly. "Not here. You must go. Find a place where we will be undisturbed." Her eyes were dark with entreaty.

After a moment he nodded. "My carriage is outside. I will send a man round to fetch it. Wait for me." He planted a slow, goading kiss upon her lips and Geneva felt her body stiffen, answering his passion. But he put her from him, laughing softly. "Soon, my lady."

Then he opened the curtain and disappeared.

Jagged images filled Dominic's head, images of sadness and anger and a woman's soft sigh. Snatches of dreams played through his mind like distant music, familiar and yet not quite familiar.

Or were they memories?

Geneva was standing by the window, pale and determined, when Henry Devere returned.

"He was the one?"

For a moment Geneva did not move. A man's honor and his very life flashed before her. "What will you do with the information if I tell you?"

"Do?" Devere smiled coldly and motioned into the corridor. Six men appeared, all burly and unsmiling. "Why, I shall see him transported to Paris, to those who will pay most dearly for his person. And then I fear we will see our Rook plucked publicly by Madame Guillotine."

"No," Geneva whispered, her hands on the amber cameo she had recovered from the floor.

"Don't think to trick me, my dear." Devere caught her arm and glared down at her. "If you lie, I will soon know it—and your sister's life will be forfeit." His fingers tightened. "Now the truth, was it he?"

Betrayal. A man's death delivered in a single terrible stroke. But what was her choice? If she was not very careful, her sister would die the same way.

Geneva nodded slowly, her face sheet white.

"Excellent. Your assistance has been most valuable." Devere gestured curtly to his crew, who moved into hiding behind the curtains while he settled upon a large settee. "Now we must wait for our hero to return."

Their prey was not long about it. Less than ten minutes had passed before his tall shadow fell over Geneva's shoulder as she stood, still and unsmiling, by the fireplace.

The man known as the Rook halted on the threshold, seeing Henry Devere seated in a wing chair beside Geneva. "Was this man bothering you?"

Geneva shook her head.

"It is as well, or his life would be gone."

"Nonsense," Devere said easily. *"Miss Russell and I were merely discussing—"* He looked at the woman motionless beside the fireplace. *"Why, we were discussing Roman history, I believe. And she was regaling me with stories of Julius Caesar."* His colorless eyes swept Gabriel's tall form. *"Dear me, why have you changed your attire, Lord Ashton? That toga rather suited you."*

"Not where I'm going," Gabriel said curtly. For a moment he surveyed the room, frowning. Then he moved to Geneva's side. A diamond stickpin gleamed among the lace at his neck. *"But the lady grows tired. We shall bid you adieu, Devere."* He pointedly took Geneva's palm and raised it to his lips, turning his back on Devere.

Geneva's throat tightened. Don't kiss me, her heart screamed. Don't trust me. Run. Run while you can. Run before I must betray you.

But she didn't speak. Isabel's image swam before her, holding her to aching silence.

She watched Devere raise a questioning brow.

And although she knew the memory would torment her forever, taking away all joy and happiness and hope, she nodded her terrible betrayal.

One gesture was all Devere required. With a growl, he pulled forth a silver pistol and called to his crew, who charged toward Gabriel.

"Run," Geneva gasped, her hand rising to shove at his chest. *"Run, before it's too late!"*

Gabriel's eyes burned in fury. His fingers tightened on the fragile bones at her wrist. *"Jezebel,"* he said hoarsely, the word hurled through her heart, killing her dreams as surely as a bullet would have ended her life.

And then he plunged through the door, with Devere's men yapping at his heels like a pack of unruly dogs.

"Damn you, you'll pay for this trickery," Devere hissed. *"And your fine sister will pay also, when her head flies bloody onto the French cobblestones."*

Geneva didn't move as Devere ran out. She did not even breathe in that moment.

She felt nothing, saw nothing, heard nothing, for she was totally dead inside.

A single tear glistened on her cheek, the crystallized loss of all her dreams. And in her palm the Ashton diamond torn from the Rook's neck gleamed cold and cruel, locked between her bleeding fingers.

Ten ~

Dominic twisted to his side and pommeled his pillow. Cursing softly, he tried the other side, but with no greater success.

He sat up, groggy as if he'd been drugged, with fragments of dreams still drifting in his head. He remembered angry voices, stamping feet.

And a vow betrayed.

Sunlight fell through the window as he shoved to his feet. The sunlight made him think of Cathlin's eyes. Damn it, how had she worked her way under his skin like this? His lower body tightened with a jolt of desire.

But that feeling, like all others, would have to be denied. Over his long years of professional service, three unshakable rules had kept Dominic alive in the shadow world that had taken him from one hot spot of the globe to another, and he was counting on those rules to get him through now.

The rules were the same as always.

Don't let it get personal. Don't let them see you sweat. And when you leave, don't ever look back.

Dominic scowled off at the distant gleam of the channel. He'd already broken two of those rules with Cathlin.

He didn't even want to think about the third one.

* * *

They spent the day apart, by mutual consent.

Cathlin searched Seacliffe from attic to cellar, looking for any old documents that might shed some light on Geneva Russell. Dominic spent the morning sawing through the fallen tree and dragging it from the drive. When he came back, dirty and windblown later in the day, Cathlin still had found nothing.

"Forget it. Go sit down while I clean up and then I'll make something to eat."

"You?" Her tone was decidedly suspicious.

"Don't be such a chauvinist, O'Neill." Dominic's eyes glinted. "You might just be surprised."

She was.

The man could cook.

He sorted through the meager contents of the refrigerator and lined up ingredients neatly on the old pine table. Then he went to work, silent and intent, competent in this as he was in everything else.

Cathlin watched, amazed. First a handful of crushed mint leaves and the juice of two crushed limes went into a bowl. Next came a trace of garlic, a single piece of rosemary, and freshly ground pepper.

The man could *really* cook. What's more, he actually seemed to like it.

Dominic smiled, enjoying her shock. He'd learned at his mother's knee all the arcane mysteries of stockpot, roux, and *foie gras* and was utterly comfortable in the kitchen. Some of his warmest childhood memories, in fact, were of her big, window-lined kitchen filled with sun and wonderful smells, fresh eggs in handmade baskets and a hundred different copper pans.

But Dominic shuddered to think what Danielle Ronsard Montserrat, *nouvelle cuisine* virtuoso and sister to one of the best known chefs in all France, would have thought of *this* particular meal.

It certainly didn't help that the electricity was still out and he had to work by the light of four candles shoved onto cracked porcelain saucers in the dark kitchen. He cursed as he nearly set his cuff afire wrestling a plate of grilled salmon with lime sauce out of the old gas stove. He was even less happy with the thought that Nicholas's letter to Cathlin was missing from his jacket. Most likely he had lost it out on the marsh, when he'd fallen by the bridge. But he couldn't be certain, and that thought bothered Dominic. If the letter fell into the wrong hands, the news of Gabriel's will would soon become public.

And that would put Cathlin in real danger.

As these thoughts churned through Dominic's head, Cathlin sat silent at the end of an eighteenth-century pine table. Chin in hands, she watched his swift, efficient movements, utterly hypnotized. The fish was perfect, crisp on top, crowned with a light sauce and freshly cut lime slices. She had brought the fillet from London, but had been too tired even to think of cooking since she'd come to Seacliffe. Not that her efforts could have come anywhere near this.

But the amazing thing was how different Dominic looked here in the kitchen wrestling pans and juggling spatulas. He seemed quieter, self-sufficient. Entirely self-absorbed, in fact.

Happy.

Cathlin didn't know what made that word come into her head. Or what made her think he wasn't usually happy.

Uneasy at the inceasingly personal direction of her thoughts, she turned to pour two glasses of the French vintage La Trouvaille which she'd also brought from London.

It was her only contribution to their lunch, in fact, since Dominic had insisted she rest while he worked.

Now he turned, two steaming plates in hand. "Lunch, such as it is, is served."

Cathlin studied the grilled fish, golden slices of pan-fried French bread, and bananas cooked in brown sugar with walnuts and whipped cream. "Amazing. It smells absolutely wonderful."

"There wasn't much to work with. Two limes, a handful of crushed mint leaves, a banana, and a single salmon fillet don't exactly make a full larder." He set the dishes on the table, raising a brow as he saw Cathlin's contribution. "Chateau Climens '71?" There was a gleam in his eyes. "You shouldn't have, Ms. O'Neill."

"I *didn't*. Not on my salary. We can't all be born with a silver spoon, you know. But this La Trouvaille will do very nicely. In fact, I've always thought red wines make a perfect complement to full-flavored fish, and rules be damned."

Dominic set her plate before her, his face unreadable. He raised his glass. "Here's to good wine and rules be damned."

Their glasses glinted in the candlelight. Outside the wind whispered through the elm trees along Seacliffe's south front. The etched crystal touched, clinking softly.

Dominic's hair glistened from the shower he'd taken after his efforts with the fallen tree. A few drops still clung to the dark strands at the neck of his opened shirt, of faded but beautifully tailored blue on blue herringbone cotton.

His damp skin smelled slightly of lemon and cloves. Cathlin wanted to inch closer and see if he felt as good as he smelled.

She caught a ragged breath at the unruly path her thoughts were taking and looked away, busying herself with the salmon. "I'm impressed. You didn't tell me you were a cook."

Dominic shrugged. "I've picked up a few things here and there."

A few things? This was world-class cuisine and

Cathlin knew it. What other secrets was the man hiding from her?

"So tell me about this great wine you've discovered." He held up the glass and studied the rich crimson liquid. "Looks pretty ordinary to me."

"Hardly. It's got a unique nose—a mix of raspberries and smoke. Great tannin."

Dominic sniffed. "Passable," he said.

"Better than passable. Try it."

He did, his eyes on her face.

"Well?"

"Good body. Deep color. A rather pleasant little mix of fruit and moss."

"Pleasant? It's extraordinary," Catlin protested. "And it's got wonderful staying power."

Dominic smiled slightly. "Do you happen to hold shares in this vineyard, Ms. O'Neill?"

"Of course not. It's simply my job to recognize a good wine when I find one." She swirled the liquid thoughtfully. "My prediction is that this will be one of the very best. If it's handled properly, maybe even a legend."

Dominic made a muffled sound that might have been a cough and set his glass down sharply on the table. "A legend. You mean that?"

"It *is* my job to know wines, Lord—"

"Dominic, please. I think your saving my life entitles us to progress to first names."

"Very well, Dominic. You sounded happy at my assessment. Maybe *you* have shares in the vineyard," she said teasingly. "But I happen to know that the reclusive owner of La Trouvaille is very old and very bad tempered. He sees no one, and he's a perfectionist when it comes to his wine." She frowned. "Come to think of it, Serita mentioned something about your owning a vineyard."

Dominic's eyes darkened. He started to speak, then looked down at the wine in his glass. "Would it change anything if I were someone else, if my vine-yard were as exceptional as La Trouvaille, perhaps?"

"I judge my friends by who they are, not what they own."

"I expected something like that." Dominic laughed grimly. "No, my acres are nothing extraordinary. I'm just one more playboy earl trying to make ends meet in this day of a shrinking British economy and crippling death duties."

Your idea of economy is probably giving up the second pastry chef and the twelfth gardener."

Dominic gave a tight smile. "Just remember, O'Neill, I can always take away that food you're devouring at roughly the speed of light."

"Okay, I give in. You have perfect notions of economy." Cathlin made a protective movement with her hands. "And this salmon isn't going anywhere except into my mouth, I warn you." She studied Dominic. "By the way, where *did* you learn to cook like this?"

"My mother. She was wonderful in the kitchen, always with bread rising somewhere and a bit of candy or fruit tucked away in one of her big pockets to reward curious fingers. She believed in having children learn right along with everyone else. I could make a soufflé before I could ride a bicycle, I think. A most un-English childhood, believe me."

"She sounds wonderful."

Dominic heard the question in Cathlin's voice. "She died four years ago," he said. "Swift but painless. It was very hard on my father, for they were very much in love even after all those years." A muscle flashed at his jaw. "My sister, Alexis, bore the worst of it, because I was—away."

"I'm sure they understood if your work kept you from them."

"They might have understood, but I'm not sure I did. At least I got to see her, before . . ." His voice drifted away as he ran his finger along the rim of his glass. When he looked up, his voice was steady. "And what about you, Cathlin O'Neill? What secrets are you hiding behind that brash American exterior?"

"Nothing very exciting, I'm afraid. My father was . . . in the English government."

"Someone I'd know?" Dominic asked casually.

"No. Just one of the nameless, thankless drones," Cathlin said bitterly. "My mother died when I was ten. Donnell was a wonderful father. He taught me all the important things."

"Oh? I'm afraid to ask."

Cathlin gave Dominic a challenging smile. "How to palm a card. How to spot a counterfeit bill. How to tell diamonds from Diamonique. It was rather important in his line of work, you see."

"He was a government jeweler?"

Cathlin laughed softly. "No, he was a jewel thief, among other things. Then he went straight. If you can call government security work going straight," she added grimly.

"Not interesting? You've beaten my tale to shreds, O'Neill. Tell me more."

"There's not very much." Not much that Cathlin knew, at least. There had been long months in the Far East and Arabia, but Donnell never spoke of them when he returned and Cathlin knew not to ask. It seemed that the tension had just begun to leave his eyes, and he started to laugh again, when the call would come dragging him off. "He worked for the government and was away a great deal of the time." Her voice hardened. "No son of mine will ever have that kind of life," she said flatly. "It destroys too many lives. That's assuming I ever have a son, of course."

Their eyes met. Heat flared. Cathlin cleared her throat and took a bite of the salmon she'd been pushing around her plate.

"What if your son *wants* a job of that sort? Wouldn't the choice be up to him? Just hypothetically, of course."

"No." Cathlin toyed with the last piece of banana. "Not if I could help it. I've seen too closely the kind of pain it brings."

"I see."

"Do you? I had a father I never knew. And when I finally had the chance, when we both needed each other most, they still wouldn't let him go. They called him out again, always just one more time. Only one time he didn't come back." Her voice wavered, then grew strong once more. "Sorry. Maybe we should talk about something else."

A muscle flashed at Dominic's jaw. "Maybe we should. Tell me what you found today?"

"The short version? Nothing. The long version? Dust and dirt and then a whole lot of nothing." She sighed and ran her hand through her hair. "I've searched everything but one small closet of my father's and found nothing. If there are any records in this house, then they must have been hidden by an expert."

Dominic frowned. "I'll call someone in London to look into the official records. Marriage licenses, wills, property transfers, that sort of thing."

"Isn't that rather a long shot?"

"Do you have any better ideas?"

Cathlin gnawed at her lip. "If your Mad Uncle Gabriel and Geneva Russell were truly close, maybe we should spend more time looking into his life. Maybe you can trace his friends and acquaintances from their letters or one of the family diaries."

"You're right, of course. I have an aunt who has whole trunks full of that kind of thing. I'll have to put her on it." He smiled wryly. "Of course, Great Aunt Agatha would love nothing better. You're brilliant, O'Neill."

Laughing softly, he bent forward to brush a strand of hair from her cheek. Cathlin stopped, fork midair, her eyes very wide and very dazed.

And Dominic knew why. Years of experience had taught him to recognize that the arrested look he saw there, the look that shocked her just as much as it did him, was pulse-slamming desire.

He pulled away as if burned. When had a simple touch become such a complicated prelude to utter disaster? "I'm sorry."

"Don't be." Cathlin looked down. "It's not your fault that I'm acting like a fool. It's just that I don't usually—what I mean is, it's been a long time since—" Muttering, she tossed down her napkin and stood up quickly. Her hands tightened on the carved back of the pine chair.

Dominic was around the table in a second. "Sit down, damn it. This is enough to drive any sane person crazy. I wouldn't be surprised if Mad Uncle Gabriel arranged all of this just to poke his nose at his family when they finally thought they were rid of him. In fact, maybe he and Geneva ran away and eloped, then died in blissful obscurity in some little hamlet in the Cotswolds."

Cathlin gave him a pained look.

"No? Then perhaps they just fell out of love. People do, you know. Perhaps your Geneva married another man and had ten children and lived happily ever after. Gabriel might have continued his reckless, dissolute life, only to discover that he had no one else he cared for enough to leave his wine to."

"But what *was* his end?"

Dominic frowned and rubbed his temple, which was aching slightly. "I haven't a bloody clue. But I'll tell you one thing. Something happened to you when you put on that gown. And something happened to me when I saw you in it. We've got to find out what, and the only place left to try is Draycott."

Cathlin stiffened. "I'm not sure I want to think about this. I came down here to rest and deal with Seacliffe, not with Draycott Abbey."

"Maybe you've got no choice," Dominic said grimly.

There was a hiss and pop as the electricity returned. The refrigerator gurgled and then whined back into activity.

A moment later the phone near the door began an incessant peal.

"Let it ring, Cathlin. We have to talk."

But Cathlin pushed away. "It might be Serita. I have to take it."

Dominic glared at her as she lifted the phone. After a moment she smiled sweetly. "Richard? How nice to hear from you. Oh, nothing major. A storm knocked out the power here. No, everything's fine."

Dominic's hands tightened.

"No, it wouldn't be a bother. I have the cases here anyway. Three o'clock? Fine. Of course, I remember. See you then."

She'd barely put down the phone when Dominic was beside her, his shoulders braced and determined. "You're not going."

Cathlin's brow climbed. "Oh? Since when are you telling me what to do?"

"This is important, Cathlin."

"And my business isn't?" Her foot tapped angrily against the polished wooden floor.

"Be quiet."

"Who are you to—"

"*Be quiet.*" Dominic's fingers clamped down on her shoulder.

Outside the window the lavender bushes rustled.

"Get down and stay down." Dominic moved, pinning Cathlin to the floor.

"But—"

His palm lodged over her lips. "There's someone out there."

Cathlin stiffened. She had just seen what Dominic had seen.

A man was standing outside the kitchen. He was dressed in a hunting jacket and boots and looked like the usual country gentleman out for an outing.

Then Cathlin saw the revolver in the man's fingers.

She swallowed, watching Dominic inch along the wall toward the door. He slipped out into the corridor, knees to his chest and body low to the floor.

As she watched, Cathlin went very still. Her father had taught her just such a movement a year after her mother's death. "Keep low," he'd ordered. "Focus your weight forward so you're ready to run if necessary. Try to make the smallest target in case of an attack."

Oh, yes, Cathlin remembered. Now she watched the man she'd rescued from the marsh moving exactly the same way, a professional in every sense of the word.

The realization left her cold.

Dominic Montserrat was one of *them*, the men who had stolen her father from her and held him captive in their nasty shadow world.

And that meant she couldn't trust a single damned thing he'd told her.

Later Dominic would wonder about the raw instinct that made him turn and shove Cathlin to the floor.

Even after three years in France, some deep part of him had registered the cues and responded instantly. He didn't even like to think about that fact. But now, with adrenaline racing through his veins and anger tightening his throat, he didn't think, he only *moved*.

When the man outside the window disappeared,

Dominic waited for instinct to kick in. Almost immediately it did.

Around to the back.

He headed for the front, meaning to circle back through the dense woods bordering Seacliffe. In the process he'd also have to verify if the intruder was armed, if he had backup, and what kind of transport he had hidden.

Dominic went very still as all the old reflexes went into play. His fingers dug into a polished chair leg as one part of him watched and analyzed, calling on the long years of grim experience that had kept him alive in too many back streets and parade grounds and government cavalcades.

The other part, the saner part that had struggled to be free of that dangerous life, stood away, sickened by what he'd become.

His superiors in Whitehall would have been delighted at how easily he slid back into the old patterns. It seemed that the years in France had made no difference. Maybe his retirement had come too late, or maybe the pattern was part of his nature. He didn't have the answers to explain it, and God knows he'd spent three years trying.

The truth was that he would never be free of this world. He'd been in too deep for too long.

Silently, Dominic eased the front door open, his fingers itching for a gun he didn't have and a holster he couldn't even remember. Following the dictates of dark memories, he worked his way outside and then sprinted soundlessly toward the woods.

Knowing already that some part of him had gone dead inside.

Ten minutes later, hidden within a tangle of yew trees, Dominic stared down at the set of fresh prints left in the soft earth. Whoever had been outside the kitchen window was gone. But it had been a professional, that Dominic knew. The man had been dressed casually, like a tourist who'd lost his way upon the marsh and stopped to ask directions.

Except for the Smith & Wesson in his right hand. Something chambered for .357 cartridges, which stayed accurate even at long distances.

Dominic's jaw hardened as he felt the old adrenaline high begin again. He'd been slow in the kitchen. He'd lost more precious time at the door, thinking about a past he had tried hard to bury.

And because of it the man had gotten away.

Nicholas had been only too right. The news of the wine discovery had gotten out, possibly from someone who'd been watching him when he'd fallen by the bridge and gone through his pockets to find Nicholas's letter explaining the discovery of the wine and the terms of the will. Now Cathlin would be in danger every second of every day.

And it would be his job to keep her safe, whether she liked it or not.

He walked in, tired, disappointed, and very angry. If he thought he was going to be thanked for his interference, he soon realized he was wrong.

"You lied to me." Cathlin's hands were stiff at her sides and her face was white. "You lied to me all along. You're one of *them*, aren't you? One of the men from my father's world."

"Cathlin, listen."

"No, I don't want to listen! I saw how you went after him, your whole body a weapon, your mind cold and hard as a computer. You have all the same moves that Donnell had. All along, you sat there and listened, nodding. Lying. How much more is lies, Dominic? *How much?*"

"None. I meant to tell you, Cathlin. Then you mentioned about your father and I decided you weren't ready to hear the truth."

"Ready? Who are *you* to make that kind of decision?"

"It was necessary, Cathlin."

"You bet it was. You had to lie to me, to manipulate and steer me just where you wanted." Her fingers locked. It had all been a lie, the story of his mother and his playboy life. Yet he'd made it all seem so believable, shredding her careful defenses. "When were you going to tell me, Dominic? Or maybe I should say *Officer* Montserrat."

"Officer will be fine," Dominic said grimly. "Because from now on I'll be giving the orders. We each stand to gain at least half a million pounds when the terms of that legacy are fulfilled, Cathlin. I was carrying a letter of explanation from Nicholas Draycott and I'm afraid it's been stolen. That means that the news of the will has gotten out, and the danger is now very real."

She laughed tightly. "Because of one case of old wine?"

"How many men do you know who would kill for a 1792 Château d'Yquem?"

Cathlin did a rough estimate and felt a sickening jolt in her stomach. Wine collectors were a fanatic lot. It was part of the reason Cathlin liked them. Yes, she could think of quite a few who would go to any lengths to possess such a treasure. "So I might be in danger. Do you want me to apologize? Very well, I'm sorry, Officer Montserrat. I only fell for part of your lies, not the whole lot."

"Cathlin, listen. I made a decision. It might have been the wrong one, but I never meant it to hurt you."

"Tell that to my father." She spun around, tears glinting on her cheeks. "No and no and no! I hated that world then and I hate it now. I don't want anything to do with it."

Dominic looked at her hands, locked on her soft

floral blouse. At her eyes, blazing and gold and haunted.

"I don't need you here and I don't need that wine, not if it involves going back to Draycott. So just stay out of my way and let me do my work."

"I can't," Dominic growled, his eyes on the satin skin exposed at the neck of her flowing blouse. "You see, you *are* my work right now. Where you go, I go. What you do, I do. And no matter what I tell you, you do it, since it could be the one thing that saves our lives until this business is finished. By God, I'm going to keep you safe, whether you like it or not."

"What gives you the right to—"

He cut her off harshly, pulling his gaze from the creamy skin that left a hot pulse pounding at his groin. "That letter from Nicholas Draycott gave me the right. Either you go with me and do things my way or you don't go at all. And then we're both out half a million pounds." He shoved to his feet, muscles tense. "So what's your answer?"

"What choice do I have?"

"None at all," came the flat answer.

"I don't like you, Officer Montserrat. I'm inclined to say that I hate you right at this moment. Which doesn't make much of a basis for a week's stay anywhere in close quarters." In her anger, Cathlin sat forward, shoulders stiff. Her blouse moved, revealing a satin curve of skin and the shadow of one perfect, dusky nipple.

A muscle flashed at Dominic's jaw. "I'll survive, O'Neill. But maybe you'd better remember that I've got perfect eyesight."

Cathlin looked down, saw the gaping fabric, and sat back abruptly, hot color in her cheeks.

"Don't let it worry you," Dominic said coldly. "I've guarded more women than I can count, and none of them has ever gotten through to me. The sex can be great when you're in that kind of life, don't get me wrong. The danger and adrenaline push everything to the edge and make even a kiss explosive. But when I'm in bed with a woman I want to know it's not just adrenaline that's making the high between us. So you can relax, O'Neill. You might as well be dressed in a habit and a crucifix, because from now on it's business, just cold-blooded business between us."

"Oh? And what's the good news?"

"That *is* the good news."

Again the swift flare of color, this time sweeping down to Cathlin's chest. "I'm delighted to hear it, Officer Montserrat. Now maybe you'll get the bloody hell out of my kitchen."

"One more thing. You're not going to see Severance. Not alone, anyway. Not after what just happened."

"Any other orders?"

"If there are, I'll tell you, O'Neill. And you'll obey them." His voice was cold. One hundred percent professional. "Because that's the only way we're going to get out of this whole bloody mess."

Cathlin watched him stride from the room. "Like hell I will."

Down the hill, hidden beyond the ragged line of trees at the edge of the marsh, a man eased back into the shadows. Carefully he flipped out a transmitter. Then he began to speak softly.

Eleven ~

Dominic sat down on the old rosewood desk and frowned at the sunny study filled with pictures. Pictures of Donnell O'Neill, looking happy but as if he were thinking of something else. Pictures of a beautiful woman with golden eyes. Cathlin's mother, no doubt.

And then there were the pictures of Cathlin, riding her first pony, climbing her first tree, going to her first tea dance in high-heeled satin pumps.

Something twisted in his gut.

Muttering darkly, he picked up the phone and jabbed out a number. "Nicholas?"

"Right here. Any luck with Cathlin?"

"I'm working on it. Things have been a little chaotic here, I'm afraid."

"The same on this end," his friend said grimly. "We've had a call from my solicitor in London. Someone has been asking about the reports we had to file locally after the discovery of Gabriel's remains. We've asked the people here to keep it quiet as best they can, but I'm afraid someone's gotten wind of the story. It was only a matter of time, I guess."

"I'm not surprised to hear it. We had a visitor today, too. An unexpected visitor," Dominic said flatly. "And that letter you wrote to Cathlin has disappeared. How long do we have until the newspapers get hold of this, Nicholas?"

"Who knows? I'll do what I can. I still have a few friends on Fleet Street I can trust. But I think you'd better get Cathlin down here now, so you start fulfilling that week of residence. Meanwhile, Kacey and I have begun looking into the documents here, trying to track down anything about the elusive Gabriel Montserrat. So far, no luck, however."

"Ditto here. The whole thing's damned strange. Cathlin's attitude isn't going to help either."

"Attitude?"

"She hates anything to do with the work that killed her father. And unfortunately, that means me."

"You'll bring her around," Nicholas said confidently. "You always do."

Maybe not this time, Dominic thought. And maybe this was the only time that really counted.

"Dominic, are you still there?"

"Right here, Nicholas. By the way, there's nothing you aren't telling me, is there? No other crazy stipulations that Gabriel put on this bequest."

There was a tiny pause. "What makes you ask that?"

"You haven't answered me, Nicholas."

His friend cleared his throat. "Look, I've got to go. Kacey's just come in with Genevieve. I'll talk to you when you get here, Dominic. And make it soon."

She'd bloody show Dominic Montserrat, Cathlin thought.

She would be pampered, perfect, and beautiful when she left this room. And just let him *try* to stop her from conducting her business. Serita had friends, after all, friends in the very highest places. They would dispose of a nasty little insect named Dominic Montserrat in a second.

Frowning, Cathlin dumped a packet of expensive

French bath powder into the big old tub and turned the faucets on high, letting the fragrance rise in rich clouds around her.

Angrily, she settled into a froth of bubbles and forced her mind to business, something she'd woefully forgotten in the last twenty-four hours since Dominic had come charging into her well-ordered life. Cathlin sat back and began a mental tally of her current inventory against the desires—and ruthless dictates—of her well-heeled clients.

No Sauternes for Alexandra, the banker's wife. Her third husband had recently absconded to parts unknown, taking the family diamonds along with him. And since *he* had adored Sauternes, now *she* couldn't abide the sight of them.

Next was her German diplomat. No more vintage champagne there. Poor Herr Schmidt had recently been involved in a scandal with a hot-blooded but underaged heir to a French champagne dynasty. As a result, he'd had to pay a cool two million to buy his way out of the nasty legal proceedings the family threatened him with. Yes, only fine robust burgundies for Herr Schmidt from now on. Cathlin decided that an elegant Clos St. Denis 1969, silky and rich with fruit, would make a perfect offering for the fastidious Herr Schmidt.

That left only the Château Lafite. A very upscale restauranteur in Brighton had been pestering her for a new shipment of first growth burgundy. After lunch she'd place a call and see if Marcel still wanted—

Abruptly, all thought stopped as Cathlin watched the bathroom door inch open. Maybe it was the intruder. Or maybe it was—

Dominic eased into the room, silent and cool. Only his glittering eyes showed his fury. "Just what the hell do you think you're doing?"

Cathlin made a lunge for a towel, missed, then

sank low into the now-churning water. "It's bloody obvious, I should think. Get out!"

A muscle flashed at his jaw. "I didn't know where you were. I called a dozen times, but you didn't answer."

"Next time I'll post a schedule." Cathlin slid lower, bubbles frothing around her. "I'm fine, as you can see. So now you can get out."

But Dominic merely angled one broad shoulder against the doorframe. He was naked from the waist up, his bronze chest dusted with dark hair. Cathlin felt her cheeks flame as he studied her from the end of her toes emerging from a froth of bubbles to the damp black hair curling at her neck. "I got worried when you didn't answer. Didn't you hear me calling?"

"No. Now are you satisfied?" Foam sloshed across Cathlin's shoulder, skimming the curve of one breast.

"Not in the least."

Cathlin felt her face burn.

Dominic said a raw word and grabbed the towel hanging over the edge of the door. "Get dressed, damn it. I need your help. I've found something up in the attic."

"What?"

"You'll see." The towel flew toward her and landed in the scented foam with a soft hiss.

Cathlin lurched up, bubbles sculpting her breasts and thighs as she dived to rescue the now sodden towel.

Dominic's gaze followed her every inch of the way.

"Get *out!*" Cathlin stormed, her cheeks crimson, the wet towel clamped protectively to her chest and thighs. "Unless you want a broken neck to go along with those bruises on your head!"

"It might just be worth it," he said softly. His eyes flowed over the towel. Her every wet curve lay molded in its damp, seductive drape. Then his gaze moved lower, to the creamy legs that ran up to—

Dominic bit back a curse and turned away. "Hurry up. Unless you want me to come in after you and bleed on all those nice bubbles."

Somewhere down the hall the phone began an incessant clamor.

"Damned bloody phone." Jamming his hands into his pockets, Dominic strode off, muttering a stream of curses that left Cathlin red-faced. But worst of all was the way her heart was slamming as she clutched the damp, entirely useless towel to her chest.

Because even though she wanted to hate him, even though she was struggling desperately hard, she still wasn't able to manage it.

Dominic slammed down the phone. Wrong bloody number. It didn't help that his head was pounding and his shoulder ached from crawling around that bloody attic searching for her cameo.

Then, when Cathlin hadn't answered—

He frowned, not wanting to remember the fear that had kicked in at her silence. He'd plunged up the stairs, head down and shoulders low, in a textbook stance as he braced for a concealed attacker. Even now, his nerves were screaming, and he was riding a wave of adrenaline. He'd crouched just outside her door, then reached for his shoulder, just at the spot where a revolver would have been holstered.

Only there was no gun. Dominic had sworn there'd never be a gun there again.

But here he was, making all the old moves. And there had been no one better at those moves than Dominic Montserrat.

Right up to that day in Rome when four kidnappers had moved in on the car where Dominic was escorting the twin children of one of the queen's lesser-known cousins to a horse show. Dominic had shoved the towheaded eight-year-olds behind him and dropped to one knee, then squeezed off six quick shots.

It had all happened before he'd known it.

When he'd turned the bodies over, he'd discovered that three of the men were still in their teens. And the fourth "man" was really a girl of barely sixteen.

He'd gotten through the rest of the tour, then gone back home and fallen apart. He'd gotten stinking drunk and stayed that way for nearly a week.

After that he'd turned in his resignation. And he'd never worn a gun again, nor wanted to.

Until now.

He jabbed shaky fingers through his hair, sick at the old memories. Outside the window, wind shook the trees that bordered the tidal plain. Seacliffe was a desolate place, but it had its own kind of beauty. It was a place where a man could find himself. A place whose solitude forced a man to face his private demons.

The only question was if the man *liked* what he saw.

Dominic was wondering how he'd gotten pulled into this mess when he caught the faint scent of flowers behind him. Something subtle. Lilacs, he decided.

And then she was behind him, fast and utterly furious. "Let's get one thing straight right now, Macho Man." Cathlin poked his chest and the cold, wet towel, newly rescued from her bubble bath, slapped him in the face.

"Nice aim, Irish. Almost as nice as those long legs of yours. But come to think of it, I prefer the sight of your high, full—"

"I don't care what you like!"

His hands rose in surrender. "I'm all ears. Well

maybe not all ears. I'm a flesh and blood male, after all. There are some parts that are—"

"Shut *up!*"

Dominic complied, crossing his arms and watching more of that damnably enchanting color sweep Cathlin's cheeks. It left him thinking about what it would take to make her blush like that again.

In soft, hidden places.

Places he'd graze and stroke until—

Forget it, Montserrat. It's all business now, remember? "Whatever you say, Cathlin. I put myself entirely into your hands."

Again the color, rising through her cheeks. "If you did that, you'd be sorry, because right now I'd consider it a great pleasure to snap several bones into neat little pieces. And *that's* just for starters."

His eyebrow rose. "Sounds painful."

"Blast it, you—"

His eyes slid over her robed body. "Hadn't you better get ready? You're seeing your debonair friend in an hour."

Cathlin tossed the wet towel right in his face. "You're right, I am. And I'm going alone. And that's one order you're *not* going to worm your way around, *Officer* Montserrat."

When Cathlin walked out the front door, she was tugging on a jacket of Harris tweed. Dominic noticed how the smoky golden plaid brought out the turbulence in her eyes. He also noticed the pallor in her face and the set to her jaw. Attitude.

"Let's go," he said curtly.

"This is business. You're *not* coming."

"From now on, where you go, I go, O'Neill."

"What gives you the right to interfere?"

"Interfering is my job," Dominic growled. It was only too true. Interfering was the heart of close protection, because protecting someone meant being unpleasant. It meant pointing out problems. It meant being nosy and curious and meddlesome while you were busy suspecting anyone and everyone.

And Dominic had been damned good at that part of his job. Before it had nearly eaten a hole through his soul, that is.

"Your job? You mean along with repairing roofs?"

"Taking care of a woman has always been a man's job."

She pushed past him. "Maybe this woman doesn't need protecting."

"Too bloody bad." Dominic strode after her. "You're forgetting something else, Irish. Half of that money is mine, and I need *you* to get it."

Cathlin swept her hair from her face and called back over her shoulder. "I'm loading Richard's wine. If you're not in the car when I get back, I leave without you."

Dominic watched her stride off toward the Jeep. Until he had something more concrete, he was going to keep Cathlin O'Neill close. It was only logical, given the amount of money involved in Gabriel Ashton's will.

Good try, Dominic thought. *But we both know that it's already gone a whole lot further than the money.*

Cathlin had just shoved the last case of wine into the back of her Jeep when Dominic strode down the drive. His long legs ate up the distance, and his casual elegance in an old leather jacket gave him the look of a movie star traveling light. Mirrored aviator sunglasses gleamed silver beneath his wild, dark hair.

Cathlin barely allowed him time to sit down before slamming the car into gear and roaring down the drive.

"Tell me about Severance."

"There's nothing to tell. He tried something once, but I wasn't interested. Now it's strictly business."

"Let's hope *he* knows that."

"Oh, he does. We have an understanding, Richard and I. I understand that he's an irresponsible, arrogant jerk, but I need his business. He understands that if he tries anything out of line, he's going to lose a few teeth."

Dominic laughed. "Very well, enough about Severance. Tell me about this wine you're taking to him. No doubt it's going to cost him a lot."

"A shocking amount." Cathlin smiled faintly. "The case comes from Bordeaux."

"I believe I've heard of it," Dominic said dryly. "I've also heard that half the Bordeaux vintages are worth little more than the bottles they're housed in." It wasn't quite true, but Dominic wanted to hear her talk, even if it was only to refute him.

"Sometimes they're overvalued. In 1972 an exceptionally poor vintage was foisted on the world at record prices. Buying a name-brand château that year was a major mistake. It's a question of land and continuity, you see."

Dominic sat back and listened to Cathlin slide into her subject. She thought she was being boring and obnoxious, but Dominic was intrigued by her passionate knowledge of all things related to wine.

"The old houses, or châteaux, usually have the best soil and ideal growing conditions. Because of that, over a long period of time their wines will be consistently better than any others."

The lady was good, all right. It seemed that anything she didn't know wasn't worth knowing. But her concern spread beyond crop yields and pesticides and harvesting schedules. Clearly Cathlin O'Neill had a heart for wine and a love for the land. Both came through even in this bland description of vintage controversies and vineyard soil conditions.

Dominic sat back and let her deluge him with facts and figures. As she described the fields of Bordeaux, he pictured green vines climbing over a rolling hillside. He saw the low mists that clung to the valleys, shielding the grapes until they reached perfect maturity.

Yes, Cathlin O'Neill was damned good. And she was good because it came from her heart, not her head, which was where too many well-heeled vintners and arrogant wine connoisseurs failed. Dominic had learned all this from his French mother.

Danielle Montserrat had taught him that a very fine wine should not be coddled, worshiped, or bartered as a simple commodity. Wine, she had always insisted, should be treated like a fine old friend. It should be savored and appreciated, enjoyed in the heat of a fine summer afternoon and in the last cool slide of velvet evening.

Dominic had always made that his credo at La Trouvaille. He wanted to create wines that were rich but subtle, with a power and elegance that lingered. And apparently he'd succeeded. Cathlin herself had pronounced La Trouvaille a success. He didn't suppose it was because of trends either. Cathlin O'Neill would never be a slave to fads. She would judge a Château Lafite with the same honesty that she accorded the most anonymous French *vin de pays*.

And a part of Dominic Monsterrat honored her for her cussed independence. That kind of stubbornness had no doubt created any number of problems for her, given the conservatism of the wine world. But she'd survived.

Dominic knew he could learn a great deal from that kind of tenacity.

As they drove on through bars of golden sunlight and a haze of bright spring wildflowers, Dominic found himself wishing he didn't know her name or her past or anything about her. Then he could simply pull her into his arms and kiss her the way his hardening body urged him to do.

But that was impossible.

She was business and nothing else, right up until the will was honored. Somehow he was going to have to remember that.

An hour later they turned up an oak-fringed drive that overlooked the sea. A pink granite palace squatted at the top of the hill, its banks of modern windows ablaze in the setting sun. The beautifully manicured lawns were marred by two tennis courts and a garish black flagstone swimming pool.

Money, Dominic thought. Lots of it. Money that was screaming to be seen. "Remind me not to look up *this* guy's decorator."

Dominic saw Cathlin frown and run her hand absently over her neck, as if it ached.

A uniformed guard met them just beside the gatehouse. Obviously, Mr. Millionaire didn't like to have his privacy threatened.

"Name?" the guard said, trying to eye Cathlin's legs.

Dominic had to restrain the urge to give him a savage right uppercut.

"Cathlin O'Neill to see Mr. Severance."

"I'll have to phone up to the house." The man frowned, scanning Dominic. "Who's he?"

"My assistant," Cathlin said silkily. "He'll help me with the wine cases."

The guard shrugged, then turned away to his radio. A moment later he gestured over the trees. "Drive to the top of the hill. Park at the servants' entrance," he added maliciously.

As the ornate wrought-iron gates slid open, Cathlin pulled in and started up the drive. "You stay in the Jeep. You'd never pass for a workman, not in that jacket and those glasses. Definitely not with that attitude."

"What's wrong with my attitude?"

"You're too arrogant."

Dominic shrugged. "We bodyguards have an image to keep up after all." Cathlin pulled into the parking area, but made no move to get out. "We're here, O'Neill. Or hadn't you noticed?"

"I noticed."

"Then you'd better get going. Mr. Lifestyles of the Rich and Famous isn't going to like that pricey Bordeaux throwing phosphates from the heat."

Cathlin muttered and reached for the door.

"Damn it, O'Neill." Cursing softly, Dominic caught her cheeks in his hands and pulled her against him.

God, but she fit his arms perfectly. And her scent . . .

Slowly, he ran his hand through her silky cap of black hair. It danced against his fingers, warm and electric. Then he reached beneath and slid something around her neck.

Cathlin didn't speak. She seemed to be struggling with a wave of conflicting emotions. Hell, Dominic knew that *he* was.

"I found your cameo. I thought you should wear it, as a reminder of that old house you love—and of the way you can save it." It was playing dirty, but Dominic didn't care. He was going to get through to her any way he could.

"Dominic, I don't—"

He didn't give her time to be angry. He just pulled her head back and then crushed his mouth over hers in one hard motion.

This had to be what summer tasted like, he thought dimly. Hot and endlessly sweet. His fingers tightened. He wanted and wanted and wanted.

But Dominic knew he couldn't have what he wanted. This was as far as it was going to go. When he pulled away, her face was flushed and her hands were fists.

"What was *that* for?"

It took Dominic a few heartbeats to recover enough control to answer. "It's for the man who's staring at us through those windows. I want him to know exactly what we were doing out here."

Twelve ~

Cathlin tried to force her heart back between her ribs.

Who was she kidding? She wasn't even *close* to normalcy. Her mouth was still tingling from the burn of Dominic's lips, and the cameo hung cold and heavy at her neck.

Cathlin shoved open the door of the Jeep and tugged her satchel over her arm. Once again the man had outflanked her and left her speechless.

Forget him, O'Neill. You've got work to do.

She tugged her satchel higher and ran a hand over her hair, but she needn't have bothered. She did not look like the cool professional as she hoped, nor the level-headed wine expert.

At that moment Cathlin O'Neill looked like a dewy-eyed beauty, like a woman lost in love after being kissed by the man she adored. The fragile cameo at her neck above her soft blouse subtly complemented that image.

Dominic had planned it that way, of course.

Richard Severance was a picture of casual elegance in raw silk trousers and an Armani jacket carefully selected to exaggerate the width of his unimpressive shoulders. He received Cathlin warmly, all smiles

159

and curiosity to see this case of Bordeaux she wanted to sell him. But as Cathlin cradled the sample bottle, Severance's hard eyes settled on the smooth curves beneath her blouse. From there, they ran to the long, slim thighs and rounded calves beneath her blue jeans.

His lips curved in a smile.

His cordiality lasted ten minutes. By the time Cathlin began tendering bills of sale and import documents, the London merchant banker and socialite prince had waited long enough. He cornered her by the Louis XIV writing desk as she was working a cork out of her first sample bottle.

"I thought you'd like a taste before you made your decision."

"How true. I always sample anything I consider buying." His eyes narrowed as he moved toward her. "You really do have the most beautiful mouth, Cathlin. I wonder if it tastes the same as last time." He caught her waist and pulled her into his arms.

"This is not amusing, Richard!"

"Simply part of the sampling." His tongue thrust between her lips. His hand flattened over her breast.

Cathlin shoved at his hands. "Stop this, Richard. I told you last time, it was strictly business and you agreed."

"I'm afraid I lied," Severance said coolly. "Dear, sweet Cathlin, why else would you have come back? I knew that little scene last time was just to get me crazy. And it worked, love. I haven't been able to get you out of my mind."

"I came for the wine, Richard. Nothing else."

"For Christ's sake, I saw how you came on to your young stud out there in the car. You two looked like you were going to make it in the front seat. So don't tell me you're not interested."

"What you saw was—a mistake."

"Good. I'll please you more than he did. Besides, it always pays to keep your clients happy."

Cathlin's face paled. So it had all been a game. She was part of the package—otherwise, no deal. "I don't have time for these antics."

"Of course you do, Cathlin. You know you want it. Judging by the way you kissed your friend in the car, you were primed, loaded, and ready to fire." His fingers pushed under her blouse, working at the delicate layers of lace beneath.

Cathlin felt a memory stir deep in her mind, an image of hard hands shoving her into a dark room. She closed her eyes, fighting to stay calm, fighting to remember. But there was nothing more.

She shook her head as Severance pulled her closer. "Let me go, Richard."

"Damn it, Cathlin, I haven't been able to think straight since I met you. It's long past time that we—"

Cathlin sent her fist into his stomach. Severance bent over, gasping in pain. "You'll be sorry for that. I've got friends, damn it."

Suddenly Dominic charged through the doorway. "Cathlin, are you—" He stopped when he saw Severance doubled over, his suit awry.

Cathlin put a restraining hand on his arm. "Go away, Dominic. Things are fine here."

"Fine? Your blouse is up to your chin and your cheeks are bright red and you say you're *fine*? What in the hell was he doing?"

"Nothing that matters. Now if you will please leave, I'd like to finish here."

"Finish what?" Dominic glared at Severance. "The man was muscling you over. He wasn't interested in any bloody wine."

"I know that," Cathlin said calmly.

Dominic crossed his arms at his chest. "Go ahead and finish. I'm not leaving without you."

"This is my fight, Dominic."

"Not anymore, it isn't. The second that bastard laid a finger on you all bets were off."

Severance tugged his coat straight and scowled at Cathlin. "Get this person out of here so we can talk, Cathlin. Otherwise I—"

"Otherwise what, Richard? You'll warn off all your friends? Serita and I will survive, I assure you." Smiling grimly, Cathlin ripped her bill of sale into tiny pieces and tossed them over Severance's head. Then she very carefully overturned the vintage Bordeaux across Severance's beautiful carpet. "There's your wine sample, Richard. It was an excellent year, by the way, fruity and quite intense. I hope you enjoy it, because that's the last one you'll be getting from us."

"You bloody little—"

Severance never finished. Dominic's hand smashed into his jaw, and sent him staggering backward onto the floor.

Cathlin slid behind the wheel, her hands trembling. "I told you not to interfere."

"Too bad," Dominic said tightly.

"I don't want anything from Richard Severance. Nor do I want anything from *you*. I can manage by myself."

"Sure you can." Dominic's fingers tightened on her door. He took in her stiff shoulders and pale face. She was prickly and stubborn and grade-A impossible.

And he still wanted to pull her against his chest and kiss her breathless.

No mistake about it, Montserrat, he thought grimly. *You've really blown it this time.* So much for all that impartial bodyguard routine.

He glared down at Cathlin, angry at the desire still battering his body. "Slide over," he ordered. "I'm driving."

Cathlin's hands tightened. "I told you, I'm fine."

"Like hell you are."

Cathlin couldn't ignore him, no matter how hard she tried. His eyes were smoky and his body was rigid. He looked angry and frustrated and determined to protect her—even from herself. And his strength was seductive, tempting her to give in, tempting her to let him take charge and smooth her way, like the professional he was.

Only Cathlin knew one other thing. This was all just temporary. She'd let down her defenses and learn to rely on him, and then one day she'd wake up and find him gone, off to Tashkent or Bogotá or Timbuktu, just like her father had gone.

And she'd be the one left behind, drying her tears and fighting her pain, trying to pick up the thousand shattered pieces of her life.

No. Not ever again. "Forget it, Macho Man. I'm just fine."

"Fine? Your hands are shaking and you can barely see straight, O'Neill. I don't intend to die from your reckless driving. Now move over."

Cathlin thought about arguing with him, but the cold light of reason told her he was right. Her hands were shaking so hard that she'd probably have them wrapped around a tree inside of two minutes.

So she'd do it. Just this once. But she didn't have to like it.

Scowling, she slid into the passenger seat, trying not to notice how his shoulders filled the seat, how his strong fingers worked themselves around the steering wheel.

Blasted, competent male. "You didn't need to come barging in. I was managing just fine. And I certainly didn't need you decking one of my best clients."

"One of your ex-best clients. If that snake gets near you again, he'll spend some serious, quality time getting to know the traction equipment in an intensive care ward."

"Stay out of my life, Montserrat. If I do decide to go to Draycott and listen to Nicholas Draycott's explanation, you'll be the first to know. But that's all you're entitled to, understand? Everything else is mine, my business, my house, my life. I can take care of myself. I've had a lot of practice, you see, and I don't need any lessons now." Now that the adrenaline rush was fading, Cathlin felt a wave of numbness begin to climb up her legs. Seconds later a tear inched down her cheek, but she shoved it away.

"Damn it, Cathlin." Cursing, Dominic pulled the car onto the shoulder and pulled Cathlin against his chest. One tear worked into two and then more, but she made no sound. He held her anyway, feeling the heat of her tears on his shirt, feeling her soft breasts wedged against his chest, feeling her stiffness and her fury. He fought back the intense desire he felt and only held her, one hand buried beneath the warm shadow of her hair. When she finally pulled away he found a tissue and held it out to her.

She gave a defiant sniff and blew her nose. "Drive. I'll be fine."

When Dominic saw there would be no more tears and certainly no explanations, he shoved the Jeep into gear and roared away from Richard Severance's monstrous palace.

As he did, he caught the faint scent of lilacs.

Another trick of his imagination? There was a logical explanation, of course, but right then it was beyond him. All he could think of was Cathlin. The way she'd forced her chin up. The way she'd tossed the contents of that bottle over Severance's carpet. The way she left him hungry and hard and crazy to kiss her.

But in doing that, he violated the first and oldest rule of his profession: Never, ever let it get personal.

He moved away from her and closed his hands

around the wheel. To his fury he saw they were trembling slightly.

They didn't talk. Both of them knew they had too much to say and too little hope of ever saying it.

After fifteen minutes, Cathlin insisted on taking the wheel and Dominic finally agreed.

She drove the Jeep along the narrow roads by instinct rather than sight. She drove too fast and she knew it, but the shadows moving down into the valleys left her with a sudden uneasiness and an urgency to be back at Seacliffe—and away from the man beside her. The man Cathlin couldn't seem to stop thinking about.

As they rounded a bend, two sheep lumbered out of the gathering shadows and Cathlin jerked the wheel to avoid them.

"Slow down," Dominic said harshly.

"Go to hell," she snapped back.

His hands clenched. "Are you trying to kill yourself?"

"I'm simply trying to get home. And to get as far away from you as possible."

Dominic's eyes went hard. "Cathlin, don't. Not like this." He caught her shoulder.

She shook his hand away, frightened by the hundred wild emotions even that single touch conveyed.

It had all happened, just as she feared. He had gotten too close, and he was making her remember, making her feel things she didn't want to feel. Not ever.

And somewhere deep inside her, Cathlin O'Neill knew that to feel again, real and deeply, she would have to brave the dark gates of her childhood memories. She could feel them there sometimes in her dreams, but nothing ever remained the next morning when she awoke. It was safer that way, she told herself firmly.

So she would keep things just as they were. No strings, no emotions, no attachments. And needing Dominic Montserrat was just not going to happen.

She scowled into the rearview mirror and saw two headlights loom up out of the twilight. She eased to the left of the narrow lane, hoping whoever it was would slow down, in case there were any more sheep wandering past. The ditch at the edge of the road was bordered by a high stone wall which left little room to maneuver. No matter that she was born and raised in England, she'd learned to drive in Philadelphia, and being on the left still made her uncomfortable.

Behind her the lights kept coming, and they were coming faster.

Cathlin frowned.

"I see it, O'Neill. Ease into second and get ready to turn."

Cathlin swallowed, hearing the iron in Dominic's voice. This couldn't be happening. He was overreacting again, just trying to frighten her, hoping to find a reason to interfere in her life. "You're joking, right?"

"Eighty percent of all professional kidnappings take place from cars, O'Neill. This is no bloody joke."

Cathlin heard the roar of a motor and knew that slowing down was the last thing on the mind of the driver behind them. "What if there's no place to turn?" she said hoarsely.

"There will be. Just hold it steady. If we have to ram them, we will."

"*Ram* them?"

"I added some reinforcement to your front and rear bumpers, just in case. It will hold, don't worry."

Ram them. Cathlin swallowed. "Great."

Dominic scanned the wall to their left. "There's a sharp left up ahead, as I remember. Just after that, you'll make a quick right down a lane between two cottages."

He *remembered?* "Tell me when." Behind them the lights loomed closer. Cathlin blinked, sliding out of the line of reflection, concentrating on the road. Beside her, she heard Dominic search under the seat. "What are you doing?"

"Evening the odds."

Cathlin heard a click, but didn't dare take her eyes from the road.

"Steady, Irish. We're almost there. Just a few seconds. And—*now.*"

The same second Cathlin jerked left, he pulled a canister from the seat and leveled a high-intensity beam of light straight back into their pursuers' eyes. Desperately Cathlin braked and then skidded to the right, praying Dominic's memory was as sharp as the rest of him.

The road was there, right where he said it would be. Gritting her teeth, she floored the Jeep and shot between the darkened cottages.

"Good. Now get ready to pull over and cut your lights."

Cathlin's fingers were trembling on the wheel. Dimly she felt Dominic's hand grip her knee for a moment. "You're doing fine, Cathlin. Remember, they need us in one piece. That's the only way they'll get that wine."

She swallowed, nodding but not feeling very much better.

"Now."

She pulled left just behind an ancient overhanging oak, braked sharply, and then cut the lights. The car settled with a hiss of gravel and the pop of cooling metal.

Darkness closed in. In the sudden silence Cathlin heard the sigh of the wind and the rush of oak leaves overhead.

But no sound of a car.

She looked questioningly at Dominic, barely able to make out his hard features in the darkness.

"Give it a few seconds. If it stays quiet, then take this road straight on into the village."

"But how—"

"It's my business to know, Cathlin."

Business. Of course it was. She looked away, her fingers clenched on the wheel. Just business. She had to remember that.

The seconds ticked past. No lights. No shouts. No noise.

"Let her rip."

The engine answered her movement, thundering back to life, but it didn't match the thunder of Cathlin's heart. Then she heard the sound of a door opening. "Dominic? What—"

"Drive straight ahead and stop just past the church. Lock your doors and wait for me there. I'll meet you in ten minutes, after I take a look around."

Ten minutes could be a very long time.

Cathlin found it was time enough to be born and die and be born again, not a dozen but a thousand times. She learned it was ample time to taste your own fear, feel your sweat, and force yourself to desperate decisions. It was also time enough to see just how dangerously entangled her life had become with Dominic Montserrat's.

She was beyond fear, beyond feeling much at all, when the light tap finally came on the far window.

Dominic's face loomed up from the darkness and she shoved open the door.

"Drive," he said, noncommittal. Impassive.

"What happened? Were they—"

"Later."

She knew he was right, but it only made her angrier. She didn't want to drive; she didn't want to sit here in her own sweat. She certainly didn't want to be in this crazy situation.

But she started the Jeep in silence, knowing there was nothing else she could do.

He didn't talk until they were well beyond the coast road and Seacliffe loomed dark up the hill. "There was one car. You lost them in the village. They doubled back, looked around, then turned north and I lost them." He sounded angry.

"Who were they? What did they want?"

"My best guess is that someone heard about the wine and wanted to assess how well protected you are. Once the news of the discovery leaked out, and you were identified as the inheritor, it wouldn't take them long to track you down. After all, there must have been a few thousand people at that auction at the British Museum. Your picture was in several newspapers the next day. Anyone there could be behind this, and now they all know your face," he finished grimly.

"I'm not running." Cathlin said flatly. "I'm not hiding."

"You'll do whatever I tell you has to be done."

"Dream on, Ace." Cathlin swung into the graveled circle beneath Seacliffe's darkened windows and yanked open her door. "Right now I'm going up to bed. If you want to argue, fine. Stay out here and argue with the wind."

Dominic made no move to stop her. He had enough demons of his own to fight without adding her to the list. He'd been slow and stupid and missed things no beginner should have missed.

But as he went over the night's events, frame by frame, thoroughly analyzing every detail, he couldn't get one thought out of his mind.

It had all been too bloody easy.

Thirteen ~

"**I**n the trunks? That's wonderful." Dominic was on the phone with his Great-Aunt Agatha the next morning explaining what kind of documents he needed when he heard Cathlin's light step on the stairs. "Just a minute, Aggy." He covered the phone. "We're in luck. Aggy says she remembers an old packet of letters that might be from Gabriel. They're stored away in one of her trunks. She was just going to—" His voice fell as he took in Cathlin's pallor and the dark shadows under her eyes. "What's wrong?"

"I'm going back to London, Dominic." Her voice was tense and determined. "I'm done with this cloak-and-dagger business. I'll stop on the way and talk to Viscount Draycott out of respect for a woman I've never met and never heard of before, but don't expect anything more of me."

"Not alone. Remember what happened yesterday."

"Yesterday was a bad dream. Today is—reality."

"Damn it, Cathlin, listen to me."

"No, *you* listen. I don't want to hear the explanations and the excuses. No doubt they're all brilliant, but I've heard them too many times before. My father never told me exactly what he did, but I'll tell you this, he was exactly what you'll be in twenty years, Officer Montserrat. Cool and smart and fatally

170

charming. In fact, there was only one problem with my father. He was always off on some fantastically important business on the other side of the globe and never here, where we needed him. And even when he *was* here, his mind was a thousand miles away." She looked at the walls lined with framed family photographs, her eyes resting on a picture of her father caught in a smile that didn't reach his eyes. "So I'm not interested. Not in you, not in your wine, and not in this crazy mess you've steered me into. I'll go to Draycott Abbey because I owe it to myself and to my mother. Then I'm renouncing any claim that I or my family holds over that wine. Forever."

"You can't do that. It's your past, Cathlin. It's also your future. You don't walk away from something like that."

"No? Just watch me."

From the receiver in his hand, Dominic heard his aunt's voice rise in quavering questions. "Yes, Aggy, I'm still here. Yes, that's wonderful about those letters. I know it will be a load of work and your arthritis is devilish these days, but we're really counting on you. Now I'm afraid I really must run. What? A woman?" He cleared his throat. "No, afraid not, Aggy."

By the time he put down the phone, the study was empty. So was the hall. When Dominic ran outside, he cursed darkly.

It was already too late. Cathlin's Jeep was hurtling off down the gravel drive.

Cathlin slammed the old Jeep over the rutted coast road. She coaxed and nurtured her anger, even as she felt the pain choke her. Anger was the only safe thing, because she was free inside her anger as she never could be in affection.

But Cathlin found that she was draining the well

dry. What she'd find beyond, where the shadows began, she didn't want to think about.

As she drove over the little stone bridge where Dominic had been wounded, she wondered just for a moment what things might have been like if they were two different people with two different pasts.

If only . . .

No use. No bloody use, O'Neill.

She brushed at her cheek, jabbing the gears and grinding them angrily. She knew that she was bolting, running away from fifteen years of shadows.

Seacliffe no longer held any protection for her. A jade-eyed man had brought the holes in with him, pulling up the questions and unveiling the shadows she'd managed to plug up every night with work and lists and fine, detailed dreams.

Now there were shadows everywhere. An old mystery had forced her to face a more recent one. What had really happened that day fifteen years before? Her father had never found any answers, which meant that Cathlin was the only one left who could find out the truth.

In that instant, with the ocean glinting before her and the wind rippling the canals behind her, Cathlin realized something else.

She was looking for the child, the grieving child who had lost her mother too soon and been left with a father she'd never really known. No matter the pain, Cathlin knew she had to become that child again. Without opening up to that ache, she'd never be whole again. The woman stood just beyond that door of shadows, waiting for the child to open it; only through the child could the woman come truly alive.

Her hands were trembling as she headed north, the wind whipping at her hair and cutting the salt tears into her cheeks. She listened to the thunder of the motor, the whine of the wind, the fury of her heart.

As she did, she felt the child reach around that big rusty knob and slowly, slowly push open a door that had been closed far too long.

A door of shadows that led to a bridge of dreams.

PART II

A Bridge
of Dreams

Fourteen ～

Cathlin didn't know what she had expected. After fifteen years the abbey was bound to look different, and her memories had been brief.

Stone, probably. Dampness and crumbling age everywhere. A marshy pool, trees and untended grass, and the terror of irreparable loss.

But she didn't find that, not on this day in the sunlight of a spring morning.

Instead she found . . .

Eternity.

Seacliffe had prepared her for age and grace, but not for great gray walls, flower-hung and vast. Not for swans sliding through a shimmering moat. Not for mullioned windows twinkling in the sheer sweep of the long gallery.

Draycott Abbey, she thought wonderingly. She was fully prepared to hate this place and, looking around her, she tried very hard. But it was hard to hate something that was so beautiful.

The weathered gray walls floated above the Wealden hills like a summer dream, playing on all her senses with almost tangible fingers. She blinked, caught by the rose-rich air, mesmerized by the gentle swirl and lob of the moat.

And then Cathlin saw the small stone bridge,

banks of lush white lilacs teeming over its granite foot. For an instant memory shivered through her mind—heavy, dark and formless, like thorns hidden by the petals of a rose.

Just as swiftly, the image vanished, burned away by the sunlight and the flare of the moat.

Cathlin remembered something her mother had once told her. One could live many years in a place of such age and beauty, but it would take lifetimes to understand.

Cathlin frowned. She didn't *have* lifetimes. All she was prepared to spend here was one day. She would walk and watch and listen, hoping that she found the answers she wanted. But if nothing came, she would turn her back on Draycott Abbey and never come back.

That, too, she owed to her mother.

A movement pulled her eyes to the ground. There among the blooms, drowsing against the warm gray blocks, lay a cat, great and gray, at ease, as if this bridge and all else were his realm and his alone.

Standing in the magic of a bar of sunlight with the wind soft in her hair, Cathlin could almost believe it was so.

She set her single bag on the car and sank down on the soft grass, listening to a bird sing over the ancient trees, listening to her heart.

And there she heard again the dim strains of old memories.

Here. It was all here. What Dominic had said was true, then. She would finally have her answers.

If she wanted them . . .

A door of shadows, she thought, looking through the vast oak door that opened into the gatehouse.

A bridge of dreams.

Did she truly want those answers?

She was tugging hard at the grass, her eyes half-blinded by the glint of the sun on the moat when she felt something warm and soft slide past her leg.

The cat ghosted next to her, amber eyes keen and clear, giving Cathlin the oddest idea that he was waiting for something. And that he might have waited here forever.

She ran a hand uncertainly over the sleek fur, smiling when the creature turned imperiously and shoved against her opened palm. "You are one real beauty, aren't you?"

A quick, sharp hiss of sound. Protest.

"Oh, I see. Handsome, I should have said."

A quick flick of the tail. The keen eyes blinked.

"I am sorry. Truly."

The creature settled back on velvet paws, one eye on the moat. Cathlin could have sworn his other eye stayed on the tiny path that ran through banks of lilacs and roses twisting down from the bridge above.

She shook her head. Coffee, that's what *she* needed. Not daydreams. Lord, anything besides these odd, fanciful sensations. The wild idea that—

"Were you looking for someone in particular?"

"Oh, heaven!" She jumped to her feet, hand to heart. "You—you frightened me!"

He was a tall man, dressed all in black. A certifiable English eccentric, Cathlin thought. With a home like this, she supposed a man could afford to be eccentric. His face was all hard planes and unforgiving angles, not handsome in any usual sense of the word.

But it was an utterly compelling face just the same.

He bent to his knees and ran his fingers through the big cat's sun-warmed fur. "Did I? I'm vastly sorry for it."

"You were so quiet. It sounds mad, but, well, you seemed to come from nowhere."

A smile, faintly sad. "Maybe I did at that."

Cathlin felt a lump in her throat. "Strange."

"Strange?" he murmured, picking up her conversation as if they had known each other for years.

"I know someone else who has that particular trick of silence."

Sharp eyes the color of cold gray walls probed her face. "And it bothers you, does it?"

Cathlin shrugged. "It might. If I let it, which I won't." She looked up. "Do you own all this?"

The hard lips curved. "You might say that."

Might? Either he did or he didn't. Definitely eccentric, in the best English tradition.

"You like it." Oddly, it wasn't a question.

Cathlin frowned. For a moment she'd had the strangest feeling that those granite eyes were looking right through her. Seeing things that she couldn't see herself.

Memories.

Dreams.

Thoughts buried so deep she didn't even know they were there.

The cat at her leg purred softly.

"Yes, I do. More than like it."

"And that frightens you." Again, it was no question.

"No." Something about the keen eyes called for honesty. Cathlin sighed. "Well, perhaps a little. Maybe even a lot. Because I can see the shadows behind all this beauty. Sometimes they even keep me awake at night. I . . . lost someone here, you see, a long time ago."

The gray eyes narrowed. "Your mother."

Cathlin nodded. It was hardly a secret.

"And still you can find it beautiful?"

"I didn't want to," she said frankly. "I expected to hate this place."

"And you don't. Very interesting." He nodded. "My abbey does seem to have that effect on people. Especially my roses."

"They are lovely. You must be very proud of such—" She searched for the word. Something about the man demanded she get the word right. "Power. And beauty. Beauty that will last an eternity."

He looked down at the cat. "Ah, this one is good, Gideon. She sees much more than one would expect."

The cat's tail flicked slowly, a study in elegant geometry, all smooth arcs of gray.

"No? I don't agree at all, you know."

Cathlin found herself smiling in spite of the rank improbability of it all. A granite abbey? A man in solid black who spoke to a cat who looked intelligent enough to talk back?

Definitely, coffee is needed here, O'Neill. And fast.

"You will be here long?"

"Long enough to poke around in your cellar and see if that wine you discovered is authentic." Cathlin looked out over the haze of green hills. *And to find out if this wretched story about a murdered man and two lost lovers has any truth to it.* "I only wish I knew more about the man who left the wine there."

"Gabriel? Yes, he was a most complex man."

"Do you know very much about him?"

The expressive hands stilled for an instant, pale against the cat's sleek fur. "What would you like to know?"

"Everything. Dominic—that is, Lord Ashton—led me to believe no one knew anything at all about his Mad Uncle Gabriel."

"Is that what he calls him? How amusing. And how very much Gabriel would dislike that term."

Cathlin was growing impatient with this vagueness. "Can you tell me how he died?"

"I'm afraid not."

"Then why was he interested in the wine and why did he end up in the cellar?"

"These are useful questions." Her companion nodded slowly. "The why is always the most important thing."

"I was hoping for some answers." Cathlin frowned. "After all, you must know this place better than anyone."

"Much better," he affirmed.

"So what's your guess? Why would a man do something like that?"

The dark eyes narrowed. For a moment Cathlin felt their force through every molecule and atom of her being. Divining. Assessing.

"Love. Hatred. Jealousy. Revenge." He smiled bitterly. "All the usual reasons."

"We know who he loved. She was my ancestor, Geneva Russell. But her life is just as sketchy as his. Did they fall in love, only to fall out again? Or did something come between them?" Each question seemed to leave things more tangled.

"I expect there must be records of some sort," her companion said absently, stroking the great cat. "There usually are. Damned nuisance, too, don't you agree, Gideon?"

The cat popped open one keen eye and blinked at Cathlin.

"Ah, well, *you* would."

Did the man always speak in riddles? "Do you know where I might look? For the records, I mean."

"There are many treasures in this ancient house, Miss O'Neill. And the greatest treasures of all are those that cannot be seen. I suggest you remember that."

Unseen? Oh, that was going to be *really* useful, Cathlin thought irritably. Couldn't the man give a single straight answer?

"Beyond that, I'm afraid I can't help you," he said, somehow answering the question she had not asked. "Ask the right questions and you'll find the right answers," he added cryptically. "But all the an-

swers—and all the questions—must come from you."
He smiled faintly. "And from *him*."

"Him?"

Again the smile. "The one with that trick of silence
you're not going to let bother you."

"Dominic? But how did you know—"

"We are remote here but not entirely out of contact
with the rest of the world, my dear. Besides, you
have a most expressive face. I suggest that you forgo
prevarication."

Cathlin swallowed. The wind trailed over her hair,
enveloping her in a cloudlike scent of roses and lilacs. Maybe he was right. Maybe she hadn't been
asking the right questions at all—about this wine or
about her own past. As a bee droned from one heavy
bloom to the next, she considered that possibility.

And the seconds stretched out, full and silent and
companionable in the warm sunlight.

After a long while her companion nodded to the
cat. "Yes."

Cathlin hadn't any idea what he had said yes to.
It might have been to her or to the day, or even in
some strange way to the keen, imperious cat who
seemed so comfortable here.

It might even have been a yes to something much,
much more.

But before she could ask, the cat stirred and uttered a low cry.

"I must go."

She felt a sudden tug of disappointment. "Must
you?" There was power in his company. A strange
comfort.

He laughed, a sound as soft and fluid as the moat's
swirl. "I'm afraid so. But there is one thing you might
do for me, if you will."

"Of course." She studied the hard face, the face of
a man who had tasted far more than his share of
pain and pleasure, anger and despair. "Anything."

"Anything?" The hard lips curved. "I suggest you be rather more careful with your promises, my dear."

"Why? Should I be afraid of you?"

"Perhaps. Perhaps not. For now at least, you are quite safe. As it happens, my request is harmless."

"I'm listening."

His eyes narrowed. Again that faint tug of lip that seemed to send light into every corner of his hard face. "Tell him I send my greetings. And my blessings." At his feet the cat stirred, suddenly restless. "Yes, I know, my dear Gideon. But blessings, I send nevertheless. Such good as they are. I have every confidence that this mystery, too, will be solved, just as all the others were. And you will be part of its solving, my dear."

"But how? And whom should I tell—"

The cat ghosted past her ankles and vanished into the tossing lilacs, silver-white against the weathered stone. Something about those movements was lulling, effortless, almost . . . hypnotic.

"Who . . ." She tried to speak, had to swallow first, fighting a pull of sleep such as she had never felt before. It was only the sun, of course, bounced a hundredfold back across the moat. Only the high, sweet trill of a bird somewhere in the high hills.

Only her heart, full of peace in this odd, beautiful place.

"I can't just—" She spun around.

He was gone.

As the roses tossed in the wind, Cathlin caught a glimpse of black through the tangle of leaf and bud. And she could have sworn she saw white lace flutter at his dark wrists.

A man in a black suit and lime green running shoes was clipping crimson roses from a hedge as Cathlin carried her single bag toward the weathered gatehouse. He stopped when he saw Cathlin. "Miss

O'Neill?'' He tugged off his gloves and held out his hand. "I beg your pardon, but I should have introduced myself at once. I am Marston, Lord Draycott's butler. Let me take that for you, please."

Butler? Cathlin had to repress an urge to pinch herself. Butler. Of course. "Shall I trade you for the roses? The bag's not heavy, since I won't be staying for the night. I'm only here to look at the wine Lord Draycott discovered."

The butler frowned as she handed over the bag. "But his lordship is definitely expecting you to stay. He and his wife will be very disappointed otherwise."

Cathlin shrugged as waves of glorious scent filled her lungs. "The viscount seems to be an unusual man."

"Ah, you've met him, have you?"

Cathlin nodded. "I ran into him by the moat as I came in. He is a most . . . interesting man."

"Indeed he is." Marston led the way across the forecourt toward a wall of rose-covered granite. "I have prepared a room overlooking the courtyard. I thought you might like the roses. Will veal with strawberries and asparagus vinaigrette be satisfactory for luncheon?"

Satisfactory? Was the man serious? "It sounds wonderful. But I'd like to wash up and take a look at the wine cellar first."

"Ah, yes, the wine." Marston shot her an assessing look.

"Is something wrong?"

"Pardon me, but you seem so very young to possess the amount of expertise that you have."

"Not all wines need age to develop body or character." Cathlin had used the phrase often in her first tough years carving out a consulting business in London.

"You're right, of course. Forgive me."

His sincerity made Cathlin feel a little small. "Only if you let me carry some of these lovely roses."

That won her an answering smile. "Very well. We'll call it even. And perhaps you would be so kind as to have a look at our cellar conditions. There are two or three old clarets that I fear may be showing signs of damaged corks. Perhaps there is a problem with the humidity."

Cathlin looked sideways. She had a fair idea of this man's character and doubted that he cared to ask advice from anyone. Either he was trying to compliment her or he was treating her as an equal.

Both sounded good to her.

"I'm rather looking forward to poking around down there. Draycott's wine cellar has quite a reputation, you know."

"Indeed." Marston looked pleased. "It was largely the work of the eighth viscount, you know. So were all these roses. According to legend, he led an unhappy life and devoted his rather considerable skills to building up Draycott for his heirs. There are a number of Sauternes and champagnes that he personally selected, along with some particularly fine vintages of Lafite. There is even an 1825, I believe."

Cathlin's brow rose. "You'll have to watch for cracking of the glass there. Those old commemorative bottles are the devil to protect."

Marston nodded thoughtfully. "I shall relay your instructions to the viscount. He's just been out riding, so he will wish to change before he greets you himself."

Riding? Dressed in formal black? Another mark of eccentricity, Cathlin decided. If so, it was no business of hers. "You needn't trouble him to show me around. We can talk later, after I've looked through the cellars."

Marston looked genuinely horrified. "Not show

you the abbey personally? His lordship would not dream of it."

Protocol, O'Neill. Cathlin thought of the man in black, a man with eyes like granite. He would be the sort to live by all sorts of ritual and formality, she decided. And he probably had an ironclad sense of honor to go with them.

She decided there was a lot she had to learn about the Draycotts and their abbey.

"Does that great cat go everywhere with him, by the way?"

Marston faltered for a moment. "I beg your pardon."

"The cat," Cathlin prompted. "The one with the gray fur and black paws. I found him dozing beside the moat."

Something came and went in Marston's eyes. "I couldn't say, miss."

Couldn't say? Either the cat did or he didn't. Cathlin sighed. No good getting upset. Good butlers were notoriously tight-lipped, after all.

"You say you met—the viscount? With his, er, cat?"

Cathlin nodded. "They seemed great friends, although I know that will sound odd."

A frown worked between Marston's eyes. "Did you happen to note what the, er, viscount was wearing?"

"All black, actually. He looked very—rugged."

Marston looked off in the distance, his eyes narrowed. "About ten minutes ago, would you say?"

"More or less."

"I see."

You see what?

But he didn't say anything more. By then they were at the great oak doors covered with trailing roses and Cathlin felt her heart tighten.

Memories. Or were they simply shadows?

She turned her head, forcing herself to look at the abbey and really see it, not as a place of shadows and dread, not as the image of childhood memories, but as it truly was.

From here she could see every cleft and fissure of the sun-warmed stones, their ancient faces speaking in a language she could not hear but only feel. And it felt like peace, like abiding age. Like a vast will that had walked every foot of Draycott's ground and left an indelible mark there.

Oh, it was definitely time for coffee, Cathlin told herself, shaking her head. But memories teased her as she followed Marston over the small granite bridge, through the sunny courtyard, and into the rich darkness of the abbey. Her pulse only quickened as she walked past walls hung with priceless Tintorettos and Whistler *Nocturnes,* past rooms bright with costly old tapestries. It was the antique fabrics which had drawn Cathlin's mother here fifteen years before, and Cathlin had never forgotten their fragile beauty.

But there were also differences. Now there were roses everywhere, arranged in old porcelain jars and crystal bowls that filled the house with fragrance. Tapestry pillows brightened fragile gilt wing chairs. Sunlight spilled through opened curtains, bouncing off polished wood and casting a mellow glow over the ancient rooms.

Peace.

Again the thought came to her, playing over her senses like summer sunshine, like a sweet and very heady wine.

Steady, O'Neill. There are shadows, too. And memories. Don't forget those. Frowning, she shoved a strand of hair from her cheek and looked at Marston. "I've changed my mind, Marston. I'd like to go straight down to the wine cellars, if you don't mind."

The butler smiled faintly. "Lord Ashton predicted that you would," he murmured.

Lord Ashton. Cathlin's eyes narrowed. "Lord Ashton might be wonderful at stalking around dark alleys and snapping off assassins' heads, but he doesn't know me as well as he imagines."

Marston gave her a sidelong look.

"I'm sorry Marston. It's been a long day and I'm—" *Thinking about shadows. Thinking about dreams and a mother I barely had a chance to know.* She swallowed. "I'm anxious to see that wine."

"I quite understand. The stairs to the wine cellars are right over here." Marston pushed open an oak door that had to be at least six feet tall and flipped on a light.

Cathlin stared in disbelief. A passage of solid granite stretched before her, hacked out along with the abbey's original foundation hundreds of years before. The structure had been built to withstand the attacks of raiders, invading armies, and rival political factions, and it had certainly succeeded.

Cathlin shook her head. "This is some building you've got here."

"So it is," the butler said proudly, "and if I may say so, you haven't seen anything yet."

"Holy, holy heaven."

Cathlin stood at the bottom of the stone steps and studied the shadowed recess stretching before her. Like everything else about Draycott Abbey, the cellars had been built on a vast scale, in an age when high rank commanded huge amounts of manpower. Cathlin tried to conceive how many men must have been needed to hew these stone walls, but her imagination failed her.

"I suppose you've heard how the wine was discovered? About . . . the body?"

Cathlin nodded, fighting a stab of uneasiness as she looked down and wondered exactly where the remains had been found. "And there's been no other information? Nothing that explains how Gabriel Montserrat came to be buried behind that wall?"

"I'm afraid not."

Cathlin thought of a dying man writing his will by candlelight, while shadows closed in around him. As Marston led her past rows of neatly stacked bottles that ran twice her height, she found herself praying she would find an answer here amid the wine that had been his only companion for two centuries.

Assuming this was not some kind of hoax.

Around her lay the treasures collected by proud generations of Draycotts. First growth claret. Château Pétrus. Clos du Mesnil champagne, from a walled vineyard in existence since 1698. Neaby ran the old Krugs themselves—the superbly sweet 1928 and the big, textured 1945.

And on and on.

Beyond the champagnes came the clarets, housed in graceful, wide bottles that themselves had become collector's items. Another long wall held eighty prime vintages of Lafite, the *pièce de résistance* a commemorative bottle of 1825 with a handmade ground glass stopper. Cathlin could think of two dozen men who would kill to possess that treasure alone.

Perhaps her mother had been right. A person might truly spend a lifetime here and still not understand this vast, beautiful abbey.

"Is something wrong, Ms. O'Neill?" Marston was staring at her oddly.

"I think I'm in shock, Marston."

"There are several more rooms to the left. But you will wish to see the Château d'Yquem, I imagine."

"I don't think I can wait another second," Cathlin confessed unsteadily.

"Of course. Come right this way."

As Cathlin followed Marston through the semidarkness, trying to ignore the priceless wines stretching away on each side of her, she noticed a dozen wires snaking over the old granite to terminate in digital thermometers. She smiled. Though the cellars might look like a medieval set piece, the current viscount had gone to a good deal of expense to upgrade them to current standards. A good thing, too, since he was probably sitting on several million dollars worth of wine down here.

At the end of the room the stone walls narrowed and the ceiling dropped until it was almost within Cathlin's reach. "How was the hidden room discovered?"

"It was all most extraordinary, miss." Marston's voice was low, in unspoken awareness of the body that had been found here. "Recently we've had a number of problems with the water pipes that feed the south end of the house. When they were tracked to this segment of the cellars, the viscount called in a specialist."

"And he got rather more than he bargained for?"

The butler nodded. "As he was working, a section of the wall simply crumbled and he was left staring into darkness—into a grave that had been sealed for nearly two hundred years. I've never seen a grown man look more frightened in my life," Marston said quietly. "He kept talking about feeling as if something were down here with him." Marston shook his head. "Absurd, of course. Not that there aren't a host of odd stories about this old place."

"And no one knows how or why it happened?"

"I'm afraid not."

Just like my mother, Cathlin thought, suddenly aware of the shadows and the heavy, looming silence of the damp cold walls.

"Watch your step, miss." They were moving lower now, and much of the floor lay in total darkness. "There's a particularly bad stretch here where the floor dips. One of the workmen took a nasty tumble here on the day of the discovery."

But Cathlin seemed to have no trouble negotiating the passage. It was almost as if she could sense where the stone floor would dip in front of her. As if she had been here before.

Crazy, O'Neill. No doubt all old houses affect people this way.

A click. Suddenly light covered the damp stone walls that loomed up out of the shadows. Close to the ground Cathlin saw a jagged opening in the stone. She looked questioningly at Marston. "Here?"

The butler nodded. "The skeleton has been removed, of course. The remains were interred at the Ashton estate near Tunbridge with full church rites."

Dominic hadn't mentioned that. Somehow the news didn't make Cathlin feel any better. The shadows felt oppressive, and a nearly palpable sadness brushed at her neck. A sound beside her made her turn. "Yes, Marston?"

"I'm afraid I did not say anything, miss."

"No?" Cathlin frowned. She *had* heard something. It had come in that moment while she'd studied the jagged hole at the far end of the cellar. And it had been a single word.

Gabriel.

She took a steadying breath. Time to stop dodging ghosts and get to work. "May I?" She pointed to Marston's flashlight.

"Of course."

"Is there an alarm working?" She balanced one leg on the stone ledge, flashlight in hand.

"Only a simple electronic affair." Marston moved off to the wall and flicked a switch on a matte gray box.

Cathlin moved deeper into the shadows, shining light over the uneven stones. Dust skittered around her feet as she bent close to the cold granite floor.

And there she froze, her body rigid.

Rising from the shadows was a mold- and dust-encrusted wooden case filled with eight bottles cushioned lovingly in a nest of straw.

She was staring down at Gabriel Montserrat's legacy.

Fifteen ∽

Cathlin's palms began to sweat.

Château d'Yquem 1792. She knew it instantly. Her heart told her all that her scientific analysis would take days to resolve.

The wine was real; she could feel it in every screaming pore of her body.

She raised the flashlight, forcing her mind to its work. The wine looked authentic enough. The glass was of the proper texture and weight for that period. The bottle lips were full, another sign of authenticity. Her heart hammered, loud in her ears. Had Gabriel Montserrat truly died to bring this case here two hundred years before? And if so, how was her own ancestor involved in the mystery?

Chewing on her lip, she crouched over the priceless find. If the wine was indeed authentic, as all her senses screamed, then the demanding work of conservation would begin. She would have to check the bottles for hairline cracks, pitting, and corrosion before moving to a delicate scrutiny of the corks. Even in the cool damp air of the abbey cellars the corks would have turned brittle. Old wines needed to be recorked every quarter century as standard practice, and these had had no such care.

Yes it would be the greatest challenge of her career.

If she stayed, of course.

Cathlin ran her finger carefully over the case, touching the dust that had accumulated for decades, probably for centuries. How could she possibly leave until she'd had a chance to verify scientifically that the wine was genuine? And how could she ignore the tragic mystery of Gabriel Montserrat's death in this place of cold shadows?

Dominic was right. It was too rare an opportunity for her to turn her back. There was no doubt that the intensely sweet white wines of the Garonne had been prized for centuries, and no less a figure than Thomas Jefferson had visited the area and sung their praises. She recalled a letter she had once seen. "I have persuaded our president, George Washington, to try a sample. He asks for thirty dozen [bottles], sir, and I ask you for ten dozen for myself." Cathlin knew that there was no record of either American receiving his shipment that year. Was it just possible that this case came from the order commissioned long ago by Jefferson?

Trying to control her excitement, she pulled out a fine brush and cleaned the dust from the closest bottle. As her fingers touched the cold glass, a tiny, electric jolt ran through her. Heaviness seemed to gather at her heart, like the French valleys she had seen filling up with mist. She shivered, fingering the cameo at her neck, which had grown suddenly cold.

Nonsense, Cathlin told herself sharply. It was just a hidden tunnel that sent cold air slashing against her face.

But she was intensely aware of the shadows pressing around her. And she found herself wondering which shadows belonged to her and which were Draycott's.

He watched her from the shadows. Even in the dim half-light of the narrow tunnel, her hair had a glow of vitality. As she bent protectively over the old wine, using a fine brush to remove two centuries of dust, Dominic Montserrat understood just how vast was Cathlin O'Neill's love of fine wine.

Yes, this was the perfect opportunity for her, if only she could be persuaded to take it. Suddenly Dominic found himself praying that the case was authentic, because he wanted to see the excitement blaze in Cathlin's eyes when she astounded the wine world with her discovery. She deserved that joy. The abbey owed her that much, after taking her mother from her.

Without warning, tension stirred along Dominic's neck. Crouching low, he spun about, prepared for an attack.

But none came. There was no movement around him, nor sound of any sort. He was alone here beneath the damp stones, ringed by shadows. And something about those gray walls with their leaden darkness made sweat touch his face.

Something was wrong.

Habits too deeply ingrained to deny screamed out that he was not alone, that someone was watching him. Only his imagination, Dominic tried to tell himself as he eased upright.

Twenty minutes later Nicholas Draycott tracked Dominic down in the middle of the gently sloping lawns that led away from the moat. The viscount smiled wryly as he watched his friend go through sharp jabs and impossibly high whipkicks, covered with sweat and looking mean.

The man was a master and no mistake, Nicholas thought.

And just as well.

They all were going to need that expertise to survive when the news of this discovery got out.

"You're looking damnably fit, Dominic."

Dominic wiped his forehead with a towel and held out a hand. "Not too bad for an old playboy vintner. You look lean and mean yourself."

"Oh, my Thailand days are over, I assure you. The most exercise I get these days is chasing that scapegrace young daughter of mine around the abbey grounds."

"There could be worse ways of getting exercise."

Nicholas nodded. "You ought to try it. Kacey has little Genevieve in town, while she does some research on the local records, but you'll see them tonight."

Dominic looked off over the hills. "I'm glad for you, Nicholas. For this. And for how well everything has worked out."

For a moment the silence stretched out. Then Dominic bent over the wooden fence and lowered his body into a thigh-stretching warm-up. "And it's about time you showed up, considering that you finally have me where you wanted me."

"Not alone, I hope."

"No, Cathlin's here, too. She got in an hour before I did, but I'm not sure how long she'll stay. She's down in your cellars right now nursemaiding that bloody case of wine." Dominic broke into a series of dancelike high kicks coupled with shadowboxing jabs. Fists raised, body moving, he jabbed, then lunged into the *chassé* kicks that made French kickboxing, or *savate*, so lethal. "Nothing could tear her away, in fact."

"Is that irritation I hear?"

Dominic glared at his friend, as sweat ran in beads down his broad chest. "You're damned right it is. The woman's impossible. Not time nor prayer nor divine intercession is going to change that. She hates me, she hates my profession, and she hates Draycott."

"She's here. That's a start."

"Against her every wish, she's here. Even after what happened at Seacliffe, she refuses to believe she might be in danger."

"Something happened down there, did it?"

Dominic pounded at an invisible opponent, dipping and bobbing, his face grim. "Which incident are you referring to, the time I lost the prowler with the semiautomatic revolver or the time that someone nearly ran us off the road on the way back to Seacliffe?"

Nicholas whistled soundlessly. "That bad already? I'd hoped we'd have a little more time."

"Well we don't. I discovered that your letter to Cathlin was missing my second day at Seacliffe. Whoever took it knows every detail of the discovery and Gabriel's will. Someone wants that wine and my guess is they're willing to kill to get it."

"Instinct?"

"Like a kick to the gut." Dominic's eyes hardened. "You remember that last winter in Thailand? How I was sent out alone?"

Nicholas wouldn't ever forget. It had preceded his own captivity by mere months. "I remember."

"Well, I'm feeling that same way right now, and I don't like it." Dominic stabbed at an imaginary opponent and frowned. "I never wanted back into this life, Nicholas. There are too many shadows. And now, on top of that, there are the dreams ..." He cursed and turned away.

"What dreams?"

"Something—nothing. Blast it, I don't know, Nicholas. Maybe I'm just too rusty. But my dreams aren't your problem. I don't know why I even mentioned them."

"Maybe because we're friends. By listening, I also ensure a continuing supply of that wonderful wine of yours. If you'd put more fields into production, I wouldn't have to bribe half of the Garonne Valley to save a few cases for me."

Dominic looked shocked. "Bribe? I never knew. The volume is low to keep my quality high until I can expand in an orderly fashion. But you could have called me anytime, Nicky, and I would gladly have—"

"Not a bit of it. You've made a wonderful success of La Trouvaille in three years, and I'm perfectly willing to grease a few palms if it will make the French functionaries look on you more indulgently." Nicholas's smile faded as he looked at the old Jeep parked near the stables. "And now I think it's time I spoke with Ms. O'Neill. Marston tells me she has every look of intending to stay in the cellars for hours. I want to see that she is given every courtesy here, Dominic. It's the least I can do, considering ..." His voice hardened. "Considering all she lost here."

"I understand." Dominic spun a sharp right hook at an opponent only he could see. "I just don't want you surprised if she doesn't stay around very long."

Nicholas stared at the roses dancing beside the moat. "Then I suppose we'll have to find a way to change Ms. O'Neill's mind, won't we?"

There was a marked firmness to his jaw as he strode off toward the abbey a few moments later.

Dominic was finishing another series of flying high kicks, oblivious to the world, when a slender form homed in on him with the ferocity of a Scud missile.

"Dominic Montserrat, I want to talk to you!"

"You want to pull out my nails slowly, one by one, more like," he muttered, giving his chest a swipe with the towel hanging on the fence nearby.

Cathlin puffed up, arms akimbo, black hair waving in the wind. "Just what do you think you're doing?"

"I believe I'm exercising," her quarry said calmly. Cathlin caught a breath, pulling her eyes away from the broad expanse of Dominic's bare chest. "Are you trying to deny it?"

"I might, if I knew what you were talking about."

"I *knew* you'd deny it!"

"If you'll just calm down, Cathlin—"

"That's *Ms. O'Neill* to you, Officer Montserrat. Or have you already forgotten your riveting little speech about everything being business between us from now on?"

"I've forgotten nothing," Dominic said. Softly.

"Don't you threaten *me*."

Dominic reached past her for his shirt. "What's got you so furious?"

"*This.*"

Tossing his towel over his shoulder, Dominic picked up the tabloid pages Cathlin was waving in the air.

The headline was brutal and bold. "Dead lord comes back from grave to uphold family curse." Below the blazing headline was a very out-of-focus photo of Nicholas Draycott, hollow-eyed and gaunt after his return seven years before from a hellish captivity in Thailand. Next to Nicholas was overlaid a grainy shot of an oil painting in the National Gallery.

The hair was long, the eyes were hard. Discounting the black satin and the diamond stickpin, the man might have been Dominic Montserrat's twin.

"Mad Uncle Gabriel, I presume?"

Dominic nodded. "This one is by a lesser artist than the portrait at home, but the likeness is accurate."

"You two could be twins," Cathlin said accusingly.

"I'm a regular throwback, all right, demons and all. Where did you find this?"

"Under your seat in the Triumph."

"Searching my car now, Irish?"

Cathlin colored. "I had to get something from the Jeep. Your car is parked right next to mine and I happened to notice the headline. When were you going to tell me about this?"

"When it became important."

"Dead lord comes back to uphold family curse? I'd say that was fairly important."

Dominic sighed. "It's just nonsense. Some bright person got the idea that Mad Uncle Gabriel had lost the Ashton diamond through treachery and had cursed whoever possessed it. It's just family legend, Cathlin."

"And I found the Ashton diamond at Seacliffe." Her eyes darkened to burnished gold. "Do you think he gave it to Geneva?"

"We're here to look for facts and records, Cathlin, something that makes sense. Not family legends."

"Maybe legends are all we're going to find. Maybe that's all you have to go on when the facts are lost over time. Or when they're hidden," she added bitterly.

Dominic fingered the towel slung over his shoulder. "Are you talking about Gabriel or your own past now?"

Cathlin frowned out at the shimmering waters of the moat. "Both. I need to know what really happened here, Dominic. Without that piece of my past I'll never have a real future."

"What if it gets dangerous, Irish? When news of the will leaks out, a lot of people are going to be interested in your whereabouts. A fanatic collector might consider trying to steal the wine from the abbey, but it would be much easier to get the wine through you."

"Kidnapping?"

"Possibly. Or some nasty coercion. Even a barter, if one of us gets taken. What I'm saying is that things are going to get rocky."

"Then do your job. You're a bodyguard, aren't you?" Cathlin's voice was cold.

"Even bodyguards make mistakes. And when that will becomes public knowledge, every two-bit criminal and out-of-luck thief in England will be trying to get his hands on that wine. Or on *us*."

"Like the men in that car?"

"Maybe." Dominic cursed softly, tired of having to field questions he couldn't answer. "But the conditions are still the same, Cathlin. If you stay, you do what I say, when I say. Nicholas will back me up on this."

"Don't count on it," Cathlin said flatly.

Dominic's eyes hardened. "You know that Gabriel's murderer was never found, don't you? No one knows what happened that last night down in the cellar. And Aunt Aggy tells me—" He stopped.

Something about the hardness in his eyes made Cathlin frown. "What, Dominic? What did she tell you?"

"You're not going to like it."

"Tell me."

"She found some letters in an old hatbox in the back of her armoire. It appears that all London was abuzz with gossip in the spring of 1794."

"So?"

"So the story circulating was that Gabriel Montserrat had finally gone past the line by kidnapping a respectable young woman from the safety of her own house." Dominic looked out over the moat, past the tangle of old roses. "And then he murdered her."

"No," Cathlin whispered. "Why would he murder her, then mention her in his will? It doesn't make sense."

"Maybe it does. Maybe guilt drove him to make up in death for what he'd done to her in life."

"You can't believe that."

Dominic shrugged. "I don't know what I believe. And I don't know if we'll ever have the answers."

When he turned, his face was hard. "Nicholas said to tell you we're dining at eight in the Yellow Salon." His eyes glinted for a moment. "Wear something special."

Sixteen ～

"Damned, stubborn woman."

Dominic watched Cathlin stride over the gravel path along the moat.

A dozen tasks awaited him. He needed to go over the inside security arrangements, then discuss them with Nicholas. After that he wanted to take a look at the cellar and see if anything had been overlooked down there.

Yet here he stood, thinking about the past, thinking about a woman with haunted amber eyes.

Dominic's shoulder began to throb. Too much boxing. But someone who came up from behind wasn't going to care if his shoulder hurt or not.

He reached into his pocket and pulled out a fragile piece of fabric. Light broke over the Ashton diamond glinting on his palm, cold and beautiful.

Dominic twisted it thoughtfully, wondering why such a precious gem was attached to a piece of simple white cambric. He had taken it from Cathlin's chest at Seacliffe, sensing he might find answers somewhere in those cold facets.

He stared down now, watching the diamond sparkle, thinking about his hard-faced ancestor and his strange bequest.

Feeling the images form into memories . . .

                        *   *   *

*Geneva Russell crossed the polished floor and sank down
on the gilt chair before her dressing table.*

*Her face was pale, her eyes haunted as she slid off her
gown and tugged on a cambric wrapper.*

*Though a week had passed, she could not forget the fury
in Gabriel's eyes, nor the fierce disgust in his voice.*

Jezebel. How right he had been.

*Listlessly she pulled the pins from her hair and brushed
out the rich black curls, barely aware of her movements.
Devere had come to see her twice already, braying and
blustering that he would have Isabel de Verney carried to
the guillotine.*

*But not yet. Devere needed Geneva's sister alive, as a
means to threaten Geneva. It was the Rook he wanted,
and he needed Geneva to lure the shadowy hero of a hundred forays out of hiding.*

*It was for that reason that Geneva was leaving London
tomorrow for Seacliffe, the family's estate near the southeast coast. The grand old house overlooked the barren
sands and tidal pools of Romney Marsh and not even
Henry Devere would bother her there.*

*She stared down at the exquisite leather trunk neatly
packed beside her bed. Inside were the jeweled shoes and
satin gown she had worn at the masquerade. With them
was the cameo that Gabriel had given her. Geneva would
never wear any of them again. There was too much pain
in her memories of that night.*

"Will you be wanting anything else, miss?"

*Geneva smiled at her maidservant, hired along with this
furnished house in a very elegant part of London. "No,
that's all, Amelia. I shall close the trunk and you can see
it loaded onto the carriage to go with us to Seacliffe
tomorrow."*

*The young woman nodded. "Very well, miss." She
dropped a quick curtsy and went out as silently as she
had come.*

Geneva barely noticed. Carelessly she pulled off her

wrapper and studied her reflection in the mirror. Her face was as pale as the white cambric nightgown she wore. The only light and animation about her came from the diamond stickpin she wore at her neck. Geneva would wear it always to remind herself of her perfidy and the grim look in the eyes of the man she had betrayed.

A shadow slid into her vision, captured in the mirror. A shadow with glinting eyes and a hard jaw.

She spun around, her hand at her lips. "You!'

It was the only word she uttered before Gabriel Montserrat pulled a snow-white cravat from his pocket and bound her mouth. His eyes moved over the curves hinted at beneath the fragile cambric. "So you think to mock me, do you? You even wear my own jewel. But I shall see you repaid for your treachery, my sweet, in ways you can't imagine." He ignored the burning desperation in her eyes, ignored the way her face paled to white. In tight silence, he found her gown, tugged it over her shoulders, and drew the laces up the back. "We are going on a trip you see, my love. We have a great deal of business to finish, you and I."

He looked at her one last time, saw the hint of the diamond at the edge of her gown, and with a curse he tore it free. "I'll have that back now, my dear."

But Geneva kicked him wildly, every movement filled with desperation. Cursing, Gabriel dodged the blow.

And in the process the Ashton diamond dropped unnoticed from his fingers, landing in the chest beside Geneva's bed.

Grim-faced, Gabriel caught his captive over his shoulder and strode down the stairs. "No more tricks, my love. We've a long coach ride before us, so I suggest you cool your anger." Through the quiet house he stalked, Geneva draped over his shoulder like a sack of flour, her bare feet kicking. At the bottom of the stairs he was met by a wide-eyed servant, his clothing all awry.

"Miss Russell! My lord! What are you—"

Gabriel slid a pistol from his pocket and leveled it at the man's chest.

"But you can't—" The butler looked at the pistol and swallowed. "That is, you really shouldn't—"

"But I am," Gabriel said flatly. Then he strode out into the London night, his kicking hostage held tightly in his arms.

Gabriel's coachman had been waiting for his signal. Immediately a high-stepping team raced around the darkened square. Gabriel bolted down the steps and slid Geneva to the ground.

His eyes burned silver as he removed the gag from her mouth. "There is no use screaming, my dear. I am taking you where you cannot betray me."

"But you can't!" Geneva's eyes were wild as she studied the darkened square behind them. "Devere has been watching the house all week, hoping that you would come after me. That's why I was leaving for the coast."

"An unsuccessful lie, my dear."

Geneva pounded his chest, her small hands fisted. "He'll come, I tell you! The French have put too high a price on your head for him to resist."

Gabriel's eyes narrowed. Was this another of her tricks? He studied the darkness around them, watching for any sign of movement.

None came. So much for that, he thought grimly.

Not that it mattered. An hour's ride would see the dust of London's streets long behind them. Soon they would be beyond the reach of Devere or his minions.

Gabriel was just on the verge of telling Geneva to save her breath when he heard an old wooden shop sign hammer across the square.

Clang-clang, it cried, creaking in the wind. The noise reminded Gabriel of the windmill in Dunkirk, sails straining in a channel gale. He had heard the sound just before he discovered the three dead children. He knew the sound would haunt him always.

Suddenly a crack split the night. Gabriel shoved Geneva inside the carriage, while the coachman fought to control the team.

Another shot exploded past as Gabriel leaped within and wrenched the door closed behind him.

He tried to ignore the press of Geneva's soft breast where she lay beneath him. He tried to ignore her lilac fragrance and the way her hip rode against his thigh.

"I tried to tell you," she said raggedly. "He knew that you would come."

Gabriel smiled coldly. "I have naught to fear from Henry Devere. He'll never find us where we're going."

As they took another jolt, he saw Geneva wince. Cursing, Gabriel pulled her onto his lap and wrenched back her cloak.

He stared down in horror at the trail of blood on her gown. "They hit you."

Geneva's hands were white where she gripped the folds of her cloak. "He will never give you up. The French have promised him a fortune for your capture."

Gabriel pulled her against his chest, cursing softly. He couldn't go all the way out to his estates near Tunbridge with Geneva bleeding. He had already closed up his London town house, in preparation for his departure.

Which left only Draycott House.

Gabriel sat forward and called curt directions to the coachman as Geneva twisted restlessly in his arms.

Geneva Russell's shocked servant watched the carriage race from the square and shook his head disapprovingly.

He had thought it most peculiar when the woman had called upon his services as a butler. No respectable female lived alone in a house without family or a single chaperone. He supposed that's what came of her growing up in the heathen climates where her father had been a high official in the East India Company.

Yes, Edward Wilson hadn't liked it then and he didn't like it now. There had been something very peculiar about

Miss Geneva Russell. Respectable ladies simply did not set up housekeeping by themselves in London.

His muddy eyes narrowed. This was just the sort of information that gentleman Mr. Devere had asked him to report. The servant straightened his collar and pulled on his cloak. Yes, he would see that Henry Devere learned the news of this outrageous affair from his own lips. No doubt there would be several gold guineas in it for him.

His thoughts were full of greed as he set off for the address that Henry Devere had been careful to leave with him two weeks before.

The windows at Draycott House were ablaze with light as Gabriel's coach lurched up to the front door. Gabriel prayed that his reprobate friend, the viscount, was not holding one of his wild parties. As he pounded up the front steps with Geneva in his arms, the door of Draycott House was thrown open. A dour figure in black appeared.

"Let me down," Geneva protested raggedly. "I can walk."

"No, you can't."

Templeton, the old butler, gave a sniff of disapproval, eyeing the woman in Gabriel's arms. "I shall fetch Lord Draycott."

Frowning, Gabriel crossed the beautiful marble foyer and made his way to Adrian Draycott's study. After lighting a candle, he pulled back Geneva's cloak.

"It is nothing, I tell you. But you must leave. Henry Devere will follow you here."

Gabriel snorted. "Let him try. Meanwhile, stop fighting me, woman." In the light he made out a jagged line of blood, the path of a shallow bullet.

He was muttering a stream of graphic curses when the door opened behind him. "My dearest, Gabriel, what an unexpected pleasure. Templeton tells me that you have now taken to kidnapping gently bred females from the London streets." Adrian came to a halt as he saw the white-faced woman on his settee.

"It's a shoulder wound from a ball meant for me."

"I am quite well," Geneva said faintly. "And I pray you will not speak of me as if I were not here."

Adrian smiled. "So you have the same sharp tongue as ever, Miss Russell."

At the doorway Templeton cleared his throat anxiously. "Will your lordship be desiring brandy?"

"No, hot water and fresh linens, Templeton." Adrian looked down at Gabriel. "What happened?"

"Henry Devere decided to let Miss Russell act as his bait to trap the Rook. Unfortunately it worked." Gabriel's breath caught as a scrap of blood-soaked lace came into view.

"Let me alone," Geneva protested.

"Another word and I'll bind your mouth again, hellion."

Adrian smiled slightly at this byplay, watching Gabriel turn Geneva against his chest and strip away the lace of her chemise to bare her shoulder.

But she didn't complain, not by a single word. In fact, Gabriel looked worse than she did, sweat covering his brow as he studied the wound.

"It's jagged but shallow, thank God," he announced finally. "I'll have some of that brandy, Adrian."

Adrian Draycott, rake and hardened cynic, looked rather pale himself as he held out a glass decanter with the Draycott crest of interlocked dragons.

Gabriel splashed some of the brandy on Geneva's shoulder, then pressed the linen tight. As he worked, she began to struggle in his arms.

"Steady now," he murmured. "It's almost over." After binding fresh linen over the wound, he sat back, with Geneva still cradled against his chest.

After draining the rest of the brandy, Gabriel carried Geneva upstairs to rest.

When he returned, Adrian's eyes were thoughtful. "I'm afraid this isn't the best time for your identity to come out, Gabriel. Not after that last pamphlet bearing the

Rook's name. One can't go around calling for the arrest of most of the members of Parliament without expecting a nasty reaction. I agree with you that something needs to be done to stop the bloodshed in France, but it won't happen that way."

"Then what way? How many more children have to die before something's done?"

"You're doing all you can, Gabriel. I've stopped keeping track of the times you've nearly lost your life over there. Isn't that enough?"

It should have been, but it wasn't, Gabriel thought grimly. Not after walking the bloody streets of Paris and seeing the horrors committed daily in the name of equality and liberty. "I shall have to go and search for her sister, of course. But what am I going to do about Geneva?"

Adrian toyed with the lace at his cuff. "Take her to Draycott Abbey. She'll be safe there. I'll send word ahead to let them know you're coming."

"No," Gabriel said sharply. "Only you and I are to know our final destination."

Adrian's brow rose. "You suspect a traitor here?"

"I was betrayed once, Adrian, and three children died because of it. I'll never make such a mistake again. From now on I trust no one."

"Not even me, Lord Ashton?" The fluid, cultured male voice had something foreign about it as it drifted from the doorway. The speaker was a tall man with a high, arched nose and eyes of keen, cutting blue.

Gabriel stared at the American statesman who had already made a name for himself in England and France. "Is that you, Jefferson? Lord, it seems an age."

"Too long. Templeton tells me you've charmed another woman off her feet."

"She wasn't swept away by charm," Ashton said grimly. "A ball did that to her. A ball meant for me."

"A ball meant for the Rook, you mean."

A hard look passed between them.

"We must leave London tonight. Now that Geneva knows my identity, she won't be safe here."

Adrian nodded. "Of course."

"But what brings you back to London, Jefferson?"

The American looked thoughtful for a moment. "As it happens, I'm here to track down some wine as a gift for our president. Of course, it must be something very special and I have a partiality for some Château d'Yquem I found in the Garonne Valley some years back." He accepted a glass of sherry from Adrian and sat down on a leather settee by the window.

"Perhaps I can help you. As it happens, I have other business that will take me to the area."

"I don't suppose that this business of yours has anything to do with rescuing emigrés from the guillotine, does it?"

"I can't imagine why you would think that." Gabriel's voice was full of calculated boredom.

"Because I've heard nothing else since my arrival in England but stories about this man who defies death time and time again, a man who speaks French like a Parisian. It's said that the Rook could pass for a sans culottes even if he were stopped by Marat himself."

Gabriel's eyes darkened. "As it happens, he has been stopped by Marat himself."

"Now there's an encounter I would like to have seen," Jefferson said intently.

Gabriel poured himself a glass of Madeira and settled one broad shoulder against the mantel. "Tell me exactly what you require from the Garonne, Jefferson."

"Six cases of Château d'Yquem, since my friend particularly enjoys the Sauternes. But it is no place for an Englishman, Gabriel." Jefferson frowned. "Even a Frenchman may find his welcome uncertain in these trying days."

Gabriel's jaw hardened. "You need harbor no concerns for me. I know my way about."

After a moment, Jefferson nodded. "I shall, of course,

leave you a draft on my Paris bank. I am more than happy to pay you a fee for discharging this business, of course."

"Just consider it my small repayment for the enjoyable hours we've spent discussing the ideals of freedom and equality." There was a cynicism in Gabriel's voice that had never been there before.

Jefferson and Draycott exchanged a look.

At that moment there was a whisper of silk from the doorway and the soft scent of lilacs drifted on the cool, still air.

Gabriel's jaw hardened as he looked up.

Geneva stood in the doorway, silhouetted in the golden light of the hall lantern. Her hair was a black cloud against her shoulders and her white hands were clasped against her waist. But it was her eyes that held him, eyes that were filled with pain, eyes that were a thousand miles away.

"I must go—I must find her before it's too late."

He was beside her in a second, his arm circling her shoulders.

Geneva's slender hands shoved blindly at his chest. "Must go."

Cursing, Gabriel caught her as she swayed. The bandage at her shoulder was dotted with fresh blood. With infinite gentleness, he lifted her into his arms and brushed a lock of hair from her face. "Stubborn little fool," he said in a tone of vast tenderness.

Jefferson's eyes hardened. "I think I will have a talk with this man Devere tomorrow. Do you care to join me, Adrian?"

"Without a doubt. It will be a decided pleasure."

At that moment Templeton appeared, livery awry. "There's a man below demanding to see you, my lord. I told him you were not receiving, but he insisted he would not go away until he'd seen you himself. He said his name is Devere," the butler said tightly, as angry footsteps exploded across the marble entry.

"He'll be looking for Geneva," Gabriel said grimly. "I'll take her upstairs."

Adrian smiled coldly. "What do you say, Jefferson?"

"I've seen nothing of any woman. Nor have I heard of anyone called the Rook."

Adrian laughed lazily. "No doubt Devere will be far too busy to concern himself with questioning an upstart American."

"You English persist in your mistakes, don't you?" came the American's utterly confident reply.

"No doubt in time you Americans will teach us to rectify our behavior."

Then Templeton was at the door. "Mr. Devere," he announced, his voice stiff with disapproval.

A big man with small, hard eyes stood in the doorway, fingering a long silver cane. "Who is the owner of this house?"

Two pairs of eyes looked him up and down with lazy disdain.

"I demand an answer."

Adrian stared haughtily at the intruder. "I am Viscount Draycott, although I can't image what business it is of yours."

"I'll tell you what business it is. A woman was seen being carried into this house less than an hour ago. I demand that she be released."

Adrian toyed idly with the lace at his cuff. "Into this house, you say?" He looked at the butler. "Templeton, don't tell me you've taken to prowling the High Road for bed partners again."

The old servant broke into startled coughing.

"No? Then you must be mistaken, Mr. . . ." Adrian let the word linger in a question.

"Devere, damn your hide. And I won't be fobbed off with fine stories. I have witnesses, I warn you. I'll have a warrant, so I will."

"Next you'll be demanding satisfaction in a duel, I suppose."

Devere's face darkened with anger. "I wouldn't spill my precious blood for a wastrel like you."

Draycott's brow rose. "It is just as well, since I only duel with gentlemen."

The barb hit home. Devere's hands clenched to fists. "Do you give her up or not?"

"There are no women in my house, more's the pity. It's been damnably lonely of late."

"I warn you, I mean to make a thorough search before I leave." Devere peered sharply around the room and gave a crow of triumph, "There! Blood, if I ever saw it. She was brought here, just as I said."

"Are you in the habit of shooting women, Mr. Devere?" Adrian's voice was elegant in its mockery.

"I merely protect my own. The woman tried to escape after robbing my house and I mean to see justice done."

"You're lying, Devere," Adrian snapped.

Gabriel now appeared in the far doorway. "Devere," he said. "I don't suppose you happen to be of the Hampshire Deveres?"

"I have no relations in that area."

Gabriel eyed the cut of Devere's jacket. Although the garment was made of the highest quality materials, it hung awkwardly over his protruding stomach. "Then perhaps you are one of the Oxfordshire Deveres?"

"Never heard of them," Devere snapped. "And I'll play no more of these games." Scowling, he grabbed up the scrap of bloody linen and waved it angrily. "She is here, I know it. I'll have the law down upon you, see if I don't!"

"You quite mistake the matter," Gabriel said icily. "The wound is mine." He held out his hand, revealing a bloody palm.

"This is your blood?" Devere's eyes were full of suspicion.

"A mere scratch. I was enjoying the merits of my friend's Château d'Yquem far too much to bestir myself."

"Scratch?" Devere looked down at the blood on Gabriel's cuff. "You're mad, the lot of you! But don't think your lordly and arrogant tricks can hide her for long. I'll be back, you may be sure. And I'll see that Miss Russell

*is made to pay for flouting my authority in this manner!
I'll also find out all that she knows about this man called
the Rook,"* he hissed, glaring straight at Gabriel. *"There
will be no questions as to his identity."*

Around Dominic, the abbey lay quiet, drowsy in
the late afternoon sun. Only the roses swayed on the
warm granite walls as a great gray cat slid through
the lilacs by the little bridge.

He looked down. Blood covered his palm where
the Ashton stickpin had torn his skin.

But he had no memory of the pain. He was aware
only of a fleeting trail of images and the angry hum
of distant voices.

And a network of danger that felt close enough
to touch.

Beyond the moat, beyond the Witch's Pool and the
rows of dancing roses, shadows gathered. Overhead
the sky darkened to crimson and then to deepest
indigo.

And as the last fleeting rays of daylight fled before
the night a single bell began to chime across the distant hills.

Ten times. Eleven. Twelve.

And then once more.

High in an abbey bedroom Cathlin stopped to listen, brush in hand as she changed for dinner.

Stepping out of the shower, Dominic heard and
scowled, telling himself he was imagining things.

And Nicholas Draycott, standing before the
opened French doors with the curtains drifting
around him like mist, looked out at the darkness, a
frown etched upon his brow.

For on this matter the abbey legends were only too
clear. When the church bells rang twelve times—and
then once more—the ghost of Draycott Abbey was
called forth to walk the grounds.

Not out of love.

Not in search of joy.

But because some new danger threatened his beloved ancestral home. As it did now.

The wind whispered.

Shadows trembled.

Somewhere in the night, darkness gave way to black satin cuffs and pristine white lace.

As the last bell faded, the abbey's guardian ghost stepped out of nothingness onto the cool stones of the parapets. Eyes agleam, he turned his head and studied the first stars, just glinting upon the velvet sky. "Again it begins, my old friend."

A great gray cat ghosted over the roof, purring.

"Yes, I must agree. What we seek is not new but very old, something hidden but never quite forgotten." Frowning, he looked out over the abbey's stark walls, his eyes as impenetrable as night itself. "They are strong, these two. But their strength makes them weak. In their strength they are content to see with their eyes, and not with their hearts."

The cat moved, rubbing against his master's booted foot.

"Too late? It is never too late, my old friend. But your concern is real. With every day lost, every hour wasted, this danger grows."

The cat's tail arched.

"Gray?" Adrian Draycott thought of the woman he loved, a woman who had shown no fear before a madman's treachery. As she had shown no fear in death.

His jaw hardened. "She says we must *make* them see. Alas, it is not so simple, is it, Gideon?" Adrian ran his hand over the cat's sleek fur. "There are some things that cannot be given and some choices that must not be rushed. Even when time crowds close." He looked out over the wooded hills, formless in the gathering darkness. A shooting star flashed and left a trail of silver through the silent night. "No, not even by such creatures as we are, my friend."

With a sigh, the black-clad figure turned and paced the cold stones. Beside him the great cat flicked his tail and waited, eyes agleam, sharp with intelligence. A cat and yet far more.

Overhead the moon pulled free of the clutching black fingers of the woods and rose in chill splendor, its beauty mocked by a racing curtain of clouds.

Somewhere in the great, restless beast that was modern London, a figure sat hunched in darkness, listening to the quiet voices.

It always began with the voices.

So it did this night. They were never much at first, just a whisper in the shadows or a sigh in the chill light of dawn. But they never stopped there.

The figure in the darkness frowned, trying to hold back the light and the memories.

And the voices.

But it never worked. The pictures were too sharp, the voices too shrill. In a wild dance they rose, racing ever closer till they broke in a feverish rush. Only then would the blessed silence return. The nothingness, once more. The peace.

Until it began all over again, with a whisper or a hiss.

Just as it had tonight.

Just as it always would, until the traitors were made to bleed, to weep, to pay for all the pain they had caused.

Now—and two hundred years before.

Seventeen ～

Cathlin caught a hard breath. She didn't want to be here. The abbey was lovely, the will an unbelievable godsend, but Draycott Abbey left her throat raw and her pulse lurching.

It wasn't because of the portraits glaring down in cool arrogance from the silk-covered walls. It wasn't because of the scattered roses or the fragile tapestries that her mother had loved so well.

It was the past and its memories that Cathlin couldn't bear. Every room, every corner carried shadows that reminded her of the mother who had died here.

She looked at herself in the cheval glass, seeing the pale cheeks, the stormy eyes. Seeing a face full of shadows.

Just one night, she told herself.

The sun had melted over the western hills and reddish gold light poured over the old Aubusson carpets and gilt chairs. The Yellow Salon was lit by a massive crystal chandelier and candles set in silver candelabra. Four people stood gathered by the opened French doors as Cathlin entered.

The chandelier flashed. The crystal gleamed. All was peace and order.

Except for the spot where pain was eating a hole through Cathlin's heart.

She tugged uneasily at her dress, a fitted shimmer of amber silk that perfectly matched her eyes. Modest and demure in front, the dress turned dangerous at the back where it plunged straight to Cathlin's slender waist.

It was the sort of dress you didn't wear much under. Cathlin had meant it as a challenge to a man who had challenged her too often lately. Now, looking at Dominic, who was looking dangerous himself in a black turtleneck, smoky tweed jacket, and black trousers, she decided she might have made a slight miscalculation.

She shrugged. She could handle one arrogant bodyguard just fine.

About Viscount Draycott, she wasn't so sure. She tried to force away a wave of uneasiness. He was a tall man with thoughtful eyes and hair that showed the faintest sprinkling of gray. His young daughter was tugging at his hand, and he caught her up on his shoulders, heedless of protocol or the very expensive Hermès tie he wore. As he turned, Cathlin realized this was not the man she had seen by the moat, accompanied by his gray cat.

So the man liked his anonymity. Probably he let some member of his staff play at being viscount when there were visitors about. Very clever.

She looked around her, aware of the abbey's golden glow of age and wealth and unerring good taste. And though she hadn't meant to, Cathlin smiled softly. There was love here, love that whispered in the corners and gathered around her heart and clung tightly. Maybe something about this beautiful old house would accept nothing less than love.

As the blond-haired viscountess stood up and tickled her daughter's toes, Cathlin felt a burning in her eyes. She had had that kind of happiness once, only to lose it.

Here at Draycott Abbey.

Her hands tightened. She shouldn't be here. She couldn't face this. She was turning to leave when she felt Dominic's hand on her shoulder.

"Don't run, Cathlin. They won't bite." He took in her pale face and the glistening in her eyes. "Besides, you look spectacular in amber satin. Let me introduce you."

"I can't," Cathlin said flatly. "It was an abstraction before, just a name and a place. But seeing the three of them here, so happy, and knowing this is where it all happened . . ." She swallowed. "I'm not up to this."

"You would hurt Nicholas unbearably if you left now."

Cathlin brushed at her eyes. "Maybe I would hurt myself unbearably if I stayed."

"It never pays to run from shadows." Dominic pulled her hand under his arm and tugged her forward. "Another one of Ashton's laws."

"Two were gray and two were black with white spots. They were squirmy and soft and all covered with straw."

Cathlin sat by the windows an hour later, Genevieve Draycott beside her describing the nine baby kittens they had just discovered mewing in the old stables. The viscountess sat nearby, radiant in a simple Thai satin sheath as she watched her five-year-old daughter charm the room.

"I think it's time we put Archibald to bed, don't you think, my love? He looks very sleepy."

Genevieve looked down at her battered stuffed turtle. "Archibald doesn't look sleepy to me." She frowned. "I think he would like to stay up and have dinner with the grown-ups tonight."

The viscountess ruffled her daughter's curls. "Did he tell you that? But what about the nice bed we've made for him in Uncle Michael's old fishing basket? I'm sure Archibald will want to try that out."

Genevieve brightened. "Oh, I forgot. Let's go right now." She took her mother's hand and smiled at Cathlin. "Maybe I can show you the kittens tomorrow." Her brow furrowed. "If you're still here, that is. Papa said you might not stay for long."

Cathlin felt a pang of regret. "I'd love to see them, Genevieve."

The little girl's head cocked. "I like your eyes. They remind me of a ring Papa gave me. He told me you can see all kinds of wonderful things frozen inside it, and that if I look very hard, I can look right back into the past. Archibald and I do hope that you'll stay to see our kittens." With that, the girl skipped from the room, Archibald dragged carefully behind her.

Cathlin's throat tightened, burning with tears shed long ago. She had to go. She had to leave this beautiful, unbearable room before—"

"Ms. O'Neill, a toast." Nicholas Draycott was holding out a fragile Murano glass goblet. The rippled design, spun diagonally, shimmered in the candlelight. "It's not a Château Climens '71, but I think you'll enjoy this particular champagne."

Cathlin gave a jerky smile and accepted the fragile vessel.

"To the return of old friends," Nicholas said, raising his glass. "And to the welcome of those who will become new ones. While you are here, my home and everything in it will be at your disposal."

Crystal clinked. Candles glowed. The champagne slid down Cathlin's throat, velvet and fruity and flawless. A Roederer Cristal '77, intense, full, and sweet.

It might as well have been vinegar.

The pain in her chest grew and grew. As if from a distance she heard Nicholas Draycott clear his throat. "And now, I have something I must tell you both. I'm afraid that Gabriel left another condition in his bequest."

Dim, so dim, Dominic's muttered surprise. A tight, sharp question. Cathlin didn't hear, walls heavy and looming, her head hammered by memories still formless.

"Seven days . . . abbey . . ."

Dominic's voice, louder this time. Sharper.

She could barely hear. Her throat was burning and Cathlin was afraid she was going to be sick. Get away—had to get away. *Mother, where are you? I'm alone and afraid and you're not here. Where are you? Why is everything so quiet?*

Her fist pressed at her mouth, holding back tears, holding back pain, holding back fifteen years of stark shadows.

"Together . . . very specific. You must pass one week here in the manner of husband and wife . . ."

Dominic's voice rose to a harsh curse. ". . . should have told us . . . utterly ridiculous . . ."

Cathlin heard no more. Pushing unsteadily to her feet, she shoved past the drifting curtains, past the rose petals strewn over the flagstones by the wind, and out into the blessed darkness.

"Cathlin."

She turned away, her legs curled on the damp lawn, her cheeks slick with tears. "Go away."

"We've got to talk. Then I'll go away."

"It's too late to talk. You knew. You *knew* about that stipulation of Gabriel's, damn you!"

Dominic's voice tightened. "I didn't know. Turn around and look at me, Cathlin."

"Go away. Go away forever."

"No."

Cathlin stumbled to her feet and shoved past him.

He caught her at the cool weathered granite of the abbey's south wall. Near their feet the moat gurgled softly and a pair of swans left tracks of silver in their wake.

"It's not too late. Talk to me now."

"You want a peek, is that it? You want to see the tears and touch the pain. You want the full spectacle, blood and all." Her cheeks glistened, silvered and wet in the moonlight. "Well, you can't. No one can, not even me. It's all locked away somewhere, deep in a place where even I can't find it. All that's left is a hole, Dominic, a great jagged hole that tells me something's missing. Only God help me, I don't remember what."

She twisted, her face to the cold stone. Dominic turned her slowly, his fingers gentle at her waist.

"Let me go."

But he didn't release her, and Cathlin shoved at him wildly. Her fists tightened, hammering at his chest.

And he let her. Silent. Thoughtful. Unmoving. His eyes full of an emotion Cathlin didn't want to see.

After a long while she caught a ragged sob. Her hands slowed, then sank to her sides. "I miss her. Oh, God, I miss her every second, every hour." She took a ragged breath. "I'm an adult. I have charge cards. I know about balloon rates and term insurance. I handle wines worth hundreds of thousands of dollars, and here I am crying like a fool over something that happened fifteen years ago. Something I can't even remember."

Dominic's fingers wound through her hair. "She was your mother, Cathlin. Bone and blood memories like that don't go away. Maybe they just get buried."

"Why, Dominic? Why did he plan all this in that will of his? Why does he want us here together for a week?" She shivered. "Sometimes I almost think he's here, watching us."

"Because the tragedy never really ended, Cathlin. Gabriel knew that better than anyone. Maybe it's up to us to end it by finding out the truth. That could be why he wanted us here." He brushed her cheek. "The bottles are authentic, aren't they?"

"A complete chemical analysis and corroborative research will take weeks, but I can tell you the answer already. Oh, yes, they're real and they're nearly priceless."

Dominic let out his breath slowly. "If we don't agree to go along with the stipulations of the will, Cathlin, Nicholas has to dump that wine into the moat."

"He can't!"

"But he will. He's absolutely serious about all this. It was the last expressed wish of a dying man—possibly a murdered man. Nicholas is dead set on honoring every single word."

"But then—" Cathlin closed her eyes. "I still can't."

Dominic eased a damp strand of hair from her lips. As his fingers brushed her mouth, he cursed softly. "Cathlin," he whispered.

"Yes?"

"Heaven help me, I want to . . ."

Kiss me. Cathlin's heart did a funny lurch in her chest. *Please. Now. Before I can think.*

His fingers slid around her neck. His eyes burned, all smoke and jade, but he gave her time to move away, to pound his chest, to curse him for a blasted fool.

None of which Cathlin did. Somehow her hands were wrapped around his lapels and she was easing him closer.

"Cathlin?"

"No. Don't talk."

Their lips hovered, brushed, fitted lightly. It was like coming home, only a thousand times better, deep and sweet and full.

"I'm . . . sorry." Her words melted over his open mouth. "About hitting you."

"I'm not. I think that particular storm"—a pause to lick the ridge of her lip with his warm tongue—"has been too long coming." He slid his legs between hers, pulling her into his heat. "And I'm very, very glad that it broke over me."

"I won't do it." Cathlin's voice was husky, lost in arousal as he moved against her, smooth and slow and perfect. "Not here. Not for a week. I can't, Dominic."

"Then you can't. Finished. End of lot, end of category."

"Why aren't you shouting at me?"

"Because I'm far too busy kissing you, Irish. And damn, but you're good to kiss."

Her fingers eased into his hair. "I . . . am?"

"Wonderful."

"Dominic?"

"Hmmmmmm?"

"I tried to hate the abbey. I tried so hard, but I couldn't. It's too beautiful and there's too much love here. But there are shadows, too. I try to tell myself it's just me, and then I see something flicker out of the corner of my eye. I catch the hum of a voice or a hint of fragrance and I wonder is it her, is it some memory, or am I simply losing my mind."

"Irish, one of us here is losing his mind, and it isn't you." Dominic eased away, his body too hard, his eyes too hot. "You're not losing anything. It's coming back, don't you see? That's bound to hurt at first. Maybe you don't have any more choice about how or when it comes."

"Maybe not." She studied his features, stern, beautiful, awash with silver in the moonlight. "What are we doing here, Dominic? What happened to the nun and the rosary?"

"You want me to stop?"

A universe of thinking. Asking. Taking time to be honest. "No."

"Good." A low groan. "Very good. Because I think I might go on kissing you forever, O'Neill. And when I'm not kissing you, I plan on being busy touching you in the most amazing ways." His hand eased over the naked skin at her back and he fitted her to his awesome arousal.

"I bet you tell all your clients that."

"No." Dead serious, his hands rigid. "Not one. Not ever, Cathlin. It's important you know that."

"I do." Her fingers traced his lips. Her sigh was loud in the silence of the night. "Meanwhile, I suppose we'd better get back inside or Nicholas Draycott will think we've fallen into the moat."

"Maybe I feel like I have. But you're right. Any longer out here and I might do something monumentally stupid. Fantastic, but very stupid." Smiling softly, Dominic smoothed Cathlin's hair and straightened the neck of her dress. "Let's go."

Nicholas was toying with a row of jeweled Fabergé miniatures when Dominic and Cathlin came inside. His eyes narrowed as he saw the hardness at Dominic's jaw. "I'm sorry I didn't tell you sooner, Dominic, but I was afraid you wouldn't come if you knew."

"I wouldn't have."

The viscount's steady glance took in both of them. "What about now?"

Dominic looked at Cathlin and took a deep breath.

"Yes," she said.

"No," Dominic snapped.

Their eyes met, startled.

Nicholas smiled faintly, noting Cathlin's disordered hair and swollen lips, along with Dominic's rumpled lapels and the hint of lipstick at his cheek. "I'm delighted you're in agreement, just as I'm certain that Gabriel Montserrat would be, were he here." The lights in the hall flickered for a moment. "Sorry. That happens sometimes when the wiring gets damp. Now I suggest that we move things along as fast as possible, before the value of this wine is made public. Meanwhile, my wife, Kacey, will continue to go through the county archives along with church records of marriages and deaths." He refilled their glasses with a flourish and turned, smiling broadly. "And now, to a toast to your upcoming wedding."

Dominic's eyes darkened.

"I have checked with the vicar and he is free to marry you tomorrow. Whatever happens after that will be . . ." He cleared his throat. "That is, I leave the practical details of your marriage up to you."

Wind gusted through the study and the abbey's lights flickered. A moment later the room was plunged into darkness.

Eighteen ∽

Dominic cursed.

Long and fluently. In English, then in back-alley Thai, then in very eloquent French. He couldn't see a thing.

Cathlin's fingers slid to his arm. "Is this another idea of Marston's? I hope he's not going to wheel in crêpes flambées."

"I doubt that Marston had anything to do with this." As he spoke, Dominic inched toward the wall. "Nicholas?"

"Right here. What's going on?"

"I don't know yet, but I soon will."

"Good. In the meanwhile, I'm going up to check on Kacey and Genevieve."

Cathlin reached out blindly. "Dominic, wait. I'm coming with you." Silence. "Dominic?"

But Dominic Montserrat had already disappeared into the darkness.

Dominic inched down the rear stairs, his mind racing. Swift and methodical, he ran through all the permutations of exits, entrances, and electrical sources. He was at the last step, easing alongside the first row of shelves, when he heard a low whisper at his ear.

"Dominic?"

"Cathlin? Why in God's name—"

Her voice was a wisp of sound. "Because something's wrong and you're going to need my help. I know this place better than you ever will."

"After only one afternoon?"

"One long and very thorough afternoon spent in the cellar. And I remember every detail, believe me. Right now we're standing beside a row of claret bottles. That means there's a power source just a little over four feet to the left on the south wall."

A creaking sound came somewhere to their right. Instantly Dominic's fingers tightened on Cathlin's shoulder, motioning her to silence.

He bent close, lips to her ear. "Stay here."

"But you can't just—"

"*Stay.*"

She didn't hear him slip away. As always, he moved in utter silence. All Cathlin felt was a whisper of wind against her skin.

Her heart pounded as she crouched in the darkness of the ancient cellars, thinking about death and betrayal, about nightmares that wouldn't stay buried.

Thinking about ghosts past and present and a sad and lonely man named Gabriel.

Her senses were screaming and her nerves stretched to the breaking point when she finally heard the hiss of a match being struck. Through the neatly stacked rows of bottles Cathlin made out a shadowed figure bent over one of the wine racks. She was inching closer when she heard bone strike flesh. The wine racks shivered with the impact of a blow. But there were no words, no voices at all. Only later would Cathlin realize the significance of that silence, the mark of two professionals who gave nothing away even in the direst circumstances.

Cathlin didn't stop to think about what she was doing next. She reached deep, calling up her memory of the cellars. Before her were three rows of claret and a row of Madeira.

The muffled thud of bodies grew louder as Cathlin worked through the darkness. She felt a ridge of wood at her feet, a small wooden step stool pushed out of reach.

Her hands closed around the rough wooden legs. It would be heavy enough to deal a stunning blow, if only she could figure out where Dominic was.

She took a breath and then repeated one of Dominic's French curses, one of the few she had understood. She heard a quick gasp. Close by, a harsh voice, raw with pain, grated out an answering curse.

Dominic was slightly to her right, next to a rack full of priceless claret. Cathlin waited, praying, then she hurled the footstool with all her strength.

After a satisfying crack, Cathlin heard a sharp curse, followed by footsteps. Glass shattered and a shoulder rammed into her chest. She gasped as a hard body shoved her to the ground and charged off into the darkness.

"Cathlin, are you there? Talk to me, damn it!"

"I—I'm fine, Dominic." Cathlin clenched her teeth against the pain in her side. "I think he's gone."

Nearby a match flared. Cathlin frowned as she saw Dominic propped up against one of the wine racks. His jacket was gone and his cuff was splashed with blood.

"You idiot," Cathlin sputtered. "You complete and utter idiot."

"Don't get upset, Irish. Some of this blood is *his*." Dominic's fingers tightened. "Though maybe not so much as I'd like. I see you inflicted a little damage yourself." He frowned down at the glass splinters spread over the floor.

"Who was he?"

"I don't know, but he was good. *Too* bloody good

for any amateur thief." Grimacing, he headed for the stairs.

"What are you doing?"

"Going after him. It's my job, remember?"

Nicholas was pacing the drawing room, looking grim, when Dominic returned. "Did you find anything?"

"Footprints leading to tire tracks. Not much help, I'm afraid. At least you managed to get the electricity working again."

Nicholas rubbed his neck. "Someone had thrown the circuit breaker. Obviously, the news is out, and we're going to have to take some precautions. What do you suggest?"

"You need a new alarm system up and running by tomorrow. I know a man in London who can handle it. We'll also have to establish some other procedures. I want to know where everyone is at all times." He looked at Cathlin, who was sitting pale but composed next to Marston. "That means at *all* times, understood? I'll arrange to have radio transmitters for each of us." He turned to Marston. "Nothing goes in or out without my seeing it first. Not books, not groceries, not a single matchstick."

"Understood, Lord Ashton."

"I have a question," Cathlin said tightly. "When are you going to do something about that blood on your cuff?"

"Later." Dominic's voice was hard. "Any more questions? No? Then go up and rest. Nicholas and I will take watch down here until I can get someone to help in the morning."

"You're bleeding again."

Cathlin frowned as she followed Dominic out into the hallway.

No answer.

"Dominic, you can't just go around *bleeding* on everything."

Still no answer.

Cathlin grabbed his uninjured arm and pulled him to a halt. There were lines of tension at his mouth and forehead, lines he couldn't hope to conceal. Her eyes widened with disbelief as she ran her fingers over the front of his jacket.

It was wet with blood. "So when were you planning to do something about this?"

Dominic shrugged. "You'll be the first to know."

"It's all a game to you, isn't it? All about seeing who's faster or smarter or braver. Well, I'm not playing. Not now. Not ever." Her eyes were dark and haunted. "I've already lost one man I loved that way, you see."

Restless and unable to sleep, Dominic stood on the middle of the stone bridge, rubbing his neck. All the entries and exits were in good shape. Only two windows needed new locks and rewiring for the upgraded laser security system.

Now he had to try the places that weren't so obvious. He looked out over the darkened hills, trying to think with the mind of a man who would do anything to possess the wine in the abbey cellars.

A thief would automatically assume electronic protection was in place and look for a way to cut it. Next he'd go for backup generators—which Draycott didn't have. After that, he'd go for the bodyguard.

Dominic's eyes hardened. Being a target didn't frighten him. He'd done it too often before to be afraid of a bullet he couldn't prepare for. But the thought that he might fail and allow Cathlin to be hurt scared the living hell out of him.

Abruptly he turned. "Nicholas?" he called, scanning the darkness behind him.

No answer. Nothing moved amid the shadows.

Dominic inched toward the gatehouse. But the doorway, too, was empty.

"Of course no one's out there, Montserrat. You're losing your mind, that's your only problem. And all because of a woman as changeable as quicksilver, a woman who's smart and irritating and has suffered too much pain in her life already."

Muttering, he made his way over the bridge. Everything was peaceful. Not a shadow moved on those manicured green slopes. So why didn't he feel safe?

High overhead Vega flashed sharply against the deep velvet of the sky. To the north the Big Dipper dangled in a perfect silver chain, pointing to some long-forgotten mystery that only primitive man had understood. Dominic thought about newer mysteries, about white dwarfs and red giants and black holes so dense not a single speck of matter could ever escape their vast intractable pull.

Right now he felt drawn that way to the woman upstairs.

Around him the soft night sounds of wind and water drifted and ebbed. Dominic took a slow breath and told himself to relax.

Cathlin had gone up to bed hours ago. From the bridge he had watched her shadow move back and forth against the curtains. Her slim body had been silhouetted against white lace, a tantalizing sweep of curves and hollows, before the light had gone out.

He tried not to think about her undressing, then sliding down against the quilt, her hair loose and glossy around her face.

Roses tossed beside the moat, filling the air with perfume. The moon burned, unblinking over the wooded hills.

Only night. Only silence. Only the darting silver images of moon and stars, reflected in the ever-changing currents of the moat.

Suddenly something made the back of Dominic's neck tighten. "Marston?"

But it wasn't Draycott's eccentric butler who stood in the stone courtyard before the abbey's huge front gate. It was Cathlin O'Neill, wearing some damned jersey that barely covered her thighs. It wasn't feminine. It wasn't fetching or flirty or seductively silken.

But it might as well have been, because Dominic took one look and felt something burst into hot, furious life inside him. He envisioned her in white lace and peach satin. In a long gown that swept the floor and a navy velvet cloak with a soft hood.

Just like the sad-eyed woman in his dreams.

And then he imagined her in absolutely nothing at all.

"Sweet God above, Montserrat, get up off all fours and start trying to be reasonably human, will you?" Frowning, he pushed away from the stone railing.

And then he froze. Cathlin was moving toward him. He whispered her name, but she didn't answer. She moved haltingly over the arch of the bridge, then cocked her head, listening to the silence.

Dominic felt a chill at his heart as she sank to her knees at the top of the bridge and inched protectively against one of the stone columns. And there she sat, huddled in the shadows, her eyes huge, her hands twisting.

It took several moments to realize exactly what those white fingers were doing. They were scraping desperately, trying to wash off a stain that only she could see.

Dominic knelt slowly beside her. When she didn't look up, he touched her shoulder softly, waiting for some hint of recognition.

"Is it time?" she asked, in a voice that was hers but softer. Younger. "Can I go yet? I want to go."

Dominic felt something cold and sharp go in just beneath his ribs and twist hard. She was caught in the past, caught in the nightmares of her mother's death. Had she held a killer's identity trapped in her mind all these years? "You can go, Cathlin. Anytime you want. It's all over now, I promise."

Her hands twisted sharply. "You said that before. You told me I could go, and then you locked me in."

Dominic tasted a rage that threatened to overwhelm him. What kind of sick mind would torment an innocent child?

Somehow he bit back his fury. "Not now. There's nothing to hold you now, Cathlin. Look around you. All you have to do is walk over that bridge and you'll be free."

"But I can't. If I do, they'll know. And then—oh God, then—" Her hands slid to her mouth as she tried to hold in a muffled sob.

Had they threatened her? Had she been afraid to make a noise? "I'll take you wherever you want. I'll take you home, Cathlin. I'll take you back to yesterday or on to tomorrow. No one will ever stop you again, I swear it."

After an agonizing silence, she pushed to her feet. When she walked back across the bridge, there was no recognition at all in her face.

Dominic's throat tightened as he watched her climb the stairs and make her way back to bed. There she curled into a ball and pulled the covers protectively around her.

As if they could hold out a lifetime of shadows.

Dominic slumped in a chair beside her bed. When dawn finally broke over the Wealden hills, he had decided two things. He was going to keep out those shadows for Cathlin O'Neill, whether she liked it or not. Nothing was going to stop her from being free ever again.

And if it took a wedding performed at the order of a man who had been dead for two hundred years to accomplish that, then the abbey was damned well going to have a wedding that no one ever forgot.

Nineteen ~

It took Dominic two hours on the phone and Nicholas another three, but by eleven o'clock, everything was arranged.

The vicar was on his way. Serita was coming from London and several of Nicholas's friends had been invited. The wedding plans were set.

Cathlin had protested when Nicholas told her the ceremony was all arranged. She wanted to help solve the mystery of the will, but refused to believe an actual wedding ceremony was necessary. But Nicholas held firm. This was Gabriel's last wish, and he would see it carried out or the wine would indeed go into the moat.

When Cathlin had looked at Dominic, she'd seen a similar determination on his face. His reason was more practical: he wanted Cathlin cooped up at the abbey where he could keep an eye on her. His final words had been unequivocal.

It might be the wedding from hell, but it was going to take place whether she liked it or not.

It was a lovely wedding. The bride wore black and the groom was bleeding.

The study was bright with centifolia roses arranged in cut crystal bowls. Marston looked upon the proceedings with patent pride beside Nicholas and Kacey Draycott.

First to arrive was Michael Burke, one of Nicholas Draycott's closest friends and his neighbor to the north. With Michael came his wife, who was looking rather pale after a bout with the flu. Soon after, Serita McCall made a grand entrance in a jumpsuit of gold lurex and seed pearls.

Introductions were completed and sherry passed by the discreet but ubiquitous butler. Nicholas was just helping himself to a glass when the vicar rushed in. "So sorry to be late," he apologized haltingly. "There was an accident on the A28, and I'm afraid it's rather upset me. The fellow wasn't hurt, thank the Blessed Father, but the poor man's truck was left in most distressing condition. If I'm running on, do forgive me."

Nicholas hid a smile. "Quite understandable under the circumstances."

The vicar passed his hat and coat to Marston, then rubbed his hands and looked about him. "Now then, where is the bride?"

Draycott and Marston exchanged a quick look and Nicholas cleared his throat. "I expect she'll be down shortly, Vicar. Last-minute affairs to be taken care of and all that. Why don't you have a sherry while you wait?"

Right on cue, Marston passed a goblet to the vicar. The polite flow of conversation ensued.

Only someone looking very closely would have noticed the faint frown working down Nicholas's forehead.

Cathlin pulled open the door to the closet and glared at the clothes inside. Muttering, she ran over her choices, on loan from Kacey. A simple but very elegant cocktail dress of ivory satin?

Too formal.

An off-the-shoulder designer knock-off from Paris, made in a clingy knit of striking amber that perfectly matched her eyes?

Too slinky. Cathlin wasn't about to give Dominic any reason to think she *liked* this idea of his.

Next came two simple suits in dark fabrics.

Possibly.

And then Cathlin's lips curved up in a smile. She'd marry Officer Montserrat all right, and it would be in clothes from her own bag.

And when she did, it would be a ceremony he *never* forgot.

A half hour later the clock was chiming as Cathlin started down the stairs. Through the doors to the study she saw a dozen or so people talking quietly, trying to pretend it was the most normal thing in the world for a man to marry a woman he barely knew because of the will of an ancestor he'd never met.

An ancestor two hundred years dead.

The sun poured golden through the abbey's great mullioned windows as Cathlin looked down and smoothed her black silk blouse. Her black flowing trousers. Her black silk scarf.

She smiled faintly. The message should be clear enough even for a hard case like Dominic Montserrat.

Dominic was alone in the front hall when he looked up and saw Cathlin at the top of the stairs. The chandelier cast glints of gold, red, and amber through her hair as she moved down the steps, smiling.

Dominic blinked. Silky hair. Satin blouse. Flowing trousers.

All black.

A muscle twitched at his jaw. Even as he registered the solid black of her attire, Dominic felt a jab of admiration. No shy, awe-filled bride here, he thought ruefully.

Somewhere in the house a clock began to chime.

Dominic's arms tensed beneath his perfectly tailored jacket. Motionless, wary, he stared at Cathlin, dressed in black. At the jeweled satin rose in her hair, also black.

He found himself torn between fury and disbelief. *Very well, my dear, if it's war you want, it's war you'll get.* He took a step forward, poised for battle, a hard-faced warrior clad in impeccable evening dress that played up the rich bronze hue of his skin.

Cathlin studied him coldly from head to toe. "Heavens, I seem to have made a terrible mistake. I'm dressed all wrong for the occasion."

"I'm sure it was no mistake," Dominic murmured, taking her arm. "Rather an unusual way to dress for a wedding, isn't it?"

"Is it, Officer Montserrat? I wouldn't know, having never been married before."

"I'm not exactly a veteran myself. However, the guests have arrived, the vicar is waiting, and Marston is positively on the verge of a crisis of nerves. So let's just get the damn business over with, shall we?"

"Of course," Cathlin said tightly, trying to pull free of his hand. But he slid his arm under hers and guided her inexorably toward the noise and lights of the study.

Dominic was attuned to her every emotion now. He felt her slight tremor and knew the moment that her step faltered. His fingers tightened, firm but gentle, as he guided her forward.

"Is—is Serita here yet?"

"Offering healths to anyone who'll listen. She's already got Nicholas's promise to tour the wine cellars later. And Nicholas's friend, Lord Burke, has asked her over for a consultation next week."

"That sounds like Serita." As Cathlin spoke, the

flower above her ear swayed and slid to the floor. Dominic went for it at the same instant she did, and their shoulders butted beneath the five-hundred–year-old chandelier casting warm sparks over the oak floor.

Pain streaked through Dominic's shoulder, his memento of yesterday's scuffle in the wine cellar. He winced as his fingers closed on the satin flower. Already he could feel blood seeping beneath the bandage on his arm, but he'd be damned if anybody got the slightest hint that he was uncomfortable.

"Turn around," he ordered.

"Why?"

"So I can put this damn bow back in your hair. Since you seem so intent on wearing the bloody thing, it's the least I can do to see that it stays put." He caught her shoulders and spun her around, and his long fingers smoothed the hair back from her cheek and slid the anchoring pin deep into her hair. It felt like satin in his fingers and left his blood on fire. "Stop moving, damn it."

"I'm *not* moving!"

"Then stop breathing. Since you've gone to all this trouble to tell the world exactly what you think of this wedding, dressed like some sacrificial virgin going off to be beheaded and deflowered, the least you can do is stand still until this ugly flower is back in place."

Cathlin's shoulders tightened. "It's not a wedding. At least not a real and proper one. I just wanted to make my opinions clear on that."

"Oh, you've made yourself crystal clear, O'Neill. I expect everyone will be thinking you're a widow rather than a bride-to-be."

Her eyes glittered. Color slashed over her high cheekbones. Oh yes, it would be a lovely ceremony all right.

Dominic scowled, wanting to shake her, wanting

to order her to be careful. Wanting to kiss her, until she gripped his shoulders and poured over him like slow, still water and he had his fill of her.

Except something told Dominic he'd *never* get his fill of this woman.

He bit back a curse as Marston came through the study doors, magnificent in a black coat and new orange running shoes. "It appears as if we are ready, my lord. You will be wishing for the ring, of course."

Dominic opened the case Marston gave him. Inside lay a square-cut emerald, outlined in tiny pavé diamonds. "Thank you, Marston."

The ring had been passed down through his family for centuries, maybe even back as far as Gabriel's time. Family legend said the emerald had come from somewhere in the Sri Lanka hill country and that the stone changed hands a dozen times within the first two hours of its discovery.

Dominic looked down, remembering how it had flashed on his mother's strong, capable hand. She had given it to him, smiling tenderly, only an hour before her death.

"My stubborn, serious son, take this and believe. Believe that you'll find her, the one who is the other piece of your heart. You'll know who she is because she'll fit into your soul, completing something you didn't even know was missing until that moment." She had waved her hand, dismissing his protests. "Hush, my love. Let me finish, for my time is nearly gone." Dominic could still remember how the ring's sharp corners had cut into his skin. He had been repulsed at the thought that the only way the ring could be his was with his mother's death.

"When you find her and your heart whispers that she is the one, listen, my love. And give her this. When you do, I'll know it. Somehow you'll feel it, too, my dearest Dominic. Somewhere you'll know I'm smiling."

As her fingers had closed over his, her eyes had flickered shut. An hour later she was dead.

Dominic wondered if she was watching now. If so, what would that calm, practical Frenchwoman make of this bizarre ceremony performed at the wish of a man dead for two centuries.

He wasn't sure he wanted to know.

"Shall we begin, my lord?" The balding vicar moved from foot to foot, clearly ill at ease. Nicholas had explained the whole odd story to him, and in the end he had given way before Nicholas's persuasion, contenting himself with a single, muttered, "most extraordinary."

The heady scent of roses filled the air where the French doors stood open to the golden valleys.

Dominic felt a sudden pressure in his chest. He ignored it, just as he had been trained to ignore anything without relevance to his job. "Your hand, my dear."

Only Dominic saw the swift burst of color that filled Cathlin's cheeks. Only Dominic felt the tremor that shook her fingers, then was quickly suppressed as his hand closed over hers.

Dearly beloved, we are gathered together here in the sight of God . . ."

Dominic's jaw hardened as the vicar began to speak. A will was a will, after all, and a million pounds was a million bloody pounds. Oh yes, it would be a lovely ceremony, he thought grimly.

Especially if the bride and groom managed to keep from murdering each other before it was over.

". . . to be joined together . . ."

Cathlin's knees felt like Seacliffe's disintegrating roof beams.

". . . in holy matrimony . . ."

She was really here. She was really consenting. This was *really* happening.

". . . an honorable estate, instituted of God in paradise . . ."

The air was full of the scent of roses. She could feel the cool slide of her satin blouse, heavy against her sensitized skin. She caught every smell, registered every noise and movement around her, however small.

". . . not to be enterprised, nor taken in hand unadvisedly . . ."

She took a quick, steadying breath, ignoring the strong hand on hers, ignoring the urge to look sideways, toward the man whose startling eyes reminded her of a pine forest at dawn, full of secrets.

But Cathlin discovered that she didn't have to look to see Dominic.

Every detail of his face was already burned into her memory.

Fifteen minutes later it was done. The vows were said, the oaths exchanged. Dominic's elegant emerald ring now sat gleaming upon Cathlin's slender finger.

The whole ceremony had gone smoothly, in fact, if one discounted the tension between the bridal pair so thick it could be cut with a knife.

Nicholas and his wife looked on in high good humor, delighted by Cathlin's unusual style of dress. The vicar, downright uncomfortable, limited himself to a few uncertain smiles.

As soon as the service was done, Dominic had given her a firm but very swift kiss. Almost immediately she turned away and moved to greet Serita.

After a hug, Serita studied her friend intently. "I hope you'll be happy, Cathlin. I know this wedding is just a formality, part of that crazy will, but your eyes are sparkling and your cheeks are flushed. And don't tell me it's just from anger, because I won't believe it." Her voice fell. "You're entitled to be happy, you know. Both of you are." She squeezed

Cathlin's hand, then offered her a glass of Dom Ruinart champagne.

Cathlin emptied her glass, determined not to think about vintage or acidity or carbonation levels, only to enjoy how the champagne tickled all the way down the back of her throat.

When Nicholas and his wife walked up two glasses later, Cathlin gave the viscount a blinding smile. "A lovely ceremony, wasn't it, Lord Draycott?"

"Call me Nicholas, please," the viscount said with a smile. "And yes, so it was, Lady Ashton."

Lady Ashton. Cathlin met Dominic's eyes and felt color flare through her cheeks.

Nicholas's wife smiled. "Just yesterday I had it from the head of Harrods Wine Department that you are the best source of information on old Sauternes in England."

Cathlin caught up another glass of champagne from Marston's tray and drained it rather wildly. "I'm afraid Mr. Grandville-Jones is in my debt because I saved him from wasting a great deal of money on a consignment of what was supposedly fifty-year-old Sauternes." A smile played around her lips. "I tracked him down mere seconds before the auctioneer's hammer fell."

"And in the end who purchased this overrated and overpriced grape juice?" Dominic asked.

"It was a corporate purchase by a rather dour group of financiers from Osaka. But I doubt they will have noticed the problem with the wine. They were buying strictly for investment purposes." Cathlin's tone conveyed exactly how little she thought of such transactions.

"You don't like the idea?" Dominic found he enjoyed watching Cathlin leap in to defend the things she believed in.

"With wine, really good wine, becoming more expensive by the day, I can see the necessity of investment acquisitions, but I don't have to like it."

Serita laughed. "Oh Lord, now you've got her talking about wine. No one will be able to get a word in the rest of the night. Never mind, I'll rescue you all. Here's a toast." She held up a beautiful goblet of handspun glass whose stem was worked in gold. Marston had told Cathlin the set had been in Dominic's family for generations, and he'd sent for it specially for the ceremony. "I offer a toast to two friends." Her eyes gleamed with mischief. "May their wine be sweet and their nights be long."

A storm of color swirled through Cathlin's cheeks. She refused to meet Dominic's eyes as she raised her glass. Crystal tinkled amid a murmur of salutes.

Then another voice cut through the pleasurable stillness. "Dominic Montserrat? My dear boy, it has been far too long since I've seen you."

Dominic turned, his eyes hard. The new arrival sported a perfectly cut tweed jacket and a smile that did not quite reach his eyes. It had been three years since Dominic had last seen him, but James Harcliffe looked exactly the same. "What are you doing here, Harcliffe?"

"Oh my, things really haven't changed, have they?" James Harcliffe, thin and balding, clicked his tongue. "As you guessed, I'm here for business, not pleasure." He gestured toward the man beside him. "Have you met Jeffrey Hayes? He's a particularly good chap in our department."

Dominic looked over the powerfully built man whose eyes were the color of muddy ice. "I've heard the name," he said coldly.

"Jeffrey, do be helpful and fetch me a glass of champagne, won't you?" Harcliffe's cool voice held the edge of command that had allowed him to rise high in the government security apparatus. Hayes nodded and disappeared.

"You haven't changed a bit have you?"

"I expect not." Harcliffe smoothed his lapel. "Nor have you, my dear old friend."

"Friend? We were *never* friends," Dominic snapped. "Now tell me what you're doing here."

"I have some papers for you. I think you'll find they make enjoyable reading." Harcliffe's eyes were full of malice. "I left them in the viscount's study."

The others had moved away.

"I don't want files, I want answers," Dominic growled. "That's why I called you last night. Who was in that car? I gave you a license number and now I want a name."

"We're working on it."

"Working's not good enough, Harcliffe. Someone was after Cathlin, someone clever. I want to know who."

"What makes you assume that the attackers were after Cathlin? Perhaps, my dear Dominic, they were after *you*." Harcliffe's eyes narrowed. "After all, you've left a great many enemies in your wake."

"Why would they come all this way when they could track me down in France? No, there's a knot in my gut that tells me this has to do with the wine."

"Ah yes, that much vaunted instinct of yours. It has proved extremely valuable on occasion, I admit. It has also given you some very influential admirers, people in very high places who are interested in acquiring that priceless wine in Draycott's cellars. So listen to me and listen well," Harcliffe commanded. "This is out of your hands. The palace wants that wine, and that makes this a government operation. Are you following me?"

Dominic bit back a curse. Was there anything that James Harcliffe didn't know? "I'm following."

"Then I expect you to go by the book. Keep that wine safe and see that Cathlin completes the authentication that the palace wants." Harcliffe smiled thinly. "Otherwise, I'll see that Hayes replaces you in charge of security here at the abbey."

"Hayes? The man is totally unreliable and you know it. He bungled that last case in Manchester and nearly got a whole airport blown up in the process."

"Too bloody bad. Mr. Hayes is all we have available right now." There was smug triumph in Harcliffe's voice.

"What about those three harassment suits lodged against Hayes by women he was protecting? You and I both know they had total validity. Pulling the full force of the branch was the only way you got them dropped."

Harcliffe clicked his tongue. "Pure hearsay. Like any other man involved in a dangerous job, our Mr. Hayes feels the need for an occasional release of stress."

"You call it a release of stress when he forced that nurse from Brighton into his car and kept her bound and gagged for six hours?" Dominic growled a curse. "By God, there was hospital testimony to support physical evidence of assault."

"Nonsense, Dominic. It was all amicably resolved out of court. Now I really must insist that you stop dredging up unpleasant aspects of Mr. Hayes's past. It's either him or you."

"Then it's me and only me. Meanwhile, I need backup here. Men, equipment and anything else I happen to think of."

"It can be arranged."

"Tonight, Harcliffe. Not in two weeks."

"I suppose you're right. The press will soon have all the details of that wine. By the way, how is your wife holding up?"

"As well as can be expected."

"What's the problem? All our records say that Cathlin O'Neill has permanently repressed those memories of her mother's death."

"And just what else do those records say? Do they tell you how it felt to be ten years old and see your mother lying dead in front of you? Maybe you even got a sample of the woman's blood for the files."

"Don't let it get personal." It was a cold, flat order. "You know the rules as well as I do, Dominic."

"It *is* personal. I'm the one who brought her back here. How would *you* like to take responsibility for her sanity, Harcliffe?"

"I wouldn't. But then I don't have to. You have always been the favorite with the Royals. You racked up highest scores in every class. Firearms, threat analysis, close escort and evasive driving—you were always the best and they took you in as one of their own, didn't they?" For a moment there was hatred in Harcliffe's voice, hatred born of jealousy that he himself had never been able to break into that royal and rarefied world. "But it won't help you one damned bit now. You're back and you're going to stay back, Montserrat. And while you're here, you're mine to control."

"You've waited a long time for this, haven't you, Harcliffe?"

"Longer than you know," came the flat answer. "So shut your mouth and get back to your duties, Officer Montserrat. Unless you want to see Hayes replace you."

"What if Cathlin blows from stress? Then you've got no bequest and no one to carry out the verification work for the palace."

"She won't. We've got her complete psychological profile, and I've already gone through the debriefing notes made after the death of her mother. At the time there was some suspicion it might have been a political killing in retaliation against her father's government activities. Donnell O'Neill was very useful to us, you see. But that idea was scrapped. In the end, the conclusion of a panel of experts was that

Ms. O'Neill knew nothing of importance—and anything she might have observed at the abbey was permanently blocked in her subconscious as a result of the trauma. Don't you think we looked into every possibility? As a matter of fact, my wife was the expert of record in the case and she did nothing else for weeks. If there was a chance, even the slightest chance, that Cathlin O'Neill could remember something of use, you can be bloody certain that we would have pursued the possibility."

"And then what would you have done, Harcliffe? Pumped her full of hallucinogens? Given her pentathol? Sweet God, to a ten-year-old child?"

"If it would have resulted in useful ends, that's exactly what we would have done." Harcliffe's eyes were utterly cold.

"By God, sometimes I think you're mad. Sometimes I think *all* of us are."

Cathlin watched Dominic stride away from the balding man who'd just arrived from London. Was it something about the wine? She was going after Dominic when she felt a hand on her arm.

"Don't go yet."

Cathlin looked up into soft brown eyes. There was something sad about the woman's faint stoop and the strand of gray hair trying to escape from her prim chignon.

"You do remember me, don't you?" The woman frowned. "I see you don't remember at all. I am Joanna Harcliffe. Dr. Joanna Harcliffe." She looked at Cathlin, her head cocked, as her husband moved off in search of more champagne and new prey. "I'm afraid my husband has managed to irritate Dominic Montserrat yet again."

"Again? I don't understand."

"You didn't know? My dear, they worked together for years."

Cathlin stiffened at the reference to a world she continued to hate. "I see."

"Good heavens, you *do* have the look of your mother, especially when you're angry. I would have thought it impossible."

"You *knew* her?"

"Oh, yes, I knew Elizabeth O'Neill." Joanna Harcliffe said the words slowly, as if they held a host of memories.

Cathlin's face paled. "You knew her well?"

"Oh goodness, yes. We were up at St. Hilda's together—Oxford, you know. We read English before she developed an interest in art. Then she leaped right ahead of me. She was quite brilliant, your mother." The older woman's voice tightened. "Don't let anyone tell you anything different."

"But I don't—"

"No, of course you don't. How could you?" Joanna Harcliffe's eyes softened. "It's been fifteen years, after all. And perhaps it's far better this way, with your having no memory."

Cathlin felt a heaviness in her chest. "You know about that? About how she—she died?"

"I'm afraid I do, my dear." The woman hesitated.

"No, don't stop."

"You see, I'm a doctor. A psychiatrist. The—police called me in afterward."

"And you were called in for me." This time, it was a statement, not a question. "My God, I talked to you about it." Cathlin's eyes darkened, locked on the elegant Baume et Mercier silver-link watch on Joanna Harcliffe's wrist. As if in a dream, she watched the second hand sweep toward the top of the silver face.

Eight.

Nine.

Ten.

Cathlin swallowed. "For a moment it was all there, so close. Oh, God, I almost had it."

Eleven.

Twelve.

Cathlin felt darkness settle over her with light, scraping fingers. Memories drifted, then faded. "How can I make it come back? How can I remember?"

The psychiatrist shook her head. "I'm afraid it isn't that easy my dear, no matter what the television serials imply. It takes hours and hours. It takes hard work and complete commitment and *wanting* to remember."

"But I do want to remember!"

After a moment the woman smiled. "I believe that you do, Ms. O'Neill. But forgive me, I should be saying Lady Ashton."

"Why?" Cathlin said flatly. "It's just for the will. In a week this marriage will be over and I'll be Ms. O'Neill again."

"You sound wistful."

"You're wrong about that!"

"Am I?" Again the faintly sad smile. "As you will. But I fear I must be going now. My husband and that intense Mr. Hayes are returning. For some reason, I can never feel entirely comfortable around that young man."

James Harcliffe cocked his head as he strode up, with the young man in question a careful pace behind him. "So sorry if I'm interrupting anything, my dear."

"No, nothing. I was simply telling Lady Ashton how lovely she looked. So very refreshing to see someone take charge of her own wedding, dressing just as she likes without all this folderol and expense." She smiled and Cathlin felt as if they were sharing a private joke.

"Yes, quite lovely," James Harcliffe agreed indifferently. "Rather unorthodox however."

"Nonsense, James. She looks wonderful." Joanna

Harcliffe took her husband's arm, effectively cutting him off in midsentence. "But we really should be off. It would be nice if we could make your sister's party without being disgracefully late for a change."

After a stiff farewell, Harcliffe moved toward the door, only to halt and turn back. "Your gloves? How the devil should I know? You never lose things, Joanna."

His wife came back toward Cathlin. "Here they are, just as I thought. I'm afraid it's all true, my dear," she said, patting Cathlin's hand. "The memory really is the first thing to go."

Cathlin watched the unlikely couple move off, Harcliffe doing all the talking and his wife doing all the listening. Suddenly she felt something prick her palm. Looking down, she saw that Elizabeth Harcliffe had pressed a business card between her fingers listing her office number and a twenty-four-hour answering service.

It takes hard work and complete commitment. It also takes wanting to remember.

Cathlin felt something pull at the pit of her stomach. Did she have that kind of commitment? Did she really want to remember, no matter how painful the result?

She wasn't certain, not even now.

"You look a thousand miles away." Silent as usual, Dominic had come to her side.

She shrugged. "I suppose I was."

"Want to talk about it?"

Cathlin looked at his long, tanned fingers wrapped around an etched crystal champagne flute. How could he always look so strong, so handsome, so damned competent? "No," she said flatly. "But I will take some of *this*." She reached for his glass and emptied it.

"Delighted to be of use," Dominic said dryly.

"Oh, you're bound to have any number of uses.

Carrying wine cases and chasing away intruders is just a start." Cathlin snared another glass of champagne. "Cheers," she said, raising her glass. "And here's to the departure of that terrible man."

Their eyes locked. A wave of hunger flooded Dominic's face.

The force of it left Cathlin reeling. "Why are you looking at me that way?"

"What way?"

"Like you can't decide whether to kiss me or deck me or drag me away somewhere?"

"Maybe because I can't decide whether to kiss you or deck you or drag you away somewhere."

Too smart. Too fast. Definitely too *dangerous,* Cathlin thought. "Forget it, Officer Montserrat." She was determined to remind him this was business.

"Dominic," he said huskily. "Barring that, try 'husband' or 'my dear.' "

"Don't count on it anytime this century."

Again the hungry gaze. Cathlin blinked and gulped her champagne.

"More champagne, my lady?" Ghostlike, Marston appeared, carrying a bottle of nicely misted Dom Ruinart Blanc de Blancs.

"That would be lovely, Marston."

Dominic arched a brow as Cathlin tipped the pale, creamy froth to her mouth. "Going a little heavy, aren't you, Irish?"

"Nonsense. Drinking is my job. Well, tasting at least," she said scrupulously. Her head cocked. "Are those two people friends of yours or Lord Draycott?"

"Both, actually. Michael Burke is a good man. But I should call them the marquess and marchioness of Sefton, to be precise, even though Michael prefers his old naval title. His wife's an archaeologist by trade and a magician by birth, if half of Michael's stories are true."

Cathlin looked at the softly laughing couple. They

were standing very close, their hands entwined. "They look very much in love." Her voice was wistful.

"So they are. And they deserve it. They've both had a rough time."

Cathlin shrugged. She wasn't going to think of shadows. She definitely wasn't going to think about a man with bottomless green eyes, on whom she was coming to rely entirely too much. What she was going to do was snare another glass of that wonderful champagne.

"Are you sure you want that, Irish?"

"Absolutely." She waved her hand, narrowly avoiding Marston's shoulder.

Dominic frowned. "Have you eaten anything today?"

"Of course," his new wife said grandly. "Huge amounts of food."

Marston edged past, tray in hand. "Half of a croissant for breakfast, my lord. Two strawberries for lunch," he said helpfully.

"I see," Dominic said slowly, watching a very becoming flush slip over Cathlin's neck and chest.

"Quite, my lord," Marston murmured.

"What?" Cathlin frowned and steadied herself with a hand on a nearby chair. "*What* do you see?"

"Everything, I should think." Dominic took the empty goblet from her fingers and set it on Marston's tray. "No more, thank you, Marston."

"What, had enough, have you?" Cathlin studied Dominic smugly.

"I believe I have."

"Well, I haven't." Cathlin threw her hands wide, narrowly missing a priceless Tang ceramic horse. "I could go on drinking Dom Ruinart all night."

"Not tonight." Dominic's eyes darkened. "Not on our wedding night."

Cathlin frowned and reached for another glass. As

she did, Dominic turned, managing to jostle her arm so that the champagne landed in a potted orange shrub.

"Really, Dominic," Cathlin said crossly. "If you can't tolerate alcohol, you shouldn't drink."

"How right you are, my dear." A smile ghosted over Dominic's face as he took her hand. "Maybe you'll be kind enough to give me a steadying hand."

"Of course. No reason I shouldn't—" Cathlin stopped abruptly. "Where are we going?"

"It *is* our wedding night. People are rather expecting us to leave," Dominic said gently.

"*Can't* leave with all these guests still here." Again she gestured broadly.

Dominic eased a priceless Sèvres figurine out of her striking range. "Rude, is it?"

"Absitively." She blinked, then cleared her throat. "Rude, I mean. Couldn't possibly leave. Not yet."

"And just how long are we supposed to stay?" There was a glitter in Dominic's eye.

"Don't ask me. Never been married before." Cathlin eyed him uncertainly. "Have *you*?"

"Not that I recall," Dominic said dryly.

By now he had a secure grip on her arm and was guiding her through the room.

She sniffed.

"Try some of this lovely champagne," she advised Serita as they moved past. "It's doing wonders for me."

Serita frowned. "Cathlin, have you eaten today?"

Marston ghosted past. "Half a croissant for breakfast. Two strawberries for lunch," he murmured.

"Why does everyone keep talking about food? Where's the champagne, that's what *I* want to know." Cathlin took a step, frowned, then put a hand on Marston's arm for support. "Could you find me another glass of that divine Dom Ruinart?"

"Er, the champagne, my lady?" The butler looked

at Dominic, who gave a tiny shake of his head. "Alas, my lady, I fear it is—all gone. Yes, it was a great hit. A very good suggestion of yours to serve it. May I compliment you on your taste?"

"Don't know why. It was *your* idea, though you were amazingly clever about making me *think* it was mine." Cathlin peered at him. "Are all butlers like you? If so, I can't imagine how anyone in England manages without you."

Marston's cheeks went bright pink. He murmured something incomprehensible and strode off, glasses rattling audibly on his silver tray.

"Come on," Dominic muttered. "Marston has something he wants us to see in the kitchen."

"But why did he leave? Did I say something wrong?"

"I expect he's not used to compliments from beautiful women," Dominic said smoothly. "Meanwhile, no more champagne for you."

"I'll have whatever I want. Don't think this ridiculous ceremony entitles you to order me around."

"The wedding doesn't, but my job here does." Dominic's voice was grim. "Until this is over I need you one hundred percent sober."

They were still arguing when they made their way back into the kitchens, where rows of copper pots gleamed from hooks above a pristine white marble counter.

"Marston's domain, I take it."

Dominic nodded. "He won't thank us for disturbing anything. I warn you, he's a true dictator in his realm."

At that moment the butler appeared, his face impassive. "I believe you informed me I should beware of anything unusual, my lord. Boxes, bags, packages and things of that sort. If you'd care to come this way, there's one particular item that's had me more than a little curious." He pulled open the door to a massive sixteenth century French armoire at the end of the kitchen and lifted out a cardboard box. "I found this on the counter just before the wedding ceremony today. I was curious because there were no deliveries expected."

Dominic's eyes narrowed. "What did the card say?"

"That's just it, my lord. There wasn't any card."

"You were right to alert me, Marston."

The butler started to open the box, but Dominic caught his hand. "Don't."

"But why—"

"Not yet." Dominic reached into his pocket and pulled out a metal box which he ran carefully around the outsides of the box, watching the dial.

"A possible electronic triggering device?"

"It never hurts to be prepared," Dominic said grimly. When his search revealed nothing, he pocketed the electronic sensor and pried open the top flap. Inside was a mass of folded white tissue paper. Dominic frowned. "You two had better move back."

Then he began to unroll the white tissue, every motion slow and controlled.

"You're wrong, you know. It's probably something totally ordinary like a cake." Cathlin smiled crookedly. "Or a bottle of merciless zinfandel."

Dominic frowned, remembering other seemingly innocent packages that had escaped detection only to blow up in their recipients' faces twenty minutes after their arrival. He happened to know that one small briefcase could hold enough *plastique* to blow up the whole abbey. "I'm not taking any chances."

Layer by layer the tissue parted. He felt sweat beading his forehead as he ran through the various devices that could be used to trigger a detonation from a remote location. None of them took up much space or weight.

The last layer of tissue slid free.

And then Dominic stood, staring speechless at the bottom of the box as a wave of heat climbed to his face.

"Dominic, what is it?" Cathlin moved closer, trying to see into the box.

"Nothing important." He shoved the box out of reach. "Just forget it."

But Marston outmaneuvered him, sliding past Dominic and lifting out the box's contents, his expression deadpan. "Excessively dangerous, my lord. Most lethal indeed."

From Marston's fingers dangled a nearly transparent froth of black lace and satin ribbons. It was the sort of nightwear bought by sinfully elegant women in sinfully expensive Parisian boutiques. Marston's eyebrow rose as he lifted another item from the box, this one a single piece of black nylon meant to cover the male anatomy—but just barely. "An anonymous wedding gift, my lord?"

Cathlin pulled the smaller garment from Marston and tugged it between her fingers, frowning at its size. "But how would you, that is, how could this *possibly—*"

"Never mind," Dominic growled, snatching away the two items and tossing them back into the box. He glared at Marston. "And if I ever hear one word said about this, Marston. One single, bloody word ..."

The butler looked affronted by the mere suggestion that he would ever breach a confidence.

"Come on, Cathlin," Dominic said harshly. "Let's say good-bye to the guests. Then there are some security arrangements for the wine that I want to discuss with you."

"But what about these lovely gifts?" There was a wicked gleam in Cathlin's eyes. "I adore black, and something tells me you'll look positively unforgettable in—whatever that bit of nylon is called."

Dominic muttered something sharp and unrepeatable. "*Now*, damn it."

As Marston watched the pair storm out, a smile crept over his lips. "Yes, altogether a most satisfactory day." Marston was still smiling a few moments later when Nicholas and his wife strode into the kitchen.

"Mission accomplished?"

"Quite satisfactorily, I would say, your lordship."

"Wonderful." A smile softened the viscount's angular features.

"Nicholas, you didn't! What a beastly thing to do to them."

"I am afraid, your ladyship, that he did." Marston smiled broadly at the viscountess. "It was most interesting to watch a grown man blush, by the way."

Nicholas gave a bark of laughter, while his wife managed to look disapproving. "You two are impossible, you know. Just like two children."

"Yes, I expect so," the viscount said happily. "Perhaps this will make up for what Dominic did to me the last time we were in Bangkok."

His wife's eyes widened. "What is that supposed to mean, Nicholas Draycott?"

"I couldn't possibly repeat it," her husband said coolly. "It would be a violation of A-level state secrets."

"I'll violate a great deal more than state secrets if you don't tell me all about it this minute."

"I suppose I might be persuaded to talk," Nicholas murmured. "Under great duress, of course. Seduced by the wiles and intrigues of a trained enemy agent." Heat filled his eyes as he looked down into his wife's smiling face.

Kacey inched closer. She slid up onto tiptoes and whispered something in Nicholas's ear. The viscount looked skyward and shook his head. "Some torture is definitely beyond a man's capacity for resisting." He took his wife's arm and guided her toward the corridor. "Very well, Mata Hari, it all began some time ago ..."

"Is Michael Burke in this story?" his wife asked eagerly.

"As it happens, he was there too."

Kacey clapped her hands in glee. "Perfect. I want every single detail. And I am prepared to pay well, of course," she added wickedly.

Nicholas slanted a pleading look skyward. "Definitely more torture than any red-blooded man could bear. Maybe we'll have to leave for London sooner than I planned," he murmured, as his wife pulled him out of the room.

Twenty ~

Darkness gathered in the valleys and slipped over the silent hills. Somewhere in the night an owl cried, long and shrill.

"I'll rest easier now that there's a backup generator in place." Dominic and Nicholas stared at the dark hills. Dominic's old associate from London had worked through the day, and the system was now complete. "At least we won't be having any more unexpected visitors."

Nicholas studied his friend. "You're sure you want me to leave, Dominic? I could change my plans, if you think—"

"No, I'll handle things here. Now that the power is guaranteed, we'll be fine. Harcliffe has promised to send some more men down in the morning, along with whatever equipment I need. So shove off, Nicky. Take your wife and daughter off to London, as planned, and stop fretting."

The viscount sighed. "Very well. I just hope you know what you're doing."

"I do."

"But what about—"

"Good-bye, Nicholas." This time it was a flat order.

* * *

"What an extraordinary wedding."

All the other guests had left, and now Cathlin and Serita stood in the rose-filled courtyard before the gatehouse. Cathlin watched a swan part the sleek waters of the moat. "Too bad it wasn't real," she muttered.

"It could be, you know. That's up to you and Dominic. There's something else you should know. La Trouvaille is his."

Cathlin's eyes widened. "I don't believe it. What about all the stories?"

"Just a smoke screen. He wants total privacy and no interference until he's convinced the wine is as good as he can make it."

"But it's wonderful!"

"Try telling Dominic that. My guess is he's still feeling shaky about whether he can pull off such a huge change in his life." Serita frowned. "He's a good man, Cathlin. Not at all like the image he projects. That was all part of his work, to allow him to mingle among high-profile celebrities and Royals, with no one the wiser. Underneath the flash, he's very kind—and very careful."

Cathlin sniffed. "He would be. He likes to be in control of every detail. I suppose that's what makes him such a good bodyguard."

"*Made* him," her friend corrected. "He's out of that life for good, from all I hear. It took this wretched will to force him out of retirement."

Cathlin frowned. "There's something else, isn't there, Serita? Something you haven't told me."

"Dominic carries around a lot of ghosts, Cathlin. On his last job in Royal Protection duty I understand that the car he was in came under attack. When the bullets started flying, he did what he was trained to do—shoot first and ask questions later."

Cathlin swallowed. "And?"

"I don't know the details. They're classified. But I

know people died that day and ... Dominic considered himself responsible. He left the profession he was very good at."

Cathlin closed her eyes and shivered.

"He turned in his resignation after that. I understand that Harcliffe has come after him again and again—he's never gone back."

"Why won't they leave him alone?" Cathlin asked bitterly.

"That's James Harcliffe as much as government policy, I expect. I have heard that once Harcliffe has his claws in someone, he never pulls them out. It's a matter of principle with him." A shadow fell across the weathered flagstones. "But I expect I'd better be going. Just you remember what I told you, Cathlin."

"I will."

Dominic was framed in the broad oak doorway, his face cast in shadow. He looked at Cathlin for long moments. "You'd better come in now. The alarms are all triggered."

Cathlin nodded. But still she did not move.

Are you carrying around the memories? she wanted to ask. You gave up your gun but did you give up everything that goes along with it?

But Cathlin said nothing. She wanted nothing more to do with the shadow world that had stolen her father, because it had brought her far too much pain already. And as Dominic stood unmoving, his face hidden by the shadows of the cloud-veiled moon, Cathlin decided he would hardly be likely to entrust her with any confidences.

She turned away. "I'm going down to have a last look at the wine."

"Fine."

Standing in the courtyard with his hand on weathered stone ten centuries old and the wind in his face rich with the scent of a thousand roses, Dominic wished he was someone different, someone without ghosts and a past, someone who could be anything it took to make Cathlin O'Neill smile and laugh and feel whole again.

Someone who wasn't plagued by memories.

But there was a job to be done and Dominic meant to see it through. Until it was completed, there was no time for dreams or carelessness or emotion—not if he hoped to protect Cathlin's life.

He scowled down at a section of flagstone, nudging it with his toe. A section of rope lay half-hidden in the shadow of a stone. Small, cleanly sliced at both ends, it was twisted into a rough loop handle.

Dominic picked the rope up and turned it idly. The loop was like those used by French farm workers to carry cases of wine.

Frowning, he turned the rope to and fro in the moonlight. Then he saw the dark blotch of blood near one end.

Blood from their recent intruder?

Cursing, Dominic turned and ran for the cellars.

"Cathlin?"

She wasn't in the cellar. She wasn't in the foyer. She wasn't in Nicholas's study. Fighting down his fear, Dominic hammered up the stairs to her room.

No sign of her.

A wild instinct brought him around with a start. "Cathlin, answer me!"

He raced along the hall to the kitchen and pounded down the stairs. She was standing before the broad rear windows, watching moonlight spill over a bank of white lilacs. There was a box on the table beside her and a glass in her hand.

Dominic knocked the elegant crystal goblet from her lips just as she was about to drink.

"Are you *crazy*?" Cathlin gaped down at the shattered glass.

"Did you drink any?"

Cathlin just stared at him.

"Did you *drink* any, damn it?"

She shook her head. "What's wrong with you? That was exceptionally old and rare—"

"Poison, unless I miss my guess." Dominic's mouth set in an angry line.

"Poison? I don't believe it."

"It's my job to be right, Irish. To spot things that are wrong, even when they look entirely unimportant. And it's always in the little things." Grimly, he shoved open the wooden case and studied the bottles inside. "Where was it from?"

"The card was from the Wine Department at Harrods."

"Was it addressed to you by name?"

Cathlin nodded. "The gift of an old colleague of mine who works there now."

"You're absolutely sure of that?"

"I know his stationery, if that's what you mean. We've worked together several times in the past. Dominic, this is ridiculous. You can't really believe that a perfectly respectable wine expert from Harrods would try to poison me."

"Someone tried to drive us off the road two days ago, remember? Nothing is impossible, O'Neill. You'd better remember that." He lifted the cork and studied it carefully. "No cracks or needle marks." He sniffed the rim. "But there's a slight excess of acidity that shouldn't be there, even in a markedly dry vintage like this. A few minutes longer and the aroma of any contaminants will have entirely dispersed."

Cathlin frowned. "For an amateur, you know an awful lot about wine." *But then he wasn't really an amateur, was he?*

"Maybe." Dominic shrugged as he wrapped the cork in cellophane. "Meanwhile, this goes up to London for testing."

"Who, Dominic? Who would want to poison me?"

"Just about anyone. You're the heart of this whole business, Cathlin. Without you, that wine doesn't get certified and it loses its importance as auction material—or as the political football it might soon become. To bring in another expert with your credentials would take a fair amount of time, and by then, the wine would probably be gone."

"Dear God." Cathlin caught a sharp breath. "Was it . . . someone here today? Someone at the wedding?"

Dominic wasn't about to share his worries with Cathlin, not when her face was sheet white and her fingers were trembling where she'd locked them at her waist. "I doubt it. Direct involvement like that is far too dangerous. Whoever did this was probably careful to put a dozen steps between this wine and himself."

He ached to run his hands through that vibrant black hair, to pull her against his chest and hold her until he felt the tension slide away.

But he didn't trust himself to do either. He had already gotten far more emotionally involved than was safe for either of them. "There's no sense brooding, Irish. Tomorrow we'll know more." Jade eyes burning, he took in Cathlin's pallor and her faint edge of fear. "Steady Irish." His hand cupped her chin.

"Then someone tried—tried to poison me. It's true." She caught a ragged breath. "I'm frightened, Dominic. And I hate being frightened almost as much as I hate owing people—and I owe you for saving my life yet again." She caught a tight breath. "Was it the same men who were in the car near Seacliffe?"

Dominic thought of lying, but gave up. She'd see through a lie anyway. "I can't be sure. Not until James Harcliffe gets back to me with some answers. Now it's time you were in bed."

"What about you?"

"Not yet." His face was grim. "I've still got a few things to clear up down here."

"By that you mean calls you don't want me to hear."

He didn't deny it. "Get some rest, Irish. Something tells me you're going to need it tomorrow."

Yes, it had been one hell of a wedding day, Dominic decided grimly.

Sitting in the abbey's dark kitchens, Dominic made three calls. Each was to an old friend, each a man whose life he had saved over the years during his career as a bodyguard. And each man was delighted to repay an old debt by coming to the abbey and helping Dominic keep the vast grounds secure, no questions asked.

But when he was done, Dominic didn't go upstairs. Instead he pulled out the folders Harcliffe had given him, folders that laid bare the inside of Cathlin O'Neill's young mind, as recorded just after her mother's death.

The reports were chilling, and made even more chilling by the cold, precise, and utterly impersonal language they used.

. . . *deep trauma . . . unpredictable formation . . . uncertain prognosis . . .*

Dominic read through page after page of clinical reports that recorded everything, but explained absolutely nothing.

The conclusion? Cathlin O'Neill's memory of that night was clean, swept bare by a trauma that a ten-year-old mind was beyond enduring. The prognosis, couched in five pages of extremely technical language, was that any answers the police hoped for would have to be gotten elsewhere. The girl would never remember what had happened that day at Draycott Abbey.

Except in one unlikely condition.

Dominic sat forward, frowning as he read the sentence over and over again. One condition might trigger Cathlin's memory, and that was if she experienced another trauma of equal and similar severity.

Dominic leaned back and let his breath out slowly. Was that the purpose of these threats to Cathlin? Had someone learned of her past and hoped to trigger those lost memories? Severance, perhaps, as a perverted form of revenge? Or had it been one of the smug, tanned faces who had smiled at Cathlin in London at the charity auction, then gone home to arrange for her murder?

Too many bloody questions.

Grimly, Dominic checked the entrances once more and then the alarms, though he knew they were all in perfect order. After that he made his way upstairs, drawn inexorably to a room with red roses, where moonlight played over the polished floor.

She was sleeping, her hands flung out, her hair a dark veil against the white pillow. He moved closer, feeling faintly guilty, yet unable to take his eyes away. She twisted as he watched, shoved at the sheet, tugged at the pillow.

Staring down, he heard Cathlin's soft breathing and the wind in the branches outside the window.

Memories, again. How strange that he should have too many memories and she too few. And Dominic wondered what she was seeing in those restless dreams.

Silence. Panic that ran through the darkness on sharp little feet. Her heart, pounding like knives in her chest.

The little girl sat up, fingers clenched on the strange sheets in the strange bed in the strange, beautiful old house.

No one there. No one but shadows.

She pushed out of her bed and ran to the door, with the

wind from an opened window blowing her hair like cobweb strands across her eyes.

Fingers tight, she ran past the hard-faced portraits, past the tapestries her mother had come to study, past all the pretty rooms with all their pretty things.

At the great oak door she stopped.

It lay open, open to darkness, open to shadows and the murmur of the moat.

She ran into the night, calling for her mother, calling wildly. And then she saw.

A dark shadow was spread against the lawns. Beneath the folds of her favorite amber plaid lay her mother's body. Unmoving. Arms twisted, legs bent.

All wrong. Wrong, wrong, wrong . . .

And then ten-year-old Cathlin O'Neill began to scream.

Afterward, all she could remember was the blood.

The window was open again, curtains drifting. Just as before, her hair played over her face, faint as cobwebs. She ran out of her room, drawn to the faint glow of light, her eyes wide, full of shadows.

"Dominic?"

No answer. Dimly she heard the hammer of water. She shoved open the bathroom door. "D-Dominic."

The water stilled. "Damn it, Cathlin, what are you—" His anger died as he saw her face, her rigid stance. "Hold on, Irish." His eyes never left her face as he tugged a towel around his lean body and strode through the drifting steam. "I'm here, love. What's happened?"

She moved against him, oblivious to the beads of water that ran against her chin and seeped through her gown. "A dream. Just another stupid, silly dream." She caught a ragged breath, hearing her heart pound.

Hearing his heart pound.

Feeling his muscles, tight and damp beneath her cheek.

Wanting him. Oh, God, wanting him more than she'd ever wanted anything.

But there was something wrong. Ever since she'd met this man, he'd drawn upon the shadowed part of her mind, pulling images out of the vacuum of her past. And every day she spent in his company the pull grew worse, until Cathlin knew one day she'd shatter.

"It's okay, Irish. You're safe now."

"Am I?" Cathlin gave a shaky laugh, her eyes locked on the drifting mist, on a blur of blood she could never quite forget—even when she remembered nothing else. "And if I'm safe, it's only because you're *not*. And, I—I don't think I could stand it if any more blood were spilled here. Do you understand? It's gone too deep."

Dominic's fingers slid into her hair, cradling her head. "Does this mean you've remembered something?"

Cathlin shook her head. "Only the old dream. The blood, just like always. And then—nothing. But now it's worse, because the memories are only inches away. Waiting. Hanging."

Callused fingers smoothed over her lips. "Take it easy. They'll just keep coming, Cathlin. That's part of remembering."

"I thought I wanted this, but I didn't expect it to hurt so much. I didn't expect to feel like I was a child again."

"Shhh." He eased his arms around her waist, his long damp body warm against hers.

Cathlin took a ragged breath. Her head rose. "Could I make you forget if I tried, Dominic? Could I make us be two strangers, just for one night?"

A muscle beat at his temple. "You don't know what you're saying, O'Neill. It's late, and you're exhausted."

"I know, Dominic. I know exactly what I'm asking. So do you."

The air shimmered between them, heavy, slow, electric.

As if compelled, his hands slid lower, trapping the pulse that throbbed at her neck. "The timing's wrong. Damn it, all wrong."

"I don't care."

Slowly, slowly his head bent over hers.

And she leaned into him, leaned into the unbowing strength of his body, into the mystery of his arms and the unbearable pleasure he was making her feel.

All the denials crumbled. All the protests fled.

All that was left was heat and hunger and a hundred kinds of needing. Lips, light and hot, feathering her skin. Her heart racing.

"Dominic, I can't—breathe. It's not supposed to—to feel like this."

"Like what?"

Trembling, her fingers inched into his hair. "Like . . . forever."

"Who said?"

She made a low uncertain sound. Her hands slid deeper into his hair. Dimly, she realized she was pulling him closer.

And Cathlin didn't care. She wanted him close. She wanted their bodies meshed, with only sweat and skin between them.

She wanted *him*.

With all his demons and his fears. With all his flash and his careful brand of honor hidden beneath.

Warrior's honor. Warrior's heart.

She raised her hand, smoothing the crease at his brow. She saw the face of a man who'd looked into his heart and found his strengths and weaknesses. Each cold memory had left another line etched on that face. But the victories were there too, each set into the proud, sensual flare of his mouth.

And her skin was aflame as he caught her mouth with his. Lips hard, he slid across her, shaped her to his passion.

No fear. No room for fear. Too much need.

He made a low, rough sound. A sound of pain that left her utterly possessed.

"Please, hurry. Don't let me think. Don't let the dreams get through. Just once. Just tonight."

Silent like the warrior he was, he moved behind her. Hands across her waist, he pulled her against him. "Sorry, Irish," he whispered huskily. "Tonight hurrying's the last thing on my mind." He found the hungry little hollow behind her ear and planted slow kisses down to the bend of her shoulder. There he nudged aside the soft gown.

"Can't you . . . go a little faster?"

His low chuckle drifted over her naked skin. "Not a chance. Hell, Irish, I've got whole continents to discover." His voice darkened. "And paradise to claim."

"Dominic, something else. Serita told me."

Silence.

"About your last job in Royal Protection. She also told me about La Trouvaille."

More silence.

"What I'm trying to say is I'm sorry. You're doing wonderful things over there, and I'm just making all this harder for you." Her hands tightened. "I'm sorry you had to come back to a world you hated."

More silence. Thicker now.

"Dominic?"

A raspy breath. "Not now, golden eyes. Only this now." He turned her face and his tongue swept hers. "Only the heat to stop the nightmares." Lace shifted. Linen rose.

Then only her heat, melted against his. Only her soft, muffled breath as he carried her to her room and laid her on the chintz settee beside the window. Moonlight pooled against her skin below curtains that drifted like ghostly fingers. The air carried the perfume of a thousand roses mixed with the warmth of lilacs.

He was confident in this as in all else, his hands sure in their possession. Cathlin watched his face, one side silver with moonlight and the other cast into darkness. She wanted then to be the one who pulled him from those shadowed memories. She wanted to be the one who made the laughter brighten his eyes and smiles crinkle his hard mouth.

She wanted. Oh, how she wanted. But he was moving too fast, spinning his dark enchantment over a body that was fast turning into a stranger's. Wanting struck her and a hot, sweet melting.

"Dominic, I—"

"Not now, Irish. I'm . . . busy." He bent, his mouth to her throat, to her collarbone, to the high, sweet arch of her breast.

"Dominic, why—"

"Do you always talk this much?"

Only when I'm frightened. Only when my heart is about to slam right out of my chest. Because it feels like I've wanted you this way forever and nothing has ever felt more natural than your skin touching mine.

"Sometimes," she lied, wondering why his scent was somehow familiar. Why his eyes shone with a brilliance Cathlin seemed to have known somewhere before.

Or sometime before.

The sheer impossibility of it left her chilled for a moment. What was happening to them here in this lovely, dangerous place with too many secrets and too many shadows?

Then Dominic's mouth coaxed the warm skin at her shoulder and Cathlin forgot about secrets and shadows.

The only mystery she cared about was the mystery

of skin brushing naked skin, of fingers twining and thighs caught in silken discovery.

Dominic seemed to have the same idea. His palm opened over her waist, drawing her back against him.

And he felt like forever. Like all the questions she'd ever had, answered in one hot, jerky breath.

With a strangled sound she raised her hands to the hard planes of his face. Her linen gown parted with a low hiss. Cathlin went utterly still, breath jammed in her throat as Dominic feathered tiny kisses over the high, full swell of her breast.

Desire slammed through her, finely edged, shining like a blade. Dominic nudged aside lace and linen, easing his way down to one swollen crest.

Champagne bubbles raced up her spine. "I don't think—this is anywhere in the rule book, Officer Montserrat."

"To hell with the rule book," her bodyguard said hoarsely. "Damn it, you taste fine." Slowly he kissed his way up the curve of her throat. "Let me have all of you, Cathlin. Let me have your taste in my mouth. I want you to be part of me."

Heat again. Delicious and amazing. Utterly tormenting. How could she possibly resist? "Dominic, I've never—that is, it's never felt so—"

Like forever. Like coming home.

Like we've done this a hundred times before. "Good," she finished lamely.

"No, perfect," he growled.

"But you, haven't you ever felt—"

"No." He frowned, studying the perfect crimson thrust of her, rising hungry to his lips. "Not like this." His voice fell. "Not the way it feels with you. But I'm going to feel it now." His breath caught. "With you, Cathlin."

The old house slept, silence in the corridors, silence

in the rose-filled courtyard. Only two shadows moved in the moonlight.

The wind played over her through the opened window, sweet and light as Dominic's fingers. Sweet as the dreams that pressed, full of heated memories.

Of yesterday and a hundred other yesterdays.

Cathlin caught a ragged breath as he kissed the hollows of her spine, then turned her slowly in his arms.

"Cathlin. Sweet God, you're so . . ."

So perfect for him, perfect against him as he found the curve of her and then her hidden heat. Pleasure welled through her heart, coursed through her veins, and she unfolded to him like a flower.

Forever.

That's what he gave her in his touch, in his hot, dark words poured against her yearning skin.

And forever was the place she struggled to find, anchored in his arms. But fighting wouldn't take her there, not when the memories followed, chill and leaden and all the more frightening because they had no form and no face.

Around her the curtains rose and fell, silent ghosts that mocked her for her fear.

Was he Gabriel, their spirits somehow linked, carried through time by laws older than simple human understanding? And was she the woman Gabriel had kissed, there in a candlelit drawing room on a smoky London night two centuries before?

Images lapped at the edges of Cathlin's mind, images of another warrior and another pair of strong, callused fingers that had bared her body to racing pleasure.

Forever.

"I can't. Dominic, please, this isn't—"

"You *can*, Irish. Because my love will take you there." She felt the silken slide of his fingers, firing her heat, wooing her silently until she arched in restless abandon. "Now, Cathlin. While the moonlight plays around you. Let me take you beyond dawns and darkness. Through that door of shadows you never dared to open."

A low groan. Maybe his, maybe hers, or maybe it belonged to them both. She tightened around him, head flung back, mind and spirit shimmering in a wave of breathless pleasure.

But it didn't end. He wouldn't let the pleasure end. Some instinct told him just how to move, where to skim until the light rocked her again and the last shadow fled, banished by his love, banished by his care and joy. Her breath swelled in a choked cry of discovery. Of love.

Forever.

No more shadows. Not in the still, silent house where the curtains drifted. Not in the slanting bar of moonlight, which crept across the floor and filled the room with beauty.

Not even in Dominic's eyes, which followed every inch of her wild journey with an urgency that signaled his own discoveries.

As the roses danced, as swans coursed the moat, Cathlin gave herself up to his wild pleasure, to his knowing touch and his dark, whispered praise, knowing that somehow she had loved this man forever, that somewhere she had vowed to find him and heal him and give him back his joy—even if it took uprooting his life and tearing his calm composure into tiny little shreds to do it.

Today.

Tomorrow.

And a thousand dawns to come.

"Dominic?"

He pulled her against his chest.

"Why—"

"Hush."

"But you—"

A husky laugh. A lopsided smile that shattered her heart in the quiet moonlight. "Sleep, Irish. There'll be time. A century of nights like this to come, I promise."

"But you didn't—"

He knew one way to silence her, and he used it, pressing his lips to hers, his body hard, his fingers even surer now. And when her pleasure came again, she cried his name in wonder.

She slept at last, curled against his chest. Their bodies were blocked by only a thin towel—and an ironclad code of honor that kept Dominic Montserrat motionless even when his mind screamed for him to take her, pounding and hard, until they both discovered the taste of forever.

But he didn't.

Though it was truly torture, he held her gently, unmoving.

Because at that instant it was the very best way this warrior knew to protect her when the shadows came back.

And as the moon slid toward the horizon, it wasn't Cathlin who twisted in dark dreams.

It was a man with eyes like jade and smoke.

A warrior with too many memories to fit inside one lifetime.

Twenty-one ~

*T*he sky was still dark when a heavy coach moved out of the mews behind Adrian Draycott's London town house. Slowly it lumbered around the corner and came to a halt at the front of the house. Black lacquer doors bright with the Draycott crest were thrown open and a woman, heavily veiled, came down the stairs, leaning on her companion's arm.

"To the East India docks," the liveried footman called out crisply. "And make it sharp."

Across the street, hidden by a mass of ugly wrought-iron railing, a man in a dusty greatcoat smiled grimly. So they were making for the docks, were they?

Henry Devere would pay him well to see that they never completed their journey.

For long moments Gabriel Montserrat stood in the darkness, listening for sounds of pursuit. Only when he was satisfied that he was alone did he motion into the shadows behind him.

Geneva Russell, swathed in a hooded gray cloak, moved into the cobblestone lane, assisted by the tall American from Virginia.

"We'll leave you now," Lord Ashton said. "I wish I could see Devere's face when he realizes his prey in the

279

Draycott coach is an inebriated butler and a woman who is far from a lady."

"You're going to have to forgo that pleasure, Gabriel." Adrian motioned into the mews and a swift traveling chaise, without identifying crest or insignia, pulled out of the shadows. He helped Geneva up the stairs.

She pressed his hand for a moment. "How can I possibly thank you for your help? You have been kindness itself, Lord Draycott. You, also, Mr. Jefferson. But do not underestimate Henry Devere. He is more than a little mad and has never been bested in any goal."

The American patted her hand. "We are more than equipped to defend ourselves against a bounder like that, my dear. Now you had better go, for these spirited grays do not care to be kept standing." He raised his hand in farewell. "Godspeed," he whispered as the carriage rumbled into the night.

Gabriel stared down at the woman across from him, moonlight silver on her cheeks. She sat silently, her body cast into shadow.

Outside, the crowded thoroughfares gave way to quiet hamlets and then to long, rolling hills. Beyond the city the coach picked up its pace, jolting over the pitted road. At a particularly large rut, Geneva was tossed forward and Gabriel saw her face illuminated for a moment in the moonlight.

Her cheeks were pale. Her mouth was set in a thin line. "He will come after me, I know it. He is ruthless and has powerful friends. I have brought my own ill fortune down upon all of you."

"Why, Geneva? Why did you betray me?"

"For my sister. As I fear I might betray you again, for every thought brings her face before me."

"I will bring her to England, Geneva. I make you this promise."

Gabriel gathered her against his chest. "And I will see

*you to safety before I go, in a place where Devere can do
you no more harm.''*

"You don't understand. He is not sane." Geneva caught
a jerky breath. Her face was a blur of light against the
darkness.

A lock of her hair trailed over his hand, and he could
feel her hips pressed against his hard thighs. With every
jolt of the carriage her breast thrust against his chest.

Desire slammed through him. They were alone, far from
prying eyes. She had already offered him the pleasure of
her body in return for his assistance. His thighs tightened
at the thought of pulling away her lace fichu, of loosening
her stays until her creamy breasts sprang free and filled
his hungry fingers.

He caught a sharp breath. What kind of blackguard had
he become? She was innocent, completely in his care.
Nothing could take place between them.

"Why do you frown?"

"Because it is time you rested." He pulled her head
against his shoulder. *"Don't argue,"* he growled as he felt
her body tense in protest. *"You didn't win before and you
won't win now."*

Slowly her hand relaxed its grip on the folds of her
cloak and Gabriel heard her sigh. From the softening of
her shoulders he knew that she had fallen asleep. But it
was not that which left him reeling, shaken to his very
core.

It was the way she curled close to him in her sleep,
utterly trusting, then ran her hand along his chest and
tucked it gently in the curve of his shoulder.

Overhead the sky was full of stars. They were in open
country now, level fields stretching out into silent forests.
Gabriel estimated they had three hours of traveling before
they reached Draycott Abbey. Careful not to awaken the
woman asleep in his arms, he sat forward to get a better
view of the countryside and the road behind them.

No vehicle was to be seen. The road was empty and they were safe.

For now, at least.

He looked down at Geneva's face and frowned. Soon Devere would discover Templeton's masquerade and send his men in search of any other carriages which had left the mews.

If only they could make Draycott Abbey in time.

Dominic was sweating. His fingers clutched at dreams as he saw another place of moonlight and plunging horses and a shutter crashing somewhere in the night.

He tried to pull free, to gain a footing in the dark chaos of his dreams.

No good. Too many noises. Too many memories. Too many broken promises. And a danger that tracked him through time, even in his dreams. . . .

They didn't make it to Draycott Abbey.

They didn't even make it to Tunbridge Wells.

A trio of riders clattered into the road behind them.

"What is it?" Geneva blinked and sat up, awakened by the sound of racing hoofbeats.

"Nothing."

"It's him, isn't it? He's found us." The color bled from her face.

"No one has found us yet, and no one will." Grimly Gabriel seized her arm and uttered a sharp command to the coachman.

The wind was rising and the smell of rain hung heavy in the air. Gabriel knew that the river lay less than half a mile away. He signaled to the coachman, who put them down where they were hidden by a bend in the road. When the coach lumbered forward, the riders followed, giving Gabriel and Geneva precious time to escape.

But in the face of a rising wind, every yard was a

struggle for Geneva, even though Gabriel knew she was fighting to conceal it. "Let me carry you."

"I'll be fine." Her face was white and the rising wind tossed gravel and twigs in her face. "Is it much . . . farther?"

"Just beyond that line of trees."

Overhead a bolt of lightning cracked through the sky. A wall of wind tore at their clothes. Without a word, Gabriel caught Geneva up in his arms and carried her over the rocky slope to the river.

A quarter of an hour later the storm had raged past. In its wake a veil of fog crept over the river. Here and there a branch emerged from the drifting mist, black skeletons clutching at nothing. The dark figures broke, shouting, from the mist.

Gabriel pressed his pistol into Geneva's fingers. "Take this and use it. I'll try to lead them off into the mist." He shoved forward and then set off in a sharp angle, his footsteps purposely noisy as a lure to Devere.

Geneva watched in horror as his plan succeeded too well, and moments later he was facedown in the mud with Devere's pistol at his back.

"It is really a very simple question, Lord Ashton. I fail to understand why you refuse to answer it. Are you the man known as the Rook?"

Fog swelled up around the men standing at the edge of the river. Gabriel lay facedown, his hands bound tight at his back. A jagged bruise mottled his forehead and the corner of his cheek. "Rook? Never heard the name."

Henry Devere smiled coldly. "I fear your bravado is wasted on me." He made a sharp gesture with his hands. "Hold him down."

One minute passed. Then half again.

"Bring him up," Devere snapped. When Gabriel was pulled back onto the sand, he coughed harshly and strained at his bonds. His only reward was a sharp kick in the ribs.

"Now then, Lord Ashton, shall we try again? I repeat, are you the man known as the Rook?"

"And I repeat, you maggot, that I have no acquaintance with anyone by that name."

Devere shook his head. "I shall find out, you know. Someone will remember a voice, the set of a face. And then I'll have you."

Gabriel coughed and watched blood stain the muddy bank in front of him. "She's free, Devere. And I'll kill you for laying a hand on her."

Devere gestured sharply and Gabriel was shoved back into the muddy water.

"This time rather longer I think." His eyes flat and hard, Devere stood at the edge of the river as fog lapped around his beautifully polished boots. "One minute," he announced icily, watching with interest as Gabriel's submerged body flashed and twisted. "Two minutes." When the big body ceased to move, Devere smiled grimly. "Haul him in."

This time their victim gave no response.

"Rouse him," Devere hissed.

After three sharp kicks to his back, Gabriel shuddered and began to cough.

"You are truly stubborn, Ashton. But not half as stubborn as I am. I have had to be since whatever success I hoped to attain had to be earned with the strength of my fists and the cunning of my mind in the mud of the Whitechapel slums. And that is why it is particularly fitting that I relieve my poor French victims of all the gold that nature in its ignorance gave them in excess. Now for the final time, on pain of death, admit that you are the man known as the Rook. Miss Russell may have escaped me, but you have not. And you were what I really wanted anyway."

Gabriel spat up a mouthful of bloody water and laughed coldly. "You should have kept her when you had her, Devere. She'll suffer no more of your torment, even if I have to buy her safety with my life."

"A touching sentiment, but I fear that that is exactly what you will do." Devere stood for a moment, veiled in fog, smoothing the priceless lace at his cuffs.

"Kill him," he ordered.

He wasn't going to make it this time, Gabriel thought as the two men shoved him beneath the water.

Strange red lights played before his eyes and his throat burned, but he kept himself from moving, knowing that surprise was his only chance at escape.

But what happened next took him by surprise. Even underneath the water he heard the muffled shouts. There was a sharp tug on the rope at his wrists, and then the rope went slack.

Gabriel knew it was now or never.

With the last of his energy he pushed off the bottom. Fog lay everywhere and he gasped for breath, trying to make sense of the chaos around him. A bullet hissed past and then he heard Devere curse.

Suddenly, slender fingers seized his wrist and pulled him into the water.

"Geneva?"

"I've found a rowboat downstream. Can you swim out to it?"

"I'll manage." Gabriel followed her into the water, amazed at her resourcefulness and quiet courage. He watched her skirts drift up against the dark waters. She'd come storming into his life, overturning all his peace, but now he couldn't imagine what life would be like without her.

"What happened to Devere?"

"I shot him," she said grimly. *"He was holding his arm when the others brought him his horse."*

Moments later they reached the rowboat and Geneva climbed in, her hair tumbling in a wild cloud down her back, her satin dress molded to every curve.

Gabriel swallowed, fighting a desperate urge to take her right there, rocking in the fog.

He told himself this was just the ache of a man who had gone too long without the comfort of a woman's body.

But he knew it was something far deeper.

"I'll tend to the oars," he said, his voice harsher than he intended.

The slap of the water was the only sound as they drifted through mist and darkness, following the bends of the river. Eventually, Gabriel knew, it would lead them toward the abbey.

When his shoulders finally began to ache with strain, he pulled beneath an overhanging tree. Beyond was an old mill that looked long deserted. "We'll rest here and push on later."

Geneva gathered her sodden skirts and stepped onto the muddy bank. As she did, the boat lurched and she tumbled backward. Gabriel caught her clumsily, dropping an oar to keep both of them from being tossed overboard.

Her young body covered his. He felt the thrust of her breasts through the wet silk of her gown. She looked at him, a dark emotion in her eyes, her hair gusting black and rich around her shoulders.

Gabriel felt himself falling, falling into an ocean without any bottom, his heart spread high and wide like the sails of the swift ships that had carried him so often to France.

He wished he were a hero then, the kind of man she thought that he was. But he was no hero. A hero would have turned her away, and he could not. There was too much sweetness in her face, too much yearning in her eyes. Her hair blew about his face and all Gabriel could think of was the sweet smell of lilacs that filled his mouth, his lungs, his whole being.

He knew then that he had to have her, that all his honor could not save her, because it had gone far beyond heated thighs and rasping breath.

Now it was a thing of rushing spirit, of deepest yearning dreams, the sort of hunger that could not be denied because it went past bone and muscle to the very soul.

"I'll hurt you, damn it. I'll take you, my love, again and again, until you forget where you start and I begin. Once there's a starting, there won't be an end, I warn you. Not today. Not tomorrow. Maybe not ever."

He had hoped to scare her away, but he might have known he could not succeed. Her hands whispered over his arrogant mouth. *"I pray so, my lord."*

"Fool." There was anger in his voice along with an infinite tenderness. *"You don't know anything about me."*

"Except what counts. That you are a hero and . . . I love you."

"I can give you nothing but pain, Geneva. Through my whole life, that's all I've done to those I love most."

Then her body blocked out the night, the river, the fog, and she kindled a joy he had thought long dead.

When she touched him, he was lost. Gabriel fought for sanity, for strength to deny her, but found neither. *"Geneva, are you sure?"* His voice was harsh as his fingers moved through her hair.

"Yes, now. There, in the mill beside this dark river." And if the words had not been clear enough, then the soft pressure of her body was.

"It's wrong. Wrong and I know it." His fingers tightened, locked deep in her hair.

"Maybe, my lord," she murmured, her hands achingly gentle on his face, *"it's your knowing that's wrong."*

The mill was full of dust, but Gabriel mounded clean straw and made a bed in the moonlight. When Geneva turned, her eyes were full of love.

Her fichu, gown, and stays slid free. Beneath she wore only a chemise of finest cambric, now damp from the river and nearly translucent.

Gabriel feasted on the sight of her, on the full, rich sweep of her soft shadows beneath the moon. His throat constricted. *"So fine. So bloody beautiful . . ."*

She smiled a little sadly. *"I am too tall for fashion and*

my mouth is too wide. I have no graces and I squint."
She spoke with utter candor.

Gabriel would have laughed, could he have summoned up a single sound. He would have bellowed with laughter, for she was all that he'd ever hungered for—all that any man could ever hunger for.

"None of the graces?" he managed.

"Not a single one," she said defiantly.

"And surely not a squint."

"Just so." She demonstrated.

He thought to himself that it made her look enchanting, lending a lovely intensity to her fine, regular features. But he did not tell her so. He could not speak with any safety.

"Now you'll not want me."

It was all beyond his taking in, standing in the moonlight and talking calmly, as if she wasn't half-naked, straw at her feet.

"Besides, I smell."

"Smell?"

"I carried a bottle of perfume in my gown. It was my mother's. The bottle broke in the river." She sniffed. *"I'm certain you must have smelled it."*

Lilacs. Oh, yes, he'd smelled them. Like her they were fresh and full and everything young. They were spring come to the dark earth and joy to a hardened heart. They would help him remember this moment forever.

"Come closer and let me see."

She moved through a bar of moonlight, all whisper and heat, her shoulder extended. *"Will this do?"* Her voice was husky.

Did it do any better, he would die of her!

Gabriel nodded gravely. Bending slightly, he inhaled while the tantalizing sweep of one breast, barely veiled beneath white cambric, lay inches from his fingers.

So close. So sweet.

He found lilacs and more—courage and honesty and

fierce loyalty. Lilacs would mean that to him from now on, Gabriel thought. "I can smell it now."

She nodded gravely. "You've wanted none of me, not from the start. And why should you? You're far too grand. You can have your pick of fine, grand women without a squint and with every sort of grace."

He swept her against him, his hands lost in her hair, his mouth raining hot kisses over her face.

Geneva gave a shaky laugh. "I am too tall."

"Which means I can see your face when I do this." He caught her lip gently between his teeth.

She swallowed, her hands at his shoulder. "But my mouth—"

"Is just perfect."

He filled himself with her, and his fingers were not quite steady as he slid her chemise from her shoulders, following the fine fabric with his mouth, kisses like a storm.

She sighed as he slid the cambric away and found the impudent coral thrust of her breast.

Lilac filled his senses. Geneva filled him, heart and soul. He'd take away her pain, and with it all her doubts.

"But you are dressed and I am not. Besides, I want to touch you too. If . . . that is allowed."

He laughed, could not help himself. "Most certainly it is allowed."

She frowned for a moment. "I've lost your stickpin. I had it to remind me of the night I betrayed you. It must have fallen."

He brushed her cheek. "I'll put a curse on whoever finds it."

"Do not jest, my lord." She sank onto the snug little bed of mounded straw. "Come here."

He did. Wondering.

She tugged away his cravat, shoved at his buttons, and freed his jacket, two buttons bursting in the process.

Gabriel knew a fierce urge to give her all her heart desired, to sweep down the very stars and give them to her on a platter of beaten gold.

But he had no gold nor stars. All he had was his touch and his joy in her.

"You—are beautiful," she said, her voice low with wonder. "I'm far too ordinary for you." Her fingers touched his muscled arms, brushed the fine hair across his chest.

"Geneva," he said warningly, heat climbing.

She traced the silver trail of an old scar, earned on his first foray to France. "You've been hurt too often," she said gravely. Her lips covered the skin, bringing a pleasure more fierce than any pain Gabriel had felt when the French cavalry saber had sliced through him.

Her tongue was magic, blinding as she came slowly upward. And then she met his mouth. Inexpert. Eager. Maddeningly fine.

Too soon. He had her body yet to taste.

But she pulled him down against her, suddenly demanding, cambric fallen aside and only burnished skin before him.

"Now," she whispered, her eyes grave. "Before I can remember, I pray you." Her thigh moved along his. "Unless you have changed your mind?"

He caught her, pulled her down atop him in a sprawl. "Never," he said grimly. He palmed her thigh and moved to higher glories. "Satin. Sweet." And wet, he saw, with sharp delight. *Not that she yet understood the significance of that.*

"But you—"

"Hush." Sliding to part her, pushing deeper. *Ignoring her startled breath, he remained intent on his goal.*

Which was her pleasure.

"Gabriel—"

No words. Nothing but the joy he could show her.

Nearly there, all clinging skin. All heat that welcomed.

"Gabriel." This time her voice came in a rush of awareness. Her skin flushed warmest pink.

"Yes, my stubborn love?"

"I feel—so strange. And I don't at all understand—"

"You will."

*He taught her then, his hard hands carefully gentle
against petals lush. She flowered in the heat of his care
and love and opened her glorious amber eyes, shock war-
ring with a final instant of fear.*

*But he swept her beyond both, into a dark storm of
feeling, in a place where all memories stopped and all
wounds were healed. He felt her arch against him, a single
word on her lips.*

And the word was his name.

*It coiled around his heart, held him speechless, made
him feel a thousand times young.*

And truly the man she loved.

There was no more fighting then, not for either of them.

With a soft moan Cathlin turned, shoving blindly
at her pillow.

River.

Night.

A man whose face was hard with regret.

She fought her soft pillow, seeing trails of white
fog, feeling the heat of a lover's hands and mouth
and skin, understanding all her years of distance and
regret and fear that came from a distant time when
she had found love, only to have it stolen from her.

And in that moment of aching awareness, with one
foot in dreams and the other in waking, she saw all
the rare, remarkable things she had never had a
chance to know as Cathlin O'Neill, but had never
quite forgotten as Geneva Russell.

*Gabriel was smiling when she opened her eyes, her body
poured over his in a moonlit glow of breast and thigh.*

"You—knew? You have felt this?"

"Of course I knew."

*She touched his chest, wondering. "It is—quite extra-
ordinary."*

"There is more."

Her head cocked. "Truly? It seems beyond imagining."
A hesitation. *"You could be persuaded to ... show me?"*

A dark smile. "Very likely. With the right inducement."

Her fingers moved along his chest and then lower. His eyes closed when she found him, fire a drumming in his blood.

"Persuaded like this?"

"Maybe faster than you like."

A soft laugh. Her hair a veil across his chest. Her kisses—heaven itself.

He caught her in her flight downward.

Her smile was a luscious invitation as she eased her legs around him, fitting herself to the awesome mark of his need.

He cursed. "Geneva—"

Deeper. Encasing him in satin. Taking him to a paradise beyond his dreams.

He tried to hold her, but she wriggled free. "There will be pain, so I have heard. Yet I think it will be well worth the sight of your face now, my lord," she whispered huskily.

Gabriel frowned, trying to be sane for a few moments longer. "It is true, there will be pain. I only wish—"

She stilled his lips and moved against him, frowning when she could move no more.

Gabriel twisted, knowing it would be best finished in one swift stroke. He studied the glory of her beneath him, hair spread wild, eyes ablaze, a questioning smile on the beautiful mouth she assured him was far too wide for beauty. "As little as I can make it, my love."

She nodded, grave. Indescribably beloved.

He moved, filled her, met the barrier and then thrust beyond. As he did, she swallowed, her eyes closed, her hands tensed. But even then she did not push him away or struggle against him, her body open to whatever he would offer her.

And that very openness was the greatest bravery Gabriel had ever known.

Bending, he claimed one nipple while his hands claimed a different bloom, sliding deeper and teasing her to maddening need.

She gasped and shoved hard against him.

He met her instantly, sliding deeper through honeyed skin where now no barrier stood. Only heat leaped up to meet him. Only blazing desire.

"Wrap your legs around me," he ordered hoarsely.

"Like this?"

"Good, sweet God!"

"No?" Immediately she tried to pull away.

"Yes. A thousand times yes, my beauty."

He showed her how right it was, how much he loved her, sliding deep and finding the still, hot core of her. Finding at the same time the still, hot core of himself.

There love lay coiled, a love he'd never thought to find.

She cried out, her back drawn tight like a bow, her nails to his chest. He smiled, with his last shred of sanity enjoying her soft, choked cry of delight, the hot sweet tremors that proclaimed her cresting pleasure.

Then Gabriel followed, cast up in the wave of night, swallowed and then made whole just as she had been reshaped in the hot, still crucible of love.

And as he fell, Gabriel swore he would never let her go again.

Sleepy minutes passed in moonlight and drifting shadow.

"You sleep, my dearest, like an army on the march."

A soft murmured sigh. "And what would you know of armies on the march, my lord?"

"Too bloody much."

"You've left me exhausted." A frown. "Is that quite usual?"

"Only for those who are very lucky." He gently combed a curl back from her forehead. "But I'm not offering a complaint, you understand, since all your marching was done over me."

A flush. An enchanting dimple. "I am quite beyond redeeming, I fear."

"I have no thought of redeeming you."

His hand found her breast. Instantly she was afire again, needy for this wondrous thing he'd made her feel.

There was a moment of sadness in her eyes, and something like regret. Then she smiled and inched closer. Her thigh rose, coaxing till it found a most enchanting hardness. "Perhaps I am not so exhausted as I thought."

Gabriel slid the length of her. "Are you quite certain?"

"Without a doubt."

"In that case . . ." He drove against her, filling her in one hard, perfect thrust, delight swirling through every muscle as she crested against him anew. "How very, very glad I am to hear it," he managed, just before he followed her down into a swirling ring of pleasure.

Lulled by the soft rush of the river and the muffling veil of the fog, they finally fell back against the straw. Outside the mill an owl cried over the river and little animals curled warm and safe in their dens.

Somewhere, far in the distance, a church bell chimed.

Twelve times and then no more.

Hands entwined, breaths soft, Gabriel and Geneva finally slept.

Henry Devere sat unmoving in the darkness, listening to a church bell chime.

He liked the darkness. He could think in the darkness, plan in the darkness.

And he planned now, careful and thorough, while he nursed the wounds delivered at Geneva's hand. For that she would pay dearly, as would her arrogant lover. The Rook was almost within his grasp, along with the thousand-guinea reward the French had posted for the Englishman's capture.

His eyes glinted, hollow and cold.

He would have the Rook. Then he would begin teaching Geneva Russell how very stupid she had been to think she could escape him.

Twenty-two ∼

"There were three calls from France, two equipment deliveries, and two calls from London, my lord. In addition Lord Draycott has already called twice."

A notepad in hand, Marston stood in a beam of early morning sunlight beside the desk Dominic had commandeered in Nicholas's study. "Oh, yes, the vicar also called. He wished to offer his felicitations to you and the countess. He said that if any difficulties should arise, you must feel free to call him."

Dominic laughed. "Can he secure a frayed electric wire, do you think?"

"I could not say, my lord. However, I have always believed that with the help of the Almighty, all things are possible." With that enigmatic utterance, the butler laid a pile of parcels on the desk and turned to leave.

"And . . . the countess?" Dominic swallowed. The word brought back too many heated memories to face easily in the daylight. Things were still too uncertain between them. At least she had slept deeply. He had seen to that before he left her at the first light of dawn.

And his body still pained him for that celibate departure.

"I believe she has not come down yet, my lord. Shall I give her a message?"

"No need, Marston. I'll be cooped up rewiring this bloody security system for several hours and then I have to inspect that backup generator. It's already acting up." He frowned. "If I didn't know better, I'd almost think there *was* a ghost here playing havoc."

Marston cleared his throat, then moved off, astounding in black broadcloth and neon purple running shoes.

After he left, Dominic sat staring at the files Harcliffe had left him the day before, thinking about the stresses Cathlin must be feeling and wondering if these waking dreams of hers were a sign that she was skating near the edge of her endurance.

The phone cut short his reveries.

It was Nicholas, his voice grim. "I'm sorry to add any more pressure, Dominic, but I've had bad news. Already the heads of three European countries have expressed profound interest in at least one of the bottles of your wine—as a 'token of British goodwill.' In addition, two American senators have made discreet contact through the American embassy in London, each claiming a bottle to present to the president. Jefferson happens to be one of the man's heroes, it seems."

Dominic was uninterested in legends, living or dead. "What you're saying is that things are going to get even rockier, is that it?"

"I'm afraid so. With this kind of interest the ante has just shot up in one enormous leap. Be careful, Dominic. Be certain that Cathlin is careful, too."

Dominic frowned. He decided not to mention Cathlin's sleepwalking and the poisoned wine. Until he had answers, there was no use discussing his suspicions. "Anything new with Kacey's search of the church records?"

"Nothing yet. I'll let you know if we find anything though."

Dominic looked down and sighed as the lights flickered. "I'd better run. Problems with that backup generator already. Are you sure this place isn't truly haunted?"

Silence.

"Nicholas? Are you there?"

"Tell Harcliffe to send another one down from London."

"Oh, he's promised to help, but you know how the man is. Something might arrive tomorrow or next year."

"Blast him! Is he supporting this project or opposing it?"

"He plays his own game, as always. He has a rare, Machiavellian mind."

Nicholas said a few curt words that expressed exactly what he thought of James Harcliffe's mind, leaving Dominic laughing as he hung up.

But Dominic wasn't laughing ten minutes later. He had just finished reading the last of the fifteen-year-old files Harcliffe had left him. Between the flat lines of cold, scientific details he saw the blood and bones of a wounded mind and a horror that no child should have to bear.

Maybe it was better if Cathlin never remembered, he thought. And maybe bringing her to Draycott had been more dangerous than he'd realized.

When the phone rang again, he answered with only half his attention, the rest still caught in that chilling day fifteen years before, a day that still held too many unanswered questions.

"Slept well, did you?"

Harcliffe. Dominic frowned. "Perfectly. But I'm sure this isn't a social call."

"Quite right. Two things. I've found a mention of

this Geneva Russell of yours. According to the data our people uncovered, she was the daughter of a rich Suffolk East India Company merchant. It appears that she died in 1794. Interestingly enough, the nasty event appears to have taken place at Draycott Abbey."

Chills gathered along Dominic's neck. "How did it happen?"

"Unclear, I'm afraid. The whole affair seems to have been hushed up. Except for an odd village bookseller and an obscure researcher who has spend the last twenty-five years researching the unexplained deaths of women over twenty in the southern counties of England, we'd never have found anything."

Dominic cut him off coldly. "What about that cork I sent you last night?"

"We looked into the fragments. It's poison all right. Amazon curare alkaloids with an admixture of pepper to hasten blood absorption rate. A damned sophisticated mix."

"Did you check any deliveries made to Richard Severance's London town house?"

"Our people found a bill of sale for that particular vintage. Severance received the bottles yesterday, but there's still no way we can prove a connection. Frankly, I think the whole idea is preposterous."

"Try the delivery company. They keep records. With a little pressure someone's bound to talk."

"It's going to be damned hard. Luckily, Severance is in Brighton for the day. When he hears what we've done, he'll have a whole regiment of legal experts down on us. The man's got an impeccable reputation and all the lawyers that a million pounds can buy. I still don't understand what makes you think he's involved."

"Instinct," Dominic said flatly.

"Really, Dominic, without ironclad proof, this is going to result in one nasty scandal."

"It's a dirty job, but someone has to do it, Harcliffe. And get me those generator parts I ordered yesterday. You *are* interested in seeing that the government and royal family are entirely satisfied with the handling of this affair, aren't you?" *Especially since there might be a knighthood in it for you.*

"I suppose it can be arranged. But—"

Dominic hung up, tired of hearing protests and more bad news.

So there had been another, much earlier death at Draycott Abbey. He frowned, unable to get the thought out of his mind.

Looking down, he saw the opened files, page after page of sterile details that provided absolutely no answers to his thousand, burning questions about Cathlin. He sighed and rubbed his shoulder, which was throbbing from his tussle in the cellars. But he decided hard physical work was just what he needed to clear his head.

First he'd take a look at the malfunctioning generator, and then he'd have a look at the new alarm system. After that he'd fill in the three men he'd asked to help him out with the abbey's security.

And then, if Cathlin still wasn't down, he'd think of an unusual way of waking her.

The moat was shimmering in the sunlight as Cathlin stood by the tall window overlooking the abbey's roses, dreams that were far too real for dreams chasing through her head. Her pulse raced as she thought of memories, heated memories. And then the brush of shadows.

She reached into her pocket and traced the corner of the crumpled card she had shoved there. There was no point in waiting. The intimate encounter she had shared with Dominic had pushed her beyond her normal defenses, leaving her prey to feelings and half-seen memories that threatened to tear her apart.

She knew now that her questions would not go away. If she were truly going mad, then she wanted to know it now.

As she turned to make her way to the study, she saw an envelope shoved beneath the hall door. It bore her name and a London postmark, but no return address. She opened it slowly, then froze. Plaid. Amber plaid, the pattern that had been her mother's favorite. The same fabric that she had worn when she died.

Or when she had been murdered.

Fingers trembling, Cathlin pulled a sheet of paper from the envelope. It bore only one word, in bold block letters.

Remember?

Cathlin's heart was racing as she dialed the number on Joanna Harcliffe's card. A pleasant female voice answered.

"I'm afraid that Dr. Harcliffe is not available right now. Shall I have her phone you?"

Cathlin swallowed. "Of course." She left the abbey's number, frowning. "Do you know when she will be back?"

"Not long. Forgive me, but . . . is it an emergency? You sound rather upset."

Cathlin thought of her restless dreams. She thought of the memories jabbing at the edge of her consciousness. And now there was the unexplained scrap of plaid and its cruel message. Was the killer in the abbey right now, planning another deadly attack?

"Just have her call me," she said tightly.

Dominic had to be told next. Cathlin tried his room and the cellars, where a new laser security grid gleamed in the darkness. But Dominic wasn't there, either. No doubt he was in Nicholas's beautiful study making more of his covert calls.

But the study was empty. Only a pile of files and

an old book lay on the rosewood desk, with a gilt bookmark in the center. Cathlin opened the book idly and then froze.

A tall woman in blue satin stared back at her. Nearby stood a young girl, her eyes a blaze of happiness.

The caption was most specific: EVANGELINE RUSSELL AND DAUGHTER GENEVA. INDIA, 1782.

Cathlin felt the blood rush from her face as she stared down at those two happy faces, wondering how everything had gone wrong. Then a piece of paper caught her eye. A paper that held her own name.

Frowning, she slid the sheet free.

It was dated fifteen years before, a neatly typed transcription of some sorts of interviews. As Cathlin read further, her eyes widened. First came confusion, then shock, then pure, blazing fury.

Muttering, she pulled out sheet after sheet from the files that Dominic must have been reading. All of them held her name. All of them held the fragments of her past, recorded in dry, clinical sentences that speculated about trauma depth and recovery time and psychological prognosis.

Damn them! Damn them all!

She dropped the papers as if burned, hating to see herself pinned there like some dying insect caught beneath the scientist's knife.

What right did they have to dissect a child's mind this way? And what right did Dominic have to this kind of painfully private information, information even *she* had never seen!

She shoved the papers off the desk and watched them scatter in an angry cloud. Something about the sight made her think of fog and darkness and a danger that stalked her still. In her head, the slow ache became a savage drumming. Suddenly Cathlin felt stifled, choked.

Terrified.

Remember? the note had said. Was it her mother's killer watching her even now?

She turned, white-faced, desperate to escape from this strange old house, which held too much pain and too many secrets.

His hands black with grease, Dominic turned away from the moat.

His eyes narrowed as he heard the sound of running feet.

A premonition of fear hit him as he saw Cathlin's slender form disappear into the dark boxwood copse to the north.

Her face had been bleak with pain.

Twenty-three ~

The fog seemed to come from nowhere, drifting in little pools that hung in the hollows near the river. Cathlin ran blindly, uncaring where she stepped as the white layers grew thicker.

All the while, the cold words of the medical report danced before her eyes, along with the bold letters of the anonymous note.

Remember?

The river was below her now, a shining trail of green that ran along sloping banks of moss, streaked now with fog.

Fog.

Darkness.

The river . . .

She shook her head, shoving her hair from her face, trying to separate *now* from *then*. Mud clung to her shoes and branches scraped at her arms and face as she plunged blindly forward into the fog.

"Cathlin! Stop, damn it!"

It was Dominic's voice, but to Cathlin it was somehow unfamiliar, like the voice of a stranger. Wildly, she pushed through the thick bank of flowers, her pulse ragged in her ears.

"Cathlin, wait!"

She shoved past the lilacs, past ferns and anemones, until she came to a sheltered grove in the lee of a granite cliff. Roses danced crimson on stems that coiled all the way up the bank.

Her breath caught. Memories again—a lifetime of memories. Too many to hold inside her throbbing head.

Hard fingers gripped her shoulders. "Damn it, don't run from me, Cathlin!" She was shoved around, caught against a man's chest.

Her eyes were hazy, unfocused. Suddenly she was a thousand miles away. Or two hundred years away . . .

The sharp whistle of the wind woke him.

He blinked, feeling a strange bed of straw beneath him. Memory dawned. He smiled, sated, happy. "Geneva?"

No answer. No welcoming warmth.

He sat up, frowning at the first gray light filtering through the mill's narrow windows.

She was gone.

Gabriel found her tracks just beyond the bank, set into the soft mud. Grim-faced, vowing the worst of retribution, he stalked her past ferns and mossy stones and thickets still white with drifting fog.

The sun was just visible, burning red over the horizon as he strode over the hill, his eyes locked on the prints that showed her haste.

How could the woman think she could escape him?

Then Gabriel stopped. Here the prints were joined by a second pair.

Devere!

He muttered a curse and ran.

At the top of the next turning in the path he ran her down and pulled her around to face him. "Where is he?"

Her face was pale, determined. "I—I hid from him in the fog. They made their way on toward Stevington Ford. Devere was only wounded."

"You could have been killed!"

Her face was blurred with tears. *"Let me go!"*

"Damned if I will. Now answer me. Tell me why you ran away."

"Because I won't see you hurt. Devere will never give up. He'll send a dozen men after me if that's what it takes. He wants you, Gabriel, and your love for me is your only vulnerability. I must go!" Her voice was raw with desperation.

"You're not going anywhere."

She shoved at him, her lilac scent intoxicating. *"You don't understand. He'll never give up."*

"When we're married, he will," Gabriel said grimly.

"But—" She swallowed, shook her head. *"I cannot."*

"You are married already?"

"No."

"Then you can," he said flatly, already decided. *"And you will. I will see you safe from Devere."*

"No! You must let me go!" She pulled away and ran into a bower heavy with roses, her hair whipping out around her. *"I'll never be safe—nor will anyone who harbors me, not as long as Devere lives. He has killed men and now will exact his revenge against my sister, through his many friends in France who owe him favors."*

"I will help her to safety and see that you are safe from that madman forever. I give you my promise, Geneva."

"And in the process I will only bring you more pain; you have known so much already!" She turned and ran, her skirts trapping her as they caught in the rose briars. *"I cannot. I will not!"* Gabriel pulled her against him, even as she rained angry fists across his chest. Her cheeks were streaked with tears, her eyes haunted.

"Stop fighting me, woman."

But she was wild, lost to his words.

And the storm of her brought an answer in him. He seized her twisting body and pinned her against the trunk of a towering oak. She was beyond words, beyond reason, *gripped by fear and a terrible remorse for a betrayal she could never forget.*

Words failed, reason lost, Gabriel touched her the only way he could, with a need that was as fierce as her regret. Satin pulled free and linen fell in a heap. Geneva fought him like currents in a spring flood, pummeling his chest and twisting until he buried his hands in her hair and ground his body against hers.

Heat met heat. Wild hunger called to its match.

"No. I won't have you hurt. I won't!"

"Hurt me," Gabriel said hoarsely. "Rip out my very heart. For you I would give it gladly, don't you see? Perhaps I already have." He shoved away her gown; she had dressed in haste and wore nothing beneath. Her body was flushed, the thrust of her breasts testimony to the desire that already gripped her.

He groaned, found the pulse that beat at her neck, stroked the silken skin that hid her heat. He did not stop until he heard her cry out and wrap her hands around him.

"Don't hold me, my love. Let me go."

"I must," he said hoarsely. "All my life. Perhaps far longer than this mortal life." As he spoke Gabriel felt a sharp chill at his neck. But he had no time for chills or warnings, not with Geneva in his arms. "And I'll set my brand on you to prove it, a brand of love that carries all the joy you've given me."

She stared at him, a universe of love in her eyes as he bent his head and measured the pulse at her neck, then caught the soft skin to his lips.

With a low moan she curved toward him, impossibly lost, feeling the hot brand of desire that would mark her as his forever.

And then they were thigh to thigh, sliding to the damp, dark earth. Both tugged at her tangled satin skirts; together they shredded his shirt and then pushed away his breeches.

He took her there, bowered by roses, cushioned by soft

*moss and spring ferns with the murmur of the river to
lull them and the fog to veil their nakedness. She met him
with wild delight, driven by a desire that followed his in
equal measure. Control was beyond him and regret beyond
her where they lay among the roses, among the fingers of
drifting fog.*

"Together," he swore hoarsely, driving home to heaven.

"Forever," she answered, following him there.

*It was a promise whispered, shared and sealed with their
joined bodies as they met in mad abandon. And if sheer
force of will and human need could forge a bridge of time,
then their promise would pass beyond the bounds of
death itself.*

"Cathlin?" Callused fingers traced the tears on
Cathlin's cheeks. She shuddered, her mind on fire,
her thoughts a tangled blur, past and present no
longer separate.

"Sweet God, love, what's happened to you?"

*Gabriel. How very much he had loved her. And the
remembering made it far, far worse.*

"Talk to me, Cathlin."

"Let me go!"

"No." Dominic's hands—*Gabriel's* hands—dug into
her waist. "Not until you tell me what's wrong."

"Don't try to stop me. Not again, Gabriel." Then
the sharp gasp, the horror of realization, the gray
pain from deep in the mind that was somehow both
Cathlin and Geneva. "No, I didn't mean—"

His eyes were grim. The jaw so hard, so beloved.
She *had* to make him go.

"You're here now, here in the twentieth century,
Cathlin. You're no eighteenth century heiress fleeing
from a madman," Dominic growled.

She caught a wild breath, shoving at fragments of
memory, fighting to hold apart the two worlds still
crazily superimposed. "They're both here, caught inside my head."

"Fight it, Cathlin. Come back. I need you too much to lose you now," he said hoarsely.

Sweet words. Dangerous words.

"Why, so you can dissect my mind for that monster Harcliffe you work for?" She choked back a sob, hammering at his chest. "You knew all about me. About the bridge and how my mother died. Damn you for knowing what even I couldn't see clearly."

"You saw the files." Dominic's voice was hard with regret.

"Oh, yes, I saw them, Officer Montserrat. Did you enjoy reading about me, about that silly little girl they found crying on the bridge, trying to scrub the blood from her hands?"

"You're a fool if you have to ask me that."

Ragged laughter. "Then I *am* a fool, a fool along with everything else. How did they phrase it? 'Vestigial amnesia, trauma syndrome of uncertain outcome and unpredictable prognosis.' Fool? Yes, I'd say the word fool fits me very well."

"Stop it, Cathlin. Stop fighting and listen to me."

But she didn't. She only fought him, twisting and furious, the empty place in her head suddenly too full, too heavy with memories, each more shattering than the last.

Around them the fog drifted higher.

Cathlin wrenched free of his hands and stood at the top of the slope, her skirts playing about her, her hair a wild cloud.

Just like another woman long years before.

She pressed her forehead, fighting the rush of images. "Do you want to gloat? Do you want to laugh at the little girl who is still as crazy as she always was?" Her shoulders slumped against an ancient overhanging oak. "Dear God, what's happening to me? Why do I see too much, when for years I couldn't see enough?" She felt him behind her. "Go ahead and laugh."

"I'm not laughing, Cathlin." Dominic's voice was raw.

Around him came the sigh of the wind and the whisper of the roses. Dominic staggered before a flood of memories, images of this same bower rich with green moss and veiled with fog.

Madness, he thought. He *couldn't* remember. And yet he did. "Look at me, Cathlin."

She backed up. "I hate you. You're one of them. You turned my mind into a neat little game in one of those files. My God, you've *always* been one of them." She took another step and felt a rock at her back. "Maybe you even sent the note pushed beneath my door, with a scrap of plaid from my mother's dress."

"When did this come?"

"This morning. Of course you were nowhere to be found," she said accusingly. Then her voice broke. "Just let me go."

"Too late, Irish. Maybe it was always too late," Dominic said hoarsely as the fog swirled up between them.

Cathlin turned and ran up the slope, stumbling as her entirely twentieth century skirt caught on a trailing vine of roses. "No, Dominic, no more. I should never have come back to the abbey."

"You can't keep this buried, Cathlin. It will kill you. And you can't possibly believe I had anything to do with that letter," he said grimly.

"I don't know what to believe anymore." She felt no strength at all, only anger and confusion, like the drifting fog. Memories were coming too fast now, images and emotions bound together, seen in two times and by two different women. "How did you know about Geneva?"

"The same way that you knew, Cathlin."

"Dreams?"

"Of us. Together. Yes to all of it, no matter how

bizarre it sounds. I remembered the desire, Cathlin, and all the unbearable loneliness."

"No, you're lying. You're just like all the others. They told me to wait, that my memories would come back when I was ready. But God, they never told me about this second set of memories."

Dominic held out his hands, and Cathlin saw they were trembling. "Am I lying about *this*? Am I lying about wanting you so much I can't sleep or eat or breathe for the pain of it?" He cursed savagely. "You think I enjoy being ripped in two, feeling another man's thoughts hammering inside my head? Do you think I enjoy lying awake night after night and seeing you, cool, beautiful, and naked, waiting for me? Wanting me. Dear God, wanting me so much that I can't ever be free of you."

Cathlin shivered. He couldn't lie, not in such a tone, not with eyes that blazed with such fury. She, too, had seen his body hotly naked, wanting her in a way she'd never been wanted before. She had felt the same wrenching loneliness, a dark emptiness that reached out beyond the years, across a bridge of dreams, tormenting her with a happiness she had known too briefly and then lost.

She tried to argue. The small, sane part of her mind shouted he was lying. But she was already beyond reason. It was a matter of blood now, of yearning blood and hot wanting muscle. While the fog drifted, coiling about her legs, Cathlin finally accepted that.

Past and present swam around her, inexorably entwined, kindled minute to minute, hour to hour, lifetime to lifetime.

Dominic caught her hand to his lips. "Tell me you can't feel it, Cathlin," he challenged her hoarsely. "Tell me you don't want this as much as I do."

She couldn't. Her eyes betrayed her dark secret. His touch left her skin hot, hungry, wounded by a thousand memories.

Of Cathlin O'Neill. And of Geneva Russell.

"No!" Cathlin closed her eyes, trying to tear herself from the past, from memories that tore at her sanity.

She wore only the finest cambric chemise, now damp and nearly translucent. She was all soft shadows beneath the moon.

Dominic's eyes were a blaze of green. "You remember. You're seeing it now, aren't you? God, just the way I am."

His fingers were not quite steady as he slid her chemise from her shoulders, following the fine fabric with his mouth, kisses like a dark storm. He had no gold nor stars to give her. All he had was his touch and his wild joy in her.

"Tell me Cathlin," Dominic said hoarsely, his fingers in her hair, his lips pressed to her satin cheeks. "Tell me I'm not going mad alone. Tell me that and I'll stop."

How could she when it was true? Too many memories bound them and too many regrets.

Above them the roses danced. Fog swirled noiselessly as a great gray cat flicked his ears and then slipped off through the shrubs. A dim shimmering, the faintest trace of light, outlined the edges of the little grove.

Cathlin tried to hate Dominic Montserrat but she couldn't. She couldn't even distrust him. There was too much living, breathing past between them. And right now Cathlin's body was remembering every silken second of that past.

She felt him tense slightly. Because they were so closely attuned, she could read every one of his gestures. "Your shoulder's hurting you," she said accusingly, expecting him to lie.

Before the fog, before the river, he *would* have lied. But not now. "It . . . does hurt, but not badly."

"Why didn't you tell me?"

"Because it's not my way, Cathlin. I've been trained not to show pain—as far as possible not even to feel it. That was my career, and it became my whole life." He laughed bitterly. "Yes, that was at the very top of Ashton's rules: never let them see you sweat. Never show a hint of weakness, because there's no room for weakness when you're doing close protection at the top."

"But you gave it up, Dominic. The old rules are gone."

"I had to. It was that or lose everything I valued, everything that kept me sane." His eyes closed. "What do you want from me, Cathlin?"

"I want everything, Dominic. All that Geneva had—and lost."

"We can't go back, Cathlin. If there's anything I've learned, it's that."

"Maybe we don't have to. Maybe it's all here." She ran her hands over the warm skin atop his heart. "Deep in here. Maybe we're here to finish all that wasn't finished then." Her lips slid to his jaw.

"The timing's wrong, Cathlin. What if something happened to you now—"

"Officer?"

"What?"

She placed her hands on his shoulders and pushed him backward until he was cushioned by the mossy bank. "*Shut up.*" She tugged open his shirt. Her lips grazed the warm skin at his neck. Her hand slid down his chest, exquisitely slow.

With a low curse he pulled her beneath him, a dark gleam of determination in his eyes.

"Dominic? What are you—"

"Be quiet, beauty." His fingers jabbed at the little buttons on her blouse. He watched her skin come

free, warm and hungry and flushed. Inch by inch the
cool silk slid back, while his eyes locked on her face.

The last button pulled free. "Sweet God, Cathlin,"
he said hoarsely. She was lush ivory skin capped
with tight nipples of dusky coral. His head fell and
he took one pouting crest, smiling when she moaned.

"Dominic, I—" She swallowed. "Oh, God, you—"

He circled her wrists and shoved them to the cool,
soft moss. His body fit the perfect mold of hers as
he explored her, stroking crest and hollow and every
bit of velvet in between. He groaned to find a tiny
beauty mark just above her breast. A smoky crescent,
it inflamed him, bringing memories of another time,
another pair of lovers.

*He swept her into a dark storm of feeling, in a place
where all memories stopped and all wounds were healed.
He felt her arch against him, a single word on her lips.*

And the word was his name.

Had she worn his mark into another time, a reminder of all they had once been to each other?

Dominic closed his eyes. Every muscle screamed
out, urging him to take all that beauty revealed before him, to spread her wide and fill her. His fingers
tightened on her wrists with the fury of his need.

Not yet, he swore fiercely. Not until he'd watched
her climax in her pleasure, not until he heard her cry
out his name in wonder and delight as she had the
night before.

Her skirt was long and soft, covered with roses. It
moved easily beneath his fingers, rising over her
thighs to cluster at her waist. He pulled aside the
delicate swath of lace.

And then looked upon her, long-legged, beautiful,
with another smoky birthmark nearly hidden by the
graceful inner curve of her thigh.

He cursed darkly, at the very edge of his control.

There were no more words as he found her heat, pleasure hanging upon them like a haze. Cathlin's breath caught and she gave a soft cry. Her back arched, taut like a bow as she drove upward against him.

He watched, enthralled by her beauty, enslaved by the wanting and her elemental sensuality. With her fire summoning him, he spread her and laid his mouth against the silken skin which wore the dark mark of her beauty.

She twisted, cast against him anew, her breath a wild cry that echoed through their silent, rose-covered bower. And Dominic held her, his hands playing lovingly over her flushed skin as she fell back from heaven into the wonder of his arms.

He watched her, heat in his eyes, heat in his heart.

"Dear God," she managed. "I haven't ever—" A ragged laugh. "That is, I didn't expect—"

"I'm delighted to hear it, my sweetest love." Smiling gently, he eased deeper inside her. Instantly she opened, yielding around him, all heat and silken skin. All flushed woman.

Deeper, gently deeper. Finding, learning.

Loving.

It was all that Dominic wanted, this joy, this fine delight reflected in Cathlin's love-hazed eyes.

Moving deeper, he molded her to his conquest.

Her hands opened, nails sharp at his shoulders. "Sweet God, Dominic, no! I—"

She arched against him and cried out wildly, Dominic's name on her lips as she was hurtled into another storm of pleasure.

Slow, breathless moments later she opened one eye.

A rose, broad-petaled and red, nestled at her neck, silver with dew. Dominic's smile told her he thought of different petals.

Her eyes widened. "I couldn't possibly, Dominic."

The rose brushed her lips, then slid to her neck, crimson petals scattered in its wake. Cathlin watched, breathless, as the bloom made its way lower, petals shedding with every inch.

Dominic's smile grew darker as the lush petals traced the hollow of her stomach and eased downward.

"Dominic, I'm not at all sure that—"

But *he* was. God, how he was. Years of uninvolved emotion gave him the ironclad certainty now, and he used every shred of it in his silken conquest.

Then petal met dewy petal, crimson met softer crimson.

Cathlin's breath caught, desire swiftly rekindling. She moved to meet him, rapt.

Then her eyes opened. "Stop," she said breathlessly, shoving at his chest. "I felt a rock."

He stopped instantly, concern in his face as he slid aside.

But Cathlin was quicker. She followed her advantage instantly, slipping over him and pulling his shirt free, popping buttons with ruthless disregard. His belt hissed free and then a new set of buttons challenged.

Dominic frowned and stilled her hand.

But Cathlin tackled the buttons and watched his tantalizing inches emerge.

She reached out awed by the heat of him, the extravagant thrust of him.

Dominic cursed low and pulled her closer. His voice was like gravel, one final question necessary before turning back grew impossible. "Are you sure, Cathlin? Any more and I won't be stopping."

Her eyes rose, smoke and amber. High above them a single beam of sunlight pierced the drifting fog and slanted down into their quiet corner of paradise.

"I'm not changing my mind, if that's what you're hoping for." Her soft hands clutched his shoulders and sunlight glinted off her glossy hair. She inched against him, her eyes hazy with passionate intent. "Is this the general idea?"

"God . . ."

Lower. Soft and yielding. Hot ache spreading, joy building. Then the sudden barrier. Her eyes opened, pleading.

Dominic took a harsh breath and cupped her hips. With a hard thrust he brought himself deep and Cathlin cried out with the shocking joy of feeling him tight inside her.

Pleasure trembled, shimmered, any discomfort burned away by the fire of his fingers where they joined. She gasped and let her body fall, poured over him like a rain of roses. "Please, Dominic. All I want—is this, this with you."

Her thighs slid warm against him. Dominic drove himself into her, gentle conquests forgotten, amusements irrevocably past. Now his only need was to claim her, to possess her as completely as she had possessed him.

With every dark inch he came closer to that hot, still core, closer to the vow he had to pledge with body and soul.

Suddenly her body tensed and Dominic felt the pleasure rippling through her. His own followed, all dark fire and jagged fury, wilder than anything he'd ever known.

But in that moment he felt the mystery of a deeper joining, breaths and molecules fused, thoughts and memories and spirits bound together like sunlight amid the drifting fog.

And at that moment the scent of lilacs seemed to rise around them.

"Together," Gabriel swore hoarsely, driving home to heaven.

"Forever," Geneva answered, following him there.

* * *

Slowly the fog lifted. A pair of otters glided through the green river and a thrush called from the roses.

Cathlin fitted herself to him, boneless and replete. She curled closer against him and sighed. "Eminent body," she murmured. "Excellent breed." She moved by a silken fraction. "And a potent finish, just as you promised, Officer Montserrat." She ran her foot gently along his thigh.

Dominic cleared his throat. "I don't actually think it's possible," he said hoarsely, half laughing, half accusing. More than half-sated.

"But I say it is," Cathlin demurred, voice muffled as she began her silken foray, taking exquisite care over all the hard places that had been intriguing her. "And I *am* the wine expert here."

"There are certain time frames, you know. I expect it was so those cavemen could find the strength to get up and go—" He swallowed suddenly as her lips moved downward. "Er, to go kill a woolly mammoth or two for dinner." A low curse. "To feed all those little cavemen and cavewomen they were making right and left."

Cathlin ignored him, smiling when she felt the hot rise of him inside her. "Extraordinary stamina, too." She stared down, one brow raised. "You were saying, my lord? Something about cavemen and time frames and impossibility?"

Dominic cursed and rolled her beneath him, her dominion abruptly ended. Closing his eyes, he brought himself down to her in a sharp, swift slide. "Forget whatever I just said, Lady Ashton."

On the hill above them, beyond the circle of roses, beyond the mossy bank, a tall figure shimmered, then slid into being, all black silk and white, rippling lace.

He bent to stroke the great gray cat seated at his side. "Most satisfactory, don't you agree?"

The cat's tail flicked gracefully.

"No, I really can't agree with you there. Those two are meant to be right where they are. Just as they were meant to be together, all those years ago."

The cat meowed.

"I know that, my friend. But who would have expected Devere's resourcefulness?" Adrian sighed, his face lined, suddenly weary. "As it comes again."

Behind them a kestrel cried. The wind sighed over the boxwood and the dancing roses. Adrian's eyes softened as he heard his name called.

For a moment light outlined the graceful form of a woman in a dress of glimmering cloth of gold.

"Nosy? Not at all, my love. I am merely taking a well-deserved pleasure in the success of my little project."

Soft laughter drifted over the hill. Adrian's eyes darkened as the woman's shape shimmered away into the dark silence of the wood. "I rather think I must go, Gideon," he said shortly. "She captivates me as ever, even after all these years." His eyes narrowed and he thought of another time, of another world where the force of will and sheer human need had been put so cruelly to the test.

But he had won, he and the beautiful woman waiting for him on the hill.

And Adrian Draycott knew, as few other people possibly could, that some promises could truly bridge time, passing beyond life and even beyond the bounds of death itself.

The cat purred softly, pressing against his polished boot. Nearby the roses danced, blood red against a wall of green.

And then abruptly both cat and master disappeared.

Twenty-four ~

The silence beside the river was broken by a shrill, mechanic beeping. Dominic sighed and rolled to his back, fishing a metal box from the chaos of their clothes as static filled the air. "Montserrat, are you there?" The voice at the other end was urgent. "There's just been a call from Harcliffe. Richard Severance has been taken into custody for questioning, but he insists he will only talk to you."

Dominic frowned. "To me?"

"That's the word. Harcliffe wants you to get right off to London. He's sent a car."

Dominic sighed. "I'll be there shortly." He punched a button, silencing the receiver, then sat up.

"What does it mean, Dominic?"

"I'm not sure." But in that moment Dominic had a flash of intuition that they, like the *Titanic* drifting in the foggy Atlantic night, were heading directly toward something from which they had no chance of escape.

It took Dominic only minutes to pack a small bag. Then he turned and pulled Cathlin to him. "I'll be back tomorrow. At least I hope I will. There are three men working the grounds in shifts and one will always be in the house with you."

Cathlin brushed his cheek. "Take all the time you need. I'll be fine. Just as long as it isn't another two hundred years."

"You've got my promise on that, Lady Ashton."

Their fingers tightened. Their lips touched for long, aching moments. Then Dominic turned sharply and slid into the unmarked but very official car that James Harcliffe had sent to take him back to London.

"Were there any messages for me, Mrs. Holt?" Joanna Harcliffe tipped her wet umbrella carefully into its ceramic container and hung up her raincoat neatly.

Her receptionist looked down at a stack of papers. "A half dozen, Dr. Harcliffe. The usual, all except for this one." The woman held out a sheet of paper. As the older woman studied the message, a frown worked between her calm brown eyes.

"Yes, Mrs. Harcliffe—Dr. Harcliffe, I should say. Thank you for returning my call." Cathlin was standing in the rose-filled study overlooking the abbey's moat. Marston had finally tracked her down in the cellars to tell her that she had a call. But now Cathlin felt a strange reluctance to talk about the flood of memories and the chaos of feelings that were still painfully new.

"I expect you want to know why I called." She straightened the beautiful Fabergé egg at the corner of Nicholas Draycott's desk. "Actually it has to do with my memory. I—I think that it's beginning to come back."

"This is a very significant development, my dear. I'm sure you must find it a little shocking," the woman said sympathetically. "When did this all begin?"

"Yesterday. Oh, it didn't come all in one rush, but in bits and pieces." Cathlin looked out at the silver waters of the moat, trying to explain. "But it's not just about what happened fifteen years ago. This concerns another person—and another time." She sighed. "I expect this sounds entirely mad."

Joanna Harcliffe laughed softly. "You'd be surprised at the behavior I see in the course of my day, Lady Ashton. The majority of it is far stranger than what you've just described, and yet each of those people functions quite normally. To all intents and purposes they are quite, quite sane."

Somehow this didn't reassure Cathlin as much as it ought to. "But I'm coming face-to-face with memories of myself—as a woman who died two hundred years ago. And on top of that, the memories about my mother have begun returning."

There was a moment of silence, then the sound of papers rustling. "I see." The psychiatrist sighed. "I believe it's finally begun."

"Begun? I don't understand."

"You've finally begun to remember, my dear. Something has triggered the images that have been blocked inside you all these years. Don't ask me why, because I can't tell you. The human mind is still far from being well understood, no matter what experts like me would have you believe. And as for your memories of another person and time, all I can say is that many famous people have consciously experienced lives as other people, some as illustrious as Aristotle and Plato or Thomas Edison and General Patton."

"But it's all happening so suddenly."

"I'm sure it must feel that way, but you really needn't feel you have to take it in all at once. It reminds me of a rhyme I once heard. Let me see if I can get it right.

> *There is a hawke at my father's house,*
> *By oak and ash and bonny deer."*

The woman's voice became smooth and singsong as she continued.

> *"And though to me he sings full fair*
> *No one else can hear, oh*
> *No one else can hear."*

Cathlin frowned, struggling with a thread of memory. "I've heard that, I think." Suddenly the next lines rushed into her mind.

> *"There is a dove on my mother's hill,*
> *By oak and ash and bonny doe;*
> *And though to me she sings full sweet,*
> *No one else can know, oh,*
> *No one else can know."*

She rubbed at her forehead, wondering where that strange scrap of poetry had come from.

"I see you've heard it too." Another pause. "A silly bit of verse I suppose, but it's something I think of when I am faced with unanswerable questions. And I'm faced with them rather more often than I care to admit when dealing with the human mind. But my dear Lady Ashton, I could come to the abbey if you feel it is important."

Cathlin frowned. "No, I'll be fine. I—I'm sorry to have troubled you."

After she hung up, Cathlin stood for a while, the sunlight on her shoulders entirely unnoticed. She thought about the call and about that odd bit of verse—and then she thought about nothing at all. It was long minutes later before she gave herself a shake and roused herself from her reverie.

Joanna Harcliffe frowned at the receiver. The new Lady Ashton had been decisive enough in her assurances that she did not require any help, yet there had been something in her voice, a quiver, an edge of uncertainly that Joanna Harcliffe, experienced from years of professional practice, recognized as deep inner turmoil.

She sat back at her desk and looked at the framed diplomas that hid nearly every inch of the silk-covered walls. Steepling her fingers, she went over the conversation word by word. Outside a wave of automobiles screamed and snorted through Picca-dilly Circus, but she barely heard.

A moment later she reached forward and pushed down the button for her receptionist. "Something has come up, Mrs. Holt. I'm afraid I'll have to cancel the rest of my appointments for the day."

Cathlin frowned down at the dusty wine case. One of the precious bottles now stood on her worktable, where she had placed it after carefully freeing it from its case.

But as she stood in the cool shadows, the old glass bottle before her, Cathlin felt images surge, pressing at her consciousness with painful intensity. She rubbed her eyes, blinking. As she did, the bottle changed. No more was it dust-streaked and dirty, its cork brittle. Now its glass shone and its label was crisp.

As new as the day it was printed.

They arrived at the abbey just as night was falling. Roses filled the courtyard and climbed the weathered gran-ite walls.

Geneva lost her heart instantly to this place of wrenching beauty. They would be safe here; she felt it clearly. Even Henry Devere's madness could not reach Gabriel inside these moated walls.

For three days she explored every shadowed corner, every sunlit room. Even the cavernous wine cellars did not escape her curious eye. She marveled at the variety of the wines collected in those cool shadows and Gabriel encouraged her to choose a different bottle to sample every night with their dinner.

At last, Geneva saw some of the sadness eased from Gabriel's silver eyes. Amused by her boundless curiosity, he followed her everywhere, sharing information from his earlier visits with Adrian. With unflagging energy Geneva dragged him through the imposing portraits in the long gallery while she fired innumerable questions about the Draycott ancestors. When Gabriel could bear no more history lessons, he pulled her off to the moat, where Geneva dangled her toes and returned his teasing kisses.

But when night filled the valleys and stars shone in the shimmering moat, Gabriel fed a different kind of curiosity as he pulled Geneva against his hard body. Her breath caught when he carried her to the huge poster bed that overlooked the rose gardens, though neither noticed the view through the beautiful mullioned windows.

Their joy was in a different world, a place of endless discovery and boundless love where Gabriel taught Geneva pleasures beyond imagining.

And in their reckless joy, neither noticed the eyes that watched from the darkness.

"I could stay another day. I would just have time." Gabriel stood exquisite in navy silk and crimson damask on Draycott's gravel drive. Behind him a groom held the reins of his restive mount.

"No, you must go. We could have no peace, not while my sister's life hangs in the balance. And though it breaks my heart, I must let you go for you are the only one who can save her. Otherwise, I would hold you here forever, my love." Geneva straightened her shoulders and looked up at the man she loved. "But there will be time, endless time for us when you return from France." With a little choked cry she flung herself against him, her hands thrown around his neck. "Be careful, my love. They know you now and will be watching for you. Be watchful also for

Henry Devere. He may well be a greater threat than any of the French Tribunal.''

"No one will find me. I've put all my cleverness to use this time. I have every intention of returning, now that I know there's an incorrigible hoyden with an unquenchable curiosity waiting in my bed."

Caught in emotion, Geneva didn't think to scold him for his plain speaking in front of the groom, who turned away, careful to look as if he had not heard.

She caught a ragged breath and then her chin rose. "Go now, my love. Go quickly and Godspeed. I'll be waiting, waiting here in the shadow of the abbey's roses. Remember that and come back safe to me."

A dark, unnamed emotion crossed Gabriel's face. As the wind sighed through the roses, he pulled Geneva close and pressed a hard, desperate kiss upon her lips. Then he flung himself up into the saddle and galloped south to the coast, where a sleek cutter was waiting to run before the tide to France.

Cathlin stood in the half-light, feeling the memories burn through her hand where she touched the old, dusty bottle. They tore at her with aching force, until it seemed she was reliving every agonizing moment of the past.

And as she stood she heard the faint sound of a woman's breathless sobbing.

Gabriel did not make the next county, nor even make the next valley. They caught him as the sun burned over the horizon, twenty men with muskets ready.

He fought them long and well, sweat on his brow as he cut down one after another. But in the end he was no match for this cutthroat crew hired from London's cruelest slums.

As darkness fell, he was bound and gagged and shoved into a carriage bound for London. There Henry Devere waited in keenest expectation of his arrival, and of the look *on Geneva Russell's face when she saw her lover lying dead at her feet.*

Dominic showed a badge to the board officer sitting behind the desk in the cavernous office building he hadn't visited in years. "I'm looking for Richard Severance."

"Then you found him. He's right over there."

The international jet-setter and financier was being held in a narrow room with a single desk and chair. Dark lines of strain bit into his face. Even a few hours of questioning could do that to the toughest people, Dominic knew. And something told him Richard Severance was far from tough.

Severance came to his feet immediately. "There you are, Montserrat. It took you long enough to get here."

Dominic leaned back against the battered table. "What's the idea of dragging me into this? It's a simple enough case—attempted murder. We've found the company who delivered that wine to you before you added your poison. There's no reason for me to be involved."

"That's where you're wrong." Severance turned and paced the narrow room. "She's got the same hold over you, hasn't she? I know how it works. I saw her, and from that minute on I couldn't get her out of my mind either." Severance laughed grimly. "I've seen that same hunger in *your* eyes."

"So?"

"So I didn't give in without a fight. I made it my business to find out everything I could about Cathlin O'Neill. I studied her father, I studied her mother, and I studied her past. Oddly enough there wasn't that much to find, which made me curious. With the kind of access I have to people in high places, I'd expected to find more."

"Get to the point, Severance."

"I'm not certain *what* Cathlin has in her past." Severance frowned and pulled a hand through his now disordered hair. "Oh, there were a few fragments about her mother's murder at Draycott Abbey, but after that nothing. Stranger still, I found out that someone else had been along that same paper trail. Whoever it was made damn sure to sweep every detail clean after him."

"Which only made you more curious."

"You're bloody right it made me curious." Severance shrugged. "I won't say I loved her. I won't even say that I liked her all the time. But I couldn't seem to get Cathlin O'Neill out of my mind. Especially her eyes. All I could think of was seeing them hot with passion, just for me." He cursed softly. "Yes, I was damned curious. I've made a great deal of money by being curious, Officer Montserrat. Business is about information, after all. So I pushed and then I pushed some more and bit by bit the pieces of Cathlin's past finally began to emerge."

Dominic sat back, waiting to hear the rough outlines of the story Cathlin had already told him along with some of the details he had learned from Harcliffe's file. "Go ahead, Severance, astound me."

The other man studied Dominic. "Tough, aren't you? But you weren't so tough in Rome, not when those three teenagers died from your gun. And you weren't so tough when it turned out that one of them was a girl."

Dominic's jaw hardened. Less than half a dozen people knew about that bloody episode. It had been carefully covered up, not out of concern for Dominic's reputation but as a precaution in case other members of the royal family might be attacked. "Just how the hell do you know that, Severance? Not that I'm agreeing there's any truth to it, of course."

"I have access to the best sources, Montserrat. I'm not talking about receptionists or clerical staff here, but about highly placed cabinet-level contacts. These people owe me all kinds of favors. That's how I began to fit the clues about Cathlin together." He began to pace again, his expression growing more and more tense. "And finally those pieces began to make sense."

"Why did you go to so much trouble? Certainly not just because of a pair of remarkable eyes?"

"At first that's all it was. Then it changed. My instincts began screaming that there was more here than met the eye. Secrets are power, Montserrat, and power is what keeps me where I am." Severance laughed grimly. "Or where I *was*." He frowned at Dominic. "You still don't believe me, do you? You think this is all a scheme to work my way out of the charges. But this is absolutely true. Someone else was going to a great deal of trouble to destroy the details of Cathlin's past. Those psychological files of hers are not available even to fellow physicians. They're considered national secrets, don't you see? There's only one reason that would happen."

"Because Cathlin knew something important?"

"Exactly! Do you understand now? Somewhere in that jagged, tormented memory she holds a scrap of information that someone considers very, very deadly. That's why they want her past erased."

Dominic sat forward, his eyes narrowing. "Tell me who."

Cathlin stood in the wine cellar, her hands locked at her chest, images of past and present flooding her mind. Around her lay piles of rubble, remnants of the wall that had been Gabriel Ashton's lonely tomb.

A wall that reminded her of the jagged hole in her own mind.

Fragments. Images. So much of the past she could never get away from. As Cathlin moved over the floor, something glinted from the shadows. Bending down, she sifted through the dust and picked up a small metal link, the kind that came from a piece of expensive jewelry.

Cathlin studied the piece of silver, turning it in the light. Something about it nagged at her memory, but she couldn't decide what. After a moment she slipped the smooth link into her pocket, where her fingers continued to turn it over and over.

What had happened to Gabriel? And what had happened to the wistful amber-eyed woman that he'd left behind at the abbey?

Frowning, Cathlin touched the old bottle. The glass was cold, dust-streaked, heavy beneath her fingers, but now it held no answers, its secrets locked in the same tomb that had held Gabriel's bones.

Behind her the new generator popped sharply. She heard a faint hiss. A moment later the cellar was plunged into utter darkness.

Twenty-five ❦

"A nice story, Severance, but you're wasting my time. I need facts, not speculation."

The rumpled financier gestured irritably. "Get me some coffee, for God's sake. I've been cooped up in this place for six hours. The least you can do is get me something to drink."

A stalling tactic? Dominic shrugged and moved to the door, spoke softly with the man outside, then returned. "I need something specific if you want my help. This kind of empty speculation won't get you an extra blanket on your prison bed."

"It's far more than speculation, you fool! It's about secrets, damn it. The kind of secrets that keep governments afloat—or shatter them."

"I need a name or I can't help you," Dominic said flatly.

Severance rubbed his neck and cursed.

At that moment there was a tap at the door and a uniformed man brought in a paper cup. Dominic noticed he was a different guard from before. "Where did the other officer go?" he asked.

"Off duty," came the bored answer, coupled with a shrug.

Severance turned the cup nervously in his hands and took a quick drink. "Help me, Montserrat. That wine was just to scare Cathlin. When I saw her with you in the car I went a little crazy, I admit it. But I never meant to kill her. There wasn't supposed to be enough poison for that."

"Says you."

Severance stared into the steaming coffee, as if looking for hidden answers. "My God, you still don't understand!" He took another swallow and rubbed his throat. "It was all planned. *All* of it, don't you understand? Someone knew." His fingers tightened on the coffee, which sloshed over his wrists.

There was another tap at the door. The uniformed guard beckoned to Dominic. "Mr. Severance's lawyers are upstairs," he explained softly. "He is to be released in fifteen minutes. Mr. Harcliffe wanted you to know."

Dominic bit back a curse. Did Harcliffe expect him to get answers before Severance walked? He turned back, his face expressionless. "If there was someone involved, tell me how. Then maybe I can help you."

"That's just it, I never found out. And I should have been able to find out. Whoever buried Cathlin's records had access at the very highest levels. He *also* had the power to keep his involvement totally hidden." His eyes widened, desperate. "But I did learn one thing, Montserrat. The palace was never interested in that wine you're shepherding down at Draycott Abbey."

"What wine?" Dominic's tone was cool.

"That Château d'Yquem 1792, you fool! I told you, information's my business. When I found out, naturally I was interested as a collector. But no one at the palace was showing any interest and that bothered me, since it could mean the wine was a fake. When I looked into it, I found out the palace was told discreetly that the wine is only a modern copy."

Dominic's palms began to sweat as he felt a noose

of betrayal slipping around him. "Why should I believe you're telling me the truth?"

"Because I need you too much to lie." Severance's fingers were trembling and his voice was agitated. "That man you caught the day before yesterday at the abbey was my man. I sent him for pictures of the wine. I wanted verification. Of course, he wasn't as good as you, Montserrat. He barely made it out, bleeding badly."

"Tell me about the palace. Where did you get this information? No one on their staff leaks information for long."

"You're right. But this time an old associate there called me. It seems a member of the royal family was searching for a fine wine to give as a family birthday gift. He knew I occasionally obtain unusual vintages and can be counted on to be discreet. I can assure you, he had *no idea* that the wine in the abbey's cellar was authentic. Which means, Montserrat, that someone is double-crossing you." Sweat covered Severance's brow and his face had gone pale. "So now will you help me?"

Dominic tried to hide his fury. Severance couldn't be lying, not when so many of his facts were correct. And that meant someone had betrayed him. Harcliffe? Or someone even higher? "What about the car that tried to run Cathlin off the road? Were you behind that, too?"

"Car?" Severance ran a hand clumsily over his brow. "I don't know anything about a car. The poison was just to scare Cathlin and make her leave the abbey. Something's wrong there, don't you believe that now?"

He did believe it, Dominic thought grimly. But who was the person who stayed one step ahead of him?

"Did you send Cathlin the letter with the scrap of plaid?"

"What plaid?"

Another dead end. Dominic rubbed his shoulder idly, feeling it burn. "Maybe you can be useful to me, Severance. When you're released from here, I want you to do something for me."

"Anything. Just get me out."

"I want you to start asking questions again. Pull in all your old debts and make it clear that answers will be well rewarded."

"You want me to be the bait, is that it? To make my interest clear and see who comes looking for me?" He nodded slowly. "Risky, but I'll do it. Just give me your assurance that in return, you'll—" His hands lurched. A shudder ran through him.

"What's wrong?"

Severance's body tensed. He swayed toward the desk. His coffee cup fell to the floor and liquid ran in a brown stain across the dirty tiles.

"The woman," Severance muttered. "Harcliffe. Might be—" Abruptly his eyes closed and his body twitched convulsively.

And then his head slid back and he did not move again.

Dominic's face was grim as he watched the medical team carry out Richard Severance's body. "What was it?" he asked the doctor making notes in a small black pad.

"Impossible to say for certain, not until the blood tests and tissue samples are complete." The man closed his pad with a snap. Dominic thought his eyes looked tired and slightly bitter. "Myself, I suspect a fast-acting alkaloid. Probably something in the curare family, since you say it happened over a matter of minutes."

"What about the guard?"

The doctor shrugged. "He's in the clear. Someone phoned down and told him to come upstairs in order to show Severance's lawyers down here, in preparation for his release. He waited until a relief guard took his place and then he left."

"And that relief guard who brought the coffee has long since disappeared, no doubt," Dominic said grimly.

"Right again."

Dominic looked down at the floor. There were still a few beads of coffee dotting the old, cracked tile. The paper cup had been removed for evidence, of course, but Dominic doubted there would be any found. Whoever was behind this wasn't the sort to leave any clues.

Slowly he sank onto the table, his hands clenched. Who wanted Severance out of the picture and had the knowledge to see it done so cleanly?

And then Dominic sat forward. *Cathlin.* Whoever had gotten to Severance could just as easily get to Cathlin. He had to get back to Draycott.

The tired man with the notepad watched him rush from the room, then sighed and went back to his grisly report.

Cathlin moved quickly as the wine cellar was plunged into darkness. She crouched by the new security system and punched in the code Dominic had programmed to retrigger the alarm. At least its secondary power source was secure for the moment.

Nearby she heard a thump, the kind that came from a body stumbling into something heavy. Tensely, she pinpointed the noise, four yards to her right. If she made her way along the far wall past the champagne racks, she would be in reach of the stairs.

She caught her breath and inched through the darkness. When her fingers met the cool wood of the stair rail, she threw caution to the winds and bolted straight up, calling hoarsely for Marston and the friend of Dominic who was supposed to be on watch by the front door.

But neither the butler nor the other man was anywhere to be seen. The abbey was empty.

"My dear, what's wrong? You look quite distraught."

Cathlin spun around, gasping in relief as she saw Joanna Harcliffe's anxious face. "Where's Marston? There's someone down in the cellars and I have to get help."

"Oh, I assure you no one has gone down there. I've been sitting here for at least twenty minutes. Marston said he had to go into town with that nice friend of your husband. I believe they had to pick up some new equipment. Marston seemed quite delighted to be involved, actually." The older woman touched Cathlin's arm. "You're not looking at all well, my dear. Come into the study and sit down while you tell me all about it."

Perhaps she *had* been mistaken, Cathlin thought. Lord knows, her nerves were stretched thin these last days. Given her anxiety in the darkness, she might merely have imagined the noise.

She followed the older woman into the study, sank into a chintz armchair, and took the glass of water that Joanna Harcliffe had poured from a nearby carafe.

"I was certain I heard something. Just my imagination, I suppose. I've been imagining all *sorts* of strange things since I came to the abbey."

"Have another drink."

Cathlin took the glass, studying the woman's competent hands. She noted every line and texture, from the square, unpolished nails to the expensive but out-of-date Baume and Mercier wristwatch.

"Just close your eyes. It will help, you know. It will let you forget."

Cathlin stared at the silver watchband flashing in

the sunlight as Joanna's Harcliffe's voice murmured on, soft and rhythmic. "Sleep. Sleep now." Sunlight glinted back and forth across the silver links. It was the kind of expensive and classic watch that would last a lifetime, Cathlin thought dimly.

Then her eyes sank closed. Her breathing grew deep and regular.

When the phone rang, the older woman reached out and unplugged it. "There's no need for us to be disturbed," she said gently. "Just sleep, Cathlin, my dearest. Close your eyes and sleep. Exactly the way your mother did."

James Harcliffe knocked at the door of his wife's study, then pushed it open. He did not go into this room as a rule. Medical confidentiality had to be strictly preserved, as his wife had repeatedly explained to him. Because Harcliffe had his own office at home, this had never bothered him before. But lately Joanna was spending more and more time in here, and he feared she was overworking.

But today she was not at her office and she should have been home hours ago.

He looked down, surprised to see a torn sheet of paper crumpled on her desk. Nearby a little crystal jar with paper clips lay overturned.

Harcliffe frowned. His wife was usually the soul of neatness, entirely a creature of habit. It annoyed her when something was not in its place. This was not at all like her. He picked up the paper and studied the single word that ran across it, written in his wife's neat handwriting.

Cathlin.

Beneath he saw a file and skimmed the first sheet. His frown grew as he turned sheet after sheet. When he finally snapped the file shut and sank down in the chair at his wife's desk, his face was grim.

He grabbed the phone and punched out the num-

ber for Draycott Abbey. A mechanical voice came
on the line, informing him that there was a circuit
malfunction and would he please try his call again
later.

Cursing softly, Harcliffe broke the connection,
studying the unbelievable information he held in his
hands. For the first time in twenty years there was
fear in his eyes.

The sun burned away over the hills, leaving Draycott's windows a blaze of crimson. The air was still
and silence covered the sweeping hills like a veil.

Out of that veil came a shimmering wave of light
that worked into black satin and white lace, into a
face with brooding eyes and hard jaw. Adrian Draycott stood on the rise overlooking his beloved abbey,
a gray cat at his feet.

His hands clenched to fists. They had no right to
be here, severing the peace of this place, threatening
those who had come back to heal a long-forgotten
wound. He had tried to warn Cathlin and her stubborn husband, stirring their sleeping minds with
fragments of their bitter past. He had hoped that
with his warning, they might be better prepared for
the dangers to come.

But the evil that had waited for two hundred years
had only grown stronger. Now the dark past was
about to be repeated and in spite of every shred of
will and ghostly inclination, Adrian Draycott feared
he would not be allowed to interfere.

Twenty-six ~

"Yes, she was very beautiful, your mother."

Joanna Harcliffe sat beside Cathlin, her voice friendly. She spoke with the detached calm of a professional, but her eyes were expressionless and flat. It was nearly dark now, and she liked the dark best. It was the perfect time to make plans. "She had every man at Oxford dogging her steps, even those who didn't care for women. Everything was wonderful then. We were two privileged women with the grandest of prospects before us. Then Elizabeth grew immersed in her art studies and I found myself with a new set, people who had different ideas. I began to see the larger world and all the weaknesses of England. And I came to see that increasing those weaknesses was the key to making a better world for all of us." She carefully unsnapped her silver watch, then held it before Cathlin's eyes, moving it slowly. "Yes, you're sleeping deeply now, my dear. Just as you were all those years ago when we had our discussions. You remember now, don't you?"

Cathlin frowned, her fingers tensing.

"Answer me, Cathlin."

"Y-yes. I'm sleepy now, very sleepy."

"Excellent. We've gone through all this before, of course, all about your memories of that day here at

338

the abbey. And we discovered a different set of memories in our sessions, didn't we? Memories of a woman named Geneva Russell."

Cathlin's fingers moved restlessly over the chair arm, but she did not speak.

"Tell me, Cathlin." There was an iron undercurrent in the older woman's voice now.

"Yes. I remember. Geneva. Geneva Russell."

"Excellent. And do you know how she died?"

Cathlin frowned. "No, I—I can't remember. Only pieces. Painful even now . . ."

Harcliffe moved the watch rhythmically, her voice like a smooth wave. "Then I'll tell you. Listen well. She jumped from the abbey roof, distraught at her lover's death. Such a sad conclusion to the tale, just like your own past. How unfortunate that you and your mother saw me that day in London, speaking with a man I shouldn't be speaking with and giving him a file I most certainly shouldn't have been giving him. What a bad bit of luck for you that you were there by the duck pond in Regent's Park when your mother saw me. It all had to end, of course," she said softly. "I'd put far too much time into the government position I'd secured as a confidante and medical adviser to cabinet-level ministers—even to several members of the royal family. The secrets I held were of incredible value to those determined to see change brought about here in England. Nothing—nothing at all—could be allowed to interfere with that process. You do understand, don't you, Cathlin?"

No answer.

"*Tell* me, Cathlin."

"Yes, I . . . understand." It was the soft voice of a child of ten.

"And you do remember seeing me that day. It's coming back to you, isn't it? You remember the ducks, dirty and clamorous, while you tossed in the bread your mother had crumbled up for you."

Cathlin's face softened and she nodded. "I liked the ducks. I slipped and got mud on my new shoes, but she told me it didn't matter. We'd have them like new before my father saw them. She seemed worried, though. And she didn't want me to know."

"Yes, Elizabeth was quite the perfect mother. That's why I had to come up with a very special way to dispose of her." Joanna Harcliffe's eyes moved over the room, detached, analytical. "One of my new compatriots volunteered to take on the assignment. He was careful to lay all the clues to suggest it was the work of one of your father's enemies. Yes, it was a most satisfying conclusion to a nasty little problem and no breath of suspicion ever fell upon me."

Cathlin's fingers moved restlessly as the hypnotic words continued.

Abruptly the woman beside her frowned. "What are you holding there in your hand?"

Cathlin's fingers opened, revealing a small piece of silver.

"My God, you found it, after all those years. I broke my watch down there that day and had no time to find all the pieces. You didn't see me, but you heard my voice, didn't you?" Joanna Harcliffe laughed softly. "You were such a clever little girl."

Cathlin's eyes went very wide. Pain flared through their unfocused depths. After a moment she nodded jerkily.

"But I saw to that too. During our little sessions, I blocked out those memories and gave you a different set, didn't I?"

Cathlin nodded. "You—you told me I was responsible. You said if I hadn't insisted on stopping to feed the ducks that day, my mother would still be alive. You said it was all my fault."

Harcliffe sat back with a small hiss of triumph.

"Excellent. A perfect textbook case of deep conditioning that has held up perfectly all these years. Guilt made you the perfect block for your memories, right up until I gave you the code to change it. You do remember the code, don't you, my dear? We went over it so many times."

Cathlin frowned, looking out into empty space, struggling with burning memories and painful images that threatened to shred her sanity.

> *"There is a dove on my mother's hill,*
> *By oak and ash and bonny doe;*
> *And though to me she sings full sweet,*
> *No one else can know, oh,*
> *No one else can know."*

She spoke the words flatly, mechanically.

"Well done. And in the wake of those words, all the memories began coming back, didn't they?"

Cathlin nodded, her fingers tight on the piece of silver she'd found in the dust, her connection to the buried secrets of her past.

"Unfortunately, Richard Severance was also interested in what had happened to you, and he had access to information at very high levels. I soon found that he could be a formidable opponent. He had to die, of course, since he'd become a nuisance. But I had to keep you silent, too, until I was ready to clear the slate, and the best way was by keeping you off-balance, by making you question your sanity."

She looked at the watch, her face hard. "And now, my dear, we're going down into the cellars to look at that wine everyone is so interested in. It is authentic, isn't it?"

Cathlin's fingers tightened with strain. She fought the seductive force of that low voice.

"Come, now, tell me everything. I must insist."

Cathlin caught a jerky breath. She shuddered, then

nodded slowly. "Real. Priceless . . ." She swallowed, her voice trailing away.

"Excellent. They'll ensure my welcome in the rather unstable country where I'm going tonight. Yes, they *must* be real." She seemed to rouse herself. "And now, Cathlin, we will go down and you will turn off the alarm system. You know the sequence, don't you? Your dear husband must have told you."

After a moment Cathlin nodded.

Joanna Harcliffe laughed softly. "Then after we load the wine in my car, we're going to take a nice, careful walk up to the roof, just you and I. Won't that be lovely?"

Cathlin's hands clenched.

And then slowly, painfully, she nodded.

Dominic cursed and slammed his foot to the floor. His hands were white, locked on the wheel, as he went back and forth over Severance's final muttered warning.

Who? Who was behind this horror?

Frowning, he reached for the mobile telephone by his knee. Like all the other times, the result was the same, only static. Even the radio brought no response.

Damn it, where were Marston and the men he'd called in to keep an eye on the abbey? His jaw was set in a hard line as he shot past an approaching fuel truck, barely scraping his fender past in time, and roared south toward the abbey.

"Go ahead, my dear." Cathlin was in the entrance hall, her hands locked at her waist. Joanna Harcliffe carefully smoothed a few wisps of hair back into her bun and leaned closer, speaking gently. "The stairs are right behind that door. Push it open, Cathlin. It's a lovely night for an airing on the roof."

Cathlin faltered.

"Now, my dear. You must do exactly as I say."

Cathlin nodded and moved forward.

"You do see that you can't be allowed to live. It was amusing to know that I had such power over your future, that with a single string of words I could heal you or destroy you." Joanna Harcliffe laughed softly. "It was my final, perfect revenge against Elizabeth, who'd always had everything. Everyone delighted in her presence, everyone hung on her every word. After a while there was nothing left for the rest of us." The elder woman's mouth flattened, settling into an ugly line. "And now her dear little daughter is in another world, every aspect of her mind under my control. It makes a most satisfactory ending, indeed. How sad that I won't be able to see my husband's face when he finds out." She laughed coldly. "My poor, stupid, unsuspecting husband. You've done very well, Cathlin," she crooned, patting her arm. "Very well."

Behind them came a light footstep.

"Ah, there you are, Hayes."

Hayes pointed to the rear of the abbey. "The wine's all loaded. We can leave any time."

"Very good. I shall be out shortly, after I've finished here."

After a moment her husband's assistant, who was in truth Joanna Harcliffe's assistant, turned and went back out to the waiting truck.

Silently the two women entered the narrow staircase, darkness closing in around them. Dust rose in dancing flecks as they moved up the broad steps to the abbey's roof.

"Hayes is a fool, I'm afraid. I shall dispose of him, too, once I have no more use for him. By this time tomorrow I expect to be comfortably ensconced somewhere far, far away from England. I can never be happy here, in a place where I have had to fight for every advancement and every bit of security."

Cathlin kept moving.

"But you don't see, do you?" The older woman laughed coldly. "I was there too, part of that whole, tragic tale. After your unexpected regression during our hypnosis sessions, I grew curious and did a regression of my own. Most interesting, it was." Joanna Harcliffe's voice hardened. "That's how I discovered my own part in your past. I was the one who convinced you to betray the man you loved."

They had reached the top of the stairs now. "Here we are, my dear. Push open the door."

A cool wind tore over the parapets as Cathlin shoved the door open. Outside the roof was shrouded in shadows and the countryside spread like a dark velvet sea below them, a few lights shimmering in the distance.

"And now it's finally time to bring our circle closed. You do understand, don't you, Cathlin? Or should I call you Geneva?" The older woman smiled coldly. "Yes, your lover is gone, you're distraught, and everything you value in life is lost. There's only one answer for you now, isn't there?"

Cathlin's fingers moved restlessly at her waist. She scrubbed at her skirt, fighting stains that weren't visible. "I—yes, I understand."

"And what is it that you must do?"

"Jump. Jump like *she* did. Because it's my fault."

Behind her James Harcliffe's wife laughed softly. "Very, very good, my dear. The lie worked then, too. Everyone in London was convinced that Gabriel had killed the innocent Geneva Russell and then vanished. My plan was perfect, in fact. But now we're almost finished. Yes, I think this corner will do."

Below them stretched the dark tangle of Draycott's hills. In the distance the moon hung cold and silver, its light thrown in broken webs across the moat.

"It is time, my dear."

"Yes—I understand." Cathlin moved forward, her

hands restless. "He is waiting for me and I must go. First Gabriel, then my mother, now myself."

Without warning, a long shape hurtled from the darkness, ripping at Cathlin's skirts and knocking her backward, away from the roof's edge. She cried out, thrown down against sharp gravel and upturned stones, her head striking the edge of the parapet.

"Get up!" The order was sharp with fury. "You must complete the work you've agreed to."

Cathlin swallowed. Her hands pressed at her head. She looked down and saw the blood staining her palms. Looked—but did not really see. "Of course," she said mechanically.

"Be quick about it. I have a great many miles to cover before morning. I must be far away before that clever husband of yours suspects anything. Closer, my dear, that's right." Moonlight glinted on the gun in Joanna Harcliffe's fingers. "I would hate to see you change your mind now, after all this time. Yes, take another step, Cathlin." She laughed softly. "Only a few feet more and everything will finally be complete. Then your sad memories will trouble you no more."

Twenty-seven

Dominic roared up to Draycott's wrought-iron gates and leaped from the car. Instantly a uniformed figure moved to block his way.

"Sorry, sir. No one to go in or out. Strict orders."

"Orders from whom?"

"James Harcliffe, sir." The man looked nervous. As he spoke he bent down to finger the holster holding a standard-issue Beretta.

Dominic didn't give him a chance to finish. He didn't trust Harcliffe or anyone else at that moment. He spun sideways and flashed his leg up in the high, twisting *chassé* kick of *savate*. A sharp elbow parry followed a punishing right jab, and a clean follow-through brought his adversary into the full weight of his bent knee.

Dominic let him fall and took his Beretta, then ran grimly for the abbey. The moon hung like a chalk disk in the black night as he broke through the last line of trees. Now the moat lay just above him, ablaze with moonlight. When he looked up, a slender black form was silhouetted against the stark black line of the parapets.

Dominic knew as he stared upward that the bitter past was about to be repeated.

*　　*　　*

Cathlin moved nearer to the edge of the roof.

Pain burned through her palms and shoulder. She swallowed, feeling her hair flung by the wind, feeling her mind flung just as wildly by a rush of cruel memories.

Her mother. The park. The ducks quacking as they surged around her feet.

And then an older woman, her face first bland, then wrinkled and ugly with rage.

Joanna Harcliffe.

It all slid back into Cathlin's mind then, the angry words, her mother's white face as they'd left the park, though she'd tried to hide her fear from Cathlin.

That evening they had gone as planned to the abbey. The incident was forgotten until Cathlin awoke in the night and heard her mother's voice raised high in anger and fear. Cathlin had gone to the door, listening to the angry words of two women who had once been friends. With sleepy eyes she had seen a brawny man pulling her mother down the hall. Screaming, she had flung herself at him, only to be thrown back into her room with the door locked.

After that . . . only silence.

Only the horror of bleak seconds ticking past as she whimpered softly for the mother who did not come. Eventually she had cried herself to sleep, and when she awoke hours later, the house was still silent, but now her door was open.

She had run through the dark corridors, shadows at her back, calling vainly for her mother.

Then Cathlin found her.

Motionless, broken, silent, her body lay sprawled against the long grass by the moat. That image had shattered Cathlin's hold on sanity.

And the initial trauma was soon cleverly reinforced by Joanna Harcliffe's weeks of cold-blooded conditioning until the memories were completely blocked.

"Come, my dear, you are too slow. The edge is so near now. It calls to you, beckons you."

Cathlin's fingers tightened. She had to fight the words and all those years of monstrous control. The pain had helped her begin, but even now it was nearly impossible. The child in her wanted to obey, to do everything this gentle, kindly voice ordered.

Something brushed past her leg, sleek and powerful.

The cat. The cat she'd seen that day beside the moat.

Cathlin swallowed, taking courage from the warm contact. She had to fight! With her past restored, she could finally have a future.

A future with Dominic.

"Yes. I'm—coming. But my foot is caught."

"Where?" Sharp. The irritation beginning to show. "Let me see." The older woman bent over, and as she did Cathlin shoved her away, kicking wildly at the gun.

Metal struck stone and then the night blurred, speed and shadow and cool moonlight bleeding together. A feline shape hurtled through the air, striking Cathlin's shoulder, ripping out with claws bared.

Fire burned in her arm. She cried out in pain and fell backward, striking the sharp granite of the roof.

And then only darkness. A darkness were cruel memories lay waiting.

Henry Devere stood in the candlelight studying Geneva's bound hands.

"Where is he? Where is Gabriel?"

"He's escaped again, damn his soul. After he was shot,

I had him transferred to a traveling carriage with two guards. But he tossed the incompetent fool outside, then jumped himself, no matter that the carriage was at the gallop. But I'm not worried. I know exactly where he'll head—to find you, my dear, right here at Draycott. And thanks to my story about the dreaded smallpox affecting the abbey, no one will be making any visits here. Now that Adrian Draycott has gone off to escort that impertinent American diplomat to sea, we will be quite alone here."

"Monster!"

Devere only smiled coldly, playing with the lace at his cuff. "Now all we have to do is wait for your brave cavalier to return from France."

Two days passed. Then a week.

Finally Henry Devere received the news he craved: the brave Englishman had returned from his daring French mission with a beautiful Englishwoman and her three children in tow and was already on his way out of London.

Laughing wildly, Devere half carried and half shoved Geneva down to the moat. Throwing open the gatehouse door, he made her stand before him on the abbey's little bridge, with his pistol against her back. There they had stood, while the minutes ticked past, both waiting for the man Geneva loved to come plunging through the gate.

Both knowing that he would die when he did.

Geneva's hands tightened. Forgive me, my love, *she prayed.* Forgive me and know that this is the greatest gift I can give you. Accept it and remember that I shall love you always.

Beyond the gate came the sound of a horse plunging over gravel and then the hammer of boots.

Suddenly Gabriel was there, eyes wild, cloak flying. "Geneva! They said you had gone with Adrian and Jefferson. I've just left your sister in London and came as fast as I could. The wine is following by coach."

Devere stepped into the moonlight, a pistol at Geneva's head. "So I find you again at last, Ashton."

Gabriel cursed. "You can have me, Devere. Let her go and you can take me where you like."

Devere threw back his head and laughed wildly. "So simple? Come, this is hardly any challenge." Slowly his face darkened with rage. "I've outplanned you at every step, and you'll not elude me now! That reward will be mine, as all that money should have been already. I worked all those years in India, slaving for Thomas Russell in the savage heat. 'Do your work well, Henry. Keep your accounts clear, Henry. Someday if you are very good, you will marry my daughter and all my money will be yours.' " Devere laughed wildly. "But he died before I could fix her hand in marriage, blast his soul."

Gabriel saw his moment. He lunged toward Devere, who had stepped away from Geneva during his mad harangue. The blow caught Devere in the side and sent him hurtling backward against the granite bridge across the moat.

They struggled desperately, breaths hoarse. Then there was a blur of blue silk and the bark of a gun.

"Geneva, no!"

But it was too late. She lay between them, blood staining the edge of her gown. Beside her lay Henry Devere, collapsed from the force of the rock she had flung against his head.

"You must go now." Her voice was already growing weak. "Know that I love you, my dearest Gabriel, with every fiber of my soul until the very end of time." She clutched at his sleeve. "You must go now. He'll be waking up soon!"

But Gabriel didn't move. He held her head to his chest as her breath slowly stilled and her blood leaked onto the cold granite.

He was still holding her locked to him, lost in a haze of pain, when Henry Devere's gun barrel swung down on his head and the world crashed into utter darkness around him.

Brick by brick the wall was raised. Bound and gagged, blood flowing from the gaping wounds Devere had inflicted, Gabriel watched without any flicker of emotion.

It was over. Devere had won, monster that he was. He was totally mad now.

But it mattered not, in truth.

With Geneva gone, Gabriel lost his own life and any hope of happiness.

"How does it feel to be caged, Montserrat? How does it feel to know the cold is climbing inside you and your blood stains the gray stones?" Devere moved clumsily before the unfinished wall, his face wild, demonic. "You'll make your tomb in there with that wine of yours, and Adrian Draycott will never be the wiser. When he returns he'll learn only that a wall of his cellar collapsed and had to be quickly buttressed with a new one." Devere laughed coldly. "And in one week's time all London will be abuzz with the sad story of Geneva Russell, who was flung from the abbey roof by her lover in a jealous rage. Yes, the story will be on everyone's lips. I'll see to that." He stopped abruptly, his eyes anxious as he stared into the shadows of the cellar. "Who's there? Who's there, damn it?"

But no voice rose in answer. The only sound came from the mason's trowel, scraping new mortar over fresh bricks.

And then Devere's eyes darkened. His laughter echoed through the cold cellar, wild and ragged, as the last brick was set in place.

Now, two hundred years later, Dominic Montserrat stood looking up into the night sky, into the moon that hung chill overhead, feeling his blood run to ice. Memories lay sharp upon him and once again he felt fate cheating him of all that he had ever loved and dreamed of.

Above him came a cry, then the slow, silent twist of a body as it plummeted from the parapets, end over end, to strike the stones at the edge of the moat.

Catching a wild breath, Dominic plunged toward the abbey.

It took long, painful seconds for her consciousness to return. There were stones digging into her fingers and a burning pain at her neck where the cat's sharp claws had ripped through her blouse.

Cathlin slowly opened her eyes.

Nothing but shadows. Nothing but darkness and pain.

Then memory returned, and with it the chill reality of the last hours. She sat up slowly and looked around her. The roof was empty—no cat, no Joanna Harcliffe. She put her hand to her head, brushing aside a line of blood.

She was struggling to rise when the door to the roof was thrown open and a tall figure appeared, silhouetted in the light from the stairs.

"Cathlin? Sweet God, are you there?"

"Dominic!" she cried hoarsely. "I'm here—waiting for you, just as I promised, my love."

In the distance came the wail of sirens, then the roar of a car. Brakes screamed on gravel and a door was thrown open against the angry stacatto of urgent questions. Somewhere James Harcliffe's voice rose in a harsh rain of commands, countered sharply by Nicholas Draycott.

But Dominic and Cathlin heard none of it.

Their bodies were locked where they stood on the cool granite of the abbey's roof, a perfect purity of line against the burning silver light of the rising moon.

"Together," Dominic said hoarsely, his fingers buried in her hair, his heart racing.

"Forever," Cathlin answered softly. To the night. To the golden future. To the man she loved more than her very life.

Most of all, to the two lovers who had been parted here by tragedy so long ago.

And as she said the words, Cathlin felt the hole in her mind begin to close. The shadows she had lived with for so long now wavered and began to recede. She knew then that the circle had finally been broken and they had found their way home at last.

Twenty-eight

"I'm fine."

"Be quiet."

"No, really, Dominic. I'm fine."

But Cathlin's protests were ignored, muffled against Dominic's chest as he carried her into the abbey's rose-filled study. "Until I'm convinced of that, you're staying right here," he said tartly. "That madwoman came too bloody close out there. She was the one behind all of it, the intruders at Seacliffe, the men in the car, even that letter you found under your door with the ragged bit of plaid." His jaw hardened. "If she weren't dead already, I'd have serious trouble resisting the temptation to do the job myself."

Cathlin's fingers tightened on his shoulder. She didn't want to think about the nightmare of the last hours, not until the horror of the memories had begun to fade. She looked up at Dominic, seeing the lines of tension at his mouth and jaw that marked the worry that still gripped him. "You can't mean that."

"Just be glad we won't have to find out." He settled her in a chintz couch in front of the window, then sank down beside her. After a moment, he cursed and hauled her onto his lap.

"Dominic, I'm fine, really."

"Well maybe I'm not. I don't think I'll ever forget looking up and seeing the two of you silhouetted up there on the edge of the roof. As I watched, it all came back." His eyes hardened. "I saw the cellar, Cathlin. I saw the bricks going up one by one and I heard the scrape of the mortarman's trowel. And when I looked down I saw my own blood pooling over the granite floor."

"So close. Then and now." Cathlin brushed back a dark comma of hair from his forehead. "But I knew you'd come, Dominic. And until you did thank heavens the cat was there to frighten me back from the edge. The pain cut through the mental blocks somehow and when I got up, Joanna Harcliffe's control was broken."

"Cat?" Dominic frowned.

"A great creature, gray with black paws."

"Funny, I don't remember Nicholas keeping a cat here at the abbey." Dominic shrugged and eased Cathlin against his chest, trying to ignore the immediate ache that their contact kindled. "So it was Harcliffe's wife all along. No one would have guessed her capable of such tortured planning. Probably you weren't the only one she had her claws into either. In a way I can almost feel sorry for her husband, because James Harcliffe looked totally broken when he left in the ambulance with her body. Clearly all of this took him by surprise." His breath slid out slowly. His fingers crossed over Cathlin's waist. "But it's finally over now, my love. Gabriel and Geneva are at peace at last, with their old, sad mystery solved." Cathlin's fingers stole into his as he pressed a hard, protective kiss to her hair.

Outside the moon shone cloudless from a cobalt sky. Wind fluttered the roses cascading along the moat. And somewhere in the quiet darkness a nightingale began to sing.

* * *

"But something *must* be wrong. They've been in there for hours already!" Nicholas's voice was tight with worry as his wife patted his arm.

"They're fine, Nicholas."

"What if something happened to them? After all, Cathlin has been under a terrible strain. First she had to come back here and face the memories of her mother's death. Right on top of that comes this mad attack by Joanna Harcliffe."

"I'm sure that Dominic is very well equipped to soothe any trauma that Cathlin might be feeling right now."

"No, I can't take a chance, Kacey. I'm going in."

Even as Nicholas fingered the ancient silver key to his study, a ripple of muted laughter drifted from behind the closed double doors, followed by the sound of a pillow hitting the floor.

Nicholas's frown wavered, but he didn't give up. "What if you're wrong? What if Cathlin—"

"Sometimes, my love, for someone so vastly intelligent, you can be very, very dim," his wife said tenderly.

Another wave of laughter emerged from behind the oak study doors. This one was decidedly masculine.

"I suppose you might be right," Nicholas said slowly, returning the key to his pocket. "So what do we do now?"

"We do nothing at all." His wife took his arm and led him off toward the kitchen. "Except perhaps to have a word with Marston. Unless I miss my guess, those two are going to be famished when they finally come out." She gave her husband a knowing smile. "As I recall, *we* certainly were."

The viscount's gray eyes took on an answering gleam. "You're right, we were. But not for food, my love."

* * *

"Dominic, we can't. It's almost ten o'clock."

Skin moved slowly over warm skin. Sunlight spilled over the moat and filtered past the damask curtains to fill the study. "What will Nicholas and Kacey think of us?"

Dominic laughed darkly. "That we are very much in love, I hope." He slanted Cathlin a wolfish smile. "And that we're embarking on the honeymoon we never had."

"But my dress. Your shirt." Her face filled with color as she gazed down ruefully at the crumpled shirt at her feet, now entirely buttonless. Her own dress had fared little better.

"You *were* rather impatient, weren't you?"

"Me? What about *you*?" Cathlin held up the shredded remains of her lace camisole. "This isn't exactly the sign of a patient man."

Dominic's smile grew even more wolfish. "Fantastic, wasn't it?"

After a moment Cathlin's lips slid into a smile. "Entirely. Especially when you . . ." She pushed onto her toes and whispered something in her husband's ear.

His eyes darkened. "No more, Irish. Otherwise, we'll never get out of here. And I don't plan to spend another night on this cold floor, no matter how valuable its eighteenth century Peking carpet." He studied the room thoughtfully, then swept a muted wool throw of tartan plaid from a nearby wing chair. After whisking it around Cathlin's shoulders, he cinched the long folds with his belt. "Very nice. Lady Macbeth incarnate."

"Snake."

"Witch." His voice grew husky. "Enchantress. You must be, woman. You've certainly stolen my heart and all vestiges of sanity, Cathlin O'Neill."

Her finger traced his lips, light as thistledown.
"Cathlin O'Neill *Montserrat*," she corrected softly.

Dominic looked upward, as if pleading for celestial
assistance. "One look, one tiny touch, and she makes
me putty. No, she makes me the most ineffectual
mound of blancmange."

"How the mighty have fallen," Cathlin said silkily,
moving her shoulder so that the soft wool gaped and
afforded her beloved husband an intimate look at the
skin he had worshiped and explored so thoroughly
through the long hours of darkness.

The Earl of Ashton muttered beneath his breath
and tugged the tartan closed. "March, O'Neill. You
may be the keeper of the wines, but I'm the one
dedicated to protecting your luscious body." His
mouth hardened as he gathered up the shredded remains of their clothes. "If we stay in here one minute
longer, protecting you is going to be the very last
thing on my mind."

Her brow cocked. "So?"

"So you need a break. You've got beard burns over
most of your body."

"Mmmmm. The memory alone is lovely."

"Damn it, Cathlin, I saw you wince when you
stood up. And I have a fair idea of how you're feeling right now. After all, I wasn't exactly feeling very
civilized last night." Dominic unlocked the study
doors and threw them open. "I'm not very proud of
that fact," he added grimly. He looked out into the
shadowed corridor, frowning as his eyes adjusted to
the darkness.

Someone cleared his throat.

"Marston, is that you?"

"I hope I have not disturbed you, my lord." The
butler's face was impassive as he gazed at a rather
ugly eighteenth-century oil portrait just to the left of
Dominic's head. "However, I confess I am delighted

to see you. The viscount has been rather distressed, you understand."

Cathlin caught a quick breath. "Nothing's wrong, is it? Genevieve hasn't—"

"No, the family is quite healthy," Marston hastened to reassure her. "Actually, it was you two he was concerned about."

"Us? But why—" Her voice fell away and color flared through her cheeks.

"Locked in the study in utter silence for six hours, eh?" Dominic chuckled. "Nicholas, concerned host that he is, was busy imagining all sorts of tragedies."

Marston's lips took on a faint curve. "His lordship has always had a rather active imagination. But now everything is settled." With one quick look he took in Dominic's bare torso, the shredded clothes caught beneath his arm, the rosy hue of Cathlin's cheeks. He also noted the stubble that had caused that color. He nodded contentedly, then turned. "And now if you will come this way, everything is prepared."

Dominic frowned. "Prepared?"

"Quite." Impassively, Marston gestured for Cathlin to precede him. "My lady?"

Seeing no alternative, Cathlin tugged at her make-shift robe, then moved self-consciously toward the front of the house.

"The limousine is waiting at the front door."

"Limousine? Limousine for where?"

"I believe you will have to ask the viscount and his wife about that."

"Damn it, Marston, don't go bloody butlerish on me now."

No answer. Marston managed to hide his smile; he was not so successful with the twinkle in his eye.

Dominic was just steeling himself to drag the truth out of the tight-lipped retainer when Nicholas himself appeared, a broad smile lighting his handsome face. "So the recluses finally emerge. Hunger got to you, didn't it? Kacey said it would."

Cathlin's stomach gave a telltale rumble.

Nicholas pretended not to notice. "Everything's arranged." His eyes lingered on their rather eccentric attire for a moment, before he turned to lift a large woven hamper from the polished floor of the foyer. "You should find everything you need in there. Caviar. Wild strawberries. French bread and *foie gras*. Belgian lace napkins and champagne on ice." Nicholas's brow arched wickedly as he shoved the heavy hamper at Dominic's chest. "The champagne is Veuve Clicquot, of course. Sorry I didn't have any more La Trouvaille on hand. Damnably hard to build up much stock with that perfectionist in charge. I presume you *do* have enough strength left to carry all that, Dominic."

"I believe I can summon up the requisite energy," the earl said dryly.

"Wonderful. Meanwhile, Kacey has gone for your clothes. Amazing how she can predict these things." He gave a contented nod, well pleased with his plans. "Now off with the two of you. Everything is set."

"Set?" Cathlin tugged uneasily at the folds of the tartan throw at her chest. "Set for what?"

Dominic's eyes took on a shimmer of humor. He eyed the two well-worn Burberry raincoats tossed over an oak peg by the door. "Forget the clothes. We'll just take these."

The viscount gave a low chuckle. "Be my guest."

Briskly Dominic pulled Cathlin out into the rose-filled courtyard. As they disappeared toward the limousine that purred in front of the gatehouse, the viscountess padded down the stairs, an old Louis Vuitton bag under her arm. "They've gone? But they can't. Their clothes will be in no shape to travel in."

"I doubt they'll be needing any more clothes, my

love. Not the way Dominic was looking at Cathlin. Come to think of it," he mused, "she was looking at *him* the same way."

"But—"

Viscount Draycott smiled broadly and pulled his wife against him.

After a moment she laughed softly, catching his hand in hers. Together they watched the car disappear over the wooded hill. "It all worked out just as Gabriel hoped. Those two were meant for each other, weren't they?" Kacey said wonderingly. "How could he possibly have known?"

It is said that no one at London's elegant Dorchester Hotel can be surprised by anyone or anything.

Which was true. Usually.

But not on this sunny spring morning as the daffodils tossed in elegant Park Lane window boxes and waves danced along the Serpentine Lake where it lapped against the blinding green expanse of Hyde Park. When two people emerged smiling from the limousine that purred up to the venerable hotel's front steps, the liveried attendant broke into a broad grin of surprise. "Welcome back, Lord Ashton! It's been too long since you've come for a stay." The man's eyes crinkled as he nodded to Cathlin in turn.

If he thought their raincoats unusual attire for this bright sunny day, Leo was far too well trained to show it. Briskly he moved to sweep open the doors, at the same time motioning discreetly to a bellman inside. His eyes twinkled as he watched the new visitors stroll off hand in hand. Yes, *now* things would start to happen. Just the way they always did when Lord Ashton was about.

It was a pleasure to be back at the Dorchester, Dominic thought. Trust Nicholas and Kacey to plan something perfect like this. He smiled as his steps were cushioned in the deep velour plush of the art deco carpet. The hotel staff was discreet and unflappable. Nothing ever surprised or upset them. Dominic had enjoyed the elegance of this grand old hotel ever since his father had brought him for his first stay at the ripe age of eight. That first morning he had eaten crisp Belgian waffles and raspberry crepes in bed and fallen in love for life.

Now, as mellow golden light bounced off elegant banks of mirrored glass, Dominic gave a sigh and finally allowed himself to accept the happiness that had been stealing through his soul ever since he'd found Cathlin safe the night before.

"Good morning, Lord Ashton." A bright-cheeked attendant in a crisp linen apron nodded to Dominic.

"Good morning. Mary, isn't it?"

Her cheeks creased with pleasure. "So it is. I'm sure you'll have a lovely stay." Her voice dropped confidentially. "Everything is all arranged." Before Dominic could say another word, she was gone, giggling softly.

Cathlin slanted Dominic a measuring look. "Quite a regular here, are you?" She smoothed a dark strand from his forehead and feigned a frown. "Should I be upset by this?"

"I stayed here several years ago, but it was a job, simply a job, Cathlin."

"I'm listening."

"A French actress appearing in a popular London play had been receiving some nasty threats and I was assigned to protect her." He mentioned a name that made Cathlin's eyes widen.

"You worked with *her*?"

"She's not exactly what you might imagine. She was convinced that soap of any kind promoted wrinkles. As a result her, er, hygiene was somewhat less than exemplary."

"But she's *beautiful*."

"Not," Dominic said tenderly, "half so beautiful as you." He was just bending down to plant a kiss on her welcoming mouth when he heard a voice at his back.

"Welcome back to the Dorchester, Lord Ashton." An elderly woman with twinkling eyes and a serviceable navy dress smiled as she pushed a tray of pastries past.

"Thank you, Mrs. Hopkins."

Cathlin's brow rose. "*Very* familiar."

Dominic shrugged, grinning crookedly. "I did a few favors while I was here. I had to keep busy, since I was spending a lot of time avoiding being caught alone with Madame X."

"A predicament half the male population of the United States would have killed to experience."

"It was business, Cathlin." Dominic's eyes darkened. "All business. No matter what act I had to play or what lies the tabloids printed. No matter what everyone here at the hotel was led to believe. Do you believe me?" he asked, suddenly serious.

Cathlin knew what she said next was very important. "I believe you. But only because I know how ruthlessly competent you are in your work. Heaven help the female who tries to break one of Ashton's rules." Her brow creased. "She really didn't believe in using soap? Not *ever*?"

"Never." Laughing softly, Dominic pulled her close and set off for the gleaming marble expanse of the front foyer, where he was instantly hailed by a small man with very regular teeth and a suit that was a masterpiece of Italian understatement. The red rose in his lapel bobbed as he shook Dominic's hand.

"My lord, it is such a *pleasure* to see you again."

"Thank you, George."

"Things have been far too quiet since you left."

"Quiet?" Cathlin eyed Dominic.

"But madam does not know? First, there was the

crazed fan who tried to climb a rope from the balcony to the window of Lord Ashton's, er, female friend. Lord Ashton had to climb up and bring the man down when his foot got caught in the rope."

"He struggled every inch of the way," Dominic said reflectively.

"And don't forget the horse." The red rose bobbed as the hotel's concierge went on.

"Horse?"

"A circus act," Dominic said tersely to his wife, clearly uncomfortable with the trend of the conversation.

"Oh?" Cathlin purred.

"It was nothing much." Dominic shrugged. "The horse broke away from its handlers and tore into Hyde Park, then bolted across Park Lane at rush hour and raced into the lobby. I helped quiet things down, that's all."

"You caught him single-handedly, my lord," the concierge protested. "And just as he was about to mow down three duchesses and a very senile member of the House of Lords! Incomparable, you were."

Cathlin's lip twitched. "Incomparable, was he?"

"George is exaggerating. He always exaggerates."

"And then there was the time that very lovely actress friend of yours was locked out of her room—very much as God made her. You gallantly offered your jacket, but she seemed to want a great deal more from you. I had heard she was a very passionate woman, of course, but I never expected she would indulge in such a display in public."

"Display?" Cathlin breathed.

"But, yes. She was most curious to assess his lordship's, er, lordly assets before she—"

"Thank you, George. I think we can find our own way upstairs."

"But the security keys."

Dominic patted his pocket. "Right here."

"And the new codes."

"George, you offend my professional pride."

"Of course. I forgot those unusual skills of yours."

Cathlin didn't move. "So she wanted to assess your 'lordly assets,' did she?"

"It was a lifetime ago, Cathlin. And nothing happened, I assure you. Now why don't we head upstairs before—"

The dapper hotelier interrupted enthusiastically. "Oh, yes, Lord Draycott was most specific in his requests. You will find everything *molto bene*." He kissed his fingers. "And the flowers, so lovely. I myself shall escort you up."

"There's no need, truly, George. I'm certain we can find our way to the room."

"Oh, not just *any* room. To the penthouse suite, you understand."

At that moment a handsome man with mahogany skin and a rum-soft Jamaican accent strode past. "Welcome back, Lord Ashton." He gave a quick grin. "Things always do happen when you're here, that's for certain. I hear they got something pretty special waiting for you and your lady upstairs, mon. Yes, it's a true pleasure to have *you* back."

Cathlin's eyes narrowed. "Lord Ashton?"

"Yes?" Anxious. Definitely anxious.

At that moment Cathlin decided she'd had enough. She ran her arms slowly along her husband's shoulders and twined her fingers at his neck. Then she moved to tiptoes, sliding closer with every tormentingly sensual inch of her progress.

A deep silence fell over the gilt lobby. Bellboys paused over their luggage. Bemused guests slowed their steps. The uniformed attendants at the desk put down their pens and studied the new arrivals with blatant curiosity.

Cathlin made the kiss long, slow, and roughly the temperature of Cajun *sauce piquante*.

When her air finally gave out and she eased away from Dominic, she noted with satisfaction that his pupils were dilated and his pulse was definitely ragged. "Just so you don't forget that you're a married man now," she said silkily.

Dominic cleared his throat and studied her glowing face.

Behind them the silence was deafening.

"Meet my new wife, everyone," he said hoarsely.

The sound of clapping broke over the polished lobby as Dominic turned and, with a determined look on his face, tugged his wife toward the gleaming bank of elevators.

The penthouse was indeed prepared. Roses spilled from crystal dishes and china vases, filling the air with lush perfume. The doors to the balcony were thrown open, overlooking the green sweep of Hyde Park.

Dominic barely noticed. With a supreme effort of will, he pulled away from Cathlin. "I'll run a bath, then call room service."

"I'm not hungry. Not for food at least," she said raggedly.

Dominic ran a hand through his hair. "But we barely ate in the car. And after what happened yesterday, you—"

Cathlin touched his mouth. "No. Not ever again. It's done, put away in the past, where it belongs. The future is all I want to think about now. The future with you."

"But—"

At that moment the shrill clamor of the doorbell brought Dominic around, cursing. "Yes?" he demanded of the liveried attendant outside.

"Flowers, Lord Ashton. They're from housekeeping." The man held out a huge expanse of white and pink carnations. "Mrs. Morrison said to thank you again for your help with those men who were threatening her son."

Dominic gave a distracted smile, trying not to look at Cathlin. "Just a small favor," he muttered.

The door had barely closed when the buzzing began again. This time a buxom woman in a neat gray uniform held out a bottle of champagne chilling in a bucket of etched silver. "For you, *Monsieur. Merci mille fois*," she said hoarsely. "Without you, my Pierre would still be undergoing questioning for a crime he did not commit. Thank you for believing when no one else did." She wiped her eye, pressed a quick kiss on Dominic's cheek, curtsied, then withdrew without another word.

Dominic set the bucket on a gilt table beside the balcony doors. As he did, the buzzer sounded yet again. Outside a small and very round man in a pristine white chef's hat stood moving from one foot to the other.

"So they were right. You've come back, Lord Ashton." The chef shot a glance at Cathlin, who was watching this parade of gifts with a bemused look on her face. After a courteous nod, he pulled a foil covered box from behind his back. "For you, my lord." His cheeks grew red. "Not that it's half enough, not after all you did when those goons came after me. I did owe them a lot of money, of course." He looked at Cathlin and gave an unhappy shrug. "Gambling debts, you understand. Without Lord Ashton?" The man gave an expressive shrug. "No more crepes or Grand Marnier soufflés," he finished grimly. "He is a special man, this one. The truffles, they are small, for I owe him my life. That is why I want to wish you both every happiness." He pressed Dominic's arm awkwardly, then backed from the room, eyes misted.

Dominic stood staring at the foiled box in his hands, shoulders stiff, legs braced. After a moment he sighed and turned to face Cathlin. "I didn't know they'd, well—" He waved at the gifts.

Cathlin felt a burn in her throat. "Don't apologize, you crazy, stubborn man. I've been too selfish to see you as you really are. And that, my dear Lord Ashton, is wonderful. *Incomparable*."

"No." Dominic's voice was harsh as he sank into a plush damask armchair and tugged Cathlin across his lap. "I'm going to do this right, by heaven. There's something I have to tell you."

Another shrill buzz sent lines down his forehead. "Come in," he called curtly.

A uniformed teenager stood self-consciously in the foyer. "Lord Ashton? I have the package you requested from Harrods."

"Put it on the end table." Dominic's eyes didn't leave Cathlin's face as he counted out change for a tip. When the door closed softly, he gathered an unsteady breath. "The truth is that I'm a fake, Cathlin. I think I've always been a fake. I've never belonged anywhere. When I was young I felt too French among my schoolmates here and too English when I went back to my family in France. I learned to play a role, hiding my pain—no, denying it ever existed. That's why being a bodyguard was perfect. My life evolved into one great act."

"Dominic, you don't have to tell me this."

"No, let me finish. I want you to believe that the act ended that day in Italy when those teenagers died. Serita told you about it, I know. I had to face myself then, Cathlin—what I was and what I wasn't. And that sight made me turn around and never go back. You must believe that. I'm out for good. I will *never* be what your father became."

"But why didn't you tell me about La Trouvaille?" Cathlin asked gently.

"Because in a way that, too, was an act. My mind still runs back to the crowded parade grounds where

I'm watching the eyes, waiting for the flash of an automatic weapon and steeling myself to take the bullet if it comes." He shook his head. "It doesn't change overnight. But it will. One day La Trouvaille will be natural for me. The grass will feel right beneath my feet and the wind over the hill will be the most ordinary thing in all the word. But for now it's still an amazing gift every second of every day I pass there, and until that changes I guess I'll feel like a fake."

"You *are* truly blessed, Dominic. I have no doubt that your sense of being blessed is what makes that wine of yours so special."

He gave her a slight smile. "Keep telling me that often enough and I might begin to believe you, Irish. Until then"—Dominic held the box out to her—"believe that this is no act. What I feel for you is as natural as breathing—and every bit as necessary." He took out a ring with three emeralds separated by tiny diamonds and slid it onto Cathlin's finger, where it rested next to the Ashton family ring which it had been designed to match.

"This is real Cathlin. My throat goes dry whenever I look at you. My hands get clammy when I see you shove your hair back out of your eyes. I have loved you from the first moment I saw you at that blasted wine auction, so sleek and confident and utterly American. I resented that wine you were so in love with and I wanted to put that same glow in your eyes." He drew a ragged breath. "I'm making a mess of this, I'm afraid." He went down on his knee before her. "I've never been good at facing my deepest feelings, much less expressing them. But I want to now, Cathlin. What I feel for you is so real it makes my eyes burn. Somehow you reached into my chest and found the heart I wasn't sure I had. That's what I had to explain to you. I had to show you how much you've changed my life." His eyes darkened. "So will you marry me? For us, this time. Because of this feeling, not because of wine or wills or dead ancestors creeping through our heads. Will you, Cathlin?"

She rose and pulled him into her body, her eyes misty. "I will. Because I love you. Because I love how you try to hide every single good thing about yourself and then get angry when you can't. For such a big, tough guy, you're a pushover, Montserrat. And now . . ." She started to tug at the belt of her raincoat.

Dominic's eyes blazed. "No, Cathlin. Not yet. I'm not done."

"Yes you are. I've heard enough explanations for one day. Besides, if we stand here any longer that buzzer is going to ring again and a dozen new people will flood in with gifts. Then we'll never have any privacy. Just go put out the DO NOT DISTURB sign."

An arrested gleam in his eyes, Dominic did as she asked.

When the sound of jetting water drew him into the vast marbled bathroom, he saw Cathlin's raincoat discarded on the floor and her body half-hidden beneath a froth of bubbles in the creamy marble tub.

Dominic's mouth filled with cotton gauze. "I hope the ring fits." Sweat broke over his brow. "I tried to estimate your size."

"It's fine."

"And about La Trouvaille, we can split our time there. I have a handpicked staff who can manage things at the vineyards during the slack season. If you prefer to focus your work here in London, then—"

"Dominic?"

"What?"

Her toe climbed from the froth. "London's out."

"It is? So you want Philadelphia? We could manage it, I suppose. Tricky, but not entirely impossible."

"Dominic?"

"Yes?"

White foam slid back to one sleek calf. "Not Philadelphia either."

"No?" He nodded, after a moment's reluctance. "I understand, Cathlin. Your job is very important. I never meant to take it from you."

"Not *anywhere* but with you, at La Trouvaille."

Dominic's eyes took on a rush of primitive, elemental shock. "Truly?"

Cathlin rose slowly, foam in every sleek curve, her eyes awash with love. "Truly."

"You're certain?"

"Without a doubt. And now I've got a confession of my own to make."

"I knew it. You're already married?" His voice was husky.

Cathlin shook her head silently.

"You're wanted for armed robbery in three countries?"

She kept approaching; as she did Dominic's hands kept getting tenser.

"Be quiet and let me confess, tough guy." When she moved into him, it felt as natural as ice cream melting on an August afternoon.

"I'm listening," Dominic said hoarsely, his body hardening instantly at the wet pressure of her naked skin.

"What I've been trying to tell you is that you can guard my body anytime you like, Officer. In fact I've been having fantasies about your guarding me. Ever since that first day at Seacliffe."

"No kidding."

Her hands feathered over his broad chest. They kissed, long and slow. Linen fell and cotton fled. Skin melted against hungry skin.

Two bodies met the scented waters. Dominic's foot accidentally triggered the jets, which screeched into activity, water and foam flying everywhere.

He groaned as he sank into her, his blood

churning, hot and wild as the water jetting around them.

Cathlin arched against him, endlessly pliant, endlessly welcoming. She sighed huskily, taking the whole demanding length of him.

Dominic closed his eyes, fighting for sanity. "But the ring—are you sure it fits? If not I can—"

Her ankle eased over his thigh. Her muscles tensed, catching him up in a rush of pure, exquisite torture.

Cathlin's eyes gleamed. "As a point of future information, Officer Montserrat, *this* is as perfect a fit as I ever expect to find anywhere in this life."

And when she spoke, the emerald and diamond ring Dominic had slipped on her finger was nowhere in sight.

Epilogue ～

France
The Garonne Valley

It was a place of sun and stone and heat. The sky was shimmering and cloudless as the wind ran over the green hills, rich with orange blossoms and lavender.

La Trouvaille spread over the hillside and covered the valley carved out by a curve of the Garonne River. Every fertile inch was consigned to neat rows of grapes that hung on emerald vines.

A bird screeched angrily. Tired and dusty, Dominic Montserrat pushed from beneath a layer of leaves and surveyed the netting he had been tying to keep off pests. "That should do it."

"Now you're going to rest." Cathlin's face was tanned and radiant as she eased out of the spot where she'd sat to help him. Of course, Dominic could have turned the backbreaking work over to one of his staff, but by habit he chose the hardest work for himself. Cathlin had long since given up trying to persuade him to do otherwise. Stretching her shoulders, she sat back and surveyed her dusty, but very satisfied, husband.

"Not yet. There are three more rows yet to finish."

Cathlin sniffed. "I knew you'd say that. That's why I took matters into my own hands."

"*What* matters?"

"Lunch, for a start." Cathlin pulled a hamper from beneath a neighboring vine. "Caviar. Wild strawberries." Her eyes rose to Dominic's face. "Belgian lace napkins. Unless, perhaps you've forgotten a certain drive to London in a certain limousine?"

"Oh, Irish, I haven't forgotten. Not in a thousand years."

"Good. Then relax while I open this bottle. You might remember it from a certain London wine auction? Château d'Yquem 1870. Marvelous texture and wonderful finesse."

"It was a very expensive way to get your attention. And not very effective, as I recall."

"You might be surprised about that." Her eyes turned thoughtful. "I thought you had to be the best-looking man I'd ever seen." Cathlin touched the smudge of dirt at his chin. "I still think so."

Heat swept between them. The distant hum of a tractor, the backfiring of a truck, the high shrill cry of a hawk, all melted away to nothingness as Cathlin stared at Dominic's deeply tanned face and thought how lucky they were to be alive and together and here in this beautiful valley filled with golden light.

Happiness. She had finally begun to trust that it wouldn't go away, that she had the right to be happy. The change hadn't come immediately. She still awoke sweaty and breathless sometimes, expecting to hear Joanna Harcliffe's cool, hypnotic voice telling her that she was the cause of her mother's death.

But now that Cathlin's shadows had faces, she was finally able to fight them. Every day brought greater strength and deeper understanding. And every velvet night brought new textures of pleasure shared in the arms of the man beside her.

Happiness. Cathlin smoothed the soft blue linen of her dress and looked out over La Trouvaille. The reddish soil was warm and pungent in the sun and the grape leaves whispered in their neatly trellised rows astride the hills above the river.

"Dominic?" Cathlin's fingers moved in restless circles. "I have to talk to you."

"I thought we were."

"No, really talk."

The seriousness of her voice made him sit up, frowning. "You miss England, don't you? Blast it, I knew keeping you cooped up here at La Trouvaille was a bad idea. I can—"

"It's not that." Her fingers went back and forth on the sun-warmed linen.

"You want to go back to Philadelphia?" He took her face between his palms. "You should have told me, Cathlin."

"No, you don't understand." Her eyes darkened.

"Say it. Whatever you want, we'll manage it somehow, I promise."

"It's not a matter of my wanting. That is, not myself alone. It takes two to manage what I'm talking about, Dominic."

"Two? Is something wrong, Cathlin?" He sat up sharply. "Damn it, if you lifted those old casks after I told you not to—" Abruptly he went very still. "Two. Are you trying to tell me that you're—that we're—" He swallowed.

"I am. A baby."

"A baby?" He looked at her face and then his eyes slid inexorably to the slender waist where her fingers were still moving restlessly. "A baby," he whispered, half disbelieving. "You're sure?"

Cathlin nodded. "I got the results today."

A moment later she was gathered to his chest, his lips pressed to her hair. "You should have told me sooner!"

"I wanted to be sure."

His fingers tightened and Cathlin felt a long sigh of contentment heave from his chest. "Just when I thought things couldn't possibly get any better. You are seriously altering my gloomy view of the world, do you know that?"

"You're glad? Truly?"

"I have no words to tell you how glad." Their fingers locked. "I only hope she looks like you," he said in a besotted voice.

"I hope *he* looks like *you*."

"Sweet God, a baby. I think I need a drink," Dominic said blankly. "Aunt Aggy will be ecstatic. She's got chest upon chest of baby clothes she's been saving neatly in lavender. I think she'd just about given up hope on me."

"You *are* a hard man to tame. I nearly gave up, too."

Dominic gave a crooked grin. "I've been conquered territory from the first moment I saw you, O'Neill. My heart shattered the second I saw you slithering past me in that black velvet suit."

"Slithering! I did no such thing. How dare you—"

He cut her off with a kiss, fierce and hard, possessive and protective at the same time, as if he couldn't quite trust his good fortune and needed to persuade himself this was not some kind of dream. When he finally pulled away, his face was hard with desire. "Let's go back." There was no mistaking his intention.

"But it's barely noon, Dominic. We still have three more rows to finish up here."

"To hell with the vines," he said thickly. "I want to undress you slowly, and kiss you until you moan my name. I want to hear that soft cry you make when I take you over the edge. And then I want to start all over again." Suddenly his eyes narrowed. "Unless—maybe you shouldn't. Now, I mean."

Cathlin laughed huskily. "I can't imagine why not."

"You're sure? God, I wouldn't want to hurt . . ."

"We've got months yet, my love."

"We do?" He gave her a wolfish grin. "Then what are we waiting for? Come to think of it, why go all the way back down to the château?"

"But, what if one of the staff comes by? Besides, today is the day the mayor is going to—"

"To hell with the staff. To hell with the mayor, too."

The tablecloth from Cathlin's hamper hit the ground with a *whoosh*. Dominic spread it carefully, then worked Cathlin back beneath the leafy shade of the trellised green vines.

"What about that Château d'Yquem I've got cooling on ice?"

"Forget it, Irish. I've got something with greater complexity and far more staying power in mind."

"I hope you're prepared to demonstrate the proof of that statement, Lord Ashton."

"You can damned well bet I am, Lady Ashton."

The green leaves shuddered. A single cloud marched across the crystal sky. Down the hill cicadas droned from the darkness of the woods.

Husky laughter spilled from the high vines. "Sorcery, Lord Ashton? Is this primitive ritual how you manage to keep producing those amazing vintages?"

"Be quiet and kiss me, wife of my heart, mother of my child."

She did, and the love they made between them was fine and sweet and unforgettable.

Tempered in pain, anchored in joy, it was stronger than any wine that would come from even La Trouvaille's hardy vines.

They spilled out of the sunset an hour later like a ragged circus parade, two Citroëns lurching along at the fore followed by an old farm truck. Behind that, tethered with a stout rope, trotted a donkey in a straw hat with holes cut for his ears. The backfiring motors roused the two figures half-asleep beneath a row of grape vines.

"Dominic, did you hear that?"

"I bloody well did." Dominic sat up and squinted into the sun, watching a cloud of dust swirl over the gravel drive and across the mellow golden walls and blue shutters of the beautiful old château at the foot of the forest. As the lead car lurched to a halt, he held his hand to his eye and frowned. "But that's—"

"Nicholas and Kacey," his wife finished breathlessly. "And there's Marston. Did you know about this?" she demanded. "Really, Dominic you should have told me." She sat up quickly, brushing twigs from her hair. "We'll have to hurry down."

"I'm totally in the dark." His eyes lovingly ran over her body, slender and shadow dappled. "But maybe you should put something on before you go running down to greet our guests."

"Maybe *you* should too."

They wriggled into their clothes clumsily, shielded by the low vines, then went down to welcome the visitors spilling over the lavender-edged lawns of the château.

Nicholas was leaning at ease against a dusty Citroën, elegant in a sherry-colored tweed jacket and deep brown trousers. "So the recluses of La Trouvaille emerge from their vines at last." Nicholas's sharp eyes ran from Dominic's dusty shirt to the bits of grass and leaves caught in Cathlin's hair. "I trust we haven't interrupted anything," he said blandly.

His wife was frowning. "I told you we should have phoned ahead, Nicholas. If it's a dreadful nuisance, we can always go back to the last town. But the farmer insisted on showing us the way personally. Then the mayor had to come along, too." The official in question was already hailing Dominic in a torrent of voluble French, detailing the arrival of his English friends, who had clearly been lost. Meanwhile, the farmer, after untying his donkey, launched into his own account of the story, shrugging expressively as he talked.

In the midst of this cheerful chaos of explanations and hugs and kisses from a sleepy-eyed Genevieve, Marston moved off to make the acquaintance of the housekeeper, who was just emerging from the château.

Dominic would permit no talk until all were settled at the old stone tables under a pair of poplar trees at one side of the house. Cathlin's Château Climens was opened and a first glass lovingly savored.

"Celebrating something special, were you?" Nicholas asked.

Dominic looked at Cathlin. "We were, actually." He took his wife's hand. "I've just found out—" He stopped and cleared his throat. "Lord, Nicky, I'm to be a father."

Another interval of chaos ensued. Soon the two friends were perched on the old table while the farmer and mayor wandered off to argue over the best choice of name for the coming child. Kacey and Cathlin, meanwhile, moved off to the bank of the brook that wound along the foot of the forest.

The viscountess touched Cathlin's arm. "You look positively radiant, my dear."

"I can't think why. I've been eating like a pig," Cathlin confessed. "I think that's how I first realized."

"Lucky you. I couldn't eat for weeks. Besides, your husband doesn't seem to mind in the slightest. In fact, he looks utterly exhilarated with the news."

"Do you think so?" Cathlin studied Dominic tenderly as he sat shoulder to shoulder beside Nicholas.

"Without a doubt. Men have a habit of getting that way about this time. Just wait until the first dirty diaper appears," Kacey added sagely.

Insects droned from the rows of lavender and banked rosemary. The mayor and the farmer had dispensed with female names and now were moving through a weighty selection of boys' names. Didier and Alexandre had emerged as the front contenders when Marston returned bearing a tray of watercress sandwiches and a bottle of La Trouvaille.

"Marston, you are impossible. Do sit down and be waited on like everyone else," Cathlin scolded good-naturedly.

"I'm afraid I can't, my lady. Some deficiency in my character, I fear. Would you care for more wine?" he asked in the same breath, the sun glinting off his purple running shoes.

Cathlin sighed and let Kacey take a turn at trying to bully the butler into taking the vacation he richly deserved.

The viscountess was no more successful than Cathlin.

Only when Genevieve tugged at his trouser and demanded that he pour her some of that 'sparkly stuff all the grown-ups were drinking' did he put down his tray. Smiling faintly, he took her off to the kitchen in search of something 'much better than that nasty sparkly stuff that was making the grown-ups laugh so much.'

Nicholas bent closer to Dominic. "And now for my news. We've found the man who pushed Cathlin's mother. He and quite a few other members of Joanna Harcliffe's nasty little group are going to spend a long time behind bars."

Dominic looked at Cathlin, who was laughing at something that Kacey had said. "I don't think she needs to know, do you? Not yet at least. So much of her memory is returning. It's as if she's rediscovered her mother now that the mental logjam Joanna Harcliffe engineered has been broken. Thank God for it. And thank you, Nicky, for all you've done."

"I've got even better news. I've been sifting through the offers for your wine, as you asked."

"I hope it hasn't been a bloody bother. With my being away, it's been madness here."

Nicholas waved a hand. "It's been quite exciting. If Marston becomes any more impassive when he announces that the palace is on the phone, I think his face will freeze in a perpetual mask. I don't think he's ever had quite as much fun. Do you know that he got to argue with a member of Parliament and two U.S. senators yesterday?"

"Marston, argue?"

Nicholas chuckled. "He's determined that the wine should go to the Queen Mother and no one else." His eyes narrowed on the silver line of the stream. "There's no doubt that your estimate will be met, Dominic, and probably a great deal more. You see, we took apart the wooden slats of the case last week. Do you know what we found? Two pieces of paper—one from Thomas Jefferson, specifying an order of Château d'Yquem for himself and his friends. He listed a number of American patriots by name in the request, including George Washington. If that kind of written provenance doesn't drive the buyers to a bidding frenzy, I don't know what will."

Dominic's eyes played over the distant hills, wreathed in golden light. "He seemed a thoroughly decent fellow. Once again I owe him my thanks."

"Seemed? Have you been reading up on Jefferson? You speak as if you know him personally."

Dominic smiled. "You might be surprised, Nicky. Now what was that other letter you mentioned?"

Nicholas reached into his jacket and drew out a small sheet of yellowed vellum protected in plastic. "I thought you'd want to read it yourself."

Dominic took the sheet with quiet reverence, thinking of blood and loss and shadows that had finally been overcome. His eyes watered as he stared at the bold words scrawled across the old paper and he knew without a doubt that he was looking at the work of his own hand, mere minutes before his death.

If you have found this, unknown friend, then you must also know the rest. Geneva Russell was murdered before my eyes by a madman named Henry Devere as she stepped before a bullet meant for me. Now I am to die, too, and no doubt Devere will name me her killer. See that history knows the truth, my unmet friend, so that our souls may finally lie at rest. You will find the Ashton necklace pressed into a recess I made in the wet plaster at the bottom of the north rim of this wall. See that it goes to Geneva's descendant and to none other, on pain of my curse. And when that is done, friend whom I shall never meet from a time that I shall never see, then drink deep—to life, to us, and to the truth that cannot stay hidden despite all of the work of evil hearts. Know then that Geneva and I are finally at peace in that place where souls meet and dance forever in the light. I have seen it briefly, just now. It is beautiful beyond describing. Already my heart sings with an eagerness to go, for I know Geneva is there, waiting for me.

We send you our joy, unknown friend, and with it the assurance that forever is far more than just a word.

Farewell

Dominic held the page tightly, unashamed of the tears that covered his cheeks. He drew a deep breath, feeling peace steal over him, knowing that Gabriel had gone joyfully to meet his death.

He looked up to find Cathlin at his side, her eyes full of concern.

"Dominic?"

"It's nothing, love. Just an end—and a beginning, the way life always is." He brushed a black strand from her cheek. "I'll tell you later. Now I want to offer a toast to two lovers who have finally found their peace." He refilled the glasses, then raised his own. "To Gabriel and Geneva. May all their good live on."

Cathlin offered him an answering smile full of silent understanding. Even the old farmer and the mayor stopped arguing long enough to join in the toast, for love is something that any Frenchman treats with greatest seriousness. Both knew love when they saw it, of course. And they saw it now, shining in Cathlin's and Dominic's eyes as their fingers intertwined.

Far away a playful wind danced over the quiet pools and reeds along the English coast, where twilight was just beginning to gather in the hollows below Seacliffe.

Suddenly a shimmer that was not quite sun and not quite water's reflection slid along a row of roses bordering the long gravel drive.

And then a man stood staring over the sweep of hills and sea, looking far to the southeast as if he could see all the way to France.

Which, of course, Adrian Draycott could, thanks to his special awareness of anything that concerned the abbey and its owner.

"So it is finally done. The lies are broken and the past is brought full circle. It pleases me well."

Behind him the roses whispered and a great gray cat emerged into the last rays of the blazing red sun.

Adrian Draycott smiled faintly. "I expect two boys."

The cat's tail arched.

"Girls? Nonsense, my friend."

The cat sat back and studied his black-clad master with unblinking eyes.

"Three of them? And they'll grow up to do *what*?"

The cat's whiskers quivered slightly in the wind and if ever a cat could be said to smile, then this one did.

"Amazing," Adrian murmured. He fingered the fine lace at his wrist, looking at two newly carved headstones. Where Gabriel and Geneva lay side by side, a pair of roses had begun to cast up their first, tentative buds. "But now perhaps it's time for a little of my own magic, such as is left to me so far from my abbey."

Adrian's eyes narrowed as he raised his hands over the low boughs. A cloud passed across the sun and somewhere a thrush called out a persistent tune.

When the cloud moved away, there were dozens of new leaves and tight buds clustered against the pair of roses. And now a row of lilacs spilled their white blooms along the foot of a nearby wall of warm granite.

Maybe the flowers had been there before, or maybe they hadn't. Afterward no one could remember clearly.

But Adrian knew. He smiled faintly and studied his handiwork, while the gray cat pressed against his polished boots. "Rather nice, I think. And now, Gideon, it is time that we were on our way home."

Beyond the witch's pool, beyond the hill and the moat, a dying sun gilded the weathered granite walls of Draycott Abbey and light seemed to shimmer along the silent, darkened corridor that led to the long gallery. The radiance gathered slowly, settling over the hard-faced portrait of a man in black damask and white lace.

Only a sharp eye would have seen the gray cat that ghosted through the day's last beam.

Only a sharp eye would have noticed the single petal of white lilac that fell dreamlike and pale upon the old carpet beneath the painting.

And only the very keenest observer would have seen the way Adrian Draycott's mouth lifted in a smile as the great cat curled up on the carpet beneath his feet.

A carpet that now carried a rain of crimson rose petals.

Author's Note ～

Dearest reader:

I hope you have enjoyed Cathlin and Dominic's adventures. It has been a pleasure to see their ghosts laid to rest at last. As you can probably tell, I found my research on rare wines endlessly fascinating, especially the sweet white wines of Sauternes. Long the drink of kings, these expensive French vintages have been popular since the twelfth century, when Richard the Lionhearted is said to have fallen under their spell. Their production is not for the squeamish, however. When mist veils the lowland valleys at dawn and dusk, the mature grapes are attacked by *la pourriture noble*, the noble rot (*Botrytis cinerea*). Slowly, the grapes darken and shrivel as the fungus punctures the skin and evaporates the juice, concentrating the sugar while retaining the full alcohol content.

The result?

Wines of luscious sweetness, great intensity and full, honeyed flavor. Because the botrytis process occurs only when conditions are perfect, these sweet white wines are necessarily costly. The vintages of Château d'Yquem, in particular, are considered the most aristocratic of all the Sauternes family and form a suitable subject for my two-hundred-year-old mystery. Using a mix of 80 percent Sémillon and 20 percent Sauvignon grapes, this great white wine requires tremendous hand detail in its production. Because the grapes fall under the fungus's influence at different times, they must be picked at various stages, always by hand, sometimes a piece at a time. Picking continues until late November. After three pressings, the wine is fermented in oak casks. The 1971 and 1975 vintages are immensely elegant, but the 1963 and 1968 are definitely to be avoided.

No less an historical figure than Thomas Jefferson was interested in the cultivation of wine, among his many agricultural projects. While in France on government business in 1787 and 1788, Jefferson visited many wine-producing areas, including Sauternes. He introduced these sweet wines at Monticello, and under his persuasion, George Washington ordered thirty dozen bottles, while Jefferson commissioned ten dozen for his own cellars. Whether these shipments were ever made is unclear, and this, of course, forms the basis for my story.

The value of such a newly discovered case of wine in perfect condition and with a clear provenance connecting it to the great American statesman would be enormous. Recently, a single bottle of Château Lafite 1787 bearing the initials TH J was sold at auction in London for $156,000. The buyer was the son of the late Malcolm Forbes. Although the bottle's connection to Jefferson was never conclusively proved, the auction received vast publicity. Unfortunately, after the rare bottle was put on display at the Forbes Magazine building in New York City, the cork deteriorated under the gallery lights and crumbled, ruining the wine.

Nor are such old vintages the mere product of an author's fertile imagination. The cellars of many venerable French wine houses hold bottles dating back to the early eighteenth century, and these old vintages are occasionally offered for select private tastings. For further reading about this fascinating subject, look for Hugh Johnson's thorough and entertaining book, *Vintage: The Story of Wine* (New York: Simon and Schuster, 1989).

Bodyguards?

Dominic represents a disciplined breed who are becoming more in demand with each passing year. During my research, I had the opportunity to interview several professional bodyguards and learn the challenges that face them. For an intimate look at the English world of government and royal protection, see Thomas Geraghty's *The Bullet Catchers: Bodyguards and the World of Close Protection* (London: Grafton Books, 1988). A more unorthodox, yet practical record can be found in Leroy Thompson's *Dead Clients Don't Pay: The Bodyguard's Manual* (Boulder, Colorado: Paladin Press, 1984).

The question of repressed childhood memories has come into high prominence in recent years. Controversy centers around determining true memories from false, or investigator-invoked memories. One expert argues that the clearest sign of repressed trauma comes when a range of appropriate symptoms is present. In their absence, these memories are suspicious. For more information see Lenore Terr's *Unchained Memories: True Stories of Traumatic Memories, Lost and Found* (New York: Basic Books, 1994).

Of course, you will no doubt have noticed that my medieval knight, introduced in the author's note of *Hour of the Rose*, has not yet made his appearance at Draycott Abbey. Never fear, he is glaring at me even as I write these words, hefting his rather daunting sword and demanding that his story begin.

Who am I to argue with a knight?

For more information about this next Draycott book, as well as a bookmark and copy of my current newsletter, please send a self-addressed stamped envelope (the long envelopes continue to work best) to me at:

> 111 East 14th Street, #277B
> New York, New York 10003

As always, I enjoy your wonderful letters immensely.

And what better way to end than with Serita's wedding toast to Dominic and Cathlin: "May your wine be sweet and your nights be long!"

With warmest wishes,

Christina Skye

Christina Skye

Bestselling Author

CATHERINE HART

SPLENDOR
76878-X/$4.99 US/$5.99 CAN
"An absolute delight ...
Catherine Hart proves herself to be a true master"
Catherine Anderson, author of *Coming Up Roses*

TEMPTATION
76006-1/$4.99 US/$5.99 CAN
Tempted by passion, he gambled with his heart –
but a wily and beautiful cardsharp
held all the aces.

TEMPEST
76005-3/$4.95 US/$5.95 CAN

IRRESISTIBLE
76876-3/$5.50 US/$6.50 CAN

DAZZLED
77730-4/$5.50 US/$6.50 CAN

Buy these books at your local bookstore or use this coupon for ordering:

Mail to: Avon Books, Dept BP, Box 767, Rte 2, Dresden, TN 38225   C
Please send me the book(s) I have checked above.
❑ My check or money order— no cash or CODs please— for $_____is enclosed
(please add $1.50 to cover postage and handling for each book ordered— Canadian residents
add 7% GST).
❑ Charge my VISA/MC Acct#_____Exp Date_____
Minimum credit card order is two books or $6.00 (please add postage and handling charge of
$1.50 per book — Canadian residents add 7% GST). For faster service, call
1-800-762-0779. Residents of Tennessee, please call 1-800-633-1607. Prices and numbers
are subject to change without notice. Please allow six to eight weeks for delivery.

Name_____
Address_____
City_____State/Zip_____
Telephone No._____   CH 0195

NEW YORK TIMES BESTSELLING AUTHOR

Elizabeth Lowell

ONLY YOU	76340-0/$5.99 US/$6.99 Can
ONLY MINE	76339-7/$5.99 US/$6.99 Can
ONLY HIS	76338-9/$5.99 US/$6.99 Can
UNTAMED	76953-0/$5.99 US/$6.99 Can
FORBIDDEN	76954-9/$5.99 US/$6.99 Can
LOVER IN THE ROUGH	
	76760-0/$4.99 US/$5.99 Can
ENCHANTED	77257-4/$5.99 US/$6.99 Can
FORGET ME NOT	76759-7/ $5.50 US/$6.50 Can

And Coming Soon

ONLY LOVE

Buy these books at your local bookstore or use this coupon for ordering:

Mail to: Avon Books, Dept BP, Box 767, Rte 2, Dresden, TN 38225   C
Please send me the book(s) I have checked above.
❑ My check or money order— no cash or CODs please— for $_____is enclosed
(please add $1.50 to cover postage and handling for each book ordered— Canadian residents
add 7% GST).
❑ Charge my VISA/MC Acct#_____Exp Date_____
Minimum credit card order is two books or $6.00 (please add postage and handling charge of
$1.50 per book — Canadian residents add 7% GST). For faster service, call
1-800-762-0779. Residents of Tennessee, please call 1-800-633-1607. Prices and numbers
are subject to change without notice. Please allow six to eight weeks for delivery.

Name_____
Address_____
City_____State/Zip_____
Telephone No._____   LOW 0994